THE SCENE OF THE CRIME

Lynda La Plante was born in Liverpool. She trained for the stage at RADA and worked with the National Theatre and RSC before becoming a television actress. She then turned to writing and made her breakthrough with the phenomenally successful TV series *Widows*. She has written over thirty international novels, all of which have been bestsellers, and is the creator of the Anna Travis, Lorraine Page and *Trial and Retribution* series. Her original script for the much-acclaimed *Prime Suspect* won awards from BAFTA, Emmy, British Broadcasting and Royal Television Society, as well as the 1993 Edgar Allan Poe Award.

Lynda is one of only three screenwriters to have been made an honorary fellow of the British Film Institute and was awarded the BAFTA Dennis Potter Best Writer Award in 2000. In 2008, she was awarded a CBE in the Queen's Birthday Honours List for services to Literature, Drama and Charity.

✉Join the Lynda La Plante Readers' Club at
www.bit.ly/LyndaLaPlanteClub
www.lyndalaplante.com
❏ Facebook @LyndaLaPlanteCBE
✖ @LaPlanteLynda

Lynda La Plante

THE SCENE OF THE CRIME

ZAFFRE

First published in the UK in 2025 by
ZAFFRE
An imprint of Bonnier Books UK
5th Floor, HYLO, 105 Bunhill Row,
London, EC1Y 8LZ

A CIP catalogue record for this book is
available from the British Library.

Hardback ISBN: 978-1-83877-997-9
Trade Paperback ISBN: 978-1-83877-998-6

Also available as an ebook and an audiobook

1 3 5 7 9 10 8 6 4 2

Typeset by Envy Design Ltd
Printed and bound in Great Britain by Clays Ltd, Elcograf S.p.A.

The authorised representative in the EEA is Bonnier Books
UK (Ireland) Limited.
Registered office address: Floor 3, Block 3, Miesian Plaza,
Dublin 2, D02 Y754, Ireland
compliance@bonnierbooks.ie
www.bonnierbooks.co.uk

A chosen opportunity to thank all the scientists and officers who constantly give me not only their support but expertise, thank you.

CHAPTER ONE

Jessica Russell woke at 7 a.m. and spent the next hour in the living room doing her daily yoga and meditation, hoping it would help calm her nerves before her interview at Scotland Yard. When she'd finished, she rinsed the dirty crockery her twin brother David had left in the sink the night before and put it in the dishwasher. Then, she wiped down the work surfaces and table before making her daily breakfast of granola, yoghurt and blueberries. She was making herself a ginseng tea when David walked into the kitchen wearing a T-shirt and pyjama shorts.

'Not at work today then?' she asked, surprised to see him.

'I wouldn't be here if I were, would I?' He yawned and scratched his backside.

'I was just asking, that's all . . .'

'I had hoped to have a lie-in, but all your chanting woke me,' he grumbled.

'Sorry about that. Is the day off to escape that little Chihuahua that keeps attacking you on your rounds?' she laughed.

'It's not funny. The bloody thing's mad. It's bitten me twice now. I daren't give it a kick in case it drops down dead.'

'Tell the owner to keep it indoors.'

'I have, but she's eighty-six and doesn't know what time of day it is . . . she's as mad as her dog.'

'So why the day off?'

'I'm going to look at a racing bike in West Wickham. It's a Fairlight Strael, a year old and hardly used, or so the seller says.'

'How much is it?'

'Two grand.'

'For a bicycle!'

He frowned. 'They're nearer three thousand new. I'll use it for the Ride London event if I buy it. I'm doing it for Cancer Research in memory of Mum, so it'd be nice if you'd sponsor me.'

'Of course I will. Have you raised much so far?'

'Nearly three grand. A lot of my postie colleagues have donated online. I've also been a bit cheeky and asked people on my mail round.'

'Are you allowed to do that?'

'No, but I stuck to people I know well who are unlikely to report me. They've all been very supportive actually.'

'Well done, you. Send me the link and I'll donate. How far is the ride?'

'Hundred K. We start in central London, cycle into Essex and finish at Tower Bridge.'

'Do you want anything?' she asked, getting the granola from the cupboard.

'Finding your own place to live would be good,' he said, po-faced.

Jessica wasn't sure if he was being serious. 'I meant some breakfast.'

'No thanks. All I want is some water and more sleep,' he replied. As David reached for a glass, Jessica noticed him wince and then rub his lower back.

'You all right?'

'I pulled something pushing my mail trolley around.'

'I thought they were meant to make your job easier.'

'They're still bloody heavy when they're full.'

'Maybe you should ask your manager about working in the sorting office if your back's playing up.'

'No way. I like being outside in the fresh air.' David turned the cold tap on too far, splashing water everywhere.

'Mind what you're doing, David, I just tidied up.' She grabbed some kitchen towel and placed it on the floor.

'What is it with you and tidiness?'

'Old Chinese proverb says a tidy house is a happy house.'

He grunted. 'Less of your silly yoga chanting will keep me happy.'

'I've got my big interview today. I was trying to calm my nerves.'

'It's not like you to be nervous about anything. It's just another job, isn't it?'

'It's more than just a job. If I'm selected, it will be a big step forward in my career, running a team of forensic experts.'

'You'll smash it. You're bloody good at what you do.'

She smiled. 'I'm meeting some colleagues after the interview. I should be home between three and four.'

He started to walk off, then turned around. 'I was joking about you moving out. You know I appreciate everything you've done for me since Mum died, but I'm better now, so if you did want to find a place of your own, I wouldn't be upset, that's all.'

'That's OK. I'm happy here with my adorable little brother,' she replied.

'You may have popped out twenty minutes before me, but people say you look a lot older,' he said with a grin.

'And wiser,' she responded.

He yawned and rubbed his lower back as he left the kitchen.

* * *

Jessica could feel her nervousness mounting as the train arrived at Charing Cross just after 10.15 a.m. It was a cloudless but slightly chilly May morning, and the streets were bustling with people. As she joined the crowd, she couldn't help glancing at her watch again, knowing she had plenty of time.

Arriving at Scotland Yard, Jessica showed her Kent Police civilian identity card to one of the armed officers. He nodded, stepped aside and let her in. She then gave the receptionist a copy of the email from Commander Mary Williams confirming the appointment. The receptionist checked Jessica's name against the list, ticked it off and handed her a visitor's lanyard. 'Take the lift to the fourth floor, then turn left. Commander Williams' assistant's office is at the end of the corridor.'

Jessica nodded her thanks, checked her watch one more time, then went into the Ladies opposite the lifts. In the toilet, Jessica checked herself in the mirror to make sure she looked professional. She was wearing a navy-blue trouser suit, white silk blouse and block-heeled court shoes. Her thick, curly red hair was tied up in a bun. She touched up her makeup and then washed her hands. After carefully drying them with paper towels, she used the towels to clean the sink and taps.

Exiting the lift, Jessica made her way to Commander Williams' PA's office where a tall, dark-haired, good-looking man in his mid-forties was sitting behind the desk. 'I'm Jessica Russell. I've come for the Murder and Serious Crime Analysis Team Leader interview.' She handed over the confirmation email and showed him her identification card.

'I'm Jordan, the Commander's PA. You're nice and early.'

'Gives me more time to compose myself before I enter the lion's den,' she joked.

He smiled. 'I think you'll find it less formal than you're expecting. So that you know, the panel likes to call it MSCAN for short . . . it's less of a mouthful. The waiting room is just across the corridor. Help yourself to a hot or cold drink. I'll come and get you when Commander Williams has finished interviewing the other candidate.'

'Thank you. Can you tell me who else is on the panel with Commander Williams and what their rank and department is?'

Jordan smiled. 'Well done, you're the first person to ask. They all work in the homicide and major crime command. DCI John Anderson is the small bald chap. He's a Senior Investigating Officer on the Barking homicide team. The other officer is DCS Morgan. He's based here at the Yard and is Commander Williams's deputy.'

'How many people are they interviewing?'

'Eight in total, and you're the last.'

'Thanks.' Jessica entered the waiting room and got herself a bottle of water. Thankfully she already knew Commander Williams from when she was a DCS in the Kent Police before she got a promotion and transferred to the Met. Jessica had been the crime scene manager on Kent homicide cases when Williams was in overall command. She was a highly respected, no-nonsense detective with a successful track record and the Met had recruited her to improve the efficiency of investigative and forensic work in homicide and major crime investigations.

Jessica removed her phone from her handbag, switched it off, and looked at the time again; it was 10.45 a.m. She had thirty minutes before her interview and decided to review the notes she'd made in preparation. Jessica read a couple of pages, then realised it was making her anxious again, so decided to do some deep breathing instead. She was just exhaling when the door opened and Jordan entered.

'The panel is ready to interview you, Miss Russell. Sorry it's a bit earlier than expected. The last candidate's chances were pretty much over before the interview began. Commander Williams does her homework on all the applicants. She discovered the chap had made derogatory remarks on Facebook and X about the Met's senior management. He tried to deny it but had to fess up in the end.'

Jessica shook her head. She wasn't on social media herself, and couldn't believe how foolish some people could be. Jordan took her to the Commander's office, and she took a deep breath as she entered.

Despite Commander Williams's desk being positioned in front of the windows, Jessica was surprised to find her sitting in a comfortable armchair and the two male officers seated on a matching three-seater sofa.

'Nice to see you again, Jess,' Williams smiled. 'I don't expect you're used to being interviewed this way, but I prefer a less formal surrounding as it helps candidates feel more at ease.' Williams smiled, gesturing for Jessica to sit in the other armchair. Morgan nodded in agreement, but Jessica noticed Anderson's dour expression as he picked up his clipboard and pen from the coffee table.

Williams's opening question was to ask her if she knew who the other officers present were, and Jessica was immediately thankful for Jordan's tip as she reeled them off.

'And what do you know about MSCAN?'

'It was your vision to create a team of the best crime scene examiners working alongside a behavioural psychologist for the homicide and major crime command. They will deal with all forensic matters throughout an investigation, from crime scene to court. This will include crime scene analysis, reconstruction, victimology and suspect profiling. They will also consider the value and limitations of the available evidence, as well as suggesting any additional investigative and forensic opportunities.'

Williams nodded with a look of approval and wrote something on her clipboard.

DCS Morgan raised his pen. 'The Commissioner was initially reluctant about Commander Williams's idea as the Met already has its own forensic lab and crime scene managers. He was also concerned about the running costs. How do you think MSCAN will bring value to major crime investigations?'

'Having a specialised unit of experts on hand to identify and optimise the best forensic opportunities in the early stages of an investigation should ultimately be more cost-effective.'

Williams smiled. 'That's pretty much what I told the Commissioner. That said, he decided MSCAN would be evaluated after a year. If it isn't cost-effective and producing results, it could be disbanded. How would you feel about that?'

'I'd like to think that won't happen, ma'am. If selected for the team leader role, I know I can run a unit that will get results and prove its worth.'

Williams and Morgan nodded. The expressionless Anderson twirled his pen between his fingers, then pointed it at Jessica. 'What makes you think you'd be a good team leader?' he asked bluntly.

Jessica took a deep breath. 'I have good communication skills, a strong work ethic and the ability to empathise with others. Good leadership is about supporting the people around you, trusting them, and allowing them to contribute their expertise so the team can be successful.'

'Yes, I'm sure I read that definition in a manual somewhere,' Anderson glibly replied. He then flicked through a couple of pages on his clipboard before continuing. 'You are only thirty-four, and according to your CV, have been a crime scene manager for two years, which isn't a lot of experience in managing people.'

Jessica wondered if he was just trying to unsettle her or was totally against her leading the MSCAN team. Either way, she was determined he wouldn't get to her. 'The director of forensic services in Kent was the referee for my MSCAN application. He recommended me for the position and commended my crime scene management and forensic investigation skills,' Jessica replied calmly.

Anderson was about to continue, but Williams raised her hand to stop him. 'Tell us about your academic qualifications, Jessica.'

'I have a joint first-class honours degree in Psychology and Criminology and a master's degree in Investigative Psychology.'

'Was criminal profiling part of your degrees?' Williams asked.

'Yes, ma'am, for my Master's, but it was called Behavioural Investigative Analysis.'

'We haven't selected a behavioural psychologist for the team yet. How do you think they will assist murder and major crime investigations?' Morgan asked.

'Essentially, behavioural analysis studies an offender's motivation and method by examining their verbal and nonverbal actions during and after the commission of the crime. Identifying these behavioural clues at a crime scene is fundamental to developing an accurate profile of an unknown offender. It's a valuable investigative tool that detectives can use to narrow down a list of suspects.'

'Some say it's nothing more than guesswork,' Anderson said.

'A behavioural adviser should only base their conclusions on the information and documented evidence they receive from investigators,' Jessica replied calmly, not taking the bait.

Morgan nodded and made a tick mark on his clipboard.

'Do you find your behavioural knowledge helps as a crime scene manager?' Williams asked.

'Undoubtedly. I try to get inside the offender's head, to think and act like them in order to identify the correct forensic approach.'

'You have impressive qualifications, but my question is this. Have you ever actually given behavioural advice on live or cold case investigations?' Anderson asked.

'No, sir, but I have been involved in a case where a behavioural adviser was called in and . . .'

Anderson shook his head, 'The National Crime Agency has an

approved list of highly qualified behavioural investigative advisers that senior investigators can contact for advice on major investigations. Is your name on that list?'

'No, sir.'

Anderson frowned. 'Then you have no recognised expertise in using or giving detectives behavioural advice.'

Jessica noticed Williams's expression tensing. Anderson was about to continue, but again Williams stopped him. 'That's not necessarily correct, DCI Anderson. Tell me, Jess, the case where the profiler was involved, was it the murder of a young woman in Maidstone?'

'Yes, ma'am, she was strangled to death in her own house with a pair of tights. I was the crime scene manager.'

'As I recall, the senior investigating officer went with the profiler's theory, which was . . .' Williams deliberately paused. 'The husband had snuck home during a night shift, murdered his wife for the life insurance, then staged the scene to look like someone had broken into the premises and killed her. You told the senior investigating officer you disagreed with the profiler and thought someone else might be responsible, but he ignored you.'

'In fairness, he listened to what I had to say but disagreed and charged the husband.'

'But you were right, and he was wrong. Tell us why,' Williams asked.

Jessica nodded. 'For me, the crime had none of the hallmarks of a staged scene. I considered that it might have been a burglary gone wrong. A rear window was broken using a lump of wood, which we recovered nearby. I had the window pieced together, found an ear print on it, and the scientist recovered black woollen fibres on the wood, which made me wonder if someone wearing black gloves had been listening for any movement inside the premises, as a burglar might do. The husband went to work at 7 p.m. He said his wife told him she was tired and would have an early night. It was possible the wife had gone to bed and turned all the lights off, leaving the premises in darkness and I . . .'

'How could you know she was in bed at the time?' Anderson scoffed.

'I didn't, and I could still be wrong. However, I noticed the duvet on the left side of the bed was thrown back, and one of the bedroom curtains had been pulled open. Her bedside cabinet had been knocked sideways, and a glass of water was spilt on the floor. I considered the possibility the victim had heard the window break, woke up startled, jumped out of bed and looked out the front bedroom window, thinking the sound had come from the outside. The suspect heard her moving about and entered the bedroom. A brief struggle ensued beside the bed, knocking the cabinet out of position. He then took her into the living room and strangled her with a pair of tights.'

'The person who killed her could have pulled the curtain open,' Anderson suggested.

'I agree that was possible. However, I considered it unlikely that someone who had just committed a murder would pull a curtain open so wide to look outside. If this were the case, I would have expected the curtain to have been pulled back just a few inches.'

'That makes perfect sense to me. Was any property stolen?' Morgan asked, while Anderson huffed.

'The jewellery she was wearing and her mobile phone, which was on a charger in the living room.'

Morgan nodded slowly. 'And what was the evidence that led you to her killer?'

'Although we didn't find any DNA evidence to link another suspect to the crime scene, his mistake was leaving the tights around the victim's neck. I considered they might not be hers and had the crotch area tested for DNA. The vaginal fluid didn't match the victim, but it did match a local woman who had a criminal caution for a minor assault. Her boyfriend, who had a record for burglary and assault, was arrested, and his right ear matched the print on the broken glass. We also found black woollen gloves at his flat, matching the fibres on the wood used to break the window.'

'Did the girlfriend assist the investigation?' Morgan asked.

'Thankfully, yes. She said he had come home drunk on the night of the murder and had a scratch on his face. He said he'd walked into a low-hanging tree branch and became physically aggressive when she questioned him further. She also said he had sexual fetishes and liked to put a pair of tights around her neck and tighten them during sex. On one occasion, she found a pair of her tights in his jacket pocket . . . his excuse was that it made him feel she was always close to him.'

'Did he admit the murder?' Anderson enquired.

'No, he tried to blame the victim's husband but was found guilty and sentenced to life imprisonment.'

'Why do you think he killed her?' Morgan asked.

'He was a heavy drinker with a short temper and sadomasochistic tendencies. It's possible she may have seen his face and recognised him. He then panicked and strangled her, which may also have given him some sexual gratification.'

'Was the victim sexually assaulted?' Morgan asked.

'I think she may have been, but there was no forensic evidence to support that conclusion.'

'Then I guess we'll never know if your profile was correct,' Anderson said smugly, leaning back in his chair.

Jessica had finally had enough of his demeaning remarks. 'The jury convicted him on the evidence presented to them . . . not my theory alone.'

'How did you feel when he was convicted?' Morgan asked.

'I felt proud that our scene of crime and forensic teamwork had saved the husband from possibly going to prison for a crime he didn't commit.'

Williams nodded in agreement. 'Did you receive any recognition for your work on the case?'

'Yes, the trial judge commended my crime scene investigation, and I was also awarded a Chief Constable's Commendation.'

Morgan flicked through the papers on his clipboard, then looked at Jessica. 'Are you a modest person?'

She was confused by his question. 'Well, I'm not a bragger.'

Morgan continued. 'You never mentioned the commendations or the case involving the profiler on your CV. Why was that?'

'To be honest, I thought it might reflect badly on me as I disagreed with a senior officer and I . . .'

'It was exceptional work, and disagreeing with a senior officer is never easy, regardless of rank,' Morgan remarked.

Commander Williams continued. 'We will also be recruiing two forensic experts for MSCAN. If you were selected for the team leader role, is there anyone in particular you would like to work with?'

'Yes, ma'am. Diane Thomas. She's a forensic scientist specialising in DNA, blood pattern analysis and fibres. I have worked alongside her many times at major crime scenes and her knowledge and skills have been invaluable.'

To Jessica's surprise, Anderson nodded. 'She lectured on my senior investigators' course. She impressed me; her blood pattern work has solved some big cases. Who would be your second pick for the team?'

'Stephen Jones. He's a fingerprint expert who also specialises in footwear, tool and weapon mark comparisons. He's worked on numerous murder and terrorist cases.'

Williams nodded. 'They've both applied to be on the team. I've spoken to colleagues, and they are both highly respected. Have you spoken to them about working on MSCAN?'

'Yes, ma'am. I felt I should get their approval first if asked to put any names forward.'

'Would they still be interested in joining the team if you didn't get the job?' Anderson asked.

'Of course. They see it as an opportunity to get more hands-on experience rather than being called in as and when for their expertise. I'd love to work with them more permanently, but that's not for me to decide.' Jessica smiled at Anderson, who frowned and looked at his clipboard.

'Your CV states that after completing your master's degree, you worked as a trainee probation officer in Southwark, supervising young offenders to help them avoid re-offending. Is that correct?' he asked.

'Yes, sir. It was challenging as the kids I dealt with were often impulsive and tested boundaries at every level. But it was also very rewarding.'

'So why did you leave after only a year in the job?' Anderson asked, looking at her pointedly.

Jessica knew she could have just said she didn't feel it was the right job for her but decided to be open and frank with the panel. 'I was sexually assaulted by a fifteen-year-old boy I was supervising. Unfortunately, he wasn't charged, but I'd rather not go into all the details. At the time, I couldn't handle the emotional distress it caused me and found it difficult to concentrate on my work. I decided on a different career path and joined Kent police as a scene of crime officer.'

Anderson and the others looked shocked. 'I'm sorry. I didn't know that, um, you know . . .' Anderson mumbled.

'It's not something I'd want to put on my CV. Bad things happen, but you learn to deal with them.'

Anderson didn't ask another question during the remainder of the interview, which focused on Jessica 's personal life and interests. She told them that she currently lived with her brother, but was looking for a place of her own. She also explained that due to her long hours as a crime scene manager, she didn't have much of a social life but enjoyed staying fit and practising yoga to relax and stay focused.

Williams looked at her watch and said she had a couple more questions. 'If you are not selected as the team leader, would you still be interested in being a crime scene investigator on the team?'

'Yes, ma'am, I'd welcome the opportunity to be on such an elite unit.'

'And if selected for either role, how long would it be before you could start?'

'The Kent director of forensics is aware of my application, and I'd have to hand over my current cases, but I think two weeks would be a fair estimate.'

Williams nodded. 'You'll be contacted with the panel's decision on Friday.'

'Thank you, ma'am.' Jessica shook hands with each officer before leaving, and Williams and Morgan wished her well. As he gave her a limp handshake, Anderson said nothing.

* * *

Once Jessica had left the room, Williams turned to her colleagues. 'I have to say Miss Russell impressed me. She has all the requisite skills, and her knowledge of behavioural analysis is definitely an asset. What did you think of her choice of Diane Thomas and Stephen Jones as part of the team?'

'I wouldn't argue with that. Five of the eight candidates said they would like them on the team,' Morgan said, and Anderson nodded his agreement.

'If Miss Russell was on or leading the team, there could also be a cost-saving opportunity,' Williams remarked.

Anderson looked confused, but Morgan could tell what she was considering. 'Are you thinking about giving Miss Russell a dual role?'

Williams nodded. 'Yes, as the team leader, she can also be the behavioural adviser and a CSI.'

Morgan nodded. 'A team of three will certainly be more cost-effective than four.'

Anderson frowned. 'Just because it would save money doesn't mean Russell is the right choice.'

'What is your problem with her, John?' Morgan asked, clearly exasperated.

'I don't have a problem with her. She's clearly an excellent CSI, but she's not on the NCA-approved list as an analyst. I believe employing her as a behavioural analyst is a massive risk and could do more harm than good.'

Williams stood her ground. 'Behavioural advisers do not have Russell's crime scene skills and forensic knowledge. They are generally called in by an SIO a few weeks after a murder or rape by an unknown offender and never visit a live scene. They base their analysis and conclusions on scene photographs, police and witness statements. Russell would be there right from the beginning.'

'Sounds like you've already made up your mind,' Anderson grumbled.

'I haven't. I'm merely pointing out her all-round abilities. We need to discuss our notes on all the candidates before making a final decision.'

CHAPTER TWO

As she left Scotland Yard, Jessica untied her hair, shook it loose and ran her hands through it to fluff it out. She then switched her phone on and noticed a missed call and voicemail from Diane Thomas. She played it back.

'Hi Jess, Taff and I are in Champagne Charlie's. It's in the arches off Villiers Street. Let us know when you're on your way.'

Jessica had never been to Champagne Charlie's before and was pleasantly surprised by the interior, which featured high ceilings, ornate mirrors and a classic Victorian-style bar. She spotted Diane and Taff in a booth at the far end. Diane saw her and was about to wave, but Taff, his usual gregarious self, raised his voice to get Jessica's attention.

'How'd the interview go?' Diane asked as she stood up, hugged Jessica and kissed her on the cheek.

'Hard to say. I won't know the result until tomorrow. God, I need a drink after that. What are you two having?'

'No, no, my round,' said Taff.

'A large glass of Sauvignon Blanc then, please,' said Jessica.

'Same,' nodded Diane.

While Taff was at the bar, Jessica had a word with Diane. 'I'm worried that going over the interview will just make me more anxious about the outcome.'

'If you don't want to talk about it, that's fine by me, and I'm sure Taff will agree. But talking to friends about your thoughts and emotions might actually help relieve your anxiety.'

Taff returned with the drinks and a half of lager for himself, which he raised towards them. 'Iechyd da,' he said as they clinked glasses.

Jessica took her time trying to recall the interview questions and her answers. Doing so made her realise she'd answered some of the questions better than she thought.

'Sounds to me like you did OK,' Diane remarked.

'That DCI Anderson sounds like an arsehole,' Taff added.

'Do you think he might have been playing Bad Cop just to see how you'd react?' Diane asked.

'It's possible, but I think he meant every word. Commander Williams didn't look happy with the way he spoke to me.'

'Sounds like she was on your side?' Diane said.

'Williams and Morgan were charming, and their body language was positive, but Anderson had a face like a prune throughout the interview. And I'll be up against some strong competition, where my lack of management experience might go against me.'

'Do you know who they might pick for the behavioural adviser role?' Taff asked.

'Not a clue, but I'd guess it will be someone on the National Crime Agency list. I told the panel if I were selected as team leader, I'd want you both working alongside me.'

'How'd that go down?' Taff asked.

'Williams said you are both highly respected in the forensic world.'

'That's odd because Taff's always on another planet,' Diane joked.

'Even if I don't get the position, you two are in with a good shout of being on the MSCAN team.'

'It wouldn't be the same without you, Draig,' Taff said, using her Welsh nickname of 'dragon' on account of her flaming red hair.

'Even so, I'd be upset if you two didn't accept the offer. We've analysed my morning enough, so let's move on to something more important. What do you two want to drink?'

'Not for me,' Taff said. 'I've got a Zoom meeting with the prosecution barrister regarding his footwear evidence in an upcoming murder trial.' He finished his drink and looked at Jessica. 'If you don't get the job, it'll be a fucking travesty. I've never worked with a crime scene manager as good as you. Never doubt your worth or abilities, Jess, and know that me and Di will always have your back, no matter what happens.'

'Thanks, Taff. What will be will be.' She gave him a hug.

'It's not often you see him being that serious,' Diane remarked after he'd left the bar.

'Underneath all the jokes, he's got a heart of gold,' Jessica smiled.

'You want some lunch here or going somewhere else?' Diane asked.

'It's a nice day . . . do you fancy a walk, and we could maybe grab a sandwich along the way?'

'Sounds like a plan.'

'Let's get a sandwich on Villiers Street, then walk to Victoria Station,' Jessica suggested.

'I can get a train home to Petts Wood from Victoria. What about you?'

'I'll get the train to Clapham Junction and then walk home,' Diane said.

As they strolled through Horse Guards Parade eating their sandwiches, Diane asked about David.

'He's hurt his back, but otherwise I think he's doing OK.'

'Is he still off the drink and drugs?'

'It appears so. I haven't found any hidden vodka bottles in the house for a long time. He pretty much sticks to alcohol-free beer and wine now, but he's been smoking cannabis. I've smelt it on him and in the garage and garden shed.'

'Did you confront him about it?'

'I don't want to get into a row with him. I'm pretty sure it isn't Skunk again, as he hasn't exhibited any psychotic behaviour like before.'

Diane knew Skunk was made from unpollinated cannabis plants, which contained higher levels of tetrahydrocannabinol, making it stronger, and also causing nasty side effects, including paranoia and hallucinations. 'You should talk to him about it. If a neighbour smells it and tells the police, it could harm your career.'

'You're right, but I need to tread carefully with David. He often takes advice the wrong way and becomes very defensive.'

'He's lucky to have you as a sister. I hope he appreciates how much you've done for him since your mother died. I know he took it badly and went off the rails, but he seems to forget it was also a terrible time for you.'

'David's not a bad person. He's just had a tough life and . . .'

'So have you. You gave up your flat and most of your social life to look after him. You should start looking for a place of your own again, you know.'

'That's what David suggested this morning. I don't mind living with him. It helps me financially, and we get on OK . . . well, most of the time. But if I'm selected as the MSCAN team leader, my salary will increase significantly, enough to get a mortgage for a place of my own. Anyway, what about you, how's your family?' Jessica asked, wanting to change the subject.

'Not bad, thanks. Mum and Dad have been godsends since the divorce, especially with looking after Ellory. He's five now and starting primary school in September. I'm lucky they live just around the corner. But if I get the forensic scientist's role on the MSCAN team, it will undoubtedly mean longer hours and being on call day and night.'

'Have you told your parents about it?'

'Yeah, they're very supportive, even if it will mean more work for them.'

'What about your ex-husband, does he not help out with Ellory?'

'He did until he buggered off to Leeds with that tart he had the affair with. She's pregnant now. He pays me child maintenance, but he only visits Ellory once in a blue moon. You know, I'll never forgive Paul for what he did to me, but he's Ellory's father, and as much as it galls me, I won't bad-mouth him to our son.' She laughed. 'You could move in with me, then we can grow old and miserable together.'

Jessica smiled. 'I think we'd drive each other mad talking shop all the time.'

Arriving at Victoria station, they stopped and gave each other a big hug. 'I really hope you get it,' Diane said. 'And Taff and I will be working with you.'

'So do I. But if I don't get it, I'll stay in Kent as a CSM and still be doing work that I love.'

'But then we won't be working together on crime scenes anymore as the MSCAN unit only covers the Met area ...'

Jessica shook her head. 'Don't you dare turn it down because of me. It's an opportunity you may not get again.'

A departure announcement came over the station's public address system.

'Shit, that's my train. I'd better get a move on ... Ring me when you hear anything,' Diane said and hurried off.

CHAPTER THREE

Jessica walked from Petts Wood Station to the three-bedroom bungalow she shared with David in Greenfield Gardens. Their mother Eileen had bought it after an acrimonious divorce which gave her custody of Jessica and David, and she had left it to them when she died eighteen months ago. David had still been living with her at the time.

After the divorce, their father Roger never contacted his wife or children again. David had difficulties in coming to terms with what had happened, often asking where his father was and if he could visit him. The problem was, their mother didn't know where he was living, and whenever she tried to contact him at work or on his mobile, he didn't answer or just put the phone down.

Not long after they moved into the bungalow, Eileen went back to teaching at a local primary school, and though she made new friends, she never formed any serious relationships for her children's sake. She raised David and Jessica alone.

Over time, David realised their father wanted nothing to do with them and his feelings for him turned to contempt. In his teenage years, he became argumentative and moody, neglecting his studies, often staying out late, drinking and taking drugs, which caused arguments not only with his mother but with Jessica as well. It wasn't until his best friend died from an overdose that David realised the damage he was doing to himself and his family. He stopped taking drugs, regularly attended a rehabilitation group, limited his alcohol consumption and got a job as a postman. In Jessica's absence at university, David lived at home and insisted he pay his mother rent and do any odd jobs, house repairs and gardening she wanted.

Although Jessica was also upset when her parents divorced, she hid her emotions, not wanting to cause her mother and David more anguish. Her father had never been very loving or affectionate towards her, often commenting that she would amount to nothing if she had her mother's brains. Looking back, Jessica realised his comments had had the reverse effect, giving her the drive to succeed, and although he was no longer part of her life, she still wanted to prove him wrong.

After their mother's sudden and unexpected death from cancer, David suffered from depression and started drinking and using drugs again. Jessica moved back to the bungalow, but due to the pressures of her work, she couldn't always be there for him. In desperation and fearing David would lose his job, she persuaded him to spend time in the Priory drug and alcohol rehabilitation hospital in Hayes. When David was well enough, they discussed selling the bungalow, but in the end agreed it would be best to keep it and live together.

Arriving home, Jessica walked into the kitchen where she found David, dressed in cycling clothes, oiling the gears of his new bike which was upside down on the kitchen table. 'She's a beauty, isn't she,' he said proudly. 'And I managed to get the seller down another two hundred quid.'

Jessica shook her head and sighed. 'You've spilled oil on the table. Can't you do that in the garage?'

He shook his head. 'My other bike is on the stand. Anyway, I've finished now. I'm taking her for a quick spin before it gets dark.'

'What do you want for dinner?'

'Whatever you're cooking will do. How'd the job interview go?'

'Fine. I'll find out if I've got it tomorrow.' She couldn't face going over the details again.

As David lifted the bike off the table, his face tightened and he arched his back, clearly in pain. He dropped the bike, knocking the uncapped oil can off the table. As the oil began to spill onto the floor, Jessica grabbed the kitchen roll and started mopping it up. 'Sorry, I didn't mean to . . .'

'It's all right. I'll clean it up . . . as usual!' Jessica couldn't help adding.

'Why are you always so anal about tidiness?'

'I'm not . . .'

'Yes, you are. You hoover and dust in the morning before work and again in the evening.'

'No, I don't.'

'Yes, you do. In fact, at weekends, you sometimes do it three times a day!'

'It's because I'm forever having to clean up after you,' she said, holding the oil-stained kitchen roll out towards him.

He frowned. 'It's like living with Mrs Hinch. I'm off on a bike ride. I'll see you in about an hour.'

'Do you think riding a bike is wise if your back is playing up?' she said.

'I'm fine. It was just a little spasm.'

'Suit yourself. You need to see a physio or book an appointment with the doctor before it gets worse.'

'Give it a rest, Jessica,' he said as he put on his helmet and walked his bike towards the front door.

'That's going to leave wheel marks in the hallway. Go out the back door through the garage,' she said.

David sighed loudly, shaking his head, but did as she asked. When he'd gone Jessica got down on her hands and knees. There were still traces of oil on the kitchen floor. She got out a mop and bucket and started cleaning.

* * *

On Friday morning, Jessica returned to work at the Kent Police head-quarters in Maidstone and spoke with the Director of Forensics, Chris Hadham. 'You'll be a significant loss for the crime scene unit, but I wish you well. And in the meantime, I won't allocate you any major crime scenes so you can complete your outstanding paperwork.'

Jessica thanked him and went straight to her office. She was almost up to date with all her work, but she had a couple of cases she still needed to follow up on. She had her mobile on the desk, anxiously awaiting a phone call from Commander Williams. It was just after 9.30 a.m. when her phone rang. She grabbed it and hurriedly answered the call, only to discover it was Diane.

'You heard anything yet?' Diane asked.

'No, have you?'

'No, that's why I'm calling you,' Diane retorted.

'Have you spoken to Taff?'

'Yes, I called him. He hasn't heard anything either.'

'As soon as I hear anything, I'll let you know,' Jessica said, trying to sound positive.

'I've never felt so nervous . . . it's worse than being cross-examined at the Old Bailey.'

An incoming call warning appeared on Jessica's phone screen, but she didn't recognise the number. She hurriedly told Diane she had to go, ended their call and answered the unknown caller.

'I'd like to tell you about our great new solar panelling . . .'

'Piss off!' Jessica told the unfortunate cold caller, slamming her phone down on her desk. She went to the canteen and got a coffee to calm herself down, but realising she'd left her phone on the desk, hurried back to the office.

Jessica noticed a missed call on her phone from an unknown central London landline. She tentatively dialled the number, not wanting to be caught out again and was relieved to hear Jordan, Commander Williams's assistant, answering. He put her straight through to her.

'Good morning, Jess. How are you today?' Williams asked

'Fine, ma'am, though I'm somewhat nervous about this call.'

'Well, after much deliberation, it was decided that you were the best candidate to be the team leader for the MSCAN unit, so congratulations and welcome to the Met.'

Jessica almost spilled her coffee in her excitement. 'Thank you, ma'am. It's a real honour, and I'm looking forward to it.' She was about to ask who else had been selected, but Commander Williams said she had a meeting with the Commissioner and asked Jessica if she could come to her office at 2 p.m. to discuss her appointment and some other exciting news she had for her. 'Yes, of course,' Jessica replied.

'Good, see you then. Please keep things to yourself for the moment, as I've yet to inform the unsuccessful candidates. I'm happy for you to speak with your director of forensics so arrangements can start for your official transfer but kindly ask him to keep it to himself.' She ended the call.

Jessica banged her fist on the desk in triumph. 'You did it, Jess, you did it!' She desperately wanted to phone Diane and Taff but knew Commander Williams would not be impressed if she found out. She just hoped they'd also been selected for the unit.

Jessica put her phone on silent and left it in the office when she went to speak with Hadham. He seemed genuinely pleased to hear her news. 'Take the weekend off and celebrate properly, and I'll have the paperwork completed quickly so you can transfer to the Met a week Monday if Commander Williams agrees. And we'll organise a farewell drink next Friday if that's OK.'

'That would be great. Thank you.'

Returning to the office, she checked her phone. She'd missed two calls from Diane and a text message asking if she'd heard anything. She texted her back, saying not yet and she was in case meetings for the rest of the day but would let her know the result as soon as she got it. She wasn't surprised she hadn't heard anything from Taff. Compared to the two of them, he could be remarkably patient.

Jessica returned home to get changed for her meeting with Commander Williams. She tied her hair back and chose wide-leg trousers paired with a button-up shirt, jacket and pointed flat shoes, wanting to look smart, but not as if she was attending another interview. David wasn't back from work, so she texted that she had been selected for the team leader job and was going to Scotland Yard for a meeting. David quickly replied: *Congratulations! Proud of you!* She was proud of him too, she thought, the way he'd turned his life around. But now she had this important new role, she was definitely going to have to mention the marijuana.

Jessica booked herself in at the Yard and went to Williams's personal assistant's office. Jordan congratulated her and said he needed to take a digital photo to produce an identity card allowing her access to Scotland Yard, all Metropolitan Police stations, and the laboratory at Lambeth, where she would be based.

'Can I offer a suggestion?' he said. 'Untie your hair, fluff it out and let it hang naturally. You'll look a bit less severe in your ID photo.'

She was taken aback at first, then realised he was right. 'There's something I'd like to ask you too, but you might not want to answer it,' Jessica said as he got the digital camera set up.

'I won't know until you ask, so go ahead,' he said as he printed off the photo to put in a card laminator.

'Was my selection a unanimous verdict by the interviewing panel?'

He paused before replying. 'Two to one . . . but I didn't tell you that.'

'And would I be right in saying DCI Anderson was the 'no'?'

He nodded. 'But I wouldn't let it worry you. His opinions don't carry much weight with Commander Williams. As a former Kent officer, she knows many Met detectives think of county officers as country bumpkins, but she's proved them wrong . . . as will you.' Jordan finished making the identity card and put it in a small folding leather wallet with a metal Metropolitan Police crest. He handed it to Jessica, along with a plastic holder on a lanyard.

'There is quite a bit of paperwork I need you to sign for your transfer, but I'll email you a link to a secure Met website with a passcode where you can do it all online. Is there anything else you want to ask me?'

'Not that I can think of right now, and thanks for all your help and advice.'

'My pleasure. I'll let Commander Williams know you're here.'

Walking down the corridor, Jessica couldn't believe how quickly things had changed since her interview two days ago. She felt she was starting a new and challenging life. She proudly looked at her identity card and again thought Jordan was right to suggest she untied her hair, not trying to hide it away.

'I am absolutely thrilled to have been accepted for the position. I won't let you down, ma'am,' she said as Williams welcomed her into her office and ushered her into an armchair.

'I know you won't,' Williams said, sitting down on the sofa. 'However, your crime scene and forensic knowledge wasn't the only reason we selected you. You have the skills to perform a dual leader and behavioural analyst role. It will mean more responsibility and pressure on your workload, but I'm confident you can do it . . . if you are willing to.'

Jessica was surprised but quickly regained her composure. 'I'm not a qualified BIA, but I understand their methodology and investigative techniques, some of which I frequently use in my crime scene analysis. So, yes, I'd be happy to perform a dual role.'

'Excellent. Undoubtedly some senior investigators will see it as cutting corners, and I won't hide the fact it will save money. However, your combined knowledge of psychology, forensics and hands-on crime scene investigation are invaluable skills that behavioural advisers don't have and will enable you to prove any doubters wrong. I also think a behavioural analysis course would be beneficial to you . . . if you want to attend one.'

'I'd be happy to,' Jessica replied.

'There is a slight catch,' Williams smiled.

'And what would that be?'

'It's a ten to twelve-week residential course at the FBI Academy in Quantico. Would that affect your decision?'

Jessica was almost speechless, 'Oh my God, that's the most prestigious course of its kind. I'd be honoured to go on it. Would it be before I start on MSCAN?'

'No, it will probably be in a few months or early next year if I can get you on it.'

Jessica was relieved it wasn't imminent as she was keen to start in her new role.

Williams continued. 'The Commissioner has approved it, and I've been in touch with Special Agent Anna Travis, a lecturer on the course, who will make enquiries and see if you can do the course. You may have heard of her.'

Jessica nodded enthusiastically. 'Yes, I have. She was a DCI in the Met and lectured at a Chartered Society of Forensic Sciences conference I attended some years ago. She was a very impressive speaker.'

'And a formidable investigator. I got to know her well on a joint Kent and Met serial killer investigation. She married an American FBI Agent, moved there, got her green card and was selected for the Behavioural Analysis Unit. You have many of her qualities.'

'I'll do my best to prove you right, ma'am,' Jessica said, taken aback by the compliment.

'Right, so when can you start?' Williams asked.

'A week from Monday, ma'am.'

Williams looked pleased. 'I'll fast-track the transfer process then.'

Jessica was on the point of asking who the other members of the MSCAN team would be, but then realised, as Williams hadn't mentioned it, a final decision might not have been made.

'Now, Jordan, my PA, has organised a car to take us to Lambeth so you can see your new offices and laboratory facilities.'

*   *   *

The drive to the Metropolitan Police Forensics Laboratories took about ten minutes, and when they arrived Williams took Jessica to the fourth floor. 'Have you been here before?' Williams asked.

'No, it's my first time. We used different forensic labs for submissions in Kent.'

They stopped by a door with a 'Murder and Serious Crime Analysis Unit' plaque. Williams pressed 1066 on the number entry lock, opened the door and stepped to one side. 'After you, and welcome to your new home from home.'

As Jessica entered, she was impressed by the size and layout of the room. There were three large desks, each with a mini computer, monitor and iPad Pros for use at crime scenes. Beside the desks were silver crime scene cases with MSCAN embossed on them. There was a large TV screen on one wall linked to a laptop on a table below it, and along one wall were cabinets containing much of the equipment they would need. Williams opened one of them, containing an array of brand-new fingerprint and footprint recovery equipment and a variety of crime scene torches.

'This is unbelievable. It's way more than I was expecting,' Jessica said, wide-eyed.

'You and your team can sort things out as you want them. Crime scene vehicles will also be provided, but if you need anything else, equipment-wise, let me know.'

'Do we have access to the Home Office Large Major Enquiry System?' Jessica asked.

She was referring to the computer database known as HOLMES, designed to aid the investigation into large-scale enquiries and used by police to collate and cross-reference all the information gathered in a major crime investigation.

'Unfortunately, the answer is no, as none of your team will be authorised users. It can only be operated by trained personnel in the Homicide and Major Investigation team offices.' Williams pointed to a glass partitioned room with the blinds down. 'Your office. Take a look.'

Jessica opened the door. As she looked for the light switch, she jumped back as Taff and Diane suddenly appeared from behind the door.

'Your team and I thought we'd organise a little surprise for you,' Williams said, grinning.

'Thank you. I can't tell you how much it means to have these two working with me,' Jessica said, embracing them.

'We don't work with you, we work for you . . . boss,' Taff replied, and they all laughed.

Jessica looked around the room, which was furnished in a similar style to Williams's office but with different coloured furniture. She noticed a bottle of champagne, with four glasses on her desk, along with a cake with 'Congratulations' written on it.

'Time for a toast,' Williams said. 'You do the honours, Taff.'

'And don't spill any,' Diane added as she picked up a knife to cut the cake. 'We've got our own lab next door, Jess . . . you'll be blown away when you see it. There's state of the art DNA extractors, microscopes, superglue chambers, light sourcing . . . you name it.'

'It must have cost a bloody fortune,' Taff remarked as he handed them each a glass of champagne.

'It did, and I'm counting on you all to prove it was worth every penny,' Williams said, raising her glass.

'Cheers. We'll do our best,' Jessica said.

'Do the detectives on the Murder and Serious Crime teams know about MSCAN and what we will be doing?' Taff asked after he'd swallowed a mouthful of champagne.

'I've issued a circular and spoken with the senior investigators who lead each team,' Williams told them. 'They will brief their officers and civilian staff, so they won't be surprised when you arrive at a crime scene. Given that you're a small unit, attending every major crime scene in London is impossible unless you work around the clock. I believe your investigative skills are best utilised in the most serious crimes. Therefore, I have instructed all the senior investigating officers that MSCAN's assistance should only be requested for Category A and B homicides and major crime investigations.'

'That make sense,' Jessica said.

'You'll still have a heavy workload,' Williams added.

'We are all up for the challenge and can't wait for our first case,' Jessica replied confidently.

Diane raised her glass. 'I'll drink to that.'

'I was wondering, if we are going to be working long hours, does that sofa convert into a bed?' Taff joked.

'There's no way you're ever sleeping in my office,' Jessica said firmly.

'Looks like you'll have to do with the office floor then,' Diane grinned.

This was the first time Williams had observed them together. *I think we may have ourselves a good team*, she thought to herself.

CHAPTER FOUR

When she got home, Jessica could smell something familiar cooking but wasn't quite sure what it was. The oven was on, and David was sitting at the kitchen table, looking at a piece of paper. 'What are you cooking?'

He handed Jessica the paper, and she instantly recognised their mother's handwriting. 'It's Mum's chicken casserole recipe, our favourite meal. We haven't had it since she died, but I thought it would be a nice way to celebrate your success today. I'm making mashed potatoes with it, and there's a bottle of champagne in the fridge. It's from Lidl, but it's won blind-tasting awards from experts. And there's sticky toffee pudding with cream for dessert, but I bought that from M&S.'

'Thanks, David, that's so thoughtful of you. I really appreciate it. Can I do anything to help?'

'Nope. It's all under control. Ready in about half an hour?'

'OK, I'll just go and sort out the dirty laundry,' Jessica said.

'I've already put the washing on and hoovered and cleaned everywhere, even the bathroom.'

Jessica was taken aback. She knew David loved cooking, but she couldn't remember if he'd ever done any housework. 'You didn't need to do all that, especially if your back is playing up.'

'I took it nice and easy. Besides, you're always telling me a clean house is a happy house, so I thought I'd give you a break and make you happy.'

Jessica glanced at him sideways. 'Have you had your bike in here again?' She looked around for any signs of cycle oil.

He laughed. 'No, I just wanted to do something nice for you.'

'All right, I believe you,' she said and went to her bedroom. After changing into her tracksuit bottoms and a T-shirt, Jessica returned to the kitchen and started setting the table while David opened the champagne. They both said cheers and clinked glasses. She sipped hers but noticed that David quickly drank half a glass and immediately topped it up. David served the chicken casserole and mash, eager for Jessica's reaction. 'Just like Mum's,' she said, and he smiled.

While they ate, she told him about her meeting with Commander Williams, the office and the state-of-the-art laboratory facilities. When they finished, he cleared the table and Jessica did her best to hide her irritation at the haphazard way he put the dirty plates and cutlery in the dishwasher, knowing she liked them to be rinsed under the tap first and placed in the dishwasher a certain way.

As David was getting the sticky toffee pudding from the fridge, the washing machine beeped. Jessica stood up. 'I'll put the clothes in the tumble dryer,' she said.

David wagged his finger at her. 'No, you won't. I'm in charge today, so sit down. You can pour us another glass of champagne if you want something to do.'

Jessica still had a full glass and poured a bit into David's while he had his back to her. She watched as he pulled the clothes out and put them in the laundry basket, then her heart sank as she realised what he had done. She could see he'd mixed the coloured and white clothes and set the temperature dial to 60 degrees. As a result, the dye in the coloured clothes had bled out and turned her white silk blouse and underwear a pinky-grey colour. She saw her cotton jeans and a red jumper in among the load and realised they would most likely have shrunk at that temperature. Trying her best not to ruin the evening, Jessica swallowed her annoyance and said nothing. But David quickly noticed his error.

'You are a fucking idiot!' he muttered angrily to himself, swiping his hand against the sticky toffee pudding and accidentally knocking it to the floor. He looked forlornly at the soggy mess on the floor. Jessica calmly got up from her chair and grabbed the kitchen roll. David bent over and tried to scoop up the pudding, bits sliding back to the floor through his fingers. As he started to straighten up, his back went into spasm. He cried out in pain and collapsed to his knees.

Jessica knelt beside him and put her arm around his shoulder to help him up. 'You've obviously done something serious to your back. You need to see a doctor.'

'I'll be fine, it's just a bit of sciatica . . .'

'You need to rest up. All that cycling and pushing heavy mail trolleys around doesn't help. If you don't book a doctor's appointment, I will.'

'All right,' he said. 'Point taken. I'll do it on my laptop in the bedroom.'

'I'll run you a hot bath with some Radox, then I think you should go to bed and rest your back.'

David didn't argue as she helped him to his room. While he bathed, Jessica cleaned up the mess from the sticky toffee pudding and placed it in the bin before mopping the floor. She then removed the dirty plates and cutlery from the dishwasher, rinsed them in the sink and restacked them in an orderly way so they would be cleaned efficiently. Although David's sloppiness annoyed her, she realised that her need to constantly tidy and clean irritated him just as much. He said she had an obsessive-compulsive disorder, and from her psychology studies, Jessica knew there was some truth in it. She recognised that her OCD had been triggered by the traumas she had experienced. Her compulsive behaviour served as a coping mechanism, which, ironically, also happened to make her exceptionally thorough in her work as a crime scene investigator.

David hobbled in. 'Sorry for the mess and ruining the evening,' he said miserably.

'The clothes and the pudding are not important, David. It's your health I'm concerned about. Did you book an appointment at the doctor's?'

'The best I could get was a telephone appointment with Doctor Barnes on Monday morning. It's a two-week wait for a surgery appointment.'

'Well, that's better than nothing, and for Christ's sake take it easy . . . no cycling and maybe go sick from work.'

'I'm off this weekend, so I'll see how I feel on Monday.'

'Then spend the weekend in bed and let your back heal.'

He tried to stand upright and saluted. 'Yes, ma'am!'

She shook her head and laughed. 'Now get to bed and get some rest.'

'Any chance of a hot chocolate? Might help me sleep.'

'God knows what you'd do without me,' she said, flicking the kettle on. He shuffled off with a smile. When she had made his drink, she tapped on the door and went into his bedroom. She placed the big mug on his bedside table, turned to go back to the kitchen, then hesitated. 'I don't want you to get pissed off with me, but occasionally I can smell that you've been smoking weed. It's just that if I can detect it, you never know if someone else can.'

He folded his arms. 'I've not done it for a bloody long time.'

'I'm sure you haven't, but it's just a sort of warning, I need you to look out for me, even more so in my new position. It could get me into big trouble.'

'Shit, you're right, and I'm sorry, but I don't have any and there's no way I'll score any more, you have my word.'

'Thank you.'

He reached for his hot chocolate. 'Did you sugar it?'

'I most certainly did. Good night.'

* * *

Jessica spent the weekend taking care of David, insisting he stay in bed. He wasn't happy about it, saying he wanted to go on a ride with his Petts Wood Cycling Club friends. But she told him she'd locked the garage doors and hidden the key, so it was pointless trying to escape. She had also done a quick sweep to double-check he had been telling the truth and had only found an old roach under a bench. On Sunday, he said his back felt much better and that he would go to work the following morning. Jessica had noticed his occasional wince of pain and once again tried to persuade him to go sick, but he kept saying he was fine. She knew arguing with him would be pointless but warned him that he'd only have himself to blame if his back flared up again.

* * *

On Monday morning, Jessica went to her office at the Kent police headquarters. She completed and signed all the online documents for her transfer on the following Monday, and then, having finished her paperwork and case files, spoke briefly with the Director of Forensics. He said she could spend the rest of the week at the Met lab setting up her new office, and he would call her if needed. He also reminded her he'd organised a leaving drink after work at the local pub on Friday.

Jessica then called Commander Williams to inform her that she could officially join the Metropolitan Police next Monday. The Commander was delighted and asked Jess if she and her team would like to be on call over the coming weekend if a category A or B major crime occurred. Jessica said she was available all weekend and would speak with Diane and Taff later, as they were helping to set up their new offices, but she felt they would be happy to be on call.

That evening, sitting at the kitchen table, David told Jessica he'd had a phone consultation with Doctor Barnes. Unsurprisingly, she said he'd probably strained a muscle in his back at work. David didn't challenge her assessment, even though he'd never felt any pain while doing his mail round. But Doctor Barnes also wanted him to have a blood test to assess his general state of health, and he'd had a sample taken at the local chemists in Petts Wood after work. The doctor would contact him once she had the results. However, he failed to mention to Jessica that Doctor Barnes also recommended he take a few days of sick leave to recover fully.

'That's it?' Jessica asked sceptically.

'Yeah, she said it'll probably sort itself out. Right, I'm off to bed,' he said before Jessica could say anything else.

CHAPTER FIVE

It was 2 a.m. on Monday morning when the London call handler answered a 999 call from a mobile phone. 'Emergency, which service do you require?' There was no reply. 'Do you require Fire, Police or Ambulance?' As the handler repeated the question, he could hear the caller's distressed, shallow breathing. He decided to use the Silent Solution system, a procedure to filter out accidental 999 calls while ensuring the caller could alert the police and get help if the call was genuine. 'If you cannot speak but need an emergency service, please tap the handset, cough or make a noise.' A faint gurgling cough followed the request, and the handler connected the call to the police's automated silent solution system at the Metropolitan Police Command and Control room.

'This is the police. If you can't speak, please press 5 twice on your keypad,' a pre-recorded voice stated. The requested numbers were pressed, and the call was now answered by a young female civilian handler who was new to the job.

She could hear the caller struggling to breathe. 'I need to ask you some questions. To answer, press once for no and twice for yes on any button on your phone. Do you need police assistance?'

The caller pressed twice. The handler asked if the caller was injured and received another double press. When asked if they had been assaulted and if the assailant was still on the premises, the caller indicated yes. The handler, realising the caller might be in a life-threatening situation, raised her hand to get the attention of the duty chief inspector, who came over and connected his headset to the handler's unit. The handler continued the conversation.

'I can see your mobile phone number but can't pinpoint your

location. Please whisper your address, then I can dispatch the police and an ambulance to you.'

The caller started to speak for the first time, but their voice was weak and their breathing shallow, making it hard to understand the reply. The handler could pick up a few words and asked the caller to tap yes or no again to her questions.

'Did you say Victoria Park?'

There was another double press.

'Is that Victoria Park Road in Hackney?'

The caller pressed yes again.

'I know it's hard, but I need your house number . . .'

The caller started to speak, but his voice was rasping, making it difficult to hear the number.

'I heard the numbers three and eighty, but I need the last number again.' The handler requested.

The caller groaned as he tried to give the number, then cried, 'No, please don't . . .'

The handler and chief inspector could hear repeated thuds, like a fist beating against a chest, intermingled with the agonising screams of the caller, who was clearly being beaten or stabbed. Then the phone went dead.

The young handler was visibly distressed and slow to respond, so the chief inspector took over and put out an urgent response call on the radio. 'All units Central East from Control . . . suspects on premises Victoria Park Road, Hackney. The exact address is currently unknown, but it is believed to be between 380 and 389. Approach with caution, as suspects may be violent and armed. Victim unknown but male and may have life-threatening injuries. Ambulance also en route.'

Two vehicles initially responded, with one stating it was in Bethnal Green, approximately three minutes away, and the other about five minutes away. A police dog unit and an armed response vehicle said they would attend but were some distance away.

The chief inspector updated the officers travelling to the scene, informing them that the mobile cell mast identification showed the call coming from the Hackney Wick end of Victoria Park Road, which would suggest the victim lived in one of the expensive terraced houses opposite the park.

PC Sally Simpson, with full headlights on, was driving the closest vehicle, and said they would start house-to-house visits from 380 to 389. The chief inspector instructed the second vehicle to check the even numbers from three hundred and eighty upwards, which, from mapping data, didn't overlook the park and were further up the road from Hackney Wick. The other two vehicles attending were to split up and assist the officers at the odd and even numbers on arrival.

'I just hope they find him alive,' the young call handler said, close to tears.

The chief inspector gave her a comforting smile. 'Those are the sorts of calls we all dread, but you handled it well, so don't let it get to you. You can finish duty early if you want. I can also arrange counselling if you need it.'

'Thank you, sir, but I'll be fine. I want to stay and know the outcome.'

'OK, but take a few minutes off first. You did a good job and remained calm while dealing with the caller. Believe me, there was nothing more you could have done . . . but be prepared for the worst.'

*   *   *

PC Sally Simpson drove slowly up Victoria Park Road past the odd numbers. None of the premises had lights on. She reversed, parked outside number 385, and her colleague, PC Andy Reid, hurriedly opened his passenger door and started to get out. Sally grabbed his jacket. 'Whoa, not so fast, newbie. You don't go flying into these situations . . . the suspect might be armed and still be on the premises. Let control know we've arrived.'

'Sorry.' Since his initial training, he had only been on patrol for three weeks, and this was his first night shift. His heart raced as he nervously made the radio call, then looked to Sally for advice.

'You start at 380. I'll go to 389. If you see anything, don't go charging in or shout. Call me on the radio quietly or wave if you can see me. Use your torch to check the ground and door for blood as you go.'

Reid, eyes wide open, nodded and got out of the car. As Sally approached 389, she flicked on her torch and proceeded up the three stone steps to the front door. She shone her torch on the door-mat and noticed a tiny smear of what looked like blood and another small smear on the doorknob. She next opened the letter-box, shone her torch through it and could see what looked like a bloody footprint in the hallway. She called Reid on the radio.

'Get the enforcer from the car boot asap,' she whispered, refer-ring to the portable battering ram.

Reid replied, 'Received', and on hearing their conversation, the control room chief inspector asked for an update. Sally told him what she'd found, and the chief inspector suggested they wait for back up before entering in case any suspects were still on the premises. Reid, who now had the red enforcer, looked to Sally for a decision.

She pressed her radio button. 'I've got a taser. The victim may need urgent medical assistance, so we'll proceed with caution, over . . .'

The chief inspector said he would direct the other attending officers and the ambulance to their location.

'Turn your body camera on, put the door in, then get your truncheon out,' Sally told Reid.

'I've never used an enforcer,' he said, feebly.

'You're much stronger than me. Aim halfway between the doorknob and the frame for maximum force, not at the doorknob itself.'

His hand trembled as he pressed his body cam on. He held the ram towards the door, took a deep breath, swung it back, then smashed it into the door with all his might. It didn't open the first time, but he kept going, and on the third blow it did, revealing a long hallway with oak flooring and two sets of carpeted stairs at the far end, one going up and the other down. Reid put the ram down, withdrew his extendable baton and flicked it open.

'You good to go?' Sally asked calmly. He nodded and started to walk across the threshold. Sally stopped him and held up the taser. 'It's ladies first, you stay behind me. Keep to the left-hand side of the hallway to avoid stepping on any suspect footprints.'

She stepped into the hall. 'This is the police,' she called loudly. 'I am armed with a taser. If there's anyone in the house, walk slowly into the hallway with your hands raised.' She cautiously walked a few feet into the house with her taser raised. They waited a few seconds before moving forward again. To their left was an open door to a large living room. Sally used her knuckle to knock the light switch on. They could see it had been ransacked, with drawers and their contents scattered over the floor.

'Looks like a burglary,' Reid said quietly. Sally pointed to faint bloodstained footprints on the floor so Reid wouldn't step in them. He looked queasy as they moved forward slowly, stopping by the decorative archway which led to a large open-plan kitchen diner. Sally repeated the taser warning and pointed to some more bloody footprints on the tiled kitchen floor by a large marble island, which they couldn't quite see over. Sally turned the light on, illuminating a considerable amount of blood on the floor, the island worktop, kitchen cupboards and a large fridge. Reid started to move sideways.

'Don't step in the blood,' Sally warned him as they moved around to get a better view of the other side of the island.

'Jesus Christ,' Reid exclaimed. There was a semi-naked man in pyjama bottoms lying motionless, face down in a pool of blood. He had a large kitchen knife embedded in his back and a gaping wound on the back of his head. He looked as if he had been beaten and repeatedly stabbed. Reid put his hand to his mouth.

'If you're going to be sick, do it outside,' Sally said as she holstered her taser and moved forward to check for any signs of life. She leaned over to avoid stepping in the blood and put two fingers on the man's neck, then looked at Reid and shook her head. 'Looks like he's dead,' she said calmly.

'Oh my God!' Reid exclaimed.

'What, what's wrong?' Sally asked, startled.

'I just saw his finger twitch.'

Sally heard a siren. 'That's the ambulance . . . go and escort them in.' She then contacted the control room and gave them an update.

As Reid rushed outside, another patrol car pulled up. Two officers got out and headed towards the house. He told them it appeared that the suspects had gone, then spoke with the ambulance crew and directed them to the kitchen.

While the ambulance crew worked on the victim, Sally told the other officers it was best no one else entered the scene so as not to contaminate or damage any potential forensic evidence. As they didn't know in which direction the assailant had gone, Sally asked the officers to get further assistance to cordon off the street at least a hundred meters each way and both ends of Homer Road, which was to the right of the victim's house.

The control room contacted Sally and informed her that the

voters' register showed Johan and Michelle De Klerk living at the premises, and the mobile phone number used by the 999 caller was registered to a man with the same name and address. Sally, Andy, and two other officers searched the rest of the house, but no one else was on the premises.

The ambulance crew were hurriedly taking the man out face down on a stretcher. The knife was still lodged in his back, but roller gauze was wrapped around the entry site to control bleeding and secure the knife in place. The driver told Sally they suspected the man had suffered a traumatic cardiac arrest due to stab wounds in his thoracic area, and they were taking him to Homerton University Hospital A and E.

'Will he live?' Sally asked.

'It's touch and go. He's lost a lot of blood and got a fractured skull by the looks of it, but he's young and looks fit. It's lucky you found him as quickly as you did. Generally, with those types of injuries, they don't survive beyond fifteen to twenty minutes without medical assistance.'

Sally turned to Reid. 'How are you doing?'

'I'm OK, thanks. I've just never seen that much blood before. It was like a slaughterhouse in there . . . on the floor, the fridge, the ceiling, just everywhere, and then that knife sticking out of his back . . .'

Sally put her hand on his shoulder. 'There's a first time for everything in this job. You go in the ambulance and keep your body camera on. I know it's unlikely, but the victim may say something, and it would be good to have it recorded. Secure the victim's pyjama bottoms and knife as evidence when they're removed.'

'I haven't got any exhibit bags.'

'The hospital will have plastic bags you can use temporarily. If he does peg it, you stay with the body and put some bags over his hands. I'll secure the scene and start a crime scene log. I know this has all been a bit traumatic for you. If you feel you need counselling, make sure you get it . . . or you can talk to me. I'm a good listener,' she said with a reassuring smile.

Reid thanked her and got in the ambulance. Sally called control and informed them the victim was in critical condition, on his way to Homerton Hospital, and PC Reid was with him. She then requested the attendance of Forensics and the Homicide and Serious Crime night duty team.

The young handler, now back at her comms station, asked if anyone else was on the premises. Sally informed her that she and PC Reid had searched the house from top to bottom, and it was empty.

*   *   *

Jessica was in a deep sleep when her mobile phone started vibrating. It was just after 3 a.m., and she instantly knew it would be a call to attend a major crime scene. She picked her phone up then quickly got her notebook and pen from the cabinet drawer before answering. It was the duty chief inspector from the Met's Command and Control room.

'I'll keep it brief,' he said, first giving the address. 'A male, believed to be Johan De Klerk, was found with stab wounds and a knife embedded in his back, probably attacked during a break-in. He's in critical condition, currently undergoing emergency surgery.'

'Any other casualties?' Jessica asked as the jotted down the details.

'No, but the victim's wife is unaccounted for.'

'I'd appreciate it if no one else entered the scene until I arrive. At this time in the morning, it should take me about forty-five minutes. If possible, I'd like the first officers attending to remain there so I can speak to them about what they saw and did. Can you also please contact the officer at the hospital and ask him to request a doctor take hand swabs from the victim if possible.'

'Understood,' the chief inspector said, ending the call. Jessica then phoned Diane.

'We've got our first job, Di – a serious stabbing during a break-in in Hackney Wick. The victim is in hospital in a critical condition. You got a pen and paper?'

'Yes, fire away with the address.'

Jessica gave it to her. 'Time is of the essence. Can you call Taff? I'll meet you both there.'

'Will do. Would you like us to video and photograph the scene if we're there before you?'

'I'd appreciate it if you'd wait, then we can assess things together and decide on an action plan. If there is any visible evidence outside the scene, photograph and secure it. Also, identify any uniformed officers, or CID, who entered the scene, then take some elimination photos of their footwear. I'll get washed and dressed and see you there.'

Jessica hung up and quietly went to the bathroom, careful not to wake her brother. She wanted to shower, but she knew that time was crucial when gathering significant forensic evidence at a major crime scene. After brushing her teeth and gargling with mouthwash, she cleaned the sink and taps and placed the damp cleaning cloth on the bathroom radiator. Looking around, she noticed some grime in the bathtub. 'That's disgusting . . . you're so lazy, David,' she muttered, picking up the cloth and quickly cleaning the bath. Jessica applied a little makeup and tied her hair in a bun, then dressed quickly in a dark blue polo shirt, jumper, trousers and trainers.

Arriving at Victoria Park Road, Jessica parked the unmarked police SUV she had been allocated near the 'Do Not Enter' crime scene tape. She picked up her work bag from the passenger seat, then got her scene case and a protective suit from the boot. She'd attended numerous murder and major crime scenes in her career, this one already felt different. Officially working for the Metropolitan Police marked a new chapter in her life, a new beginning where she and her team would have to prove their worth to their new employer. She took a deep breath to steady herself before approaching the young, uniformed officer standing by the outer cordon. She held out her identification lanyard. 'I'm Jessica Russell from the Murder and Serious Crime Analysis unit.'

'Another SOCO?' he asked as he wrote her details down in the crime scene log.

'No, I'm head of the unit and here to oversee the crime scene examination,' she said, the words sounding strange in her ears.

The PC asked Jessica to sign the log and lifted the tape to let her through. Diane was with PC Sally Simpson on the pavement outside number 389, taking photos of Sally's shoes. She turned when she saw Jessica approach. 'I've been at the scene about 20 minutes. I can tell you that PC Reid, the officer who accompanied the victim to the hospital, was unable to get hand swabs from the victim as they had to take him straight to the operating theatre, but he did manage to get possession of his pyjama bottoms. Taff's on his way via the hospital where he's taking photos of PC Reid's and the ambulance crew's footwear, collecting the pyjama bottoms, and hopefully, the knife.'

Jessica nodded. Her team were doing their job.

'This is Sally Simpson, one of the first officers on scene. She noticed blood on the doormat, doorknob and in the hallway, so forced entry. She saw a lot of bloodstained footprints inside the house that likely came from the assailant's shoes. I seized the door-mat and did light source testing on the steps and pavement but didn't find anything to track an escape route. I've got a copy of Sally's body cam footage for you to view.'

Jessica watched the shaky video and asked Sally to go over everything from the moment they first arrived. As Sally spoke, Jessica made shorthand notes with a stylus pen on her iPad and asked the occasional question to clarify exactly where she and PC Reid were in the house and what they touched or moved.

'One other thing,' Sally added. 'The victim had a tattoo of the South African flag with a springbok on his right upper arm.'

Jessica turned to Diane. 'Are any detectives on scene yet?'

'Yes, they're making house-to-house enquiries with uniform officers and checking for CCTV and doorbell footage with any-thing of interest. As far as I can see, the victim's house doesn't have a video doorbell or cameras at the front, but I don't know about the back. Victoria Park is across the road. It's a big area that will need to be searched.'

Jessica nodded. 'Probably best to do it once it's light. I'll ask the senior investigator to organise a search while we examine the crime scene. Do you know if an SIO is on their way?' she asked Sally.

'He's in the house with his DI.'

'I did tell control not to let anyone enter until we attended. Did he say why they needed to go in before we arrived?' Jessica asked, annoyed by such a fundamental error, which risked contaminating the scene.

'You can ask him yourself,' Sally replied, tilting her head towards the doorway.

Jessica looked up and saw two men exiting from the house wearing crime scene suits, with the hoods up, face masks, latex gloves and shoe covers. She walked towards them as the man in front pulled back the hood on his suit. Before he even removed his face mask, she recognised the bald head and piercing eyes of DCI John Anderson. She steeled herself for a confrontation.

'Excuse me, sir, can I ask why you entered the crime scene before we—'

He cut her off. 'Because I'm the Senior Investigating Officer, Miss Russell. As such, I am responsible for managing the investigation . . . including the forensic strategy.'

Technically he was right, but Jessica still felt a senior investigator should know better than to enter a crime scene before forensics arrived and video recording and photography were done.

'I appreciate that, but there is the risk of scene disturbance and contamination—'

He cut her off again. 'That's why we suited up and didn't touch anything. A safe has been jemmied open in the basement study, and an empty jewellery box is in the bedroom. I'm not a behavioural expert like your good self. But my initial assessment is that this is most likely a burglary gone wrong, during which the victim was assaulted when he confronted the intruder.'

'I wouldn't like to comment before examining the scene with my colleagues,' Jessica replied.

'How long do you think your scene examination will take?' he asked in an almost aggressive tone.

Jessica didn't like his attitude but didn't want to get into an argument that would prevent her from getting on with the job. 'Hard to say. It's a big house, so maybe a day or two.'

'You can enlighten us with your findings and forensic opportunities at an office meeting with my team . . .' He looked at his wristwatch. '4 p.m. at Barking.' He indicated the man beside him. 'Detective Inspector Chapman is my deputy overseeing the house-to-house enquiries. He will remain here, and I want you to keep him up to speed with your scene examination.'

'Arsehole,' Diane muttered.

Chapman pretended he hadn't heard her as he unzipped his crime scene suit. He was casually dressed in blue chinos, a polo shirt and a lightweight jacket. He was a handsome, fit-looking man in his late thirties with dark, swept-back hair and an engaging smile. He shook hands with Jessica.

'I'm Jessica Russell, the MSCAN team leader. This is Diane, our DNA expert.'

'Your DCI's a bit up himself,' Diane remarked.

Jessica sighed. 'I think it's my presence that's pissed him off. He rejected me on my interview for team leader role but was outvoted.'

Chapman nodded. 'Anderson mentioned that when he was told you'd be attending the scene.'

'That was nice of him,' Jessica replied, frowning.

'Well, he needs to realise that Jessica was selected to lead this unit because she's the best person for the job . . . whether he likes it or not,' Diane said.

Chapman held his hands up in a conciliatory gesture. 'I'm sure he will . . . in time. And I can assure you his bark's worse than his bite.'

'So, what's his problem?' Diane asked.

Chapman paused for a moment. 'The thing is, he's not a career detective. He transferred from uniform inspector to DI, then got promoted to DCI and made SIO thanks to . . . let's just say friends in high places.'

'Are you saying he's out of his depth?' Jessica asked.

'At times, yes. His aggressive attitude is just a front to hide his lack of experience as a detective.'

'Great,' Diane grunted.

'But look, he wants to find who is responsible for the crime as much as we all do. It's just that he often goes about it in the wrong way.'

Taff pulled up in the van beside them and leaned out of the window. 'Good morning, Draig and Di. Never fear, Taff is here bearing good news.'

Jessica ignored him 'Thanks for being frank with us,' she nodded to Chapman.

'I just wanted you to understand the reasons behind Anderson's sometimes odd behaviour.'

Taff picked up on the tension. 'Have I missed something?'

'I'll tell you later,' Diane said.

Taff got out of the van and showed the team the black-handled knife that was recovered from the victim's back, which was now inside a plastic weapons tube. 'It's a Japanese Damascus 67 chef's knife, made from stainless steel and very, very sharp. I looked them up on the web. The price of a set is five to seven hundred pounds, depending on how many knives you want.'

'How much!' Diane exclaimed.

'Go figure. I got a set at Lidl for under a tenner,' Taff said. 'I also managed to get some of the victim's pre-transfusion blood for a DNA profile. I asked the ambulance crew if they removed any personal property. They didn't, but the paramedic who put a pulse oximeter on his finger noticed a watch tan line on his left wrist.'

'Meaning the intruder probably took it,' Diane said.

'What about the victim's injuries?' Jessica asked.

'Severe fracture to the skull, three stab wounds to the back, four including this embedded knife, but none to the chest. He's in surgery, but it's still touch and go. Doctor said they may put him in an induced coma if he survives, and it will definitely be a few days yet before anyone can speak to him.'

Jessica clapped her hands. 'Right, let's suit up and get to work. Taff, you can video and photograph the downstairs and basement, and I'll do the upstairs. Di can follow behind you, deal with the blood on the door and examine the hallway.'

'I'll do light sourcing for footmarks and blood, and, if necessary, I'll use luminol as well,' Diane said, referring to a liquid spray that reacts to blood the eye can't see and produces a bluish-white light that glows in the dark and enhances footmarks and blood stains.

Jessica looked at Chapman. 'You might be standing around for a while. It's a big house, so the video and photography will take about an hour. Then I'll do a walkthrough of the premises to form an initial assessment, prioritise the evidence and formulate a forensic strategy.'

'No problem. I need to brief the house-to-house officers and give them a list of questions to ask. When I've done that, I can drive to the garage and get everyone a coffee or anything else you want.'

'Thanks, that would be appreciated,' Jessica replied, removing a small wallet from her pocket.

'Don't worry. I'll claim it back on expenses. Do you want anything to eat?'

'I wouldn't say no to a coffee and bacon roll,' Taff said.

'Same for me, please,' Diane added.

'A tea and an egg sandwich if there is one,' Jessica said.

Chapman nodded. 'Got it.' He walked off.

'What do you make of him? Diane asked Jessica.

'Hard to say. Maybe a bit too friendly, considering we've just met. Best we keep an eye on him.'

'You think he's up to something?' Diane asked.

'He could be Anderson's mole, but I might be wrong.'

'That would be a rare occurrence, Draig,' Taff grinned.

'You'll should get on well with him, Taff . . . you both think you're funny,' Diane said with a grin.

* * *

While Jessica and Taff started recording the scene, Diane photographed and swabbed the blood smear on the doorknob. She also found some on the internal Yale lock and examined it closer with a magnifying glass and crime scene torch. She noticed two tiny black fibres stuck to the blood, and used plastic tweezers to retrieve them and put them in a small pill box. As there were no finger marks in the blood, she thought they might have come from woollen gloves worn by the perpetrator.

An hour later, DI Chapman called out from the front door. They joined him outside, and he handed out the food and drinks. 'Sorry about the delay, but I got some info from one of the house-to-house officers that I had to follow up on. I took a statement from Mr Elton, the next-door neighbour. He and his wife know the De Klerks quite well it seems . . . Johan is in his late thirties and a wine importer from Cape Town. According to Mr Elton, Johan likes the finer things in life and tends to brag about them, one such item being his new gold Rolex Daytona, worth sixty grand. He showed it to Mr Elton, who recalled it had a black face and a diamond-studded dial. The paramedic noticed a tan mark on De Klerk's left wrist, right? So, it looks like the intruder took it.'

Jessica nodded. 'We'll search the house, in case it's still there. Did Mr Elton say anything about Mrs De Klerk?'

'Yes, her name is Michelle. She's a barrister – a KC – but uses her maiden name of Belsham for work. I've come across her in court and she's highly respected. She's a tough operator, handling some big cases. I've informed Anderson. He's shitting himself because he knows the press will be all over the case if they find out the victim is Michelle Belsham's husband.'

'I don't see how he can stop the press finding out,' Jessica said.

Chapman shrugged. 'Well, Anderson wants everything kept low-key for now. If the press asks, he's just going to say it's a burglary where a male resident was assaulted, and he wants us all to do the same.'

'I don't get it' Taff said.

'He doesn't think it likely, but he's concerned that she might have been kidnapped. A press release could spook the kidnappers and put her life in danger. He's also hoping that your team might find something forensic-wise to identify the assailant quickly.'

'We'll do our best, but I wouldn't bank on it,' Jessica said.

'Fair enough,' Chapman said. 'Does Mrs De Klerk own a car?' Jessica asked.

'The neighbour said she drives a silver Mercedes SL sport, which I found parked around the corner in Homer Road by a locked gate leading to their garden. A number-plate check showed her as the registered keeper. Her husband's car is a year-old black Range Rover Sport, which isn't there. It might have been stolen or used as the getaway car.'

'Mrs De Klerk might be using it if she's away somewhere,' Taff suggested.

'I hope you're right,' Chapman replied.

'If she is safe and well, it will be a big shock when she finds out what's happened to her husband,' Diane remarked.

'Did the neighbour know the Range Rover's registration?' Jessica asked.

'Only part of it. Because it's a personalised plate. The first three letters are JDK. I've asked for a search on Range Rovers to identify the full registration and his insurance company. If he had a tracker fitted, it will help us locate the car.'

'I'll look for the registration and insurance documents in the house,' Jessica said.

'What's your initial assessment?' Chapman asked.

'Still working on it. I'll make it a priority to assess if Mrs De Klerk was on the premises when the crime occurred.'

'Thanks. I'll continue speaking to the neighbours and see what else I can learn about the De Klerks,' Chapman said, walking off.

'He's like a little ferret, sniffing around everywhere,' Diane remarked.

'That's his job, isn't it?' Taff replied.

'Do you trust him?' Diane asked Jessica.

Jessica shrugged. 'I'm still on the fence . . . but I do know ferrets have a nasty bite.'

CHAPTER SIX

After using different light sources and luminol in the hallway, Diane found further bloodstained partial footprints leading towards the front door. She took photos of the footprints using a scale marker and swabbed them for DNA testing. She also found clearer foot-marks on the kitchen floor tiles.

Diane showed Taff the digital photographs. He estimated that someone with size nine to ten feet left the footmarks. 'From the imprint design, they might be Adidas trainers,' he said. 'A footwear database search back at the lab will confirm if I'm right.' He then returned to the house to continue his scene examination.

Jessica exited the house, holding her iPad, and sat down on the concrete steps by the front door. She removed her mask and latex gloves, placed them neatly beside her, and then made notes of her crime scene assessment and forensic strategy on the iPad. A few minutes later she closed the pad and put it to one side before cross-ing her legs and sitting upright. She breathed in and exhaled in a controlled manner before closing her eyes and putting her hands, palms up, on her knees.

Diane didn't see Chapman approaching. 'What on earth is she doing?' he asked, making Diane jump.

She turned sharply. 'Please don't creep up on me like that.'

'Sorry. In future, I'll give you a verbal warning before sneaking up on you.' He grinned, but Diane didn't find it funny. 'Is she hav-ing a quiet moment?' he asked, nodding towards Jessica.

'She uses meditation to help her analyse the course of events. Jessica becomes the criminal and tries to visualise and re-enact everything in her mind.'

'Like watching a film with her eyes closed?'

Diane nodded, but she wasn't sure if Chapman was being sarcastic. 'She once told me, the further backwards you can look, the further forwards you can see.'

Chapman smiled. 'No offence intended, but that quote, often attributed to Winston Churchill, is incorrect.'

'Enlighten me then, Mr Know-it-all,' Diane said curtly.

'I wasn't having a dig. I heard someone say it before and googled it. The late Queen used Jessica's version in a Christmas message to the British Commonwealth . . . so even the highest in the realm get it wrong.' He cleared his throat and spoke in a low, raspy monotone to mimic Churchill. '"The longer you can look back, the further you can look forward" is what he actually said.'

Diane couldn't help laughing. 'They mean the same thing . . . and that impression was awful.'

He shrugged. 'Fair enough. I'll stick to Sean Connery from now on.'

'Please, spare me,' Diane said, holding her hands up.

'OK, seriously, I'm genuinely interested in Jessica 's thought process and how she works things out.'

Diane wondered if he was just fishing for tidbits he could take back to Anderson but decided to answer anyway. 'She develops an initial theory by assessing and analysing the scene. Then she considers the criminal's mode of travel, how they may have entered the house, their actions, motivations and exit route. As the investigation progresses, she assesses any new evidence, forensic results and how they impact her initial theory. She's also very good at understanding and analysing criminal behaviour.'

'I'm not criticising, but it doesn't sound much different from what a good detective does,' he replied.

'Do you know many detectives with a first-class honour's

degree in Psychology and Criminology, plus a master's degree in Investigative Psychology?' Diane asked.

He rubbed his chin as if in deep thought.

'I thought not.'

'What's she like to work for?'

'Great. I've worked with her on quite a few cases, and believe me, she's good, if not the best, at what she does. She's also good at taking on board the advice of others.'

'Unlike my boss,' he smiled.

'Sounds like you're not his biggest fan,' she said.

'I don't dislike him, but he always thinks he knows best, which can be a pain. Why does Taff call Jessica "Draig"?' he asked, changing the subject.

'Because of her red hair. Draig is Welsh for dragon. She accepts it from Taff, but I wouldn't start calling her Draig if I were you.'

'The last thing I want to do is offend her. Her hair is rather striking, though . . . do you think she'd be OK with Ginger Ninja?'

Diane shook her head and picked up her scene examination case. 'I better get to work on the BPA.'

'Sorry, what's BPA?'

'Blood pattern analysis.'

'Right, I know what it stands for, but what does it involve?'

'Basically, it's the interpretation of blood patterns to recreate the actions that caused the bloodshed. I examine the bloodstains' size, shape, distribution and location to form opinions about what did or did not happen . . . and I take swabs for DNA.'

'I can do the packaging and exhibit labels for the swabs if you want.'

Diane was wary of his offer and his desire to be close to everything they were doing.

'I'll need to ask Jessica. She's never keen on too many people being in a crime scene due to the risk of contamination.'

He gave her his most winning smile. 'I'll suit and boot up, and I promise not to get in your way.'

A few minutes later, Jessica opened her eyes, picked up her iPad and started making more notes. Diane approached, speaking in an undertone. 'The ferret's at it again. He wants to assist me in the kitchen and bag and tag the exhibits.'

'He's certainly persistent,' Jessica replied. She turned to Chapman. 'Thanks for the offer, DI Chapman, but I feel three of us in the crime scene is enough and—'

He interrupted her. 'I'm not here to spy on you and report back to Anderson, if that's what you're thinking. It's just that I feel like a waste of space hanging around twiddling my thumbs waiting for the house-to-house enquiry results. I'm just trying to be helpful, that's all.'

Jessica had a sense he was being genuine. She looked at Diane, who nodded. 'The crime scene suits and other protective equipment are in the van.'

Chapman smiled. 'Thanks, I appreciate it. But I have another request . . .'

Jessica frowned. 'And what would that be?'

'Can you all please call me Mike?'

'OK, Mike,' Jessica said.

'Good. So, what are your thoughts about the scene?'

'I'm still working on it. I believe the intruder was male, but I'm not ruling out more than one person.' She picked up her crime scene case and walked towards the house.

Jessica went downstairs to the basement, which covered the same square area as the ground floor and consisted of three rooms. The middle section at the bottom of the stairs had an eight-seat home cinema with a large, motorised screen, ceiling-mounted projector and red velvet reclining chairs. To one side, there was a commercial dual-zone double-door wine fridge filled with an impressive array of champagnes and red and white South African wines. Next to the refrigerator was a cabinet filled with bottles of spirits and liqueurs with a popcorn machine on top. To the right of the cinema area was a well-equipped gym, with a sauna and shower room.

Jessica went to the front room, an oak-floored study with a bay window about five feet down from street level. There was a large, modern oak computer desk with a mini-PC and two monitors on it. Jessica looked at some of the paperwork on the desk. It seemed to be mostly invoices and orders for South African wines with Johan De Klerk's name and address on them. On the left side of the desk was an overturned photograph frame. Jessica wondered if the intruder had knocked it over. Wearing latex gloves, she gently turned it over. It was a picture of a man gleefully smiling while holding a rifle and crouching down beside a large dead animal. Standing next to him was a woman who, from the expression on her face, didn't look happy about it. Jessica thought the animal might be an antelope of some kind. It had vertical white stripes on its torso, a white chevron between its eyes and long twisting horns. She sympathised with the woman in the photograph. As far as she was concerned, wild game hunting was barbaric.

Jessica searched the internet on her iPad for a picture of Michelle Belsham. She found a good one of her outside the Old Bailey and could instantly see that she was the woman in the hunting photograph. She was tall and slim with piercing green eyes, high cheekbones and long glossy black hair. Jessica then searched Johan De Klerk and found a site dedicated to his wine import business, featuring pictures of him in a South African vineyard. It was also clearly him in the hunting photo. Johan De Klerk was handsome, with blond hair, blue eyes and a rugged face. He was about six foot five inches tall, with broad shoulders and a muscular physique.

To the side of the desk was a two-drawer filing cabinet and the digital locking metal safe that had been forced open. Jessica took some photographs of the safe and then enlarged the area to get a better look at the indented striation marks on the door and frame, which could be helpful for comparison if the implement used to force it open was recovered. Jessica heard Taff calling her. 'I'm in the study room,' she called back.

A few moments later he joined her. 'Just wanted to let you know I've finished the video and photography, downstairs and upstairs. I'll examine the main bedroom now if you're happy with that.'

'Yes, of course, crack on.'

He looked around him. 'This place is something else, all mod cons and top-of-the-range stuff... must have cost a bloody fortune.'

'Just over four million a year ago,' Jessica told him.

'How'd you know that?'

'Looked the address up on Rightmove. It gives you the sales history.'

He whistled. 'The wine business must be doing well.' She showed him the photos of the striation marks on the safe. 'Could be from a jemmy,' he said. 'Lots of detail, which is good. Moving the safe won't be easy, though. It must weigh over 200 kilos.'

'You're right. But the big question is, what was inside it?'

'Cash and jewellery is what you'd normally expect,' Taff said.

'Makes me wonder if the intruder already knew it was down here,' Jessica said as she stood by the bay window and looked up towards the street. 'If the assailant had scoped the house out first, they could have seen the safe through the window. Can you please get me some nylon accelerant bags from the van?'

Taff, wondering if he was missing something, took a few good sniffs but couldn't smell any form of accelerant. Jessica saw his quizzical expression. 'The safe shelves are lined with carpet.

I'm going to remove it and put them in the nylon bags to preserve any drugs residue for testing at the lab.'

'You think De Klerk was dealing drugs?'

'I don't know, but we have to cover every possibility. How's Diane getting on in the kitchen?'

'She's still working on it. Chapman is helping her. Do you want me to video and photograph the rear garden?'

'Yes, please.'

Taff started to leave, then turned around. 'There's a laptop on the kitchen table. I'll take it for fingerprinting and a digital examination.'

'Fingerprinting is fine, but if it's the victim's, we might need his permission or a warrant to examine it. There's a technical support section at the lab. We'll have to ask them to do it as none of us are experienced enough in that field of forensics,' Jessica added.

Taff left, and Jessica opened the filing cabinet. Looking through the contents, she removed an A4 folder labelled 'J & M cars'. Inside were the registration and insurance documents for the De Klerk's vehicles. She removed the registration document for the Range Rover, photographed it and put it in a property bag for DI Chapman. There was another folder labelled 'passports and travel docs'. Looking inside, she only found Johan De Klerk's South African passport. Looking at his date of birth, she saw he had just turned thirty-eight. She took a photo of the passport, put it in the bag with the car documents and flicked through the other folders in the cabinet for anything else of interest. She found a document relating to De Klerk's Rolex watch, with the make and serial number, which she bagged so the details could be circulated on the stolen property index. Taff returned briefly to give her the nylon bags, and after putting the safe carpets in them, Jessica sat in one of the cinema chairs to make more notes on her iPad.

In the kitchen, Diane was setting up a large digital camera on a tripod, while Chapman was admiring the eight-seater glass dining table and L-shaped sofa with a large TV on the wall. Natural light flowed through the skylights and sliding doors leading onto a stone-paved patio.

'Hasn't Taff already done the photography and video in here?' he asked.

'Yes, but this is a Faro 3D laser scanner with a high-resolution DSLR. The photos are stitched to the scan using 3D construction software. I can—'

He held his hands up. 'Slow down . . . I haven't a clue what you're talking about.'

'Sorry, in layman's terms, it creates the precise measurements of blood spatter patterns for computer analysis. I can then reconstruct the scene and determine the nature and direction of the attack.'

'Now I get it.' He looked around. 'Well, there's enough blood to fill a bath, so you have plenty to work on.'

'We used to run bits of string from points at which blood droplets impact to a pre-calculated directional angle converging at the area of origin—'

'Now I know you're taking the piss,' he said, wagging his finger.

'The string bit is true. But using the Faro is much quicker and more accurate. A 3D reconstruction is also better for a jury to look at, as it allows them to better understand my blood pattern analysis. That said, the blood spatter distribution in here is confined to the area around the island, making it slightly easier to interpret visually.'

'Enlighten me.'

'I will when I've photographed and looked closer at the blood patterns.'

* * *

Having finished making notes of her observations in the study, Jessica decided to go upstairs. Standing up, she noticed a crystal tumbler in one of the front cinema seat cup-holders, and then, as she moved closer, saw another tumbler in the seat next to it. Both glasses were hand-engraved with images of what looked like South African wildlife; one was a water buffalo, and the other was a chee-tah. She leaned over and sniffed each glass. One smelt different from the other, but she couldn't tell what had been in them. She took some photos, went out and got some airtight plastic contain-ers from the van, then came back and put the tumblers in them for fingerprint and DNA examination.

Before going to the main bedroom, Jessica quickly checked the others. There were two fully furnished double bedrooms with built-in cupboards and a chest of drawers, which did not appear to have been disturbed. The fourth bedroom, a single room, was only partially decorated. The floor was bare untreated wood, but the walls had safari animal print wallpaper. A cardboard boxed cot and nappy changing cabinet were propped up against the wall, which made Jessica wonder if Michelle De Klerk was pregnant. The thought that she and her unborn child might be dead was disturbing.

She then moved on to the plush main bedroom, where the tall double-glazed Victorian windows filled the room with natural light. Taff was kneeling on the carpet by the dressing table, about to use a small electrostatic dust lifter to retrieve any invisible shoe impressions. He placed a sheet of Myler film on the carpet.

'I hate using the ESLA. It gave me a bad electric shock once . . . felt like I'd been hit with a taser,' Taff frowned.

'That's why I get you to do it,' Jessica said with a grin. Having used ESLA herself, she knew it was a high-voltage power source used to create a static electric charge. This charge attracted dust and loose particles to form a shoe impression on the black side of the Myler sheet. If your hand accidentally made contact with the sheet during the process, you would get a nasty shock, though it was unlikely to be life-threatening unless you had a heart condition.

Taff grimaced as he slowly turned up the electric charge on the ESLA. The Myler film was gradually drawn down to the surface of the carpet, and he carefully used a wooden-handled foam brush to flatten out any areas that had creased or bubbled. Turning the ESLA off, he carefully lifted the sheet and shone some ultraviolet light on it, revealing a clear shoe mark. He held it up for Jessica to see. 'I didn't find any traces of blood in here, and this footmark doesn't look like the ones in the kitchen and hallway. I'll check it against De Klerk's shoes in the wardrobe. If there isn't a match, it could be that two people broke in.'

'Yes,' Jessica agreed. 'Do you know where the jewellery box is?'

Taff leaned to one side, picked up an exhibit bag and handed it to her. Inside was a brown nine-by-five-inch mahogany box. 'It was on top of the dressing table.'

'Open or closed?' she asked.

'Closed but empty. Although the carpet in here is very soft, an intruder would be taking a big risk entering while De Klerk was asleep,' Taff suggested.

Jessica looked at the king-size bed. The left side of the duvet and pillows looked undisturbed, but on the right, it was creased and folded over to one side, as one would do when getting out of bed. One pillow was on the floor but upright against the bedside cabinet, as if it had been deliberately placed there, and the other pillow was creased and slept-on looking. It seemed that only one person had been sleeping in the bed.

While Taff continued looking for more footprints, Jessica took some iPad photographs of the room, particularly the bed and side cabinet, on which there was a bottle of water and an iPhone charging cable plugged into a lamp with a built-in USB socket. She looked in the other dressing table drawer and found a lady's hairbrush, which she put in an exhibit bag. If Mrs De Klerk had been kidnapped, they'd need it to raise a DNA profile from her hair. A matching two-seater sofa was also in the room, with a pair of trousers, shirt and underpants over the armrest and some socks and shoes on the floor beside it. Jessica assumed it was Johan De Klerk's clothing and checked the pockets of the trousers. Inside the right pocket was a wallet containing cash and credit cards in Johan De Klerk's name. She picked up one of the shoes, looked at the sole, and handed it to Taff. He compared it to the first ESLA lift. 'Yep, same shoe,' he said.

'OK, it looks like De Klerk was woken by the intruder and went downstairs to confront him.'

'That fits,' Taff agreed.

There were no closets or chests of drawers in the room, but there was a large walk-in dressing room. She looked inside the closets, but nothing appeared to have been disturbed.

The ensuite bathroom was expensively decorated with two sinks, a large walk-in shower and a Jacuzzi bath. There were his and hers cabinets containing personal hygiene products and medicines. Johan's cabinet contained various health vitamins, ibuprofen and other over-the-counter painkillers. Jessica noticed a plastic bottle with melatonin written on it. She knew it was used to help aid sleep and was only available on prescription in the UK. This bottle had a red heart and CVS Health written on it. Jessica googled it and discovered that melatonin was available over the counter at pharmacies in America. She took a picture of the bottle and wondered if Johan had taken some melatonin before he went to bed the previous night.

Jessica then went down to the living room and looked at the

contents of the cabinet drawers scattered around the room. She also deduced that the coffee table had been pushed or knocked to one side from the four visible indentation marks on the carpet. On the floor beside the table were two magazines and two remote controls, one for the television and the other for the lighting and window blinds, suggesting a struggle had taken place in the living room between De Klerk and his assailant, during which the coffee table had been moved and the controls knocked to the floor.

As she made more notes on her iPad, she heard Diane laughing. She had an infectious laugh, which made others join in, even at the most inappropriate times.

'How's it going?' Jessica asked as she stood by the archway entrance.

'I've done the 3D photography and nearly finished with the blood swabbing,' Diane said, recovering herself. 'Mike was just telling me a funny story about when he was a probationer PC . . . go on, tell Jessica.'

'It's not that funny,' he said hesitantly.

'Di clearly thought it was,' Jessica said. 'And we share the same sense of humour.'

Chapman held his hands up in surrender. 'OK, I was with an old sweat PC at a murder scene. A big pool of blood was on the parquet floor, and a cat was sleeping in an armchair. I was told to get the cat in case it woke up and walked in the blood. When I touched the cat, it lashed out and scratched my hand. I lost my balance and fell in the blood . . . and to top it off, the cat ran off through it as well, leaving a trail of bloody paw marks everywhere.'

Jessica laughed as she envisioned it happening. 'I bet the crime scene manager wasn't impressed.'

'He was livid, as was the SIO. They took my clothing at the scene and left me to find my way back to the station. I had to walk two miles wearing a white crime scene suit and shoe covers over my bare feet. The looks I got along the way made it even more embarrassing. When I got back to the station, everyone started meowing.'

Jessica smiled and felt herself warming to him. 'I think Mrs De Klerk might be away or abroad, as her passport wasn't in the folder with her husband's,' she said, getting back to the business in hand.

'Let's hope so,' Chapman replied. 'I'll tell Anderson.'

'Any initial thoughts on the course of events in here?' she asked Diane.

'Visually, the blood distribution suggests a violent struggle, which is no surprise. I think the first injury to his head occurred over there.' She pointed to the corner of the marble worktop with an overturned knife block. 'I'll come to my thoughts on the knife block in a second, but they are the same make as the one Taff retrieved from the hospital. As you can see, there are circular blood droplets on the tiled floor which have fallen from a height, suggesting the victim was standing up at the time with his back to the assailant when he was initially hit. This blow caused the first wound on his head, resulting in the blood drops on the floor.'

'He wouldn't have seen him coming then,' Chapman remarked.

'As odd as it seems, he may have,' she said. 'There are two scenarios . . . firstly, De Klerk saw the assailant coming towards him, turned, and hurriedly attempted to, or did, pull the eight-inch knife from the block, thus causing the block to fall on its side. Before, or as De Klerk grabbed the knife, the assailant struck him on the back of his head, possibly with the jemmy used on the safe. His head splits open and starts to bleed. He turns, and a struggle ensues. He stumbles forward and falls to the ground a few feet away. He is now face down and is repeatedly struck again on the back of the head while prone on the floor . . .'

'How do you work that out?' Chapman interrupted.

'From the low-level blood spatter on the cabinet door and cast-off trail on the ceiling.'

Chapman looked up and saw the blood trail marks, which he hadn't noticed until now.

Diane used her hands to demonstrate. She held her right hand out and closed her fingers. 'Think of my fist as the weapon,' she then held out the palm of her left hand, 'and this is his head.' She banged her fist a couple of times onto her palm. 'When a blunt object makes contact with a bleeding head, it forces the blood to travel outwards and upwards, causing the impact spatter stains on the cabinet door. If I swing it backwards, the blood on the object flies off and travels upwards . . . resulting in the cast-off bloodstains on the ceiling.' She again used her fist and palm to demonstrate the effect.

Chapman still looked confused. 'If he was first hit when standing by the knife block, why isn't there any impact or cast-off blood on the ceiling there?'

'Because there was no bleeding head injury when the first blow was struck, but after that impact, there would be.'

'I get it now. Thanks for explaining. It's fascinating,' he said.

Diane continued, 'From the blood smearing and pooling on the floor, De Klerk was either dragged forward a few feet or pulled himself forward. The blood spatter on the next cabinet along and on the floor suggests this is the area where he was stabbed and found by the first attending officers. The direction of matching bloody footprints implies that the assailant stepped in the blood after stabbing De Klerk. I should also add that the assailant may have pulled the knife from the block, or De Klerk dropped it, and the assailant picked it up.'

'There are signs of a disturbance in the living room,' Jessica said. 'The coffee table looks as if it has been pushed over and there are items on the floor.'

'So, the struggle could have started there,' Diane said. 'De Klerk ran to the kitchen to get a knife to defend himself and was struck on the back of the head while trying to do so.

I can't find any blood distribution that suggests the assailant was injured, but I've taken samples in different areas for DNA profiling. I found a mobile phone with smeared blood on it under the dining table, which I assume belongs to De Klerk. It's boxed and bagged for DNA and prints.'

'Will you do digital forensics on it as well?' Chapman asked.

'No one on the team is an expert in that field, but we can give it to the lab's digital unit for examination. Will they need a warrant to do it?' Jessica asked.

Chapman shook his head. 'No. There are reasonable grounds to believe De Klerk's last calls, texts and messages might contain information relevant to the investigation, so my approval to examine the data is fine.'

'What about the laptop?' Diane asked.

'We don't know if it's De Klerk's yet, so we may need to apply for a warrant there, but that's for Anderson to decide.'

Taff walked in through the patio doors from the garden.

'Good timing, Taff,' Jessica said, leaving him looking puzzled. She explained her theory about a struggle in the living room and asked Taff to examine the kitchen floor, from the left side of the living room entrance up to the knife block, for signs of bare footprints with the suspect's footwear overlaying them.

'What will that tell us?' Chapman asked.

'I can't say precisely when any barefoot prints got there, but if they are overlapped by what we believe to be the suspect's footmarks, it strengthens Jessica's theory that De Klerk went towards the knife block and was followed by the assailant,' Taff replied.

'Anything of value in the garden, Taff?' Jessica asked.

'I found a detailed footprint in the soil of the raised bedding area in the far-right corner of the garden. It matches those in the blood and the hallway. I've taken some photos but I need to do a plaster cast. The intruder must have climbed over the wall from Homer Road. There are also jemmy marks on the sliding patio door, which I've yet to photograph.'

Jessica followed Taff, briefly pausing by the sliding door to look at the jemmy marks. The brick wall looked at least nine feet high. A raised brick bedding area filled with colourful roses and plants ran along it. To her left, there was a stone-paved area with a shed, brick-built barbecue and luxury garden furniture. To her right, in the adjoining corner wall, there was a tall wooden gate that led to Homer Road.

Jessica noticed a marker cone in the bedding by the gate, which Taff had clearly placed as an indicator of the footmark when taking a photo from a distance. She looked at the mark in the soil, which was from a left foot. The right foot had landed on the flowers and crushed them. The gate had two sliding bolt locks, and the top was lined with anti-climb spiking. She looked back at the house and couldn't see any CCTV cameras or alarm boxes.

'Whoever broke in must be fit and agile to climb over that wall,' Jessica remarked.

'Can you take some soil and plant samples from the footprint and crushed plant, Taff?'

'Already done. Bagged and tagged and in the van,' Taff said.

'I'm going to have a look from the Homer Road side,' Jessica said, opening the gate and walking to the opposite side of the road. It was now clear how the intruder got over the wall. The house in Homer Road, which backed onto the De Klerk's garden, had a four-foot brick wall at the front, which abutted the De Klerk's wall, with an eight-foot metal gate attached to it, which she assumed led to the neighbour's side alley and rear of their house. She looked around, although the house opposite had CCTV at the rear, it was pointed away from the De Klerk's garden gate.

Jessica returned to the garden and spoke with Taff, who was pouring fast-setting plaster on the footmark. 'I don't think it was as difficult as we first thought for the intruder to get over the wall. By standing on the neighbour's wall, he could use their gate to pull himself up and then drop down into the De Klerk's garden.'

'OK, I'll get the telescopic ladder from the van and examine the top of the metal gate for fingerprints and footmarks,' Taff said.

'Great. I need to make some more notes. I'll be in the kitchen. Give me a shout if you need any help.'

Taff went and got the ladder. Returning to the back of the house, he extended it and ensured the locking mechanism was engaged. He propped it up against the wall and took one step when it began to slide slightly on the pavement. He called to Diane, who was by the van, and she came and held the ladder steady for him.

'The walls are crumbly on top. No good for foot marks,' he said. 'There are some glove marks on top of the neighbour's gate, though. I'll do some tape lifts for any fibres.'

'What do you think you're doing? I'm calling the police!' An elderly woman holding a broom shouted at them. Diane let go of the ladder to show the woman her MSCAN ID. 'Don't come near me, or I'll hit you with my broom,' the woman said, gripping the broom tighter.

Suddenly, the ladder started to slip away from the wall. 'Hold it steady!' Taff shouted to Diane, then climbed down gingerly. 'There's been a burglary. We're the forensics team,' Taff said, holding his own ID out. 'We think someone may have used your wall to enter the De Klerk's garden.'

'If I'd seen them, they'd have got a good whack with this,' she said, holding up the broom.

Diane smiled. 'We're sorry to have disturbed you. We should have asked for your permission to examine the gate.'

'It's all right, I understand you've got a job to do . . . do you want a cup of tea?' she asked, lowering the broom at last.

'Thanks for the offer, but we have to finish our work,' Diane replied.

'Could you do me a favour?' the woman asked.

'What would it be?' Taff said.

'Tell that arsehole Mr De Klerk to stop parking his big car outside my house. It blocks the light from my living room. I've told him three times to move it, but he just ignores me and walks off. You know they've only just moved in; we had builders and contractors here for months digging up their basement for a cinema, throwing their money around like confetti. I swear, if he keeps parking that Range Rover in front of my living room, I'll shove this broom handle right up his backside.'

'We'll see what we can do, ma'am,' Taff assured her, trying to keep a straight face.

'Doesn't look like Mr De Klerk has too many fans in the neighbourhood,' Diane remarked.

'I'll say, Taff agreed, stepping onto the ladder again. 'Right, this time put your foot on the bottom rung and keep a tight grip on it. The last thing I want to do is break my neck on our first job together!'

CHAPTER SEVEN

David Russell sat in the waiting area of his local medical practice, nervously tapping his foot on the floor and looking up at the TV screen on the wall for his name and the doctor's room number to appear.

A woman in her seventies sitting opposite him leaned forward. 'Do you mind?'

'Mind what?' David asked.

She pointed to his feet. 'The constant toe-tapping.'

'Sorry, I've had to take time off work to be here. My appointment should have been twenty minutes ago.'

'That's par for the course at this practice. Mind you, I've been here so many times I've got used to it.' She turned back to *Good Housekeeping* magazine.

David had been worried all weekend after Doctor Barnes called him on Friday afternoon and requested that he attend the practice on Monday morning so she could discuss his blood test results. After a previous blood test, all he'd received was a text message informing him the results were satisfactory and that he didn't need to attend the surgery. He contemplated telling Jess, but he didn't want to worry her when she had the stress of starting her new job. He'd told her he just had a bit of sciatica, but he was actually suffering from leg cramps and was starting to have difficulty gripping and carrying his mailbags. Over the past two months, he had lost weight and muscle mass, but he couldn't understand why, as his eating habits and daily routine hadn't changed. Feeling anxious about it, he'd looked up iron deficiency anaemia and similar illnesses on the internet. Although he had some symptoms, he didn't have pale yellow skin or get headaches when doing something strenuous. Another sign of anaemia was a rapid heartbeat, which he knew he didn't have, as he'd bought an ECG smartwatch to monitor his heart rate, blood pressure and oxygen levels.

David looked at his watch. His heart rate was slightly up, but that was probably due to being nervous about his blood test results. Without knowing he was doing it, he started tapping his foot again.

The woman lowered her magazine and frowned. 'Sorry.' David apologised then put his hands firmly on his knees to keep them still. He looked up and saw the receptionist walking towards him.

'David, the doctor is waiting for you in room three,' she told him. He realised he'd missed his name on the TV screen.

As he walked into room three, Dr Barnes welcomed him with a warm smile. 'Sit down, David. How are you feeling?'

'Not too bad, thanks. I'm still getting the leg cramps and feeling run down though.'

'Did you try the tonic water I recommended? The quinine in it helps against cramps.'

'Honestly, it hasn't made any difference. And I've been monitoring my weight and muscle mass . . . they've both been going down, which has never happened before.'

'There could be many reasons for that.' Dr Barnes turned her seat and looked at her computer screen. 'Your blood test revealed an increase in a substance called creatine kinase. It's an enzyme that exists in your heart and skeletal muscle. Any event, like an injury, that causes muscle damage or interferes with muscle energy production can increase creatine kinase levels in your blood. Even intense exercise can be a cause for the rise. How do you keep fit?' she asked.

'I don't go to the gym and lift weights or anything like that, but I'm a member of a cycling club, and my girlfriend and I cycle together regularly. I've also recently been doing longer hours delivering mail due to a backlog at the sorting office. It's made my working days more strenuous, so maybe that's got something to do with it.'

'It's possible. Kinase levels can also go up after drinking too much alcohol. What would you say your average daily intake is?'

'Very little during the week. I have to be up for work at 5 a.m. I might have the occasional bottle of beer, but it's often an alcohol-free one. I sometimes go to the pub with cycling friends on Saturday night, but it's not a regular thing.'

'What about spirits?'

'I rarely, if ever, have any.'

'This is a question I need to ask . . . please don't be offended by it. Do you take any performance-enhancing supplements, such as anabolic steroids or protein powders?'

'No, but I take multivitamin tablets and cod liver oil daily.'

Dr Barnes smiled. 'That's a good thing . . . in moderation, of course. Your work as a postman is obviously very strenuous and could cause a rise in kinase levels. Your symptoms of muscle cramps, aches and weakness could also be symptomatic.'

'So, there's nothing wrong with me?' he said, feeling relieved.

'I can't say that for certain, David. You might have a heart condition or a neuromuscular problem causing the kinase levels to rise.'

'I check my heart rate and blood pressure daily, and they've been fine.'

'Then that's a positive thing. But I am going to refer you to a neurologist who will carry out some more tests . . .'

'Why can't you tell me what's wrong with me?' he interrupted.

Dr Barnes could see the look of concern on his face. 'There may be nothing wrong with you, David. I know you must be worried but try not to be.'

'What sorts of tests?'

'I'm not a neurologist, David.'

'But you must have some idea . . .'

'There are many disorders that affect the nervous system, but there is no risk in having a neurological examination. I will also give you a prescription for some antidepressant medication.'

'I'm not depressed!'

'I know, but amitriptyline is also prescribed for fatigue and back pain.' Dr Barnes printed off the prescription and handed it to David. 'A receptionist will text you with the date and time of your appointment.'

'How long will it be before I see the neurologist?'

'I can't give you an exact date, but hopefully in a week or two.'

'Which hospital will it be at?'

'Guy's. Please, try not to worry, David. You're young and healthy, but don't overexert yourself on your mail round. For now, it would be better if you could do some internal work at the sorting office instead of delivering mail.'

'I'll ask my manager.'

'Good. I will also email you some low intensity exercises you can do to help with the cramp.'

'Thank you, Doctor.' David folded the prescription and put it in his pocket.

David went to the chemists in Petts Wood to get his prescription. He knew the doctor was trying to be helpful by telling him not to worry, but he was sure there was something she wasn't telling him. While waiting for the medication to be packaged, David looked at the health supplements on the shelves. He bought some Metatone tonic, Wellman effervescent tablets and magnesium, which, according to the labels, would help him sleep and increase his energy levels. When he got home, David sat down at the kitchen table with his laptop and started looking up articles on creatine kinase, what a neurologist does and the tests they do. He knew about CT and MRI scans, but other tests like angiography, myelography and neuro-interventional radiology he'd never heard of and sounded scary. The more he read, the more depressed and worried he became.

* * *

Having started work just after three in the morning, it was midday when Jessica said it was time to down tools and have a lunch break. The exterior crime scene tape had been removed, so Taff organised a pizza delivery to be dropped off by the garden gate on Homer Road. It was a sunny afternoon, so Taff and Diane sat at the garden table, drinking water and chatting while waiting for the pizzas. They'd been working non-stop and were glad to be able to finally relax, with their crime scene suits unzipped and the sleeves tied around their waists.

Not wanting to be distracted, Jessica sat at the kitchen table making more notes on her iPad. She reviewed everything she and the team had done and observed, knowing that DCI Anderson would want a detailed analysis of the crime scene and forensic opportunities as soon as possible.

DI Chapman had been in his car, reviewing the house-to-house forms. He called the office and then entered the house to join the others. On seeing Jessica, who had her back to him, he started to tiptoe across the kitchen floor to avoid disturbing her. She turned and looked in his direction with a curious frown. 'Are you all right?'

'I'm fine, thanks.'

'Why are you tiptoeing?'

'I didn't want to disturb you while you were meditating.'

Jessica rolled her eyes. 'I was going over my notes. We're having some pizza in the garden. You're welcome to join us.'

'Thanks. I just spoke to Anderson . . .'

'Wondering why we haven't found the perpetrator yet, was he?' she interjected.

'Actually, he's more worried about Michelle De Klerk, aka Michelle Belsham, being missing. I told him to request an all-ports warning to see if she checked in on any flights or ferries.'

'From what I saw at the crime scene, I don't think she was at the house, but I could be wrong. Whatever happened, or wherever she is, let's hope she's safe and well.' Jessica actually felt a bit sorry for Anderson as he was in an awkward position and was taking a risk whatever he chose to do about Michelle's disappearance.

'Anderson's changed the meeting time to 3 p.m., by the way.'

'Any particular reason for that?' she asked.

'Said he's got a 5 p.m. meeting at the Yard with Commander Williams. The truth is, he probably needs to get home to his wife. I met her once at a colleague's wedding. She's a bit of a battle-axe. He's under the thumb and does what he's told. He's as quiet as a mouse in her company. Mind you, so would I be,' he laughed.

'What's the address of the station?' She got out her phone and opened the Waze app.

'Fleet Road, just off the North Circular. Postcode is IG11 7BG.'

'Thanks.' They went into the garden and joined the others.

'Anything new to report?' Jessica asked.

'Maybe,' Taff said. 'I've examined the striation marks on the safe a bit more closely.

They're different from the ones on the patio doors and caused by something I've not seen at a forced entry crime scene before. I'll need to remove the safe and take it to the lab for a detailed microscopic examination.' He turned to Chapman with a smile. 'Could you help me lift it?'

Chapman held his hands up. 'I think that's a forensics job, isn't it? I wouldn't want to compromise any evidence.'

Everyone laughed.

'The intruder most likely brought a toolkit with him,' Taff said. 'Like a shoulder bag or rucksack, something easy to carry.'

'Makes sense. And he could have used it to take away any stolen items,' Chapman added.

Diane thought of something. 'He'd have had to put it down to get any tools out. I'll take some fibre tape lifts from the carpet around the safe. If we identify a suspect and recover a rucksack or something similar, we might find fibres from the carpet or vice versa.'

'Good thinking, Diane,' Jessica said.

'I haven't done any ESLA testing on the basement carpets yet, though,' Taff said.

'Not a problem,' Jessica assured him. 'The electric current will lift any loose fibres onto the Myler sheet, and once you've photographed them, Diane can extract any fibres.'

Taff nodded. 'I'll do it after lunch.'

'OK, but first I'd like to discuss what we've got so far and the forensic opportunities going forward.'

'Sounds good,' Diane said, and they all tucked into their pizzas.

When they'd finished eating, Taff put the empty boxes and water bottles in a bin bag and took them to the van to dispose of later. Chapman's phone rang, but the conversation was very brief. He turned to Jessica.

'Anderson wants me back at the office to update him. It's been a pleasure to meet and work with you all. I've learned a lot about crime scene investigation' he nodded to Diane 'particularly blood pattern analysis, even though I probably won't remember most of it. And thanks for the pizza.' He handed Jessica a business card with his mobile number on it. 'Call me if you have difficulty finding our office or need anything else.'

'Thanks. And thanks for lending a hand,' Jessica said.

As he started to walk off, he stopped and turned around. 'There is one other thing I'd like to ask you about the crime scene, Jessica, but I understand if you don't want to answer it yet.'

'Go on,' she said.

'Do you think Anderson is right that it's simply a burglary gone wrong?'

'Well, clearly entry was forced, De Klerk was assaulted and property was stolen, all of which constitutes an aggravated burglary, but a few things don't quite add up regarding what the intruder did . . . and, for that matter, Mr De Klerk.'

'In what way?'

'I'll let you know when we've finished examining the crime scene and I further review my observations with Diane and Taff,' Jessica said.

Chapman nodded. 'I guess only two people can tell us exactly what happened. One is Mr De Klerk . . . if he survives. The other is the person responsible, whom we've yet to identify. But I'm confident, having seen how well we work as a team, that we will.'

'So am I,' Jessica replied, wishing he'd stop waffling and let them get on with their jobs.

Diane waited until Chapman was well out of earshot. 'He's hard to fathom. What do you two make of him?'

Taff shrugged. 'He seems like a competent and experienced detective.'

They both looked at Jessica. She had a serious look on her face. 'He's certainly interested in everything we do. I'm just not sure why.'

* * *

Jessica, Diane and Taff spent the next hour discussing and reviewing everything about the crime scene in fine detail. They were all aware that after a detailed laboratory examination of the footwear marks, blood and other items seized, their hypothesis of the sequence of events during the commission of the crime could change.

Jessica made notes on her iPad as they discussed their thoughts and observations. Although they differed in opinion at times, they didn't argue. They stuck to the facts, remained objective and reached logical conclusions on which they all agreed. Jessica thanked them for all their hard work and, as it had been a long day, told them to continue their forensic examination until no later than 5 p.m. If they hadn't finished, she would resume and complete the outstanding examination in the morning while Diane and Taff started their lab analysis of the DNA swabs and other items seized.

'Hopefully I'll be back at the office about the same time as you,' Jessica said, 'and we can discuss what DCI Anderson has to say.'

'I've uploaded all the photographs and videos to the MSCAN internet drive and made a copy on a USB stick for DCI Anderson,' Taff said.

'Good. I'd better head off to Barking. The last thing I want is to be late. Is there anything else you can think of that I should raise at the meeting?'

'You could tell Anderson to be a bit more respectful,' Diane said.

'Don't let him get to you, Di. We can only do our best and advise him accordingly. If he doesn't want to take on board what we say, then he's only himself to blame if things go pear-shaped,' Taff commented.

'Anderson's under a lot of pressure to solve the case quickly,' Jessica said. 'Even more so now he knows Michelle Belsham is the victim's wife, so maybe give him some slack. See you all later.'

Di and Taff watched her go. Di pursed her lips. 'I'd better behave myself, then,' she said.

'You'd better,' Taff agreed. 'You know she's got eyes in the back of her head.'

CHAPTER EIGHT

Jessica was removing her crime scene suit by the van when a black cab pulled up near number 389. A woman wearing a baseball cap, a blue velvet tracksuit and white trainers got out while the driver removed a small black suitcase from the boot. Jessica couldn't quite see the woman's face as she was talking on her mobile with her head down.

'Mrs De Klerk?'

She looked at Jessica and held her hand up. 'Two seconds. Fine, I'll take the case. Leave the file on my desk and I'll review it in the morning.' She ended the call and looked up. 'Yes, I'm Michelle De Klerk. What can I do for . . .' She paused, noticing the uniformed police officer standing by the door of 389. 'What the fuck's going on?'

As a crime scene examiner, Jessica had no experience conveying bad news about the victims of serious assault. She held up her ID. 'I'm Jessica Russell, a Crime Scene Investigator . . .'

'Oh my God, is it Johan? Has something happened to him?'

'I'm afraid someone broke into your house and assaulted him . . .'

'Where is he . . . is he all right?' She started to walk towards the house.

Jessica didn't want to use physical force to stop her from entering the house and was unsure what to say. 'Johan's not there, he's in hospital.'

Michelle stopped and turned sharply. 'In hospital! What's happened to him?'

'He has a serious head injury and was stabbed.'

'No, no, this can't be real.' She started to cry, her whole body shaking.

'I'm afraid it is, and your house is being treated as a crime scene.'

'Where is he?'

'Homerton hospital. All I know is he's in a critical condition and undergoing surgery.'

'I have to go . . . I need to be with Johan.' Michelle reached into her designer handbag and fumbled for her car keys but couldn't find them. 'My car keys, they're in the house. I need to get them.'

'Understandably, you are very shocked, but I don't think you should drive to the hospital,' Jessica said.

'Yes, you're right. I'm not thinking straight. Can you take me, please?'

'Of course,' Jessica said, instinctively wanting to help the poor woman, but she couldn't help wondering if she might also be able to ask her a few questions that might assist her crime scene investigation.

'Can I leave my case here?' Michelle asked.

Jessica took it from her, handed it to the officer at the front door and asked him to put it in the hallway.

As Jessica drove to the hospital, Michelle sobbed and stared vacantly out the window, occasionally wiping her eyes with a tissue. Jessica thought about calling DI Chapman on her car phone for an update on Johan De Klerk's condition, but fearing it would further distress Michelle, she decided to do it privately when they got to the hospital.

Michelle sniffed, wiped her nose and took a deep breath. 'Sorry, but what was your name again?'

'Jessica Russell. I'm a crime scene investigator for the Metropolitan Police.'

'What happened to Johan . . . was he attacked in the house?'

'I think it might be best if the investigating officer discusses it with you. I'll try to contact him when we get to the hospital.'

'I'm Johan's wife. I have a right to know what happened to him,' she snapped back.

Jessica could see she was in distress and relented. 'Someone broke into your house through the patio doors and forced the safe in the study open. It looks like Johan disturbed the intruder in the kitchen and was assaulted during a struggle.'

She started to cry again. 'Is he going to live?'

Jessica let out a long sigh. 'I honestly don't know, but I was told his injuries are life-threatening.'

'Oh my God, I don't believe this, do you know who did this to him? Have you arrested anyone?' She started crying again.

'Not at present, but we are working on it. DCI John Anderson from the Barking major investigation team is leading the enquiry. He'll be able to tell you much more than I can.'

Having parked her car at the hospital, Jessica accompanied Michelle to the Accident and Emergency Centre. Jessica informed the receptionist who they were and asked what ward Mr De Klerk was being treated in. They were told that he was in the intensive care unit on the first floor. Arriving at the ICU, Jessica spoke with a nurse who said she would contact the doctor caring for Mr De Klerk and take them to the nearby waiting room.

'Would you like a hot drink or some water?' Jessica asked, hoping Michelle would say yes and she could contact DI Chapman while out of the room.

'I've got some water in my bag.' She removed the bottle, unscrewed it, and took a sip.

'Are you OK while I just nip to the toilet?' Jessica asked.

Michelle nodded. Jessica left and spoke with a nurse who

pointed to a ladies toilet down the corridor. Once inside, she called DI Chapman. 'Hi, it's Jessica Russell . . .'

'You lost?' he asked, thinking she couldn't find the station.

'No, I'm at Homerton Hospital.'

'What are you doing there? The meeting starts in twenty minutes.'

'I know, but I'm going to be unavoidably late.'

'Anderson won't be pleased . . .'

'I don't care. I'm with Michelle De Klerk.'

'What? How did that happen?'

'If you stop asking questions, I can tell you!' Jessica told Chapman about Michelle De Klerk unexpectedly turning up at the house, her distressed state of mind and why she felt obliged to drive her to the hospital.

'OK, you did the right thing. I'll let Anderson know. If you get the chance, ask Mrs De Klerk about the Rolex watch, and if she knew what was in the safe, then we'll know what we're looking for.'

Jessica returned to the waiting room. Michelle was on her phone, anxiously rocking back and forth in an armchair. She looked at Jessica and ended the call.

'Thought I'd better let my parents know what's happened. My mum was beside herself. Johan's parents live in South Africa. I'll call them later when I know more about his condition.'

Jessica sat down beside her. 'I know this isn't a good time, but do you mind if I ask you a couple of questions?'

'I want to do all I can to help you.'

'OK. Do you know what was in the safe in the study?'

'To be honest, I don't. Johan did all his business work from his study. I know some of his sales were cash transactions, so he probably kept money in the safe before depositing it in the bank.'

'Any jewellery belonging to either of you?'

'We've got a small safe in the bedroom we keep our jewellery in.'

'Can I ask where it is . . . just in case it was broken into as well?'

'It's a wall safe in my wardrobe.'

'I looked in your wardrobes but didn't find any signs of a disturbance . . . so I think your jewellery will still be there. I'll get one of my colleagues to double-check.'

'Honestly, I couldn't care less if it was all stolen. I'm more concerned about Johan right now.'

'We think his Rolex watch might have been taken. Would he keep that in his safe when he's not wearing it?'

'No, he wears his Rolex all the time. It's his pride and joy. I told him repeatedly he shouldn't wear such an expensive watch. People are always being mugged for them.' She banged the armrest with a clenched fist. 'Since we moved in, I've asked Johan countless times to get CCTV and security lights fitted to the house. He kept promising to do it . . . if I'd organised it, this would never have happened and he wouldn't be lying in a hospital bed.'

'How long have you lived there?'

'We moved in a few months ago, after renovating it . . . where's the bloody doctor?' she exclaimed.

'I'm sure he'll be here as soon as he's able,' Jessica said, trying to calm her. 'When did you last speak to Johan?'

'On Sunday morning. I was in Lancashire for the weekend. One of my friend's baby daughters was christened yesterday. She'd asked me to be a Godmother. I got a flight from Docklands airport on Saturday morning to Manchester. Johan was meant to come with me but cancelled at the last minute.'

'Can I ask why?'

'He said there'd been a problem with a big wine shipment which he needed to sort out urgently or he would lose a lot of money. I was annoyed with him but I . . . never expected to return to this nightmare.' She put her hands over her eyes and started sobbing.

'I'm sorry, I don't mean to upset you with all these questions.' Jessica paused, giving Michelle time to compose herself.

'It's all right. As a barrister, I know how police investigations work. In court I've had to deal with countless violent crimes. But it's so different when it happens to someone you love.'

Jessica nodded. 'Of course.' She waited a moment before continuing. 'We recovered Johan's phone from under the kitchen table, and a laptop was on the table. Would that be Johan's?'

'Yes, I took mine with me.'

'We'll examine them for fingerprints and DNA in case the intruder touched them. The calls and texts Johan made before he was attacked could be crucial to the investigation too. The same goes for the laptop, in respect of recent emails. Are you happy to give us permission to examine them?'

'If you think it might help the investigation, though I'd rather Johan made that decision about the laptop, if and when he can.'

'Did Johan say if anyone was visiting him at home on Sunday or over the weekend?'

'No, but he often had business associates and friends around.'

'The police will probably want their details at some point.'

'I'll compile a list later, but my concern right now is Johan.'

'There's no rush. Did Johan use the basement cinema area to entertain friends?'

'Yes. Johan's a film buff . . . he spends hours down there watching movies.'

The waiting room door opened, and an Asian man in his forties, with a stethoscope hung around his neck, came in and introduced himself as Doctor Babu from the ICU.

'How severe are my husband's injuries?' Michelle asked.

Doctor Babu sat down beside her. 'He's currently in an induced coma due to his traumatic brain injury. This resulted in cerebral oedema and haemorrhaging . . . that is, swelling and bleeding around the brain. These types of injuries can also cause brain damage. When Johan regains consciousness, we will be in a better position to assess his cognitive abilities.'

He paused for a moment, then continued 'In respect of his stab wounds, the prognosis is good. He has four to his back, but no vital organs were damaged. The knife embedded in his back just missed his heart, but his blood loss was restricted due to the knife itself forming a seal around the wound.'

'What are his chances of survival?' she asked, with a tremor in her voice.

'Any brain injury is challenging, and the outcome is difficult to predict. Many factors are involved, including the severity of injury, age, prior functional levels and the onset of secondary complications. Fortunately, even with the most severe cases of brain damage, there is always a chance of recovery.'

'Isn't that just another way of saying he has a fifty-fifty chance?'

'Yes, you could put it that way. But I assure you, we will do everything we can for Johan.'

Michelle started to cry. Doctor Babu reached over to a table by his side, picked up a leaflet and handed it to Michelle.

'This leaflet has phone numbers for family support services and counsellors should you need them. On the back is the ICU number . . . you can call us for an update on Johan's condition anytime.'

'Can I see him?'

'Yes, but I must warn you, he is connected to a ventilator to assist his breathing, IV drips and monitors. Due to his head injuries and swelling, he will look very different from the last time you saw him, but with time, the swelling will recede. I would recommend comforting him by talking softly and touching his hand. I will speak with the nurse, who will take you to see him.'

'Thank you, Doctor Babu, and for all the care you are giving my husband,' Michelle said. When he left, she looked at Jessica, still in tears. 'It's going to be so hard seeing him if he's unrecognisable.'

'Would you like me to come with you?'

'I don't want to keep you from your work.'

'I'm more concerned about you right now.'

'Well, if you don't mind, thank you.'

'Is there anyone you'd like me to call who can be here for you?'

'It's OK, thanks. I take it I won't be able to go into my house for a while?'

'We are still examining the scene, but hopefully we will be finished sometime tomorrow. I can arrange for an officer or one of my team to assist you in getting some clothes and anything else you need from the house.'

'It's fine, thanks. I'll go to Holly's house. She's my sister. My mother said she'd tell her what's happened, but I'll call her later.'

'Can I ask you a personal question?'

Michelle looked puzzled. 'OK . . .'

'I noticed one of the rooms in your house looked like it might be used as a baby's room . . . are you pregnant?' Michelle didn't look as if she was.

Michelle started to well up again. 'Yes, nearly four months . . . and expecting a boy.' She placed a protective hand over her stomach and seemed about to say something when she began to gasp, overcome with tears.

'With the stress you're under right now, it might be worth telling Doctor Babu. He could arrange for you to have an ultrasound to make sure everything is OK.'

Michelle nodded. 'I'll do that.' They exchanged phone numbers and Michelle gave Jessica her sister's details. Jessica also gave Michelle DI Chapman's number and explained she didn't have DCI Anderson's but she would text it as soon as possible.

As they approached Johan's bed, Michelle began to shake and Jessica put a steadying arm around her shoulder. Looking at the figure on the bed, surrounded by tubes and wires, she would never have recognised the man in the hunting photo. His face was grotesquely swollen, looking like a balloon that was about to burst.

'Oh my poor Johan, what have they done to you?' Michelle sobbed, collapsing into the chair next to the bed. She looked up at Jessica with a helpless expression. 'God, I feel so useless right now. If Johan had come with me to Lancashire, or I'd been at home . . .'

'You mustn't blame yourself in any way, Michelle,' Jessica said firmly. 'You are not responsible for the actions of others.'

'I'm frightened to touch him.'

'I'll help you.' Jessica took Michelle's right hand and gently placed it on Johan's left.

As they touched, Michelle became even more distressed. 'Please don't die, Johan. I need you . . . I can't live without you.'

Jessica felt herself welling up as memories of her mother's last moments flooded her mind. She took a deep breath, trying to compose herself, and made a silent vow to find whoever was responsible for what had happened to Johan De Klerk.

* * *

Walking to her car, Jessica recalled the last week of her mother's life, eighteen months earlier. She was fifty-seven. It was the usual Sunday get-together at the bungalow in Petts Wood. Eileen had cooked roast beef, vegetables and giant Yorkshire puddings filled with gravy.

She'd hardly touched her own plate and Jessica had noticed that their mother's skin looked yellow and she'd lost a lot of weight. When she mentioned her concerns to David, he agreed and told Jessica he'd also noticed their mum wincing in pain and struggling when walking up the stairs or doing anything strenuous. He'd asked her if she was unwell, but she brushed it off as the symptoms of menopause. David hadn't known that women generally put on weight during menopause.

They persuaded Eileen to go to her GP. The only appointment available was in two weeks, and David said he could take Eileen as it was in the afternoon after his work. When the day of the appointment came, Jessica vividly remembered her brother calling her while she was at a crime scene, thinking it was to tell her what the GP had said.

'I'm at the Princess Royal Hospital with Mum,' David had said, a tremor in his voice.

'I thought you were going to the doctor's?'

'That's why we're here. The GP said Mum had jaundice, and it might be from a liver infection. He told us to go straight to the emergency department for tests. When we got here, they took some blood and urine samples, then an hour later they said Mum's blood test showed some anomalies and she needed to have a CT scan.'

'They're probably just covering themselves. They wouldn't want to tell you one thing and then discover it's something else. At least we know Mum's in safe hands.'

'I think you should come. You know more about these things than I do.' He sounded desperate.

She remembered arriving at the hospital and joining a pale-faced David in the waiting room. 'Any news?' she asked, sitting down beside him.

'They've done the CT scan, but now they're doing an MRI.'

'Why?'

'I don't know…I'm not a bloody doctor!' he snapped.

Jessica vividly remembered the doctor entering the room, prompting David to jump out of his chair, demanding to know what was wrong with their mother. The doctor informed them that Eileen had been moved to a bed in a private side room and wanted to speak with them. As David grew increasingly frustrated, firing off question after question, the doctor just repeated that their mother wished to talk to them.

She could recall entering the room with David and seeing their mother sitting upright in bed. Eileen greeted them with a loving smile, though it was evident she had been crying. David stood on one side of the bed while she stood on the other, and Eileen took hold of their hands. What she said was forever etched in both their memories.

'I have cancer in my bones and liver, which is inoperable. The doctor said they could arrange end-of-life care for me at home, but I don't want to be a burden to you.'

David froze with shock, then broke down in floods of tears, repeatedly insisting that the doctors were wrong and that she wasn't going to die. Eileen squeezed his hand tighter.

'I'm sorry, but there's nothing the doctors or anyone else can do for me, even if I had seen them weeks ago.'

In her forensic work, through focusing on the job in hand and practising meditation, Jessica had learned to set aside her feelings when dealing with death. Knowing she had an important job to do and that her efforts often comforted the grieving also helped her cope. But when she was told her mother was going to die it felt like her heart had been ripped out.

Three days later, Jessica and David were again by Eileen's side as she peacefully passed away. It felt like their mother had been taken from them in the blink of an eye.

*   *   *

Driving to Barking, Jessica thought about what Michelle had said, how she must have prosecuted or defended men and women who were capable of violent crimes but learned to detach herself from the horrific acts they were accused of. But when tragedy is close to you, really part of you, detachment seems impossible. Jessica had learned that. And now Michelle was learning it, too.

But her mother's death, and being abandoned by her father, weren't the only traumatic events Jessica had had to deal with in her life. In her interview for the MSCAN job, she had only given brief details about the sexual assault she had suffered. And the road to recovery had been a long one. It was only through counselling and many hours of yoga and meditation that she had learned how to deal with her feelings. And, of course, focusing her attention on her work. And that, she knew, more than ever, was what she had to do now.

Having learned the extent and brutality of Johan's injuries from Doctor Babu, Jessica wondered if the person who entered the De Klerk's house had done so with the sole intent of killing or causing severe injuries to Johan. If so, had taking the contents of the safe and the watch been done to make things look like a burglary gone wrong? Although it was possible, stealing first and then trying to kill Johan just didn't make sense. Jessica tapped the steering wheel, wondering if she had overlooked or misinterpreted something in her scene analysis. And there was another question: why did someone want Johan De Klerk dead?

CHAPTER NINE

Jessica parked her car, grabbed her shoulder bag, ran across the yard to the station entrance and pressed the buzzer. She would have liked to go through the notes and photos on her iPad first but was already half an hour late for the meeting. She needed to know more about Johan De Klerk's personal, professional and social life to complete a detailed victim profile. If there was a link in De Klerk's lifestyle to his assailant, it needed to be found.

The receptionist told Jessica that Anderson's team office was on the third floor and pointed to the lift down the corridor, but Jessica opted for the stairs. Before entering the room, she paused for breath, untied her hair, smoothed it down with her hands then tied it up again before brushing herself down. As she entered, the room of twenty detectives and civilian staff went quiet as they looked inquisitively at her, clearly wondering who she was. Jessica saw DCI Anderson standing by a large TV screen at the far end of the room with DI Chapman.

'Glad you could join us, Miss Russell. Better late than never, I suppose,' he said coldly.

'Sorry, sir, but I was . . .'

'Yes, DI Chapman told me you were with Mrs De Klerk at the hospital. If you had phoned me when she turned up at her house, I could have gone to the hospital to meet her.'

Jessica knew Anderson was deliberately belittling her in front of his team, but she was determined not to react. She focused on her breathing, remained expressionless and let him continue.

'For those who don't know, this is Jessica Russell, head of the newly formed . . .' He paused and looked at Jessica. 'Remind me, what was it called?'

'It's MSCAN, short for the Murder and Serious Crime Analysis Unit.'

Anderson was about to continue, but she got in there first. 'I manage a team of experienced and dedicated forensic experts. We specialise in crime scene analysis, evidence retrieval and forensic examination. We aim to provide evidential opportunities and intelligence that will assist you, as detectives, in solving the serious crimes you investigate. We are here to help . . . not hinder.' Jessica smiled, and many in the room nodded their approval.

'And to work effectively and assist us, Jessica's team need to know what we know,' Chapman chipped in.

'I decide on what information needs to be shared, DI Chapman!' Anderson interjected.

'I was going to add, within limitations and your approval, sir.' He gave Jessica a side-long glance.

Jessica opened her iPad, expecting to be asked to brief everyone about the crime scene, her analysis and the forensic evidence they had gathered.

Anderson looked at his watch, then addressed the team. 'Carry on with your enquiries, and we'll have another office meeting at 9am tomorrow.'

A couple of detectives raised their hands. Anderson looked at his watch again and pointed to the older one.

'The first attending officer's body cam video was shaky and unclear, making it difficult to view. I was wondering if Miss Russell had any scene videos or photos we could look at?'

'I was going to ask the same question, and if the scene examination turned up anything of specific interest,' another detective chipped in.

'I'd like to discuss Miss Russell's observations and the forensic opportunities with her first, then I'll brief you in the morning,' Anderson replied, clearly flustered. He turned to Chapman. 'I need to make a quick phone call. You and Miss Russell come to my office in five minutes.' He walked out briskly.

'The missus wants him home in time for din dins,' one of the detectives quipped said, causing a ripple of laughter in the room.

Chapman turned to Jessica with a rueful frown. 'Sorry about that . . .'

'Thanks for sticking up for me,' she said. 'He's obviously got some issues.'

'Is that your assessment as a profiler?' Chapman asked with a grin.

'Just an observation. People who are insecure about their abilities often try to boost their self-esteem by belittling others.'

'Well, from the looks on their faces, the team are on your side,' he said.

Chapman knocked on Anderson's door and let Jessica enter first. DCI Anderson was still on the phone.

'I'll be there as soon as I can, dear.' He quickly put the phone down.

'Everything all right, sir?' Chapman asked.

'Um, it was Commander Williams. I'm running late for a meeting with her, so we'll have to postpone our chat until tomorrow.' He stood up, removed his jacket from the back of the chair and put it on.

Jessica took the USB stick from her shoulder bag. 'This contains the crime scene videos and photos, sir.'

'Give it to DI Chapman and he'll upload it to the HOLMES computer. I'd also like you to do a full report of your scene analysis, forensic exhibits and strategy . . . including everything Mrs De Klerk told you, then put it on HOLMES. I'll read and review it in the morning, then circulate it to the team.'

'I don't have access to the HOLMES system,' Jessica said.

He frowned. 'Then give it to someone on my team who has.'

'There are a couple of things I'd like to ask,' Jessica said as Anderson picked up his briefcase.

'Make it quick,' he sighed.

'I'd like a forensic pathologist to attend the hospital, speak with Mr De Klerk's surgeon and examine his injuries.'

Anderson gave her a look of disdain. 'He's not bloody dead yet!'

'I know, but a surgeon is not an expert in interpreting injuries, their pattern or causation. Forensic pathologists, unlike doctors, are also trained in the rules of evidence and considered experts by the courts. If De Klerk survives, a pathologist's report could be invaluable evidence.'

'Very well, I'll leave you to organise it. If that's all . . .'

Jessica hadn't finished. 'I also think a victim profile on Johan De Klerk would benefit the investigation. I've formed a rapport with Michelle, so I'd like to interview her about Johan's lifestyle, his work and . . .'

Anderson pursed his lips. 'Absolutely not. You are not an FLO or a detective. Mrs De Klerk needs to be treated sensitively and compassionately so we can gather evidence and information that will contribute to the investigation and preserve its integrity.'

Chapman knew he was quoting virtually word for word from the homicide and major crime investigation manual. He gave Jessica another covert glance.

'As you know, I have a background in psychology . . .' she began to protest.

'Interpreting a crime scene and being an FLO involve different skills. A statement from Mrs De Klerk will be taken tomorrow morning, which you're welcome to read.'

'I did the FLO course, albeit a few years ago, but I'm happy to interview Mrs De Klerk, if you're too busy to see her,' Chapman said.

'No, I've already appointed DC Owens as the FLO. As my deputy, I need you here to help run the investigation. I'll meet with Mrs De Klerk in the morning. In the meantime, Miss Russell can give DC Owens the details of their conversation at the hospital.'

'Will you be holding a press conference?' Chapman asked.

'I don't see the need now we know Mrs De Klerk is safe and well. Besides, burglaries and assaults in Hackney are an everyday occurrence, so it's unlikely to be headline news. I also want to avoid panic among the local community.'

Chapman suspected he was frightened of appearing on camera and facing probing questions from journalists. 'That may be the case, sir, but do you not think the press will be interested when they discover the victim is the husband of Michelle Belsham?'

'I'm sure Mrs De Klerk doesn't want the press camping on her doorstep, so let's ensure that fact isn't released.' He looked at Jessica. 'Have you found any evidence to help us identify the person responsible?'

'Not yet, but hopefully DNA testing and other examinations in the lab will do so.'

'Well, we are still in the "golden hour", so I suggest you find me something positive from your scene and forensic examinations, even if it takes you all night,' Anderson said.

'Yes, sir. We'll do our best,' Jessica replied, knowing the 'golden hour' was a standard police term for the period immediately following the report of a major incident.

'But my team are exhausted. They have been up since the early hours.'

'As have I,' he said, then walked out.

Chapman sighed. 'It's all my way or the highway with him.

He won't come back to the office tonight, so it's your call about continuing work at the scene. He's ignoring health and safety issues and breaking work time regulations. You are entitled to at least eleven hours of rest between shifts. If you all want to go home and get some rest, there's nothing he can do about it.'

'I'm aware of the regulations,' she said. 'I'll speak with Taff and Diane. I was going to suggest some protection for Mr De Klerk,' she added. 'If the intruder intended to kill him or De Klerk recognised him, then his life could still be in danger.'

'That's a good point,' he agreed. 'I can't authorise an armed guard, but I can ask for a uniform presence. I'll call the local station.'

He dialled a number on his mobile and spoke for a few moments. 'It's all done. A uniform officer will be outside the ITU round the clock. I'll get a couple of coffees. My office is just down the corridor, we can drink them in there.'

While waiting for Chapman to return with the coffees, Jessica phoned the coroner's officer at Hackney Mortuary and requested that a pathologist attend Hackney Hospital, speak with Johan De Klerk's doctor and examine his injuries. Jessica gave him Doctor Babu's details and asked, if she couldn't be there, for a copy of the pathologist's report.

Chapman returned with the coffee and some biscuits. 'Between us, I'm getting to the point where I feel like telling Anderson to stop behaving like a spoilt child. I don't think he realises how it affects everyone's morale.'

'Seems to me he relies on you a lot as his deputy,' Jessica said. She took a sip of her coffee. 'How long have you been in the job then?'

'Coming up for eighteen years, and a DI for five now,' he said.

'Are you thinking about promotion?'

'No, I'm happy as I am . . . actually, that's bullshit. Truth is,

I'm crap on interviews and failed the DCI promotion board,' he said, stirring his coffee.

'You seem like a confident person to me.'

'I am, but I tend to speak my mind about the lack of experience in the current crop of officers and where the police service is going, which is in the wrong direction.'

'Why do you think that?'

'You can join as a direct entry detective and be on a murder squad in two to three years. Nearly half of our team has less than five years CID experience. Meanwhile, experienced officers become disillusioned with the job and resign or retire earlier than planned.'

She nodded thoughtfully. 'How long has Anderson been in the force?'

'He joined in his early thirties and was selected for the fast-track system. He was promoted to inspector after three years, then chief inspector a few years later. He then transferred into CID, did a year on division and then got the SIO role on the homicide team.'

'His age made me think he had longer service.'

'You're not the first to say that. The point is we now have inexperienced officers leading other inexperienced officers while dealing with serious and complex criminal investigations, which isn't right.'

'The situation in Kent is the same, though there are some outstanding junior officers.'

'Same in the Met, but they're few and far between. Others lack motivation as they don't see the police as a lifelong career and fiddle about on their phones all day instead of doing what they get paid for. The standard of crime investigation is appalling, the backlog is ridiculous and criminals are getting away scot-free. Things need to change quickly because the public deserves better.'

'I must admit, I was only a crime scene manager for a couple of years before I got the MSCAN job,' Jessica said.

'I wasn't having a dig at you,' he said quickly. 'From what I saw today, you're bloody good at your job.'

She smiled. 'Thank you.'

'To be honest, I was sceptical about the whole MSCAN idea when Anderson told me about it. I've worked on cases where behavioural advisers were used. For me, much of what they concluded was either common sense or guesswork. They didn't tell us anything we didn't already know, and their advice often actually hindered the investigation.'

'I don't entirely disagree with you,' she said. 'I was the crime scene manager on a murder investigation where a behavioural adviser got it very wrong. His analysis initially caused more harm than good.'

'Seeing your work today and listening to what you said, your approach seems more sensible.'

'When I became a SOCO, I learned to combine my knowledge of human behaviour with crime scene investigation, so I tend to look at things differently.'

'But you do sort of become the offender and try to think like them?'

'Yes, you could say that.' They drank their coffee in silence for a moment.

'I don't mean to pry, but how long have you been meditating?'

She hesitated. Part of her wanted to tell him to mind his own business, but then she relented. She shrugged. 'Long time, about eleven or twelve years now.'

'What made you take it up?'

'It was something I just thought I'd try. I liked it, so I stuck with it. Can we change the subject, please?'

'Sorry. Have I upset you?' he asked.

She took a deep breath and exhaled before answering. 'No, it's just that it's personal.'

He nodded as if he understood, and Jessica thought the subject was closed, but then he continued. 'I didn't want to say anything before, but I was worried you might remember me and it would distress you.'

'What on earth are you talking about?'

'I know you were sexually assaulted when you were a probation officer. I thought . . .'

Jessica's heart started racing and she could feel her colour rising. 'Fucking Anderson told you, didn't he! He had no right to. What I said in my interview was confidential.' She stood up and grabbed her bag. 'I'm going to report this to Commander Williams. You have no idea how terrified I was that night or how it affected me. If you and Anderson think it's something to gossip about, you're both sick in the head!'

Chapman took a step back. She was so angry he thought she might attack him, but she started to walk off. 'Jessica, please wait. I swear, Anderson never told me.'

She spun round to face him. 'Of course he did. I'm not stupid!'

'I'm sorry, but I didn't say anything until now because I thought it best not to.'

'It's a bit late for apologies.'

'I was worried you might remember me, and it would lead to flashbacks and cause you distress.'

She stared at him. 'Why on earth would I remember you?'

'I was the duty detective the night you were assaulted and one of the first officers on the scene at your flat.'

'What? I don't believe this . . .'

'You told me your assailant put his hand over your mouth and said to keep quiet. You fought him and bit him, then screamed for help, and he ran off.'

'Oh my God.' Jessica groaned as her mind flashed back to that awful night.

'A female officer attended and took you to the comfort suite.' Chapman was referring to the dedicated room where victims of rape and serious sexual assault can talk to police in privacy and safety.

She had to take several deep breaths to calm herself. 'Her name was Paula,' Jessica said softly, remembering how the officer held her hand and comforted her while the doctor performed a physical examination.

'And she took your statement. She told me how brave you were.'

Jessica stared at Chapman. Everything he said was right, but she still wondered if he was lying. 'I have no recollection of you being at my flat,' she said.

'I was only there briefly. You were very distressed, which may be why you don't remember me. You told me the person who attacked you was wearing a balaclava, but from the sound of his voice and the smell of his body odour, you suspected it was a fifteen-year-old on probation and under your supervision at the time. I went to his flat that night and arrested him.'

She pursed her lips, and the anger returned. 'You could have got all this information from the old crime report. Why are you snooping into my private life?'

'I swear, I'm not. I was on night shift, so I had to hand the case over to DS Michael Blake in the morning and had no further involvement.'

Jessica remembered Blake. 'He was very understanding. Very kind.'

'He wanted to charge the boy with attempted rape, but the CPS decided there wasn't enough evidence, forensic or otherwise, to provide a "realistic prospect of conviction".'

'That was because his mother gave him a false alibi, saying he'd been in all night.'

'I know, I spoke to her when I arrested him. Unfortunately, I didn't find the balaclava which he probably threw away.'

'If you must know, as silly as it sounds, in some ways I was relieved. It meant I didn't have to go through the ordeal again in court.'

Chapman typed something into his desktop computer and turned the screen towards her. 'That's his criminal record. As you can see, it's as long as my arm.' He scrolled back. 'There's his arrest for the attempted rape. As the victim of a sexual assault, your name is redacted, and as you can see, I'm shown as the arresting officer.'

Jessica sat down. 'All right, I believe you. But why did you wait until now to tell me?'

He looked sad. 'I was the investigating officer on a horrendous rape case about ten years ago. Recounting the details in court was traumatic for the victim, but we got a conviction. The thing is, once a trial like that is over, the victim tries to move on, and you have no further contact with them. Four years later, I bumped into her in the street. On seeing me, she had a flashback to the rape and suffered a severe panic attack. It was so bad I had to call an ambulance. I blamed myself and wanted to go to the hospital to see how she was, but I was advised not to as it could further distress her if she saw me again.'

'And you thought the same would happen to me if I recognised you?' She sounded affronted.

He nodded. 'I realise now that I should have kept my mouth shut.'

She sat up straight and gave a nonchalant shrug, trying her hardest to maintain control of her emotions, determined not to show him the effect of what he had just told her. 'If you must know, even if I had recognised you, it wouldn't have upset me. Admittedly, after the little bastard tried to rape me, I suffered from post-traumatic stress and left my job as a probation officer. At the time, I didn't know how to handle it. But on my doctor's advice, I started seeing a rape counsellor, who suggested I also take up meditation and yoga.'

'Meditation sounds like something I should try,' Chapman said, trying to lighten the situation.

'It wasn't an overnight cure, if that's what you're thinking,' she said. 'Initially, I moved back home to live with my mother and brother. I was off sick from my probation work for a long time and dreaded returning. When I was able to deal with my emotions again, I decided to seek a different career path. I thought long and hard about joining the police, but at the time, I worried front line work – interviewing victims and arresting suspects – would be too stressful after what happened to me. My mother suggested I become a scene of crime officer. The rest, as they say, is history.'

He smiled. 'I'm glad you conquered your demons, and you should be proud of all you've achieved.' He had his over-serious expression on his face, and it made her smile.

'Thank you for that and I am proud of getting over it. I only wish my mother was still alive to share my success. Sadly, she died a few years ago from cancer.'

'I'm sorry for your loss.' Chapman looked at his watch. 'It's nearly time for the meeting, but I can postpone it until tomorrow morning if that would be better for you.'

'For goodness' sake, I can assure you I'm fine.'

'I'm sorry if I brought back some bad memories. That wasn't my intention.'

'I realise that now, and thank you for being open and honest with me.'

'It would have been better if I'd said nothing,' Chapman sighed.

'What's done is done, and it's time to move on. It's over, finished with, so let's keep it that way.'

CHAPTER TEN

Returning to the homicide team office, DI Chapman asked the assembled detectives and civilian staff members to introduce themselves by rank and name and briefly describe their team roles. After DC Dawn Owens introduced herself as the family liaison officer, Chapman told her that Jessica had met Michelle De Klerk, so it would be good for them to have a private discussion afterwards. Jessica was surprised at how young Dawn looked, probably in her mid-twenties.

There was a large TV screen on the wall, and Jessica asked Chapman if she could plug her iPad into it to show the crime scene videos and photographs. He helped her set it up and switched the TV on. She used Google Earth to show the exact location and streets surrounding the De Klerk's address. 'Although they only moved in recently, Michelle De Klerk had been pestering her husband to get security cameras and a video doorbell. We found estimates from security companies and it was obviously something De Klerk intended following up on but unfortunately, he never did. The house is at the end of the terrace, and there's no CCTV on Homer Road overlooking their wall or where they park their cars. Mrs De Klerk's car keys were in the hallway, so I assume that is where her husband kept the Range Rover keys and the intruder grabbed them on his way out. The lack of security at the house could be why it was targeted for a burglary, but I'll get to that later.'

'Have the house-to-house enquiries turned up anything?' A DC asked, and Chapman answered.

'So far, there's nothing useful regarding CCTV or suspect sightings. The nearest council cameras are down at Hackney Wick by the A12. DC Bingham is checking it out to see if De Klerk's Range Rover was picked up.'

The team watched the video intently as it moved from the entrance of 389 Victoria Park Road, down the hallway and into the various rooms, with Jessica describing the different locations in the house. When the video finished, Jessica said she would discuss the intruder's movements in the house using photographs they had taken to illustrate her analysis.

'Taff Jones, our footwear and fingerprint expert, concluded that shoe marks in the garden flower bed, kitchen, living room, basement study and hallway came from the same trainers, which he believes to be Adidas size ten. He didn't find matching footmarks in the main bedroom or other first-floor rooms, so it seems unlikely the intruder went upstairs. There were also visible blood-stained footprints in the kitchen and a couple on the living room carpet leading towards the hallway from the same trainers. We did luminol tests in the hallway, revealing the same bloodstained footprints.' She brought up the photographs. 'As you can see, the tread marks are quite clear and lead to the front door, which was the intruder's escape route.'

'Looks like a blue glow stick,' one detective observed.

'Glow sticks, like luminol, are based on chemical reactions that produce light, known as chemiluminescence. When used at a crime scene, we darken the room first and use long-exposure photography to record the blue glow, which lasts about thirty seconds.'

'Using luminol must make your job a lot easier and speed things up,' the detective said.

'Yes and no. Luminol will also react to animal blood, bleaching agents and other oxidising compounds, such as those found in urine or saliva, so a positive luminol test doesn't necessarily confirm human blood. We still have to take samples and do more specific tests at the lab to identify human blood suitable for DNA testing.'

Jessica played the video showing the garden's exterior and side gate entrance, explaining the intruder's entry route from Homer Road. 'We believe the intruder climbed onto the neighbour's low wall and gate, then up onto the De Klerk's wall, and lowered himself onto the raised bedding area, where he left a shoe print.'

'He must be pretty fit to have climbed up and over a wall as high as that,' an older detective commented.

Jessica agreed and had more to add. 'Taff Jones believes a right-hand glove mark on top of the neighbour's metal gate may be of evidential value.' Some team members looked puzzled, and a detective questioned how a glove mark could be helpful. Jessica brought up photographs of the glove prints. 'Woollen gloves can leave fibres behind. But in this case, Taff suspects the marks were left by touchscreen gloves that allow the wearer to use smartphones and tablets when wearing them.' Jessica explained that different kinds of conductive material are woven into the fingertips and thumb of touchscreen gloves. She said it was usually copper yarn, but some glove makers use aluminium or thermal paste. 'The marks from the palm were consistent with a decorative stitched silicone pattern that could be unique to the glove, though, with wear and tear, the original pattern of the touch screen fingers and silicone changes, and the more they are used, the more the pattern will alter from the one left at the crime scene.'

'Is it the same principle with shoe marks?' DC Owens asked.

Jessica nodded. 'We will do further research on the silicone pattern to identify the make of the glove and suppliers. We know a jemmy, or something similar, was used to force open the patio door and the safe, but from the striation marks, it appears a different implement was used on each.'

'Does that mean there were two intruders?' another detective asked.

'The footmarks and other evidence we recovered indicate a lone intruder, but I can't rule out more than one person was involved. We also believe he may have used a rucksack or other kind of bag to carry a jemmy or other tools to break open the safe. If he put the rucksack down on the carpet, there may be fibres from it on the carpet or soil if he put it down outside.'

Chapman stepped forward. 'When we identify a suspect, we obviously need to do a thorough search for the items Jessica has just mentioned.'

A detective asked if they knew what was stolen from the safe. Jessica said Mrs De Klerk didn't know what her husband kept in it, and only Johan could answer that question, if and when he recovered from his injuries. Next, she informed them about the disturbance in the living room relating to the coffee table and items that could have fallen from it during a struggle between De Klerk and his assailant.

'Taff examined the carpet and floor leading from the living room to a knife block in the kitchen. He found barefoot marks, which we believe to be Mr De Klerk's and on top of some of them were the Adidas imprints. This infers that at some point during the struggle in the living room, Mr De Klerk moved towards the knife block in the kitchen, followed by his attacker.' She brought up the photos of the area one by one.

'Jesus, it's a bloodbath,' someone commented, and Jessica noticed a pale-looking Dawn put her hand to her mouth as if she was about to be sick. She leaned towards Chapman and spoke quietly.

'As you assisted Diane, would you like to explain her blood pattern analysis and interpretation to the team? I'll project the close-up photos as you speak.'

He looked pleased as he removed his pocketbook from his jacket. 'I made notes, so I'll give it a go, but tell me if I go wrong.' Chapman spoke slowly as he repeated everything Diane said about the blood distribution in the kitchen and the likely course of events. Then, using the photographs of the bloodstains, pooling and knife block, he described De Klerk's movements and how he was repeatedly stabbed with one of his own household knives, which was embedded in his back before the assailant stepped in the blood and then left the house.

The team listened in silence, amazed yet appalled, as Chapman detailed the ferocity of the attack. He added that if it hadn't been for the quick attendance of the paramedics, De Klerk would have undoubtedly died at the scene. When he finished, he looked at Jessica, wondering if he'd explained everything correctly.

She nodded her approval. Jessica continued. 'Diane didn't find any blood droplets from the kitchen to the hallway, suggesting the assailant hadn't received an injury that bled. However, he could still have been scratched, bruised or injured in some way.'

Jessica displayed some of the electrostatic footprint lifts on the TV screen. 'These shoe prints were recovered in the living room by the ransacked drawers and the basement study. As you can see, the tread mark is the same as the other suspect marks. No traces of blood were found in them, which implies the drawers and safe were opened before Mr De Klerk was beaten and stabbed.'

'Do we know if anything was stolen from the living room?' DC Owens asked.

'Not at present, but the opening of the drawers and scattering of some of the contents may have been staged. Only the top drawers had their contents removed and thrown around the floor . . . the other drawers were open but undisturbed.'

'I don't get how that's staged,' the young detective queried.

'I would have expected a burglar searching for hidden cash or items of value to look in all the drawers and even go upstairs to look for jewellery. He didn't, which suggests the intruder already knew the location of the safe and maybe the contents but staged the living room to cover the fact. I can't say specifically what woke Mr De Klerk or made him go downstairs. I should also add that Mr De Klerk was due to be in Lancashire over the weekend at a christening with his wife, but he pulled out at the last minute due to a problem with his wine importation business.'

'So, whoever broke in might have thought he was away,' a detective observed, and Jessica nodded. Other detectives started chipping in with their opinions. One thought it odd that if De Klerk had his phone upstairs and heard a noise, he didn't he call the police immediately and lock himself in the bathroom. Another said that when De Klerk went downstairs, he'd have to go through the living room to get to the kitchen, and if the intruder was in there, De Klerk would have seen him. This led to an officer remarking that the intruder could have hidden behind the sofa if he had heard De Klerk coming downstairs or been in the basement breaking into the safe.

Jessica had considered all these things, but she wanted the team to be involved and come up with their own ideas, no matter how implausible they might be. Challenging each other's opinions was a good thing.

Chapman raised his hand. 'Enough conjecture.' He looked at Dawn. 'Make sure you ask Mrs De Klerk if they have recently employed any cleaners, handymen or builders and get their details. The property was recently refurbished, and the contractors should all be questioned too. I'm not saying they might be directly involved, but they would know the house's layout.' There were nods and grunts of assent around the room. Jessica could see that

Chapman liked being the boss in Anderson's absence, and the team respected him.

A dour-looking detective sergeant – Julian Wood, aged forty-eight and the eldest and most experienced detective – who had so far remained silent, finally spoke up. 'I don't wish to appear rude, and I don't disagree with your scene analysis . . . but all we have so far is conjecture about what might or might not have happened. There don't appear to be any forensic leads that might help us directly identify the person responsible.'

'We recovered two items, one of which might help to do that, or at least trace someone worth speaking to . . .' Jessica paused to bring up a photograph. She showed the team photos of the animal-engraved crystal glasses and told them where she found them. She added that both glasses still had some wet residue in them. 'I am not a drinks connoisseur, but the smell of what was left in each glass was different, possibly a spirit of some kind. It made me wonder if De Klerk was drinking with someone in the cinema room recently, maybe even last night before he was attacked. We will check the glasses for fingerprints and DNA. If there's saliva on the glass, we can also identify it as male or female. We will run any recovered fingerprints through the database as soon as possible and hopefully have a result for you sometime tomorrow. The DNA work will take a day or two, maybe longer, depending on the quality of it,' she said, closing her iPad. The team looked at Jessica with new respect, as this could be a significant breakthrough early in the investigation.

'You certainly like to keep the best for last,' Chapman said, grinning. 'I think we've covered everything for now unless there's anything else you want to ask us?'

DS Wood raised his hand. 'DCI Anderson seems convinced this is a burglary gone wrong. From what you've just told us, that may not be the case?'

'Technically, all the elements of an aggravated burglary are present,' Jessica said. 'However, the offender's actions at the scene also suggest alternative theories. As you've seen, some parts of the scene appear staged, the upstairs wasn't searched and the contents of the safe seem to have been the intruder's main interest. I can't rule out that he entered the premises with a premeditated intent to kill Mr De Klerk. Judging from the severe injuries he received, the intent to kill was present when he was stabbed.'

Chapman looked at one of the civilian analysts and asked her to compile a list of all known burglars who lived within a mile radius of the crime scene. Of particular interest would be any who had also carried out assaults during a break-in.

'There's a couple I've nicked before that live on the Kingsmead Estate in Hackney,' DS Wood said. 'One of them is a nasty piece of work. He tied an elderly couple up during a break-in, stole their jewellery and tortured them to get their credit card PINs. I heard he was released on parole recently.'

Jessica didn't say anything but thought the man DS Wood described was an unlikely suspect.

One of the house-to-house officers spoke up. 'The neighbour, Mr Elton, did say De Klerk likes to brag about his wealth. Could he be involved?'

Chapman laughed. 'I think we can rule him out as the intruder. He's in his fifties and must weigh about eighteen stone. I don't think he'd be capable of scaling the wall. That's not to say he didn't get someone else to break in, but it's unlikely.'

'It might be worth enquiring in pawn shops and online luxury second-hand watch dealers in case someone tries to pawn or sell the Rolex,' DC Owens suggested.

Chapman nodded. 'It's a gold Daytona, worth about sixty grand. Jessica found a document relating to it in the study.

I've already circulated the model and serial number on the stolen property index.'

An officer suggested a press release giving details of the crime and mentioning the Rolex might be productive. Chapman shook his head. 'DCI Anderson doesn't want to do a press release yet, knowing they're going to hound Mrs De Klerk, who's already very distressed as you can imagine.'

DS Wood shook his head in disbelief. 'They'll be all over it anyway once they discover who she is!' The team members looked puzzled, and one asked what he meant. Before Chapman could reply, Wood spoke out. 'As Kings Council, she goes by her maiden name, Belsham. She's affectionately known by many of us as "That Bitch Belsham", as anyone who's been cross-examined by her will tell you.'

'Bloody hell, I didn't realise it was her!' a DC replied. Many team members looked surprised, and Jessica heard some derogatory comments about Belsham being made.

Chapman raised his voice. 'It doesn't matter who she is. Someone tried to kill her husband, and so she is also a victim. The poor woman must be going through mental torment, wondering if he's going to make it. Her maiden name and profession stay within these four walls. You use her married name when you speak to anyone regarding the investigation. Is that understood?'

There was a chorus of 'Yes, sir.'

'Good. We all need to be positive. Jessica and her team are working hard and doing their best to assist us, but we can't afford to sit back and hope DNA or other forensic tests will solve the crime. Someone in the criminal fraternity will likely know about this crime and possibly know who committed it. If you have informants, speak to them and see if they've heard anything of interest. I'm sure Jessica has plenty to be getting on with, so unless there is anything else you'd like to ask her, you can all carry on with your enquiries.'

'I just wondered if you'd formed an opinion on the type of personality the intruder might have?' DS Wood enquired. From his tone and body language, Jessica sensed that Wood, like Chapman, had an unfavourable opinion about that type of behavioural analysis.

'Sorry, I don't do that. That type of profiling is often based on assumptions and generalisations about human behaviour, which can mislead detectives and the investigation. I focus on the behaviour and actions of the offender at the crime scene rather than guessing their personality, lifestyle or upbringing. All I can say at present is the offender may have previous convictions for burglary and or assault . . . and size nine to ten feet.' She closed her iPad.

Wood grinned and nodded, obviously pleased with her answer.

Chapman stepped forward. 'Thanks for your input, Jessica. I know I can say on behalf of the team that we've learned a lot about the crime scene and the intruder's actions from your in-depth analysis.' Everyone in the room nodded in agreement, but Chapman wanted them to show more appreciation and started clapping until the rest joined in. Jessica put a hand up to stop them, feeling acutely embarrassed.

Chapman was about to conclude the meeting when a chuffed-looking DC Andy 'Binky' Bingham walked in, carrying a portable hard drive in an exhibits bag and a blue statement folder.

'Any luck spotting De Klerk's Range Rover on the CCTV?' Chapman asked.

'Does a bear shit in the woods, guv,' he replied cheerfully, putting the hard drive down on his desk. 'My eyes are killing me after looking at CCTV all day,' he commented as he rubbed his face.

'I reckon it's something else making you go blind, Binky,' a detective shouted. They all laughed, and Chapman waited for silence before asking Bingham to tell them what he'd got from the CCTV.

'De Klerk's Range Rover was picked up at 2.40 a.m. this morning in Wick Road, Hackney. It was then seen on the A12 East Cross Route, travelling at forty-eight miles per hour and then at fifty-seven.'

A detective gave a sceptical laugh as he interrupted. 'CCTV cameras don't record speed, so how can you know that, Binky?'

'Because it set off two speed cameras, one in a forty zone and the other in a fifty, smart arse. Only the Wick Road camera picked up a shot of the driver.' He removed an A4 photo from the folder. The room went quiet in anticipation of a major lead. 'Sadly, the driver is wearing a dark hoodie and has his head down, making it impossible to see his face. He's also got gloves on, so I can't tell you his skin colour. As you know, the speed cameras only pick up the rear registration plate.' There was a look of gloom around the room as DC Bingham continued. 'However, there is some good news. You can't get into Wick Road from Victoria Park Road, Homer Road or Brookfield Road, which is one way. This means the suspect had to drive from Homer Road, up Victoria Park Road, right into Danesdale Road, right again into Cassland Road, then across Wick Road and onto the A12.'

'You're sounding like the voice on my sat nav,' a detective commented, causing more laughter.

Bingham continued. 'I was about to say, before I was once again rudely interrupted, there's a good chance household CCTV and doorbells in those streets recorded the car, and fingers crossed, the driver's face.'

'Good work, Binky. We can start making enquiries at the relevant houses this evening,' Chapman said.

'There's more,' DC Bingham grinned. 'There's no ANPRs on the East Cross route until just after the Green Man roundabout. The Range Rover wasn't picked up on it, so my guess is, he came off the A12 at the roundabout. Where he went after that is anyone's guess.'

'There's bus stops there. A bus or bus stop camera might have picked up the car,' DS Wood said.

'I already checked it out, as I saw them when I drove along the route. TFL CCTV cameras are not constantly recording and only do so when an operative from the compliance team identifies a road traffic infringement, like parking in a bus lane or using it illegally. I gave them the relevant times, and they said they'd check the bus cameras for the car. We might get lucky, but I wouldn't bet on it.'

'Bloody hell, you have been busy Andy,' Chapman remarked, and Bingham grinned and made a mock bow.

Jessica was also impressed. Despite his flippant manner, DC Bingham was clearly one of the experienced and painstaking older detectives Chapman had been referring to earlier.

'Could I have a copy of the CCTV, please?' Jessica asked Bingham.

'Coming right up' he said.

The room began to empty and Chapman invited Jessica and DC Owens to his office to discuss what Michelle De Klerk had said at the hospital. While Dawn got some coffees, Chapman pulled up two seats and sat down behind his desk. 'I think it might be best if you are with Dawn when she meets Mrs De Klerk and takes a statement. She's only twenty-four and hasn't been a detective long.'

'I don't think Anderson would approve,' Jessica replied.

'He never said you couldn't be present. Anderson hasn't made any effort to contact Mrs De Klerk. He quotes the murder manual at you but fails to abide by it himself. Once he knew she was at the hospital, he should have gone there to introduce himself. With her background as a barrister, she knows we will do our best to arrest the person responsible, but Anderson needs to tell her that personally. I get that family should always come first, but being on time for dinner when a victim might die at any moment is out of order.'

Jessica wondered if Anderson was worried about meeting Michelle as he lacked confidence in his communication skills and his ability to ask delicate questions without causing offence. Chapman asked Jessica if she could call Michelle, ask how her husband was and if she and a family liaison officer could speak with her in the morning. Jessica said Michelle might have her phone off or on silent if she was with her husband, so sent a text instead. She received a reply a couple of minutes later: Johan was stable but still unconscious. Michelle was going to spend the night at her sister's and would be at the hospital in the morning between 9.30 and 10. She also said she was grateful to whoever organised for a uniform officer to be present at the hospital. Jessica texted back that she would meet Michelle in the ITU waiting room with the family liaison officer, Dawn Owens.

When Dawn returned with the coffees, Chapman explained that Jessica would accompany her to the hospital and introduce her to Michelle. She looked relieved. 'I must admit I'm a bit nervous about meeting her, with her reputation. I'm happy for you to take the lead,' she said, nodding at Jessica.

After reviewing Jessica's conversation with Michelle at the hospital and Doctor Babu's observations, Chapman said it had been a long day and suggested Jessica and Dawn meet at Barking in the morning to discuss any further developments that might impact the interview.

'Sounds good,' Jessica agreed.

'Fine, and I'll prepare some questions in accordance with the family liaison manual,' Dawn said. After she'd left, Jessica turned to Chapman. 'Sounds like Dawn hasn't got much experience as a FLO.' 'This is definitely her first major investigation as an FLO,' Chapman agreed. 'Which is another reason I'd like you to be there. With your background in psychology, you'll better understand Mrs De Klerk's feelings and know when and how to ask the right questions without upsetting her.'

'Makes sense. OK, see you tomorrow,' Jessica said, leaving his office. Back on the ground floor, Jessica called Diane to ask how she and Taff were getting on with the scene examination.

'I reckon we should finish in about two to three hours, then we'll take the exhibits back to the lab and examine the car,' Diane said with a yawn.

'You sound tired.'

'I am. We've been up for nearly fourteen hours. To be honest, I'm finding it hard to concentrate.'

'I want you both to call it a day. Working when you are exhausted leads to mistakes, and we can't afford to make any. A PC will guard the house overnight so you can return in the morning and finish up.'

'I'm more than happy with that suggestion,' Diane said. 'We should be with you at the lab by about ten if we start at seven.'

'I've got a meeting with Michelle De Klerk and the FLO in the morning, but I should be back in the office about 1 p.m. We can discuss everything we've done and prioritise the exhibits for examination.'

'Would you like Taff and me to make a start on the car?'

'Yes, thanks. Just make sure you get a good night's sleep first.'

'I think I'll be in dreamland as soon as my head hits the pillow. I'll let Taff know, but no doubt he'll want to crack on.'

'Tell him I'm pulling rank, and it's an order,' Jessica said.

'How did the meeting with DCI Anderson go?'

Jessica didn't want Diane to feel any more antagonistic toward Anderson than she already did, so didn't mention his aggressive manner. 'He was better than this morning. I briefed his team on our work at the crime scene and our initial analysis. They gave me a warm welcome and were pleased with what we've done so far.'

'Was Mike Chapman being a ferret again?'

'He wasn't too bad. He didn't interrupt me anyway.'

'He left that to Anderson, I expect,' Diane joked.

'He wasn't there when I spoke to the team. He had a meeting with Commander Williams and left Chapman in charge.'

'I bet Mike liked being the boss. Was he pleased with everything we'd done?'

Jessica wondered if Diane was developing a soft spot for Chapman as she repeatedly used his first name. 'Yes, a bit too much to be honest. He even got them to applaud.'

'Nothing wrong with the occasional pat on the back,' Diane said.

'Yes, but they're going to expect miracles now. We're going to have to produce positive results soon or they'll quickly change their tune.'

'Then that's what we'll bloody well do,' Diane said.

CHAPTER ELEVEN

Jessica was relieved to get home but knew it would be hard to sleep as her mind went over the crime scene, looking for any behavioural or forensic clues she'd missed. As she went to her room to change, she heard the TV in David's bedroom. She knocked on the door, and he told her to come in. He was lying on the bed in his pyjamas and dressing gown. As she entered, he quickly closed his laptop.

'How was your first day on the job?' he asked.

'Good,' she said, 'but draining.'

'Is it a murder case?'

'The victim was badly injured. He's still alive, but it's touch and go if he'll make it.'

'Was it local?'

'No. It happened in Hackney.'

'There was nothing about it on the six o'clock news.'

'It hasn't been released to the press yet.'

'What happened?'

Jessica didn't want to go into too much detail. 'Basically, it looks like someone broke into a house, opened the safe, and attacked the owner. But keep that to yourself.'

'What was stolen?' David asked.

'We think a Rolex watch and cash from the safe. The victim's in a coma, so until he comes around, we can't be certain. Did you get your blood test results yet?'

'No, still waiting . . . probably be another few days at least. No news is good news, though,' David said with a forced smile, which didn't go unnoticed by Jessica.

'Is your back still playing up?'

'It's not as bad as it was. I took your advice and spoke with my manager. I'm working in the sorting office for the next few weeks.'

'That's good of him. Did it help?'

'Yes, today was a lot less strenuous.'

'Maybe laying off the cycling for a few weeks will also help,' she said.

David nodded. 'I made some bolognese. There's some in a container you can heat in the microwave. You'll have to make some fresh spaghetti, though.'

'That's great. Thanks.' As Jessica left the room, she glanced in the mirror and saw David slowly open his laptop. She knew he had a bad habit of searching medical websites when he wasn't well and wanted to ask if anything else, besides his back, was worrying him, but decided against it for the moment.

Jessica changed into her tracksuit and slippers before going into the kitchen. She boiled some water and added spaghetti. While it was cooking, she checked the dishwasher, removed the dirty plates, bowls, cups and cutlery David had put in, rinsed them, and systematically restacked them. After cleaning the sink and wiping the work surfaces, she checked the kitchen diary to see which bins were due for collection in the morning. It was food waste, non-recyclable refuse, paper and cardboard. Jessica slipped on some rubber kitchen gloves and emptied her bedroom and bathroom bins into a bin bag, then knocked on David's bedroom door again.

'Sorry, I'm just sorting out the bins as it's rubbish collection day tomorrow,' she said, picking up his waste bin and tipping it into the bag.

'I meant to do it earlier. Sorry, I forgot,' he said.

'No problem. Besides, you always forget to separate the paper and cardboard from the non-recyclable stuff. Is there anything else you need to bin before I leave you in peace?' She asked, holding up the bag. David shook his head.

After going downstairs, she headed to the utility room and emptied the cardboard and paper from the bin bag into the recycling box provided by the council. She noticed a paper bag with the local chemist's logo, which had been in David's bin. Curious, she opened the bag and found the contents: squashed cardboard boxes for a Metatone tonic bottle and Amitriptyline, which had a prescription label with today's date. She sighed, realising that David must have visited the doctor's surgery earlier that day. She remembered he had previously been prescribed Amitriptyline for severe depression after his nervous breakdown.

She heated the Bolognese sauce, poured it over a plate of spaghetti and sat down to eat. While twirling the pasta with her fork, she thought more about what she'd found. It was odd that he had been prescribed Amitriptyline again, as she hadn't observed any signs of depression.

'You all right?' David asked as he entered the kitchen, holding an empty water bottle.

'Yeah, I'm fine, thanks. Just got a lot on my mind about the investigation.'

'Is that why you're playing with your food instead of eating it?' he asked as he filled the bottle with tap water.

'Just wondering if there's anything I missed at the scene. You know what I'm like.'

David sighed. 'Yes, I do . . . you found the box for the Amitriptyline tablets, didn't you?'

She slowly raised her head and nodded.

'It's not what you're thinking, Jess.'

'If you are suffering from depression again, then please speak to me about it. If you bottle things up, I can't help you.'

He sat down opposite her. 'Doctor Barnes asked me to come in to talk about my blood test results.'

'And what did she say?' she asked.

'My creatine kinase levels were high. It's an enzyme in your heart and skeletal muscle released into your blood when you suffer muscle damage or over-exercise. The doc thinks it is probably job-related and said there was nothing to worry about.'

'Then why prescribe the Amitriptyline?'

'My back and muscle issues make me feel down, but it's not the same type of depression I suffered when Mum died. Amitriptyline is also prescribed for fatigue and back pain.'

'Really?' she said, raising her eyebrows.

'No, I made it all up. Stop giving me the third degree when there's nothing to worry about.'

'Will there be any follow-up tests?'

'You can't help yourself, can you? I'll have another blood test in a week, but in the meantime, I must rest and not overexert myself at work.'

'Carrying those heavy mailbags is not going to help.'

'Did you not listen when I told you I'm working in the sorting office?'

'Sorry, I've got a lot on my mind. What's the next step if your kinase levels haven't gone down?'

'I may need to see a neurologist for further tests, but from what Doc Barnes said, that's unlikely.'

'Why didn't you tell me all this in the first place?'

'Because I could see you'd had a hard day at work and got a lot on your plate.'

'I know I can be a bit OCD about things, but I worry about you.'

He laughed, 'A bit OCD. You're exhausted yet you'll go over

this house from top to bottom making sure everything is neat and tidy before going to bed. You have any idea how many times I get woken up with you hoovering at God knows what hour? You'll probably get it out tonight.'

She was still twirling the spaghetti. 'I promise I won't.'

'Yes, you will. And would you stop playing with your food and eat it, or should I put it in the food waste bin . . . or would it be the non-recyclable bin?' he joked.

'I'll put you in the bin if you're not careful,' she smiled, finally taking a mouthful. As she sucked up the spaghetti, an end flicked against her nose, leaving a red blob of sauce.

David laughed. 'If I'd done that, you'd have given me a telling-off about my table manners. You have to stop mothering me.' He wiped it from her nose with his finger and licked it. 'Good, isn't it?'

'Just-a like-a Mama used to make,' Jessica replied in a bad Italian accent.

* * *

John Wheeler sat in his underpants alone in his flat. He was a big, powerful man, but he winced in pain as he tied the nylon boxing hand wraps around his ribs, then tightened and secured them with the Velcro end. He knew proper bandages or a rib support would be more effective, but for now he'd have to make do with the boxing wraps. He went to the kitchen, got a pair of rubber washing-up gloves and put them on before counting the bundles of cash on the coffee table.

'Two hundred, two twenty, two forty, two fifty. You've hit the fucking jackpot,' he said. He picked up a handful and, without thinking, threw it in the air – and immediately felt an intense pain in his rib cage. He groaned in agony as he bent forward, clutching his side as the money fell onto the sofa and floor. He suddenly felt nauseous and, from the taste of bile in his mouth, knew that he was going to be sick.

Wheeler slowly and painfully made his way to the bathroom, holding his ribs with one hand and his mouth with the other. He couldn't kneel in front of the toilet as he knew trying to stand up again would cause him more intense pain, so he put one hand on the wall in front of him, leaned forward and threw up the sandwich and beer he had consumed earlier. Some of the vomit missed the pan and landed on his bare feet and over the floor. He couldn't bend to clean it up, so just dropped a towel on the floor and used his foot to wipe up the mess. While swilling the sour taste from his mouth with water and then mouthwash, he looked in the bathroom mirror and saw that the bruise on his cheek and left eye had now started to change from bright red to deep blue. He took a couple of painkillers, then returned to the living room, snorted a line of cocaine, leaned back on the sofa and took some slow, deep breaths until the pain subsided.

He looked at the large digital lockbox stolen from the safe. He had tried to crack the number code to look inside, but he hadn't succeeded. The burner phone he'd been given pinged. He leaned forward slowly, taking deep breaths as he picked it up, having previously ignored all the calls and messages he'd received on WhatsApp throughout the day.

Wheeler sighed. He'd avoided answering or texting a reply as he hadn't worked out exactly what to say about the situation. He had seen the lunchtime news and was surprised that there had been no mention of a murder in Victoria Park Road. He could only assume that the man he believed to be Johan De Klerk was lying dead on the kitchen floor, and his body hadn't been discovered, but he knew that at some point it would be, which would cause further complications. Wheeler composed himself as he carefully picked up the phone and pressed the redial number on WhatsApp. It was quickly answered.

'Why haven't you been answering my calls?'

'Because I'd been up all night. I put the phone on silent while I got some kip,' Wheeler replied.

'Everything went as planned then?' the man asked.

Wheeler sighed. 'No, it didn't.'

'What do you mean by that?'

'I couldn't do the job.'

'You sent me a fucking message saying the job was done!'

'I was pissed, fell over and hurt my ribs. I had to get a mate to do it.'

'You got someone else involved? Are you mad?'

'Don't worry, he's trustworthy and didn't let us down, though there were a couple of problems,' Wheeler said calmly.

'Like what?'

'Someone was in the house!'

'Jesus Christ, who?'

'I don't fucking know, and my mate didn't bother to introduce himself and ask his name!'

'De Klerk told me he was going away for the weekend with his wife, so it can't have been him.'

'Is he about six feet five, built like a brick shit house, with a tattoo of Rudolph the reindeer on his right arm?' Wheeler asked sarcastically.

'It's a Springbok, but that's him,' the man replied, sounding worried.

'Well, he caught my man in the living room and they had a fight.'

'What's your friend's name?'

Wheeler laughed, but it hurt his chest and made him cough. 'I'm not giving you his name. All that matters is that he's done the job, and he'll keep schtum.'

'Did he get the lockbox?'

'You gave me the wrong numbers to unlock the safe.'

'I saw De Klerk put those numbers in . . .'

'Then he must have changed them.'

'You better not be lying to me, Wheeler?'

'Fortunately for you, and anticipating you might get the numbers wrong, I told my mate to take my tool bag with him. He forced the safe open before De Klerk appeared and started using him as a punching bag.'

'Stop fucking about, Wheeler. Did he get the lockbox or not?'

'Yes. I've got it here in front of me.'

'If he was that good, he wouldn't have disturbed De Klerk.'

'It's your fuck ups that caused the problems, not his.'

'Was your friend wearing a balaclava?'

'Yes, he's not an idiot, but there was another big fuck up.'

'Christ! What?'

'De Klerk's dead.'

'What! Jesus Christ, you telling me he fucking killed him? Why did he do that!'

'It was an accident. De Klerk ran into the kitchen and grabbed a knife. They struggled and went over, and De Klerk landed on the knife. He thinks it went straight through his heart.'

'Then he can't be certain he's dead.'

'He's certain because De Klerk wasn't breathing. There's been nothing on the news about it, so his body must still be lying in the house.'

'Dear God, what a fucking mess. De Klerk's wife will probably find him when she gets home, and then it will be all over the media. The police will tear that house apart . . .'

'They won't find anything, so stop shitting yourself.'

'Are there any other fuck ups I need to know about?'

'He used De Klerk's Range Rover to make a quick getaway.'

'He stole his fucking car? This just gets worse and worse. CCTV cameras could have picked him up.'

'He's not that stupid. He told me he kept his hoodie up and head down when he was driving.'

'Where's the car now?'

'Don't worry, it's hidden away, and I'll sort getting rid of it.

'Why didn't he use his own car to do the job?'

'Like me, he never does, in case it's seen or picked up on camera. We always get an Uber to and from a break-in, but not door-to-door obviously.'

'An Uber. I thought you were fucking professionals!'

'Uber drivers never ask questions. If the police see a lone person sitting in the back, they automatically assume it's a cab. If they stop the car, the driver will produce his licence and the plod will happily wave him on his way.'

'Why didn't he use an Uber to get home then?'

'Besides a quick getaway, he also had De Klerk's blood on him. None of the fuck ups would have happened if De Klerk hadn't been in the house, so don't blame us.'

'All right, but you better get rid of the car and make sure nothing leads back to your friend or me.'

'Don't worry. I know what I'm doing'

'One more thing. Was there any cash in the safe?'

'My mate didn't mention finding any,' Wheeler replied, patting the money on the table.

'Your mate could have taken it and not told you.'

'I doubt it. He called me and came straight here after the job. Plus, I know he wouldn't rip me off. He could have done a runner with the lockbox, but he didn't.'

'You better not be fucking with me. I know De Klerk had a lot of money in his safe!'

'Then he must have put it somewhere else or spent it. My mate wasn't going to hang around looking for it after what happened, was he? Listen, I need more money for the job as he wants more dosh than I offered after everything that's happened.'

'That's your problem, not mine. The deal was five grand, and you've already had two up front.'

'I know, but because of your cock-up, he could have been caught, and now I'm the one who's got to sort out the mess,' Wheeler said, knowing he was pushing his luck.

There was silence at first. 'All right, I'll give you another three grand for him. I'll get one of my boys to drop the cash off and collect the box. What's your address?'

Wheeler laughed. 'No way. Do you think I was born yesterday? I'll deliver it to you at the shop during working hours.'

'I'm still out of town on business. I'll be back on Wednesday.'

'Making sure you've got an alibi, are you?'

'What I do is not your concern.'

'Don't worry, I'm not a grass. As a matter of interest, what's in the lockbox?' Wheeler asked. He had a couple of thoughts on what it might be.

'That's none of your business. And just remember, it belongs to me.'

'Nicked your gear, did he?' Wheeler said.

'I suggest you get rid of that car tonight. Ensure you delete everything on the mobile phone I gave you and chuck it in the Thames. Don't let me down, Wheeler. Sort this mess out, or you and your friend will regret it. I'll see you Wednesday morning. The shop opens at nine.' He ended the call.

Wheeler picked up the lockbox and shook it but couldn't hear anything inside, making him wonder if it contained uncut cocaine or other high-value drugs. He also realised it could contain nothing if De Klerk had removed the contents before the break-in. He opened his tool bag, removed a battery-operated mini angle grinder, switched it on, and was about to cut into the metal lock box when he hesitated. Surely whatever was in the box wasn't worth the retribution that would be coming his way if he nicked it. He already had two hundred and fifty grand after all. He smiled, confident no one would ever find out about the money with De Klerk dead. He turned the grinder off, put it on the table, picked up the Rolex watch and slipped it over his wrist.

'I'd love to keep you, sweetheart, but you're too hot to handle.' He kissed the watch with a smirk. As Wheeler stood up, the pain in his ribs flared again, making him feel faint. He staggered towards the toilet but didn't make it and was sick on the living room floor. He didn't have the energy to clean it up. Using a credit card, he cut up two lines of cocaine, which he quickly snorted. He lay down on the sofa, waiting for it to take effect. He needed to rest before disposing of the car. Pressing the dial on his Apple watch and seeing the red and blue Siri sign appear, he said, 'Set alarm for 1 a.m.'

CHAPTER TWELVE

David had already left for work when Jessica's alarm woke her at 7 a.m. Although it had taken her a while to fall asleep, she hadn't woken during the night, and after a shower she felt refreshed and ready for work.

While eating her granola and yoghurt, she watched the news on the small kitchen TV. There was nothing about the assault on Johan De Klerk, which she thought odd as over twenty-four hours had elapsed since the crime, and no one had been arrested. Curious, she used her iPad to look at the *Hackney Gazette* website and found a short article about the crime. It only stated that a break-in had occurred on Victoria Park Road, the occupier had been assaulted and his Range Rover had been stolen. It said that DCI Anderson was leading the investigation and asked that anyone with information contact the incident room at the given number.

Jessica wondered why Anderson had chosen not to reveal all the details of the break-in. She knew that police sometimes held back information on major investigations as an investigative tactic, which made her wonder if a suspect had been identified and an arrest was imminent. She thought about ringing DI Chapman but decided against it. She'd ask DC Owen when she saw her.

After breakfast, Jessica disinfected the kitchen surfaces and was about to take out the hoover before she stopped, shoving it back into the hall closet, and instead made her bed. She was about to leave the bungalow when Dawn Owens called her.

'Hi Jessica. Sorry to bother you so early, but I just got a call from Mrs De Klerk. Her husband had some breathing difficulties yesterday evening, and she's been at the hospital with him all night.

Doctor Babu managed to stabilise his breathing and doesn't think there's been any further deterioration in Johan's condition. Michelle sounded exhausted and very distressed. She wanted to go to her sister's for some sleep and a change of clothes before coming back to the hospital, so I cancelled this morning's appointment with her.'

'Poor woman, she must be going through absolute hell.'

'Yes, I'm sure she is. I told Anderson, and he said to let her have plenty of rest and leave the statement from her until tomorrow morning, but only if Mrs De Klerk feels up to it.'

'That was sensitive of him,' Jessica said.

'It surprised me as well. I'll contact her this afternoon and see if I can arrange it for the same time tomorrow at the hospital,' Dawn said.

'Do you know anything about a press release to the *Hackney Gazette*?' Jessica asked.

'Only that Anderson approved it, but I don't know why. DS Wood said it's so low key he doubts we'll get any useful information from it.'

'You haven't got any suspects or made an arrest then?'

'Not as far as I know. We're all hoping you can find something to help us identify him.'

'We'll do our best,' Jessica said as her phone buzzed with a text message from Commander Williams. 'Look, I'd better go. Thanks, Dawn.'

Jessica looked at the text message from Williams asking if she was free to chat this morning. She texted back that she was and asked when she should come to Williams's office at the Yard. Williams replied that she wanted a bit of fresh air and would come to the lab, but she didn't give a time. Jessica suspected she wanted to know how the forensic side of the investigation was going and replied that she looked forward to seeing her.

Entering the MSCAN office, Jessica noticed the lights were on, which she thought was odd, making her wonder if Taff and Diane were already there and in the canteen. She flicked the lights off and was startled when she suddenly heard a bang and someone shout, 'Ow!', from under one of the desks.

A tall, athletic-looking light-skinned black man stood up, rubbing his head. He looked to be in his early thirties, with short dreadlocks, and was dressed in a smart two-piece light blue suit, white shirt and green silk tie. Jessica noticed his tiepin had an emblem which looked like some sort of military badge.

'Can I ask what you're doing?' she enquired.

He grimaced slightly as he stood upright, almost to attention, then walked towards her with a noticeable limp. 'I'm Detective Sergeant Guy Jenkinson, your new HOLMES manager and crime analyst. I was setting up my computer equipment and sorting the wires when you came in. Sorry to startle you, ma'am.'

Jessica held out her hand, which he shook firmly. 'I'm Jessica Russell, team leader of MSCAN.'

'Yes, I recognised you from your photo on the Met Connect system. It's a pleasure to meet you, ma'am.'

She smiled. 'Please call me Jessica or Jess. Who approved your transfer to our team?'

'Commander Williams. She spoke very highly of you all. I can't wait to meet the rest of the team. I take it they are still at the crime scene?'

'Yes, but they should be here in about an hour or so for a meeting, which you're welcome to attend.'

'Thank you. I'm eager to hear about the crime scene examination and your initial analysis.'

'I had no idea you would be joining the team, but I'm delighted to have you on board.'

'Commander Williams wanted to tell you personally. She's just gone to the canteen. Would you like me to get you anything?'

'I'm fine, thanks. So, tell me a bit about yourself.'

He relaxed slightly from his upright posture. 'I was a commissioned officer in the Army Intelligence Corps. I served for seven years and nine months before I was invalided out at the rank of Captain. I then applied to join the Met as a direct entry detective. Thankfully, they didn't see my injury as a problem. I completed my probation and was transferred to the Counter Terrorism Command, where I was promoted to Detective Sergeant and made the HOLMES computer system manager.'

'Do you analyse crime scenes?' she asked out of curiosity.

'No, but I was qualified in the military to retrieve digital information from computers and phones. The Counter Terrorism Command uses a technical support unit to do that kind of work. My main job was to analyse statements and information to determine missed and other lines of enquiry before inputting it into HOLMES.'

Although Guy obviously had minimal police experience, Jessica realised his skills would be invaluable to the team. She also liked his manner. 'I hope you don't mind me asking, but were you injured in the line of duty?'

He laughed. 'Nothing that heroic I'm afraid. I was knocked off my motorcycle when an old boy in his eighties pulled out in front of me. I broke my leg and fractured my ankle. The surgeon said I broke things that weren't meant to be broken, whatever that means.'

'Does it cause you much pain?'

'Now and again, but I've learned to cope with it. Painkillers help, along with the occasional cognac.' Seeing him grimace when he stood to attention, Jessica wondered if he was playing his injury down and was actually in constant pain. 'If you'll excuse me, I'll continue setting up my equipment. I should have it all up and running before the team returns.'

'I'll be in my office, and welcome to the team. I'm looking forward to working with you.'

'Likewise, ma'am . . . sorry, Jessica.'

Jessica sat down at her desk and turned on her laptop. The previous evening, she'd started typing her crime scene report at home and had nearly completed it. She was glad DS Jenkinson was on the team, as he could load it onto HOLMES for Anderson to read.

'You've met Guy then,' Commander Williams said as she walked in holding a mug of coffee.

'Yes, ma'am. I assume it was him you wanted to speak to me about?'

She nodded. 'And the investigation, of course.'

'Thanks for bringing him onto the team. He seems highly qualified. And very dapper.'

Williams smiled. 'He's also an absolute gentleman, and completely trustworthy. Did he tell you about his background?'

'Only that he was in the Intelligence Corps and had analytical skills.'

'He's also very modest. Guy led a military team in the Middle East on a Counter-Terrorism Intelligence operation and saved the lives of a lot of soldiers whose barracks were about to be bombed. He's also skilled in exploiting and analysing social media websites to establish and track terrorist networks on the darkest parts of the internet.'

Jessica was surprised. 'He didn't tell me any of that, though he did say he was qualified in digital forensics.'

'Like I said, he's very modest. A lot of his work was secret squirrel stuff and highly classified. He's also done some outstanding work on the Counter Terrorism Command and been commended by the courts and the Commissioner.'

'Why did he leave Counter Terrorism if that's where his skills are most useful?'

'I put out some feelers about a HOLMES operator joining MSCAN. I was surprised when he contacted me personally and asked about joining the team. He wants to expand his knowledge and work in a different environment. He's very interested in forensics and well-read in the relevant sciences. His mind absorbs and retains information like a sponge. Terrorism Command was very reluctant to let him go, but they couldn't stop him . . . their loss is your gain.'

Jessica nodded enthusiastically. 'Accessing and cross-referencing information with the investigating team will certainly be much easier with a HOLMES operator.'

'I should add that Guy is also a super recogniser.' Jessica knew Williams was referring to people with an exceptional ability to recognise and memorise faces, often after the briefest glimpse. They could store facial information for months or years and quickly spot a person they'd seen before in a large crowd, even if they looked different due to ageing, facial hair or camera angle.

'He's certainly a man of many talents. Has he any skeletons in the closet?' Jessica asked.

'Not that I know of . . . unless you see being gay as a problem?'

Jessica was surprised by Williams's reply. 'Of course not, and I can assure you neither will my team.'

'I only mentioned it as some of the old sweats on Counter Terrorism were a little homophobic. It was mainly banter they thought was funny, as opposed to outright nastiness. Guy didn't complain, but a team member reported them to Professional Standards. The offending officers were given words of advice and sent back to division. Guy wasn't best pleased as it brought him unwanted attention. Anyway, I thought it best to let you know the circumstances.'

'I appreciate your frankness, ma'am. I think Guy will get on well with Diane and Taff.'

'How do you feel about DCI Anderson leading the investigation on the De Klerk stabbing?'

'It surprised me when I saw him at the scene yesterday morning to be honest. I've not had a chance to speak to him about my scene analysis as we've both been very busy.'

'Is that a polite way of saying he hasn't taken the time to sit down with you and discuss your findings?'

'No, ma'am. I was late for his office meeting as I was with Michelle De Klerk. She turned up at her house unexpectedly, and I took her to the hospital.'

'Anderson did mention it. He felt you should have called him, then he could have met her at the hospital.'

Jessica was annoyed by Anderson's childish behaviour but was determined not to show it in front of Williams. 'He didn't give me his phone number. I informed DI Chapman, his deputy, that I was at the hospital with Mrs De Klerk. Chapman was also with us during the scene examination. He was in regular contact with DCI Anderson and kept him informed of our progress.'

'I don't doubt you for one minute, and I've got my eye on Anderson. He couldn't survive without Mike Chapman and the other experienced officers on his team, such as DS Wood. Chapman is the glue that holds the team together, not to mention being an excellent and dedicated detective, though he can sometimes seem a little quirky. Anderson is keen to prove himself a capable SIO, but his management skills are lacking, and he fails to listen and learn from people like you and Mike.'

Jessica nodded. 'I just want him to realise we are here to help, not hinder.'

'I'm sure the results of your work will make him realise that.'

'I read an article in the *Hackney Gazette* this morning, but it was brief and didn't reveal much about the investigation. I was wondering if DCI Anderson had identified a suspect.'

'Sadly, no. A local reporter got wind of the break-in, contacted the Met's press office at the Yard and started asking questions. It was clear the journalist only had snippets of information which they'd obtained from a neighbour. The Press Office informed me, and I had a meeting late yesterday afternoon with Anderson about it.'

Jessica realised Anderson had not gone home to his wife and hadn't lied about the meeting with Williams. 'So, he held back information as an investigative tactic,' Jessica said.

'No, that was my decision. Playing the incident down meant it wasn't big news, and the *Gazette* wasn't that interested, so they only published a small article. Anderson disagreed. He felt that if there weren't any good leads by this morning, it would be time to give the press chapter and verse, but I was against it for several reasons. Mr and Mrs De Klerk's wishes had to be considered before information about them and the crime was released. Mr De Klerk is in a coma, so we don't know how he would feel about it, and Anderson hadn't spoken with Michelle. I also considered that this early in the investigation, a full press release might jeopardise it.'

'In what way?'

'Sometimes details about active investigations need to remain within the investigating team and not be released to the media. Criminals watch the news to see what's happening and gather information about the progress of an investigation. Whoever committed the crime doesn't know what we know. Recovering the Rolex watch and the car is vital to the investigation but finding them in the intruder's possession is what we want. So, tell me about the crime scene and your analysis.'

Jessica condensed what she'd told Anderson's team, telling Williams that she was due to meet with Michelle De Klerk to compile a victim profile on Johan, and then explaining why the appointment had been cancelled.

'I didn't realise Mrs De Klerk was Michelle Belsham, the barrister, until Anderson told me,' Williams said.

'By all accounts, she's a fearsome operator,' Jessica remarked.

'She is. But my heart goes out to her with everything she must be going through. I've just met her at social functions and attended a lecture where she spoke about the pitfalls of the poor and inaccurate evidence police officers give in court. She says she likes to "boil the frog" when cross-examining them.'

Jessica looked puzzled.

Williams smiled. 'If a frog is put into boiling water, it will jump out, but if put in tepid water and brought to a boil slowly, it will not perceive the danger and be cooked.'

Jessica winced. 'I see. And that's what she likes to do to police officers?'

'Michelle approaches her cross-examination of witnesses by gradually leading them through a series of questions, starting with non-contentious ones before moving on to more critical ones. She lures them into making small admissions without realising the impact of their answers, which ultimately leads to a significant admission or contradiction. It can seem brutal but she's only doing her job. I've always found her very pleasant outside of the courts.' Williams looked at the clock on the wall. 'I'd better get going as I've got a meeting at the Yard.'

'With DCI Anderson?'

'With the Commissioner . . . to tell him MSCAN are doing a

wonderful job, and even Anderson was singing your praises!' Williams said, and with her back turned, she waved her hand as she left the room.

Jessica laughed to herself. Williams, as always, was frank, down-to-earth and humorous. She continued with her report on the laptop.

A little later, Guy informed Jessica he'd finished setting up the HOLMES equipment.

'Great, thanks. Let's get you up to speed then.' She invited him to sit beside her so she could go through the scene, step by step, using the video and photographs she had loaded onto her iPad. Once she had given her analysis, Jessica told Guy about meeting Michelle De Klerk, her visit to the hospital and Johan's condition. She also told him she would do a victim profile.

He nodded, taking it all in. 'You're obviously very busy, so I'm happy to do internet searches about De Klerk and see what I can find about his business and associates.'

'Thank you, that would be helpful. So far, all I know is that Johan's a wine importer from Stellenbosch, South Africa. His company is called Springbok Wines. I'm unsure if he has a London office or runs it all from home, though I assume he must have a warehouse somewhere.' She showed him the internet site she found with a picture of Johan in a vineyard.

Guy looked closely at the picture. 'Can't say I've come across him before. He might use a registered UK company to distribute his imported wine. Leave it with me, and I'll do some digging. Have you considered doing victimology on Michelle De Klerk?'

'Not at present. Why do you ask?'

'As Michelle Belsham, the barrister, she may have prosecuted or defended people with previous convictions for burglary and assault. Convicted criminals often hold grudges against those who put them in prison or feel their legal counsel failed them.'

Jessica gave an approving nod. 'That's a good point and worth following up.'

'It also raises a few questions. Did the intruder intend to kill her but was unaware she was out of town, or was his intent to cause her grief and suffering by killing her husband? The whole burglary thing may be a deliberate distraction to hide his real intent.'

She nodded. 'He may even have intended to kill them both, but forcing the safe open, stealing the contents and the signs of a struggle in the living room and kitchen fit with a burglary gone wrong, as Andersons suspects. We need to consider every possibility.'

'Once you eliminate the impossible, whatever remains, no matter how improbable . . .'

'Must be the truth,' Jessica said, completing the Sherlock Holmes quote from *The Sign of Four*.

'I'll look through her old court cases,' Guy continued, 'starting with the most recent, working backwards and compile a list of possible suspects along with their photographs and criminal records. I was going to grab a sandwich and bottle of water from the canteen if that's OK. Would you like anything?'

'I'm fine, thanks.' She went back to her work. A few minutes later, she heard laughter coming from the main office. Realising Taff and Diane were back, she went to join them. She noticed they were both sweating profusely.

'What on earth have you two been doing?'

'Lugging that bloody safe up to the lab on a trolley. It weighs a bloody tonne,' Taff replied.

'Tonnes would be more appropriate,' Diane added.

'I did all the hard work because you didn't want to break one of your fake nails,' Taff retorted.

'Nothing fake about these,' Diane said, making a clawing motion towards him. They went quiet when they heard the door number pad beep and Guy entered the room, holding a sandwich and bottle of water.

'This is Detective Sergeant Guy Richardson, our new team member. He is our HOLMES manager and crime analyst,' Jessica said proudly. He put the water and sandwich down and gave them a snappy salute. 'Guy is a former captain in the Army Intelligence Corps,' Jessica explained.

'I'm afraid old habits die hard,' Guy smiled.

Diane and Taff shook hands and introduced themselves. Jessica invited Guy to tell them about his background, and he repeated what he had told her earlier, again leaving out the details of his military career.

'None of us knows much about the HOLMES computer, other than that the police use it on major enquiries,' Taff remarked.

'Actually, Taff's a bit like a computer keyboard . . . information has to be punched into him,' Diane joked.

'I'll try and avoid doing that,' Guy said, with a deadpan expression. 'Detailing all its functions would take some time, but basically, it's a cloud computer database. Information is recorded in different formats, and the system provides modules for managing documents, exhibits, actions, disclosure and case preparation. HOLMES processes the mass of inputted information and helps to ensure no vital clues are overlooked.'

'Bloody hell, who needs detectives,' Taff responded.

Guy smiled. 'It is not a magic bullet, as it's only as good as the data fed into it. If incomplete or imprecise information is entered into the database, important lines of enquiry may be missed, or the investigation led down the wrong path. Does that all make sense?'

'To me, yes,' Diane said, nodding towards Taff.

Taff shook his head ruefully. 'Will we be able to look at data on the HOLMES computer? I'm only asking in case you were out of the office.'

'Unfortunately, no. But I am qualified to give you all a view-only course, which would take three or four hours. This would only allow you to look at forensic data, exhibits and witness statements. However, I have full access and, within limits, can let you have other appropriate data that may assist you as forensic investigators, and notably Jessica as the behavioural adviser, especially regarding suspect interviews. Things like DCI Anderson's policy file, decision logs and confidential information are strictly out of bounds . . . and more than my job is worth to reveal.'

'I think we all understand your position and appreciate your openness,' Jessica said. 'I think we'd all like to do the view-only course.' She looked at Taff and Diane and they nodded enthusiastically. 'But it will have to wait as we all have a lot of work to do on the items recovered from the scene. Once we have some downtime, perhaps we could all do it together.'

'Any time which suits you is OK for me,' Guy said.

Jessica asked if they found anything else at the scene of forensic significance or that might help the investigation. Diane and Taff both said no. They felt they had thoroughly examined the scene, and there was nothing more they could do for now.

'Can the uniform guarding the scene be released?' Taff asked.

'It's up to DCI Anderson, but I will suggest he keeps the scene secure in case our forensic examination of the exhibits turns up anything we need to follow up on in the house.'

'After we've examined De Klerk's phone for prints and DNA, we'll need a digital expert to download the data,' Diane said.

Jessica looked at Guy. 'Sounds like a job for our qualified expert.'

'You do digital stuff as well?' Diane asked, clearly impressed.

'I did in the Army, and here and there in the police. I try to keep myself up to date with the latest digital technology.'

'You certainly are a man of many talents,' Taff remarked.

Guy gave another mini salute. 'What about examining De Klerk's PC and laptop?' Jessica explained that they had already seized the laptop, but they didn't yet have permission to examine it. 'We could get a court warrant,' Guy said.

'That's up to Anderson, but I'll speak to him about it,' Jessica replied.

'I called Mike Chapman about the PC. He said it was OK to take it, so I did. It's in the exhibits storeroom,' Diane said.

'Oh, I see, it's "Mike" now, is it? You got a soft spot for him then, Di?' Taff said, raising his eyebrows.

Diane rolled her eyes. 'No, he said it was fine to call him by his first name . . . and it's better being less formal.'

'On that basis, will you be calling DCI Anderson John, then?'

Diane frowned. 'I can think of a lot better names for him . . .' She noticed Jessica frown. 'But I'll keep them to myself.'

Jessica handed Guy a printed copy of her report. 'Could you put this on the HOLMES for me, please. It's quite detailed, so it might take some time to type it all in.'

'I can scan it, then use OCR to convert it to a Word document, which will only take a minute or two, then I can start researching the De Klerks, if you want me to,' Guy said.

'The research would be good. We can do it together.'

'I'll examine De Klerk's mobile phone and the crystal animal glasses for prints, then Di can swab them for DNA and Guy can do his digital magic on the phone. I've also got foot and glove marks to examine and run through the database . . . and the striation marks on that effin' safe,' Taff said.

'I'll work on the blood swabs and crystal glasses for saliva DNA.

Hopefully I'll raise a profile that isn't Johan's,' Diane added.

Jessica nodded appreciatively. 'OK, I think we all know what we are doing, so let's get to work. We'll regroup in a couple of hours and discuss our findings.'

Taff nudged Diane and stood to attention; she followed suit. They both saluted and said, 'Yes, ma'am' in unison.

Jessica laughed. 'I see Captain Jenkinson's influence is already rubbing off on you.'

Guy shook his head. 'A salute with a straight arm and palm flat to the face, as you just did, is a police salute. A military salute is done with the right arm raised, palm facing forwards and fingers almost touching the cap or beret. Like this.' He demonstrated the perfect salute.

'Why are the salutes different?' Diane asked Guy.

'There are different theories as to how the Met salute came about. One is that the standard issue cape, worn from Victorian times to the nineteen eighties, made a traditional longest-way-up-shortest-way-down salute difficult, so the arm was swung inwards instead. Another theory is that officers often stood in blue police Tardis boxes, making the traditional military salute impossible . . .'

'Are you taking the piss by any chance?' Diane asked suspiciously.

'An officer and a gentleman would never do that,' he replied with a sly smile.

CHAPTER THIRTEEN

Jessica went on De Klerk's Springbok Wines website to learn more about him and his business. His father Pieter ran a winery in Wellington, just outside Cape Town, which the family had owned for over a hundred years. The winery was in a picturesque valley at the foot of Groenberg Mountain, with the Kromme River flowing along its doorstep. From the photographs, the land, vineyards and cellars looked very impressive. They produced award-winning white and red wines, notably Chenin and Sauvignon Blancs, Chardonnays, Merlots and Pinot Noirs. Johan's brother, Duante, and his sister, Mariette, were still in South Africa, helping to run the business.

Jessica then read a recent gossip piece about Johan and Michelle. They had first met in a hospitality suite at Twickenham in 2015 when Johan was visiting the UK for the Rugby World Cup. Johan described it as love at first sight, and before returning to South Africa, he and Michelle went on a couple of dates. They kept in touch regularly by phone, and over the next two years, Michelle visited him in South Africa, and Johan came to London to spend time with her. Johan had wanted Michelle to move to South Africa. At the time, she had just been invited to join a prestigious chamber in London and had aspirations to become one of the youngest women to make silk and become Queens Council, which she eventually did. Johan was desperate to be with Michelle and approached his father about opening an import and internet wine business in London, to which he agreed. Johan moved to London to be with Michelle and set up a business supplying wine to top restaurants in London and the home counties. He described

London as one of the harshest cities in the world in which to survive, both personally and professionally, but with Michelle by his side to support and encourage him, he knew he would succeed in his new business venture. The article said they married at the family vineyard five years later, with Michelle's family and friends flying in for the wedding.

Jessica made a PDF copy of the article, printed it and gave it to Guy to read. 'Found anything interesting?' she asked him as he scan-read the article.

'Just a few interviews with him about his love of South African wines . . . and Michelle. He's clearly besotted with her. From what I've read, it looks like his business is thriving. Your report stated that Michelle thought he kept cash from business deals in his safe. It might be worth looking at his business bank accounts to give us an idea of his cash flow and how much might have been stolen,' Guy suggested.

'We'd need Anderson's approval and a court order to examine his accounts. I think we best hold on that for now.'

'There might be another way to get his business accounts and cash flow details,' Guy said. 'Under the Overseas Companies Regulations 2009, any overseas company with a place of business in the UK must register with Companies House. De Klerk would also need a licence to sell alcohol and would have to pay import duties.'

'You're certainly a fount of knowledge,' Jessica smiled.

'Companies House stores details of statutory and annual accounts, confirmation statements and change of address notifications, and it's all in the public domain, which means anyone can look at it.'

'How do you know all this?'

'I did a lot of work on the Counter Terrorism Command looking at fake companies set up by terrorists to launder money and fund their activities.'

'Well, I'll leave you to it,' Jessica said as her phone rang. She recognised DI Chapman's number.

'You busy?' Chapman asked.

'We're always busy. What can I do for you?'

'The Range Rover has been recovered and . . .'

'Hang on, let me grab a pen and paper to take the location details.'

'Don't bother. It's on its way to the lab on a total lift truck.'

'It would have been better if we examined it in situ first,' she said, surprised Chapman hadn't considered that.

'It's a burnt-out shell, and I wasn't informed until an hour ago. It looks like it was set alight in the early hours of the morning. I've been to the dump site and viewed it, or what's left of it. Anderson said to get it straight up to the lab.'

'So, where was it found?'

'In the middle of the eighth fairway by some woodland at Wanstead Flats Golf Club. It was still smouldering when some early-morning golfers came across it at 7 a.m. The area isn't overlooked by any houses or flats, so that's why a fire wasn't noticed or the vehicle found earlier.'

'If the intruder dumped the car, it suggests he knows the area.'

'I agree, and the location isn't far from the Green Man Roundabout, where DC Bingham thought it came off the A12.'

'Looks like he kept it hidden somewhere until now.'

'Yeah, probably too hot to handle, to coin a phrase.' Chapman laughed at his pun. 'The fire brigade attended and hosed it down. The club chairman was nearly in tears at the damage it's caused, not to mention the fire truck.'

'You circulated the registration at the time. Why did it take so long for you to be informed?'

'Local plods were called to the scene first, but the number plates were burnt off. They called out a scene of crime officer who checked the vehicle identification plate at the base of the driver's side pillar. It was then identified as De Klerk's car.'

'What about footmarks near the vehicle?'

'Hundreds of them, mostly golf spikes. The SOCO had a look, but it's impossible to know which way the suspect walked off as the area became so churned up from the fire truck.'

'Did the SOCO say anything about an accelerant?'

'Only that there was a strong smell of petrol. He took some samples of the interior debris and put them in nylon bags.'

'We'll be able to determine the accelerant with GC-MS testing.'

'Run that by me again?' Chapman asked, which made her laugh.

'I keep forgetting you're not one of us. Gas chromatography-mass spectrometry.'

'Sorry, but I'm still none the wiser.'

'You don't have to keep saying sorry.'

'Force of habit, I guess. I'll bring the debris bags to the lab for your gas thingy testing. Is it OK if I'm present when you examine the car?'

'If you want to, that's fine by me, but you might be hanging around for a while.'

'That's OK. I can then report back to Anderson if anything useful is found, which I doubt due to the fire damage.'

'Oh, ye of little faith.'

'Sorry, I forgot the A-Team was on the job. See you in about an hour.'

After finishing the call with Chapman, Jessica went to the lab rooms and told Diane and Taff about the Range Rover. They were pleased to hear it had been recovered, but as they were still examining some of the items seized from the house, Jessica said she'd give them a shout when the Range Rover was in the examination bay. In the meantime, she continued with her research on De Klerk.

* * *

Arriving at the MSCAN office, Chapman had to knock on the door as he didn't know the numbers for the digital lock. Jessica, who was with Guy, opened it and invited Chapman in. He handed her the nylon exhibit bags containing debris from the car and told her that the Range Rover had been unloaded and was in the examination bay.

'Very impressive,' he remarked as he looked around the room, which had brand new furniture and all-in-one wide-screen computers on the desks.

'I'd like you to meet Detective Sergeant Guy Jenkinson. This is DI Chapman, the deputy SIO on the De Klerk case.'

Guy stood up and shook hands. Chapman gave him a quizzical look. 'Are you the Holmes Manager on the Counter Terrorism Command? I've got a friend on the unit who spoke very highly of an ex-army officer called Guy Jenkinson.'

'Yes, that's me, but I'm no longer on Counter Terrorism.'

'What's your new posting?' Chapman asked, thinking he was temporarily assisting Jessica or just visiting her offices.

'MSCAN, as their HOLMES manager and crime analyst.'

Chapman looked at Jessica. 'How did you pull that off?'

'Commander Williams kindly arranged it. Guy's also skilled in retrieving and analysing phone and computer data, so we won't need to outsource the work to technical support.'

'It will also speed things up for all of us when inputting and retrieving information from the HOLMES system. I can't wait to see Anderson's face when he learns about Guy being on your team,' Chapman said.

'Will he be upset?' Guy asked.

'No, he'll be as jealous as hell,' Chapman grinned.

When Guy returned to his desk and was out of earshot, Chapman asked Jessica if he could talk privately with her about Anderson. She took him to her office.

'Bloody hell, it's twice the size of mine and you've got a sofa and armchairs. Any chance I can join MSCAN?' he said.

'Has Anderson been complaining about me or the team?' Jessica asked apprehensively.

'No. I just wanted to tell you I was wrong about him sneaking home to his wife yesterday. He went to see Commander Williams about a press release first.'

'I saw the article in the *Hackney Gazette*. Williams was here earlier and told me about the meeting with Anderson.'

'He wasn't pleased with her decision. I didn't tell him I agreed with her and thought it was right to wait for any forensic results.'

'You said earlier today that she's a bit of a battleaxe.'

'What, Williams?'

Jessica laughed, 'No, Anderson's wife. And you thought he was under the thumb.'

'By all accounts, he is.'

'Would you say she's a coercive woman? A coercive person can be described as someone in a relationship who seeks to exert dominance and control over an individual through psychological and emotional manipulation.'

'I have heard other people say she talks down to him and treats him like a lap dog.'

'If he feels worthless and bullied at home, it can affect his behaviour at work.'

'You mean by trying to act like he knows what he's doing and thinking he knows best,' Chapman said, nodding.

'On the face of it, he's had a successful career. Degree entry, fast-track promotion, moved to CID and now a senior investigator on the murder squad. Quite an accomplishment in most people's eyes.'

'I agree with you, but he doesn't listen and learn or utilise the skills of others who are more experienced. Do you think he's got some mental issues?'

'I don't know, but he may suffer from imposter syndrome.'

Chapman laughed. 'That's a very appropriate diagnosis.'

'It's not a diagnosable mental illness but Anderson may feel like an imposter because he has minimal CID experience and knows he lacks the knowledge and skills to perform the role effectively. Now he's running a major investigation team, and he's realised he has much more to learn. Inwardly, he lacks confidence and doesn't feel worthy of the rank. To counter these feelings, he is brash and tries to act like he knows what he's doing.'

'That sort of makes sense to me. But are you saying his home life causes the imposter syndrome?'

'To an extent, yes, and I don't see him as the sort of person who would seek help from others about his anxieties.'

'Is there anything I can do to help him?'

'Give him positive feedback when he gets something right or makes a good decision. If you disagree with him, tell him, but point out the pros and cons. Try to help him connect with others on the team.'

'You sound like a shrink,' he laughed.

'Well, I did study psychology at university.'

'I'll try my best, Doctor Freud, but Anderson's a tough nut to crack.'

'I'm sure he'll appreciate it in the long run. Right, we need to start working on the car.'

'Sorry, I can't stay. Anderson rang me on the way here. He's called an office meeting for one o'clock, so I'd better get going.

'We've got Johan De Klerk's laptop and PC at the lab. It might be useful to examine them to help with a victim profile. Could you raise it with Anderson and ask if he'd approve a warrant application?'

'I'll try, but I don't think he'll prioritise it, and I doubt a judge would issue a warrant at present anyway. Still, with my new-found psychological techniques, I'll give it a go,' he said with a wink.

*   *   *

Jessica, Diane and Guy put on protective clothing and face masks before entering the vehicle examination bay. The acrid smell of smoke and burnt rubber filled the air, leaving an unpleasant taste in their mouths and making their eyes sting. The exterior of the Range Rover was badly burned, and the two rear tyres had almost melted. As they approached the car, the smell of petrol hit them.

'Is it still a fire risk?' Diane asked nervously.

'The fire brigade signed it off as safe for transport, so we should be OK,' Jessica reassured her.

'You know much about photography?' Jessica asked Guy.

'A bit. I took some pictures during covert military operations.'

'I'll bet they were interesting,' Diane said. Guy smiled, but didn't respond.

Jessica removed a digital camera from a bag. 'A scene of crime officer took some exterior shots at the scene of the fire, but I need some close-ups as well . . . if you're happy to take them?' she said, wanting Guy to feel more involved.

He took the camera from her. 'Sure. Just tell me what you need, and I'll snap away.'

Jessica peered into the vehicle. The leather seats were totally destroyed, leaving only the springs and metal frames behind. She tried to force open the boot using a crowbar, but it was stuck fast, and she needed Guy's help to finally do it. Once opened, they could see that most of the carpet was burnt, leaving only bare metal. She let Guy pry open the bonnet, to find a lot of the engine parts were melted due to the intensity of the fire. Jessica tried to open the fuel cap, but it was firmly locked. She stepped back, closed her eyes, and moved her head from side to side as she pondered the extent of the fire damage to the car.

'What's she doing?' Guy whispered to Diane.

'I'll explain later . . . but don't worry, it's how she works things out.'

Jessica opened her eyes. 'Clearly, from the pungent smell, the accelerant used was petrol. I'd say, from the burn damage pattern, it was poured all over the inside of the car, the boot and on the rear and front exteriors then ignited with a match, cigarette lighter or piece of burning cloth. We'll need to remove all the debris inside the car and sift through it for any remnants of a lighter and petrol container.'

'With all that fire damage, it's unlikely we'll get any hard forensic evidence to help identify the perpetrator,' Diane remarked.

Jessica was more optimistic. 'The source of the petrol used to start the fire could help us identify the person responsible.'

'How?' Guy asked, looking puzzled.

Jessica looked at a photograph of the registration document for the Range Rover. 'It's a diesel car, so petrol can't have been syphoned from the tank, and De Klerk wouldn't have kept a petrol can in the boot.' She opened Google Earth on her iPad and entered Wanstead Golf Course. Jessica turned her iPad towards them. 'DC Bingham said the Range Rover travelled along the A12 East Cross

Route and likely came off at the Green Man roundabout, just short of a mile from the golf course where the car was found.'

Diane and Taff stood on either side of Jessica as she zoomed in on the golf course and roundabout. 'Which means the intruder might live locally and hid the car in a garage or lockup nearby for 24 hours before setting fire to it. He could have had a can of petrol at home . . . or, more likely, he went out and purchased one. There's a twenty-four-hour Jet petrol station just off the Green Man roundabout in Hollybush Hill, which is also the nearest one to the golf course.'

'You're thinking he might be on CCTV if he went to that garage,' Guy said.

Jessica nodded. 'But he could have gone to any garage in the area. All the local garages should be checked, but the one by the roundabout is at the top of the list. We know the timeline from the break-in to the car being found, so that's a big help. There'll be a till record and maybe credit card details if he bought a petrol can and filled it up.'

'He could have an accomplice who got the petrol or set the car alight,' Guy added.

Diane picked up on his thoughts. 'The intruder could have gone to the De Klerk's house with an accomplice.'

Jessica disagreed. 'If that were the case, it's odd the accomplice didn't enter the house or wait outside in a vehicle before leaving the scene together.'

Guy had a thought. 'If there were other people involved, they would need to make contact, either in person or by phone. If whoever stole the car used a mobile phone after leaving the scene, the cell masts would pick up the phone signal along the route.'

'But we don't know his mobile number,' Diane pointed out.

'We don't need to. We can ask the four leading network

providers for details of all the mobile phone numbers picked up by the masts from Hackney Wick and along the A12 to the round-about. I can then look for numbers that move quickly from cell to cell, indicating the caller was travelling in a car. If I find a number linked to cell sites along the route, we can ask the service provider for the owner's details, and any calls and texts they made . . . and its current cell site location.'

Diane looked confused. 'But surely there will be hundreds, if not thousands, of phone numbers to look at?'

'You're right, but using a computer program to search for and identify a recurring number makes the task much easier.'

'What if they made an internet call on WhatsApp or Facetime?' Jessica asked.

'It's a bit more complicated, as WhatsApp uses end-to-end encryption, but it uses the same connection to your phone's net-work to send messages and make calls, even though it's over the internet. A microchip modulates a radio wave that travels to a nearby cell tower which . . .'

'We'll take your word for it,' Jessica grinned.

'Wow, I'm so glad you're on the team,' Diane said. 'We know very little about phones and computer forensics and all the jargon that goes with it.'

'All I need is a detective inspector's authority for the service providers to give us the information,' Guy told Jessica.

'I'll ring DI Chapman from my office,' Jessica said, unzipping her protective crime scene suit.

'You can call him if you want,' she added, looking at Diane.

Diane blushed. 'No, it's fine, thanks. I'll leave it to you.'

Jessica phoned Chapman and told him about the possibility the intruder lived locally and used the Jet garage to buy the petrol used to torch the Range Rover. She also told him about Guy's idea of cell site analysis to try and identify and locate a phone that the intruder might have used.

'Great,' he answered. 'I'll get some of my team onto the garages, and I'll email you the authorisation to get the information from the mobile service providers.'

As promised, Chapman quickly emailed Jessica a signed authorisation form shortly after their call ended. She'd just put it on Guy's desk when he and Diane walked in looking pleased.

'Look what we found among the debris.' Diane held up a clear plastic exhibit bag containing something small and metallic looking.

'A cigarette lighter?'

Diane nodded, handing it to her. 'It's badly burned and a bit melted, but there's some sort of design on it and what looks like writing, which could be someone's name. I'll ask Taff if he can clean it up so we can see the engraving better.'

'Clean up what?' Taff asked as he entered the room holding a folder.

Jessica handed him the exhibit bag.

'Ah, a lighter,' He remarked.

Diane turned to Guy. 'As you can see, Taff's powers of observation are comparable to that of the great detective . . .'

'Sherlock Holmes,' he interrupted.

'Actually, I was going to say Inspector Clouseau,' she said with a grin.

'Can you clean this up enough to see what's engraved on it?' Jessica asked.

He squinted at it. 'It's a bit of a mess, but I'll have a go. Also, I've got some results for you. I ran the suspect footmarks through the database. The best match is to an Adidas size ten Ultraboost.' He opened the folder and removed some pictures of the trainers and soles he'd printed off. 'I've just emailed these to DI Chapman.'

'Quite distinctive,' Jessica remarked.

Taff nodded, 'From the amount of detail in some of the foot-marks at the scene, I'd say the trainers are reasonably new.' He removed De Klerk's mobile phone from the folder. 'I got a finger and ear print off this and swabbed it for Diane to do DNA testing. There's no trace in criminal records for a match to the fingerprint.'

Guy said he could download the phone data and compile a list of all the calls and messages, starting with the most recent. Taff handed him the phone. 'All yours.'

'Anything else, Taff?' Jessica asked.

'Yes, I think a portable battery-operated hydraulic door breacher was used to open the safe.'

'So, De Klerk had a pretty useless safe,' Diane commented.

'No safe is entirely burglar-proof,' Taff said. 'Given the right tools, skills and time, any safe can be breached.' He produced another picture from the folder, then held it up. 'They're lightweight and can easily fit in a rucksack or holdall. The one in the picture is an E-FORCE3, but it may not be the same as the one used on the safe. Firefighters use them on crashed cars. Metal doors and safes with multiple locks are no problem for this baby. You put the tip between the door and the frame, then turn it on. The tips spread apart, with an incredible amount of pressure, forcing the door open.'

'That's good work. Like the trainers, it will give a search team a good idea of what to look for.'

'I also sent details and a picture of the door breacher to Chapman, but I forgot to mention that I need De Klerk's finger and ear prints for elimination purposes.'

'I hope to speak to Mrs De Klerk at the hospital tomorrow morning with the FLO, Dawn Owens. I'll take a handheld finger-print scanner and get Mrs De Klerk's prints as well,' Jessica said.

'Didn't Anderson get upset about you speaking to her yesterday? Diane asked.

'Only because I'm not a trained FLO. If Anderson calls, say I'm out of the office, and you'll get me to call him back on my return.'

Taff tapped his nose. 'Mum's the word, but it'll cost you a round.'

'That's a deal I'm very happy to accept after work today. Are there any decent pubs around here?'

'The Rose on Albert Embankment is a short walk away. It's a lovely Victorian pub with views of the Houses of Parliament,' Guy told them.

'The Rose it is, then,' Jessica agreed. 'We'll finish at five and can head off together. Thanks, all of you, for your hard work. I feel we're getting closer to identifying the person responsible for all this.'

CHAPTER FOURTEEN

Wheeler disposed of the car under cover of darkness a few hours before sunrise, but what should have been a half-hour walk home across the golf course, through woods and a playing field to avoid houses from which he might be seen, took him an hour. The excruciating pain from his broken ribs meant that he had to walk slowly and kept stopping to catch his breath. When Wheeler got home, he took some painkillers and more cocaine, then eventually fell asleep, remaining in bed until 5 p.m., by which time the pain had subsided slightly.

He had a hot bath, which made him feel a little better, though getting in and out was agonising. Feeling hungry, he ordered some food, then turned on the TV to watch the six o'clock news. To his surprise, there was still no mention of Johan De Klerk's murder in the headlines.

The doorbell rang, Wheeler went to the door, picking up a knife from the kitchen along the way. Looking through the spy hole, he saw a man wearing a black coat and a crash helmet. Thinking the man might be about to kick the door in, Wheeler gripped the knife more tightly and took several steps backwards. After a few seconds, the doorbell rang again and Wheeler looked through the spy hole. Now he could see the 'China Moon' label on the carrier bag the man was holding and breathed a sigh of relief. Wheeler opened the door, handed the man a twenty-pound note, grabbed the carrier bag, told him to keep the change and quickly closed the door.

He turned up the volume on the TV so he could hear it in the kitchen and scooped the spareribs, sweet and sour pork and egg fried rice onto a plate. He sat on the sofa, gnawing on a spare rib, and continued watching the news. When it got to the weather with no mention of De Klerk's murder, he thought maybe it just wasn't a big enough story for the national news. As the London regional news began, the presenter started talking about a burglary in Hackney, during which the male occupant of the premises had been stabbed. They showed a house with a police constable standing by the door, and a reporter speaking to camera.

'Between 1 and 2 a.m. on Monday, the house behind me was broken into. The owner, Johan De Klerk, was severely beaten and stabbed multiple times. He was found in the kitchen by police and taken to Hackney Hospital, where he underwent emergency surgery. Currently, he is in intensive care, and his condition is described as serious but stable. His wife, Michelle Belsham KC, was not at the house when the assault occurred but has been informed. Police suspect that a distinctive Rolex watch may have been stolen and are asking the public for any information . . .'

Wheeler nearly choked on the pork ball he had just stuffed in his mouth. De Klerk was still alive. Which meant not only a greater likelihood he could end up in prison again, but his own life was now in serious danger. And that meant a change of plan was necessary. He picked up the mini angle grinder and switched it on, almost blinding himself with the sparks. Easing the box open, he took out a black velvet pouch, pulled the drawstrings and tipped out the contents. He didn't at first realise what he was looking at, but it slowly dawned on him that he'd hit the jackpot again.

Wheeler looked at his watch, picked up his personal phone and used it to book a one-way, 9 a.m. business class flight with Emirates Airways to Dubai on Wednesday morning, costing two thousand eight hundred pounds. He used his credit card to pay, but didn't care about the cost as he had no intention of paying the bill. Next, he ordered an Uber to pick him up at midnight and take him to

Heathrow. Although he'd have to wait eight hours for the flight, he'd feel safer there and, once through check-in, could relax in the business class lounge before the flight.

Having packed his bags, he poured himself a whisky and sat down on the sofa. He had been so focused on making plans that he hadn't noticed the pain in his ribs, but now he did. He thought about taking some more cocaine but chose painkillers instead, as he needed a clear head to execute the next part of his escape plan. He looked at his watch. It was 8 p.m. Wearing gloves, Wheeler used a cloth to wipe any fingerprints off the Rolex watch, lockbox and burner phone he'd been given. He then placed the watch and two thousand pounds cash in a small zip bag and put them in the front pocket of his rucksack, along with the lockbox and his zipper case of lock picks. Next, he went to the kitchen, removed a black bin bag containing clothing from under his sink and stuffed it in the rucksack.

He was all set.

*   *   *

The choice of pub had proved to be a good one, and Jessica was pleased with the way the new team seemed to be gelling, but after such an intensive day, she was glad when she finally got home. Looking at her phone, she saw a text message from Dawn Owens saying Michelle was happy to give her statement tomorrow and that Dawn had arranged for them to meet her at the hospital between 9.30 and 10 a.m. Jessica texted back that she would be there.

David, as usual, was in his bedroom, but she didn't disturb him. Changing into a T-shirt and tracksuit bottoms, she went to the kitchen and was pleasantly surprised to see David had left her a bowl of chicken curry and rice he had cooked earlier. She checked the dishwasher; as expected, he hadn't rinsed anything or filled it correctly. She wondered if he sometimes did it deliberately to annoy her as she removed the offending items, rinsed and replaced them in the dishwasher. She put the curry in the microwave and two small garlic nan breads in the toaster.

While eating her meal, David walked in. 'Thanks for the curry. It's delicious,' she said.

'Glad you like it,' he said. 'That investigation you're on. Is the victim Johan De Klerk and his wife's a lawyer?'

She was taken aback, wondering how David knew this. 'Have you been going through my stuff?' she asked, glaring at him.

He stiffened. 'Yeah, I cracked your iPad code. The guy was stabbed multiple times, found in his kitchen and rushed to hospital. Whoever did it also stole his Rolex watch.'

Jessica kicked her chair back and stood up. 'How dare you! That information is highly confidential. Have you shot your mouth off at work . . . because if you have, I could be in serious trouble and out of a job.'

David was taken aback by how angry she was. He hadn't seen her react like that in years. He sighed. 'It was on the local news earlier. If you don't believe me, watch it on catch up.' He picked up the remote, tossed it onto the table and walked off to his bedroom.

Jessica turned on iPlayer, brought up the six o'clock news and fast-forwarded to the London news. She continued eating her meal while listening to the presenter talk briefly about the crime before a reporter outside De Klerk's house gave further details. The picture then cut to Commander Williams standing outside New Scotland Yard by the famous rotating sign. Just behind her was a glum-looking DCI Anderson.

'We withheld releasing information about this horrific crime so as not to impede the investigation while pursuing significant leads. Detective Chief Inspector Anderson is leading the investigation. If anyone has any information, please contact him or his team at the Barking Homicide and Serious Crime Unit. You can also contact Crime Stoppers online or by phone. The details are on your screen, and all information will be treated as confidential. We are committed to keeping the public safe, and we will bring the person responsible for this heinous crime to justice at the earliest opportunity.'

A flurry of journalists' questions followed. Williams started to walk away, but when a question was asked about Michelle Belsham, she turned sharply and glared at the cameras.

'Johan De Klerk is in a critical condition and may not survive his injuries. I cannot begin to imagine the emotional distress Michelle, his wife, must be suffering. I'm sure at this time, she wants to be by her husband's side, so I would kindly ask you all to leave her alone and just let your thoughts and prayers be with them . . . not your cameras and microphones!'

There were no more questions as Williams walked back into Scotland Yard, quickly followed by a sheepish-looking Anderson.

Jessica got up and knocked on David's bedroom door. 'Sorry, I overreacted. I know you would never look at my things,' she said.

He shrugged. 'Forget about it. I shouldn't have been so flippant. You must be under a lot of pressure. That Commander woman on the TV was feisty, though. She put the press right in their place.'

'Commander Williams is definitely not someone you'd want to mess with,' Jessica agreed. 'The odd thing is though, this morning, she was dead against releasing those details to the press. I can't fathom out why she suddenly changed her mind.'

'Maybe that bloke who was standing behind her did,' David suggested.

'That's DCI Anderson. She's not his biggest fan. He wanted to do a full press release, but she refused.'

'Maybe Anderson leaked it, and then she had no choice but to go on TV.'

Jessica hesitated. 'I can't see Anderson being that desperate or stupid, but you've made a good point. It could be one of the detectives on his team.'

'What, for money?'

'Possibly, but some of them are not fond of Anderson, so it may have been to get back at him.'

'From the expression on his face, he didn't look very happy.'

'Probably because Commander Williams tore a strip off him. If one of his detectives had contacted the press, it's on him. I might give Chapman a call to find out exactly what happened.'

'Who's Chapman?'

'He's a detective inspector and Anderson's deputy.'

'Could it be him who told the press, looking to fill a dead man's shoes?'

'No way. He can be a bit of an oddball at times, but he's not the type of person who would do something like that.' She made as if to leave, pausing at the door. 'Sorry again I sounded off at you. Are we OK?'

'Of course, but I wouldn't like to get on the wrong side of you – you scared the pants off me.'

She left David in his room and returned to the kitchen to clean up. She considered phoning Chapman but thought it was a bit late. As she wiped down the worktops, she realised an unauthorised leak could lead to an internal investigation. If there was, she knew the finger of suspicion would be pointed at Anderson and his team and, more worryingly, MSCAN. She picked up her mobile and rang Chapman.

'Hi, it's Jessica. I've just watched the six o'clock news on catch up and saw the press release. Do you know what's going on?'

Chapman let out a deep sigh. 'The shit has definitely hit the fan here. I was in Anderson's office this afternoon when a BBC reporter called him. At first, he thought it would be something positive, so he put the speakerphone on for me to listen in. The things the reporter knew about the investigation made it obvious there'd been a leak. He asked Anderson if he had any comment, and he tried to bluff his way out, but wasn't very convincing. When the call ended, he panicked and didn't know what to do. I told him he had to speak to Williams immediately, and he flew out of the office to the Yard.'

'Any idea who leaked it?'

'Not a clue, but Anderson is convinced it was someone in the office. There are a few idiots on the team, but I can't believe anyone would be so stupid or vindictive. They've risked losing their job.'

'Will there be an internal investigation?'

'Already started. Williams has called in our Department of Professional Standards. They've spoken to Anderson and will no doubt want to speak to the rest of us at some point. Sorry to say it, but that will include your team.'

'I thought it might, but we've got nothing to hide. With all that's happened, is it OK to visit Michelle at the hospital tomorrow morning?'

'Can't see why not, but her attitude might change if she saw the press conference.'

'Has no one spoken to her?'

'Anderson should have, but I'm not sure if he did. Michelle's not called Dawn Owens, so she might not have seen the news. Anyway, that's Anderson's problem, not ours. After the appeal for information, he instructed some team members to stay in the office and answer any calls until 2 a.m. The phones were ringing non-stop after the news, but there has been no information that takes us any further forward or helps identify a suspect.'

'This whole situation must be a nightmare for Anderson. I just hope he gets a result and makes an arrest.'

'So do I. He's called an 8 a.m. meeting about the case and the internal investigation. It will probably be heated, but you're welcome to attend.'

'I think I should, then I'll go to the hospital. Taff sent you an email about the Adidas footprint and a door breacher . . .'

'Yeah, I got it, and the photos. I didn't get a chance to tell Anderson, as the press called him before I saw the email. It might cheer him up a bit when I do.'

Jessica told him about the lighter they found in the Range Rover. 'Any luck with the CCTV at the petrol stations?'

'DS Wood phoned the Jet garage and asked them to retain all the CCTV footage for the last forty-eight hours. He was going to collect it earlier, but once we found out about the leak, he had to put it on hold until the morning.'

She was about to reply but couldn't stop herself from yawning. 'Excuse me,' she apologised.

'You need to get some shut-eye.'

'There's so much going on in my head I think I'll find it hard to sleep.'

'Try meditation . . . someone told me it helps.'

Jessica laughed. 'Sad to say that someone doesn't always get it right.'

'I'll be in about 7 a.m. tomorrow. Do you want to meet for a coffee and catch up in the canteen before Anderson reads the team the riot act?'

'Thanks, that'll be good. Hopefully, he might be in a better mood by then.'

'Somehow I doubt it,' he said and ended the call.

It was just after 9 p.m. Jessica wanted to go to bed but knew Diane would be on the phone if she saw the item about the De Klerks on the ten o'clock news, so she decided to call her first.

'Why will we be investigated? We've nothing to gain by leaking it to the press,' Diane said, sounding anxious.

Jessica tried to reassure her. 'There's nothing to worry about, Di. It will be standard procedure for anyone connected to the investigation to be interviewed. They might even find out who it was before speaking to us.'

'Well, I hope so. Has Mike Chapman any idea who it might be?'

'No, and honestly, I don't think he'd tell me if he did.'

'Do you think it might have been Anderson?'

'No. He's not stupid. Anyway, I'm going into the office early to clean and photograph the lighter so I can show it to Anderson before the team meeting. Maybe that will give him something positive to focus on.'

'I think Taff might have already done it.'

'When?'

'After we left the pub. He told me it was bugging him, and he wanted to know what the engraving was before going home. You know he's like a dog with a bone sometimes.'

'Can you call him and tell him about the leak? I think I might have to put my head down.'

'No problem. And I'll ask him if he's had any joy with the lighter.' She wasn't looking forward to the meeting about the press leak and worried that Anderson would be antagonistic and accusatory towards everyone. She felt it could have an adverse effect and lead to distrust among the team, especially if one of them had leaked the information to the press. Jessica hoped it wasn't, as there were also uniformed officers and an ambulance crew who were aware that De Klerk was stabbed and his Rolex stolen. In some ways, she felt sorry for Anderson. Williams would have been livid and reprimanded him, which, with all the pressure he was under, was not good for his state of mind. If his wife was a controlling woman, the comfort of a loving home and place to retreat from the pressures of work might not be available to him. 'Fingers crossed,' she said. 'And then get some sleep yourself, Di. I think tomorrow might be a challenging day.'

CHAPTER FIFTEEN

Arriving at the Barking homicide offices, Jessica couldn't help noticing how few cars were there, and Anderson and Chapman's reserved bays were empty. Heading up the stairs, she assumed Chapman must be running late. Entering the main office, she only saw a handful of detectives and civilian staff, and they all looked exhausted. She noticed DC Bingham at his desk, his head drooping while typing on his computer.

'Good morning, DC Bingham. A bit like the calm before the storm in here,' Jessica said with a smile, referring to the upcoming meeting with Anderson.

He slowly turned and looked up at her with glazed, bloodshot eyes. 'Sorry, I missed that.'

'It was nothing. How are you today?'

'I'm knackered. I had to organise the office call centre and prioritise the information we've received since the press release. It's been chaos here . . . the phones were ringing non-stop until early this morning. I haven't even been home yet.'

'Why not?'

'We got some good information through Crime Stoppers just before midnight. Anderson was like a rat up a drainpipe when I told him about it and told me to get a search warrant pronto. The local magistrate was not happy about being woken up at 2 a.m., I can tell you. Anderson called Chapman and the rest of the team in for a 6 a.m. briefing and didn't divulge the address until just before they all left, about thirty minutes ago, to set up observation on the premises.' Bingham yawned. 'Sorry.'

'Well, that explains why the office is so empty. How long are they going to observe the premises for?'

'They're not. Anderson ignored Chapman's advice. He ordered a rapid entry and arrest, which is a bit foolhardy if you ask me.'

'Did he say anything about doing a full forensic search?' Jessica asked, surprised she hadn't been informed.

Bingham shook his head. 'Anderson wants everything kept in-house for now. DI Chapman did suggest you attend, but Anderson said he'd call you if needed. He's desperate to cover himself in glory. The problem is, if this all goes pear-shaped, he'll only have himself to blame.'

'Can you give me any details at all? I want my team to be prepared if Anderson calls me.'

Bingham looked around before lowering his voice. 'You didn't hear this from me. The suspect's name is Liam. We don't have a surname yet. He's white, in his mid-twenties, about five feet ten and bald. The informant said the suspect was trying to sell a Rolex watch to him in a local pub on Monday evening and might live in Winston Brown's flat at John Walsh Tower in Leytonstone. Council said a fifty-year-old black male called Winston Brown lives on the fourteenth floor, but Anderson reckons the suspect could be living there now.'

'Is the flat near where the burnt-out car was recovered?'

'Yes, about eight minutes in a car, thirty on foot. Please don't go, or Anderson will know I gave you the details.'

'I won't unless he specifically requests our presence. Is Dawn Owens with the search team?'

'No. Anderson told her to keep the appointment with Mrs De Klerk, get a statement, and tell her he couldn't be there because he was executing a search warrant based on a tip-off.'

'She'll want to know more than that. Is Dawn going to tell her everything?'

'I don't know, but I guess she might have to.'

'It won't look good if the information turns out to be false,' Jessica commented.

'Well, I hope the info does turn up trumps as we all want a successful result, but I've no sympathy for Anderson if it doesn't.' It was clear to Jessica that DC Bingham didn't think much of Anderson, which made her wonder if he was the source of the leak.

Jessica called Diane at the MSCAN office. She didn't want to betray Bingham's trust, so she just told Diane that Anderson had received anonymous information about a possible suspect and was executing a search warrant with his team.

'That's good news. Do you want me and Taff to go to the address?' Diane asked.

'I don't know any more than I just told you. Anderson is worried about another leak and only gave his team the details at the last minute.'

'Why weren't we asked to assist with the search? There could be forensic opportunities at the address they might miss or fail to consider,' Diane said, clearly irritated.

'I don't know, and I'm not going to call Anderson to find out.'

'Guy said yesterday that all information on a major enquiry is put on the HOLMES computer. I could ask him to look it up.'

'No, please don't do that. The last thing I want is for him to be put in an awkward position or risk being disciplined. Just let it be for now. We will be given all the details if our attendance is required.'

'Mike Chapman might tell you.'

'Can you just drop it, Diane,' Jessica said curtly. She paused, taking a breath. 'Did Taff examine the lighter?'

'Yes, and he took photos, which I'll email you now.'

'Did he work out what the engraving was?'

'It took him a while. He used the trinocular microscope to look

at it and photographed the visible bits before enlarging and piec-
ing them together. He's confident the engraving is a parachute
with wings and the monarch's crown above it. There were also
bits of writing visible, which he thinks are the words 'Utrinque
Paratus,' Latin for 'Ready for Anything'. Taff said it's the crest of
the Parachute Regiment.'

'So, the suspect might be a serving or ex-paratrooper. If he is, it's
odd that he used a personalised and probably cherished possession
to set the car alight.'

'That's exactly what I said to Taff, but he had a plausible answer.
He said it's a Zippo lighter, and when you light it, the flame stays
on until you close the lid to extinguish it. Bearing in mind petrol
was poured over the interior and exterior of the car, standing anywhere near it with a naked flame could cause an instant ignition. If
our man stood back from the car, he could throw the lighter from
a distance in through an open window and whoosh, up it goes in
flames with no danger to him.'

'That's plausible. Thank Taff for me. He's done a great job.'

'He thought you'd be pleased. I'll email you the pictures now
and get Guy to upload them to HOLMES.'

Receiving the pictures of the Zippo lighter, Jessica printed them
off and gave them to DC Bingham, who said he would inform DI
Chapman so they could ask the suspect if he had ever owned one.
Bingham also mentioned that DC Owens had called and wanted to
know if she was still coming to the hospital as previously arranged.

'I'll give her a call. Is there any update from Anderson on how
the search is going?'

'Not a dickie bird,' he said. 'I hope that doesn't mean it's bad news.'

Jessica went to the canteen to get a coffee and call Dawn. 'Hi
Dawn, it's Jess.'

'Are you coming to the hospital?' Dawn sounded nervous.

'I'm not sure it would be a good idea, especially with all that's happened since the press conference.'

'Could you call Anderson and ask for his permission?'

'I don't think he'd want me bothering him right now. Have you spoken to Michelle this morning?

'Only briefly to confirm the appointment here at the hospital.'

'Did she mention the press conference?'

'No, and I didn't ask. DCI Anderson wants me to tell her about the anonymous tip and the search he's doing.'

'What, all the information?'

'I don't know, I'm a bit confused as he didn't say exactly what I should or shouldn't say. I just spoke to Andy Bingham. He doesn't even know what's happening on the search. I could do with your help when I speak to Mrs De Klerk. Can you come to the hospital, please?' It was obvious how stressed and nervous Dawn was and Jessica wanted to support her. She thought for a moment. There was a plausible excuse she could use to go to the hospital. 'I need to get a set of Johan's fingerprints, and I've also requested a pathologist attend to examine his injuries—'

'Oh my God,' Dawn interrupted. 'When I phoned the hospital early this morning, a nurse told me his condition had improved overnight. I told Mrs De Klerk that when I phoned her . . . now I've got to tell her he's dead!'

'It's all right, Dawn. I think we'd all know if he'd died, so there's nothing to worry about. Pathologists don't just deal with dead bodies. They can assist with injury patterns and the type of knife used on living people as well.'

Dawn let out a big sigh of relief. 'I've never been to a postmortem, so I didn't know that.'

Jessica asked if Doctor Babu was still dealing with Johan, and Dawn told her he was.

'I need his permission to take the prints, so it would be helpful if you could ask him before I arrive. Tell him I'll be using a handheld scanner and not ink.'

'Should I tell him about the pathologist?'

'I left a message for him last night, so he should already know, but I'll speak with him when I get there.'

'Thank you so much, I can't tell you how relieved I am that you're coming.'

Jessica looked at her watch. It was 7.45 a.m. 'Are you still expecting Michelle to arrive between half nine and ten?'

'Yes, that's what we arranged.'

'You're there a bit early then?'

'I know. I wanted to speak to Doctor Babu about Mr De Klerk. Knowing more about his and condition will be helpful when I speak to Mrs De Klerk.'

'And what did he say?'

'Nothing.'

'Why not?'

'He's not here yet.'

Jessica closed her eyes and shook her head; it was like going around in circles with Dawn. 'I'll make my way to the hospital now. Traffic permitting, I should be there well before Michelle arrives. We can go over everything when I get there.'

* * *

The journey to the hospital was quicker than Jessica expected. On arrival, she went to the intensive care unit waiting room, where an anxious-looking Dawn sat reviewing her prepared questionnaire. Dawn looked up gratefully. 'Oh, you're here. I spoke with Doctor Babu; he told me a pathologist came to the hospital earlier.

They discussed Mr De Klerk's injuries and examined the X-rays together. Doctor Babu also gave the pathologist photographs of his injuries.'

'Did he say how Mr De Klerk is today?'

'I didn't ask. I thought it might be better if you did as you've spoken to him before and can understand technical terms better than me.'

'Did he say it's OK to take De Klerk's fingerprints?'

'Yes, but he said to get a nurse to help you . . . or I could, if you want.' Jessica needed Johan's fingers and thumbs held still while she scanned them and she worried that Dawn's nervous disposition might make the process longer than necessary or result in blurred images.

'Thanks for the offer, but a nurse would probably be best. I'll do it now, then it's out the way, and we can discuss how to approach the conversation with Michelle.'

'Will you tell her about the Crime Stoppers information?'

'I don't know much about it. That's best coming from you as a police officer and the FLO. I'll go over your questionnaire when I've taken the prints.'

'Thank you so much, I really appreciate your help.'

Having identified herself to the uniformed police officer guarding De Klerk, Jessica was allowed into the ICU. She then spoke with a nurse who said he'd assist her with taking the fingerprints.

Approaching his bedside with the nurse, Jessica commented that there appeared to be a bit more colour in Johan's cheeks and hands.

'Yes, his circulation has improved,' the nurse confirmed.

'How long is he going to be kept in a coma?'

'The swelling in his brain has gone down, so Doctor Babu hopes just a day or two longer.' The nurse then followed Jessica 's instructions, delicately placing each finger on the scanner as she held it steady. A few fingers had to be retaken as they were blurred, but the job was done after twenty minutes. Heading across the corridor to the waiting room, Jessica emailed the fingerprints to Taff. About to enter the waiting room, she noticed Michelle exiting the lift and approached her. She looked tired, with dark circles under her eyes and was still wearing the same blue velvet Armani tracksuit. 'Hi, Michelle. How are you today?'

'I'm coping a bit better, but I've hardly slept. It's still hard to get my head around what happened to Johan. How is the investigation going?'

Jessica felt it best to let Dawn update her. 'Detective Dawn Owens from the investigating team is here, she'll be able to tell you more than I can.'

'I spoke briefly to her this morning, or it might have been last night. I'm so tired I can't think straight, and didn't catch much of what she said apart from wanting to take a statement from me.'

'I expect you want to see Johan first and speak with Doctor Babu.'

'Yes, I would.'

'Take as much time as you need. I'll let DC Owens know you are here. I hope you don't mind, but I scanned Johan's fingerprints for elimination purposes with Doctor Babu's permission. I will need to do the same with you later and take a DNA swab.'

'Yes, that's fine.' Michelle started to walk towards the ICU door then stopped and turned back. From the look on her face, Jessica sensed something was upsetting her. 'I know this has nothing to do with you, and it's not part of your role as a crime scene investigator, but you might know the answer. This morning, my sister told me about Commander Williams's press conference last night, which really upset me. I can't believe no one had the decency to contact me first. As a result, I got a flood of calls from people asking me what happened and how I was. Every time the phone rang, I dreaded it was the hospital to inform me that Johan's condition had deteriorated, or worse, he had died. I had the cab driver go past my house on the way here. The road's become a journalists' fucking campsite. I wanted to get a change of clothes, but I didn't want to face a barrage of questions from the media.'

'I don't know the answer to your question, Michelle. You'd best discuss it with DCI Anderson, the senior investigating officer,' Jessica said.

'My sister said a bald man was next to Williams during the press release. Is that him?'

'Yes, it is.'

'He hasn't even had the decency to make any form of contact with me,' she said tersely and walked off. As she watched her go, Jessica couldn't help thinking that the level of stress Michelle was exhibiting was dangerous for a pregnant woman.

Jessica returned to the waiting room and was pleased to see Dawn looked a little more relaxed. She decided not to mention her conversation with Michelle as it would make her anxious again.

'I'm still unsure what to say to Mrs De Klerk,' Dawn said. 'I've heard what she's like in court.'

'You're not in court being cross-examined, Dawn. Take a few deep breaths, try to relax and have more confidence in yourself and your abilities.'

Dawn smiled. 'It's just that this is my first investigation as an FLO.'

'We all learn from experience, and there is a first time for everything, so think of your time with Michelle as part of the learning curve. There are some questions I need to ask her, but they can wait until you've finished, and I'll need to scan her fingerprints as well.'

'Thanks for your advice. It's made me feel a lot better. I'll tell

Michelle that we've had some information about the crime, which DCI Anderson is following up on, and, as yet, I don't know the outcome.'

'Excellent. You could also add that you hope to be able to give her more details once you have spoken to DCI Anderson or suggest she could talk to him in person.'

'Yes, I'll do that.' She quickly made a note.

'Try not to look at your notes or the questionnaire too much. It can give the impression you're not listening to what she's saying. Lots of eye contact is best.'

'You've obviously done a lot of this type of stuff.'

'Not with victims of crime, but I studied psychology and human behaviour at university, which has helped me better understand how we can communicate with one another.'

The waiting room door opened. DCI Anderson walked in carrying his briefcase. 'What are you doing here?' he said sharply.

'You told me to get a statement from Mrs De Klerk and tell her . . .'

'I'm not asking you, Owens! I explicitly told Miss Russell she wasn't to interview Mrs De Klerk.'

Jessica calmly removed the handheld scanner from her bag and held it up. 'I need elimination prints from the De Klerks. I was chatting with Dawn while waiting for Mrs De Klerk.'

'Well, once that's done, you can go.' With his back to the door, he hadn't noticed Michelle entering the room.

'I'd like Jessica to stay,' she said firmly.

Anderson turned around. 'And you are . . . ?'

'Michelle De Klerk.'

A red-faced Anderson proffered his hand. 'I'm DCI Anderson and . . .' Michelle walked past him and went over to Jessica.

Anderson continued. 'I apologise for not making contact or

meeting you personally until now. The investigation has been non-stop, as we have been doing everything possible to identify and arrest the person who attacked your husband.'

Michelle frowned as she looked Anderson in the eye. 'Why did you go ahead with a press conference without speaking to me first?' she asked, her head tilted to one side.

'Again, I apologise most profusely. I thought that Commander Williams was going to speak to you.' Jessica knew he was lying. It was his responsibility as the SIO to contact Michelle.

'So, whose decision, was it?'

'Um, it was Commander Williams's . . .'

'So why didn't she talk to me?'

'She was in a difficult situation.'

'What could be so difficult that she couldn't tell me?'

'I can't say at present.'

'Well, I have a right to know.'

'Commander Williams decided that . . .'

Michelle cut him off. 'Commander Williams isn't leading the investigation, you are! Why didn't you inform me about the press conference?

Anderson was flustered, 'Again, I can only apologise . . .'

'Can you imagine how surprised and upset I was when I heard it was on the news?'

Anderson's lip quivered as he tried to find a suitable answer. Dawn was spellbound, and Jessica felt like she was in court listening to the accused being fiercely cross-examined.

Anderson caved in. 'Someone leaked information to the press, forcing our hand.'

'Someone inside the investigation?'

'It could be. Our department of professional standards is investigating it.'

Jessica thought Michelle would erupt, but she remained calm and composed. 'I understand that these things happen, but I need people to be open and honest with me. I realise you're busy and have a job to do, but as the victim's wife, I have a right to know what's happening.'

Anderson looked relieved. 'Thank you for your understanding, and I assure you it won't happen again. I also came to give you some positive news.' Michelle sat down.

'After the press conference, I received anonymous information about a possible suspect and executed a search warrant early this morning. During the search, I found a Rolex watch and two thousand pounds in cash hidden on the premises.' Anderson put his briefcase on the table, opened it and removed an exhibit bag containing a watch, which he handed to Michelle.

'The serial number on the watch is the same as on the documentation I recovered from your house. I wanted to show it to you for a positive visual identification.'

Michelle looked closely at the watch face. 'It certainly looks like Johan's Rolex. It must be if the serial number matches.' She handed Anderson the watch, and he removed another exhibit bag containing bank notes from his briefcase. He held it up.

'Did your husband keep bundles of cash in the house?' Jessica couldn't understand why he was showing Michelle the cash, as she could hardly say whether it was Johan's or not. She supposed the only explanation was that he was trying to make himself look good.

'I know he did some of his business transactions in cash, which I assume he would have kept locked in the safe,' Michelle replied.

Anderson nodded happily. 'We also found other property that was identified as the proceeds of crime from another burglary.'

'Was anyone arrested during your search?' Michelle asked.

'Sadly not at present, as the premises were empty.'

'Well, that's not what I'd call positive news, then.' Michelle said.

'Because the watch and the cash were still on the premises, I don't think the suspect has flown the coop,' he said. 'I've instructed my deputy, Detective Inspector Chapman, to observe the premises and await the suspect's return.'

'Is it near my house?' Michelle asked.

'No, it's a flat in Montague Road, Leytonstone, a stone's throw from where your husband's car was found.'

'You found his car?'

'Yes, I asked DC Owens to inform you this morning.' Dawn gave Jessica a look that made it clear he hadn't.

'When and where was his car found?' Michelle asked. Anderson gave her the details and said that the forensic team was still examining the car. 'And have you found anything to indicate who did this?' Michelle asked.

'Not as far as I know.' He looked at Jessica.

Jessica took a deep breath. 'Actually, we found a Zippo lighter. It was badly damaged, but after some painstaking work, my colleague, Stephen Jones, identified an engraving on the lighter. It's a . . .'

'Why was I not informed?' Anderson interrupted.

'The work on the lighter wasn't completed until late last night. The engraving on it is the crest of the parachute regiment. I delivered photographs to your office this morning and gave them to DC Bingham.'

'Well, he failed to inform me.'

'He might have told DI Chapman if he knew you were on your way here.' Jessica turned to Michelle. 'Does your husband know anyone who served in the parachute regiment, or who used a Zippo lighter like the one I described?'

'I don't think so. He has a wine warehouse in Hackney Wick

and hired a couple of men to deliver to the restaurants he supplies. They might be ex-military, but I've never met them.'

Jessica nodded. 'Thank you. I've scanned Johan's fingerprints and can take the cash to the lab for examination. We can also do fingerprint and DNA work on the watch.'

Anderson handed the items to her. As she put them in her bag, she removed her iPad and asked for the suspect's details. If he had a criminal record, his prints would be on file and Taff could check them against any recovered from the watch and cash. If DNA was recovered, Diane could check the profile on the DNA database. Anderson looked uncomfortable.

'Unfortunately, we only know from an elderly neighbour that he's a young white man called Liam. She said he was about twenty-five, five feet eleven inches tall, thin and bald. She didn't know his current whereabouts or where he worked, so I have also circulated his description across the Met and surrounding county forces. Does his description ring any bells with you, Mrs De Klerk?'

'Not at present. My mind is all over the place, but I'll try and think about it later. I hope you find him, DCI Anderson,' Michelle said, cradling her stomach with both hands as if protecting her baby.

'I'm confident we will. May I ask how your husband is this morning?'

'Doctor Babu said his condition is improving. The swelling on his brain has gone down, and he's hoping they can wake him soon. However, it's still too early to say if there is any permanent brain damage.'

'I wish him well and a speedy recovery. Is there anything you'd like to ask me?' Michelle shook her head, and Anderson closed his briefcase and handed her a card with his mobile number. 'I need to return to the office and monitor the observation. I will let you know when our suspect is arrested. I will be interviewing him. Now we have recovered the watch and the cash, the evidence against him is strong.'

Jessica followed Anderson out of the room. As he approached the lift, she asked to speak to him about the search. 'Make it quick. I have a lot to do.'

'I was just wondering if any bloodstained clothing or other incriminating forensic evidence was recovered from the suspect's address.'

'If there was, I'd have told you. Further searching needs to be done, but I decided to withdraw and set up the observation once I knew no one was on the premises. As they say, good things come to those who wait,' he added smugly.

'What will you do if he doesn't return?'

'I don't think he'd disappear leaving an expensive watch and two grand cash behind.'

'It might be productive to have my team examine the premises once he's arrested. There may be blood and footprint evidence not visible to the eye, and fingerprints that could identify other people who may have been involved.' Jessica said.

'I'll think about it, but it won't happen until an arrest is made or I call off the surveillance, which may be some time yet.'

As Anderson got in the lift and the doors closed, Jessica shook her head in disbelief. Anderson tried to blame others for his errors, but when it came to something positive, like finding the watch, it was 'I did this' and 'I did that'. It seemed everything was about him and not the team. Jessica knew that people with imposter syndrome often tried to take credit for things to hide their feelings of unworthiness, not realising it could actually hinder their careers. Michelle De Klerk had let him off lightly.

CHAPTER SIXTEEN

John Walsh and Fred Wigg Towers were identical council-owned tower blocks in Montague Road, East London, which backed onto playing fields. Chapman and DS Wood sat in the elderly neighbour's flat on the fourteenth floor of John Walsh Tower, patiently waiting for 'Liam' to return. Wood looked out the window with high-powered binoculars while Chapman spoke to his colleagues on the radio. Four officers were in an unmarked observation van, and two were waiting in the living room of Liam's flat.

'Listen up, everyone. I want the observation van officers to let me know if you see someone matching Liam's description approaching the building. Do not approach him. Let him come up to the fourteenth floor so we can do a pincer movement to arrest him. I will watch for him through the peephole of the neighbour's flat opposite. Whatever happens, the two of you inside his flat wait for my command so we can cut him off from the fire escape in case he tries to leg it. The four of you in the observation van cover the front and rear doors of the building in pairs when we pounce. Is that understood?'

Everyone answered 'received', and Chapman said to maintain silence until a possible suspect was spotted.

'This could all be a waste of time,' Wood muttered. 'If this Liam kid looked out the window and saw all the police cars pulling up outside, he could have legged it down the fire escape and gone out the back unnoticed.'

Chapman was more optimistic. 'I reckon he'd have grabbed the watch and the cash first.'

'Not if he was approaching the building when we turned up.

Anyway, it's not your fault. Anderson is in charge and should have set up an observation from the start while making enquiries to find out more about the suspect.'

'I did raise it with him . . .'

'But as usual, he ignored your advice. Be honest, Mike, Anderson couldn't organise a piss-up in a brewery. He knew he'd screwed up when there was no one in the flat. He panicked, then beat a hasty retreat to set up the observation. He'll no doubt be proudly telling Belsham he found the Rolex.'

'To be fair, I don't think Anderson just wants to cover himself in glory. It's more a case of him trying to prove he's worthy of the rank.'

'You can't polish a turd, Mike,' Wood said.

'Do you think someone in the office leaked information to the press?'

'Is that a subtle way of asking if it was me?' Wood smiled.

'No, not at all,' Chapman replied unconvincingly.

'Look, Mike, we both know I can't stand the man, and I don't think he should be a detective, let alone an SIO. I'd love to see Anderson get kicked back to uniform, but releasing stuff to the press is not my style, and I wouldn't risk my career for the likes of him.'

'Sorry, I was out of order.'

'Not at all. Professional standards will ask me the same question, and I'm not afraid to give them the same answer.'

'Do you think it could have been Anderson himself?'

Wood laughed. 'I wouldn't put anything past him, but I don't think he's that stupid. He'll delight in telling Commander Williams that the Rolex and cash were recovered due to a tip-off after the press release. Then, when Liam is arrested, he'll have even more to boast about.'

'I don't think he's so much a big head as insecure. He can be all right sometimes.'

'Can we change the subject . . . even talking about him does my head in.'

Iris, the flat's resident, walked into the living room. She was in her late seventies and had lived alone since her husband died two years ago. Originally from Scotland, she'd been in London for forty years but hadn't lost her soft highland accent.

'Would you boys like a cup of tea and some homemade sponge cake?' she asked.

'That sounds very nice,' Chapman said, and Wood nodded.

'What's Liam done?' Iris asked.

'We need to speak to him about an incident,' Chapman replied evasively.

'Is it anything to do with what was on the news last night about that South African man who was robbed and stabbed?'

'What makes you think that?' Wood asked.

'I saw that long-faced detective who asked me questions about Liam on the telly last night.'

'That was Detective Chief Inspector Anderson,' Chapman said. 'He thinks Liam might be able to help us with our enquiries, but it doesn't mean he's done anything wrong.'

'He's a lovely lad, you know. He regularly knocks and asks how I am, and when the lifts are out of order, he does my shopping for me. You want milk and sugar in your tea?'

'Milk and one spoonful of sugar, please,' Chapman said.

'Just milk for me, ta,' Wood added. She went back to the kitchen.

'I'll bet Anderson's questions weren't exactly probing,' Wood said under his breath.

'Maybe I'll have another go, then,' Chapman replied. 'You take notes.'

Iris returned with the tea, two large slices of sponge cake and a can of spray cream. 'Hope you like the cake. I made it myself.

It's a bit dry, but the squirty cream moistens it.' She shook the can and then sprayed the cake with the cream. They each tried a bit and commented on how delicious it was. 'There's plenty more in the kitchen if you want it,' she smiled.

'Do you mind if I ask you a few questions about Liam?' Chapman asked. 'It's just that we don't know much about him.'

'Not at all, but I don't think I can help you much. I haven't known him very long.'

'My colleague DS Wood will take some notes if that is OK with you.'

'Of course, that's what detectives do, isn't it? I watch a lot of detective shows on TV, so I know the procedure.'

Chapman smiled. 'How long has Liam lived here?'

'About six or seven months now. He's a friend of Winston's.'

'Who's Winston?'

'He rents the flat from the council, but he's gone back to Jamaica and said Liam could use it.'

'Do you know why Winston went back to Jamaica?'

'His dad died suddenly. His mum's got Alzheimer's, so he needed to look after her.'

'Did he say when he might be returning?'

'No, but I think it might be a long time from what he said. He might even stay there for good.'

'How do Winston and Liam know each other?'

'Winston used to live with Liam's mum, Maria, in the flat, but they split up about a year ago and she moved out. Poor thing was an alcoholic. Winston did his best to help her, but in the end, he couldn't handle it anymore, so he asked her to leave.'

'Do you know where she lives now?' Chapman asked.

'Not a clue, sweetheart. She used to drink in The Bell on the High Road, next to the fire station, if that's any help.'

'It is, thanks. Does Liam have any regular visitors or close friends in the area?'

She shook her head. 'He's a quiet lad. Keeps himself to himself.'

'Did he say what he does for a living?'

'I think he works in a shop or something like that. He said he likes serving people and chatting to them.'

'Do you know what shifts he works?'

'Nights mostly, but I don't know what hours.'

'Could it be a local supermarket he works at?'

'Maybe, but I'm not sure. There's an Aldi on the High Road and a Tesco Express. You ask a lot more questions than that Anderson fellow.'

'Did you tell him what you've just told us?' Wood enquired.

'No. He just asked me who lived in the flat and what he looked like, then he left. Liam's done something bad, hasn't he.'

'We don't know, but we do need to speak to him,' Chapman replied. 'I don't think he'd hurt a fly.'

'I know you gave DCI Anderson a description of Liam, but it would be good to get it again, just in case he missed anything.'

'I think he's about twenty-five and your height, whatever that is.'

'I'm five feet eleven. You also mentioned that he was bald.'

'What, that wee Anderson fellow?'

'No, Liam.'

'That's because he has alopecia. The poor boy was involved in a hit-and-run accident. He told me it happened a few years ago, and he nearly died . . . that's why he lost all his hair.'

'Is that including his eyebrows?' Wood asked.

'Oh, yes.' Chapman suddenly got a call over the radio.

'Obo van to Chapman, receiving over . . .' Chapman acknowledged the call and told them to go ahead. 'Possible male target on foot approaching flats. Wearing a black jacket, blue jeans, dark trainers and carrying a backpack. Height and age fit but unable to see head as wearing a black cap, over . . .'

'Has he got eyebrows?' Chapman asked.

'What?' The officer replied, clearly confused.

'The target suffers from alopecia and doesn't have eyebrows.'

'Hang on, we need him to get closer to us, over . . .'

Wood looked out the window with his binoculars and saw the target. 'Is that Liam approaching the building?' he asked Iris.

'I can't tell from up here,' she said. Wood handed her the binoculars. As she peered through them, Chapman got a reply from the observation van, saying that the target didn't appear to have eyebrows.

'Yes, that's Liam,' Iris said, handing back the binoculars.

The officer in the van radioed that the target was entering the building. Chapman told everyone to wait for his signal, then went to the door to look through the spy hole. He waited, then watched as the lift doors opened and Liam exited the lift. As he approached his flat door, he stopped and looked at it. Chapman assumed he had noticed the scrape-marks on the door from where they forced entry earlier.

'Go, go, go!' Chapman shouted over the radio.

'Please don't hurt him!' Iris shouted as Chapman, followed by Wood, exited the flat and entered the hallway.

'Police, stay where you are!' Chapman shouted as the officer in Liam's flat came out.

Liam bolted for the fire escape, and Chapman grabbed his coat, but he slipped out of it and ran down the stairs.

'Get after him,' Chapman shouted at the two younger officers, who he knew would be a lot quicker and fitter than he was. 'All units, target moving down the fire escape,' Chapman said on the radio as he ran down after them. The observation van officers told him that the front and back entrances to the flats were covered.

Liam descended to the ground floor and, seeing the two officers outside, turned back towards the fire escape well.

'Target in lobby, now heading towards rear exit,' an officer said over the radio.

One of the officers outside the rear exit stood with his back up against the wall by the fire exit door. As Liam rushed out to escape his pursuers, he didn't see the officer stick his foot out. Liam stumbled forward, then fell and hit the tarmac face first, cutting his lip and forehead open. An officer held Liam on the ground while the other forced his hand behind his back and handcuffed him. Once he was restrained, they lifted him to his feet. An out-of-breath Chapman joined them. He saw Liam's face was covered in blood.

'What happened?'

'He tripped over his own feet,' the detective replied.

Liam spat blood from his mouth. 'You deliberately tripped me up. I could have broken my neck.'

'No, you just couldn't get away fast enough,' the detective replied.

'What's your name, son?' Chapman asked. 'It's Liam, isn't it, and you live in Winston's flat on the fourteenth floor.'

'Fuck off, I ain't done nothing wrong.'

'Then why did you do a runner?'

'Cause I thought you lot was some guys that out to get me.'

'Upset someone, have you?'

'What's this all about?'

'I think you know,' Chapman said, 'and that's why I'm arresting you on suspicion of aggravated burglary and attempted murder. You do not have to say anything. But it may harm your defence if you do not mention when questioned something which you later rely on in court. Anything you do say may be given in evidence.'

While Chapman was cautioning Liam, DS Wood joined them, panting heavily.

Liam looked stunned. 'I don't know what you're talking about. I ain't tried to kill no one . . . you got the wrong person.'

'The stolen property we found in your flat says otherwise,' Wood smiled.

'I didn't nick it. I bought it at a car boot sale.'

Wood laughed. 'I've heard some shit excuses in my time, but that tops them all.'

'What have you done to Liam?' Iris shouted from the fire exit doorway, seeing his face covered in blood.

'They beat me up, Iris. I ain't done nothing wrong,' he shouted back.

'This is police brutality, and I'm going to report you all. Don't say a word to them, Liam. I'll call my granddaughter right away. She's a solicitor's clerk, so she'll know what to do.' Iris hurried off.

'Who's the old battleaxe?' one of the detectives asked.

Chapman sighed. 'This is all I bloody well need.' He looked at the officers holding Liam. 'Call uniform, get a van to take him to the local hospital and you two accompany him . . . do not leave his side. If he has to lie on a casualty bed to have stitches, cuff him to it. Let me know when he's released from the hospital and booked in at the nick.' He turned to the two officers who had been inside Liam's flat awaiting. 'I want you to guard the flat for now, but don't do any further searching until I've spoken to DCI Anderson.'

As the officers led Liam away, Wood looked down at his trainers, still getting his breath back. 'You all right?' Chapman asked.

'I'm too old for foot pursuits. I should have stayed with Iris and had another slice of cake.'

Chapman laughed. 'You need to get down the gym and lose a few pounds.'

'I can think of better ways of wasting my time, thank you Mr Motivator. Anyway, leave Iris to me. I'm good at sweet-talking old girls.'

'Thanks. I think Liam's flat needs a full forensic search. I'm going to call Jessica Russell and her team down here.'

'I agree. He says he bought the watch, so some hard forensic evidence from his flat linking him to the crime scene could be invaluable.'

'I forgot to clock his trainers,' Chapman said, annoyed with himself.

'I did, and they're Skechers, not Adidas,' Wood replied.

Chapman phoned Anderson, who was delighted to hear of Liam's arrest but concerned about his fall. 'How bad are his injuries?' Anderson asked.

'Just a few cuts that might need stitching. He was able to talk, told me to eff off and said he bought the watch at a car boot sale.'

'Do we need to inform the IOPC?' Anderson asked, referring to the Independent Office for Police Conduct.

'No, guv. It's not an incident where they need to be involved.'

'Death or serious injury during an arrest by direct or indirect police contact is a mandatory referral to the IOPC.'

'Liam's not dead, and his injuries aren't serious. He tripped over trying to escape.'

'The CPS defines serious injury as actual bodily harm.'

Chapman was growing irritated by Anderson's lack of support for the arresting officers. 'I'd say it's borderline. He might not even need stitches.'

'Is Liam likely to make an official complaint?'

Chapman had had enough. 'Are you worried that an assault allegation might reflect badly on you?'

'I'm just following standard procedure for these types of incidents.'

'I was there when Liam was arrested, and I can tell you for a fact he wasn't assaulted. If you want to inform the IOPC and have them accuse your detectives of assault, that's up to you. But don't be surprised if it causes a lot of bad feeling in the team.'

'Like I said, I'm just following standard . . .'

'It's not always about the rule book. You don't earn respect by destroying your team's morale. You should be thanking and supporting the arresting officers. Liam tried to kill De Klerk and left a knife embedded in his back . . . he could have stabbed one of your officers during the arrest.' Anderson didn't know what to say. 'Now, if you don't mind, I've got a flat that needs searching. I'm also calling the MSCAN team in to do a full forensic sweep of the premises . . . if that's ok by you.'

'If you think it's necessary,' Anderson muttered.

'I do, and that's why I asked,' Chapman replied bluntly.

'Ask her to keep me informed of any developments.'

'I'm sure she will, as a matter of course.'

'I'll see you when you return to the office. We need to discuss the interview strategy.'

Chapman hung up and called Jessica. 'How's it going?' she asked.

'Good and bad. We arrested Liam, but I think I overstepped the mark with Anderson.'

'What happened?'

Chapman told her about the arrest and her conversation with Anderson.

'What do you think he'll do about it?' she asked.

'I don't know and don't care. I just want to get this case done and dusted. If Anderson wants me off the team for insubordination, so be it. I'd be much happier working for someone who knows what they're doing and supports his officers.'

'You never know, what you said might have hit a nerve and made him realise the error of his ways.'

'You can always dream. I want your team to come to Liam's flat and examine it . . . and before you ask, Anderson has approved it.'

'See, your charm is working on him already. I'm still at the hospital with DC Owens, taking a statement from Michelle De Klerk. Anderson gave me the Rolex watch and cash he found, so I've—'

Chapman interrupted. 'He didn't find them . . . DS Wood did. The continuity of items seized in an investigation is critical. Pathetic lies like that can cause problems and make any forensic results worthless or inadmissible in a trial.'

'Then you need to tell him that, Mike.'

'He's so self-righteous he won't listen to me or anyone below his rank. It might be better if you spoke to him.'

'I don't know him well enough. I believe he respects you and might accept what you say.'

'I'll see what I can do,' he said grudgingly. Chapman asked how long it would take her to get to John Walsh Tower. Jessica said Diane and Taff were at the lab, and she'd tell them to go to the scene. Then, when she was finished at the hospital, she'd join them. She also told Chapman that Taff would need a set of Liam's fingerprints to compare to any found on the watch, cash and other items they had seized. 'The station has a Live Scan machine. I'll make sure Liam's fingerprints and DNA are taken as soon as he's booked in.'

Jessica knew that Live Scan allowed a suspect's fingerprints to be compared with a national database and identified within a few minutes if they had a criminal record. 'Did you find any blood-stained clothing or Adidas trainers at the flat?' she asked.

'Not yet. Anderson had us withdraw and set up the observation before we could do a full search. DS Wood is with me. We can start looking if you want, but I'd rather wait until your team get here so it's all coordinated and there's no risk of contamination.'

'No problem. I should be there within the hour. Will you still be at the flat, or have you got to return to the station?'

'Anderson wants me to help him prepare the interview with Liam, so I'll have to head back.'

'Are you doing the interview with him?'

'I don't know. DS Wood will remain here to assist you. Let me know if you find anything else of evidential value, then Anderson can ask Liam about it.'

Chapman took the lift to the fourteenth floor. Inside Iris's flat, he found Wood eating another slice of cake with squirty cream with a large glass of whisky on the table in front of him. It was clear that Wood had been using his charm on the old lady.

Chapman raised his eyebrows. 'Feeling better, are we?'

'Yes, thank you. Iris said a wee dram would help clear my chest.' Chapman deliberately coughed and beat his chest with his fist.

Iris came in from the kitchen. 'Would you like one as well . . . and maybe a wee slice of cake?' she asked.

'That's very kind of you. Just a whisky will be fine, thanks.' Chapman waited for her to leave the room and turned to Wood. 'Did she call her granddaughter?'

'Yes. She was speaking to her when I got back up here.'

'So, there will be an official assault complaint.'

Wood shook his head. 'Not at present. I spoke to the granddaughter and explained what happened. I told her Liam tripped over running from the police and . . .'

'Her very upset granny called her, so she won't believe you. She'll organise a solicitor for him, a complaint will be made and Anderson will be on my back like a leach.'

'You have a bad habit of interrupting,' Wood said calmly.

'Go on then,' Chapman snapped back.

'The granddaughter won't be doing anything. She works for a firm of solicitors in Scotland whose laws, as you know, are different from ours, so she can't help or send anyone to represent Liam. If he wants a solicitor, he'll get the duty one.'

'What did you say to Iris?'

'I told her we found stolen property in his flat, and that's why he ran off, which resulted in him tripping over. She agreed it was the action of a guilty man, and he only had himself to blame for his injuries.'

Chapman looked relieved. 'Can you work your charms on Anderson?'

'I don't do miracles,' Wood replied.

CHAPTER SEVENTEEN

Chapman returned to the station feeling apprehensive. He didn't regret being blunt with Anderson over the phone or abruptly ending the call but knew his behaviour could be considered insubordination and have serious repercussions. Anderson, as his senior officer, held the upper hand, and Chapman realised he might have to eat humble pie if he wanted to remain on the investigation. Talking to Anderson about his own behaviour was now simply not on the cards.

Chapman knocked on Anderson's office door. He was sitting behind his desk, working on a laptop. 'Pull up a seat, Michael. I was just typing up my report on the discovery of the Rolex watch and the cash.'

'That was a good find by DS Wood,' Chapman said carefully.

'Yes, it was. I spoke to the officers at the hospital with Liam and congratulated them on preventing his escape. He only needs a few butterfly stitches to his head and should be at the station in an hour or so.' Chapman had certainly changed his tune about the arrest. He also hadn't mentioned their earlier conversation. Perhaps he'd taken what Chapman had said on board.

'When I arrested Liam, I got the impression he'd probably want a solicitor and might well allege he was assaulted,' Chapman said, wanting to see if Anderson's thoughts about informing the IOPC had changed.

Anderson shrugged. 'If he does make a complaint, it can go through the usual channels and be referred to professional standards.'

'So, the IOPC won't be involved?'

'They could be, but only if professional standards request it, which under the circumstances is unlikely.' Chapman knew Anderson was rightly following standard procedures but was also covering his back if a complaint was made. Although he was glad to see Anderson's change of attitude, he was still wary of him. 'I've made a list of questions I'd like to ask Liam in the interview. I wonder if you'd mind looking over them to see if there's anything to add.' He handed over the list.

Chapman had extensive experience interviewing suspects in major crime investigations and knew how complex and challenging it could be. Although a list of prepared questions could be useful, the person interviewed might give a totally unexpected answer, often requiring quick thinking and fresh, unscripted questions. Chapman feared that Anderson, having been a detective for a short time and inexperienced at interviewing suspects, wouldn't know how to handle Liam, especially if he started giving 'no comment' answers. He handed back the question sheet.

'Seems fine to me. You might want to show him the Rolex and cash during the interview to gauge his reaction.' Anderson explained that he'd given them to Jessica when he was at the hospital, and she was taking them back to the lab for fingerprint and DNA examination. Chapman asked if he'd taken photographs of the items, which he could show Liam instead, but he hadn't.

'I'll contact Jessica and ask her to email some over,' Chapman said.

'I'd also question Liam about the burnt-out Range Rover and the Zippo lighter. Pictures of them are on HOLMES.'

'I wasn't aware of that. Do you know who uploaded them?'

'Probably DS Guy Jenkinson,' Chapman said, knowing Anderson would be curious.

'Who's he? He's not on my team . . . is he?'

'He's MSCAN's HOLMES manager. A former military intelligence officer and a digital forensic expert.'

'So, he has access to the investigation and everything we have.'

'I guess so, within limits.'

'He could be the press leak. Who authorised his posting to MSCAN?'

'I think it was Commander Williams.'

'She never told me.'

'Maybe she didn't feel the need to, sir. If she posted Jenkinson to MSCAN, she must have a lot of faith in him, so I very much doubt he's the type of person who would leak things to the press. For what it's worth, I don't think anyone on her team would leak information.'

'Do you think it was someone on my team?

'I hate to say it, but it could be.'

'Who do you think it was?'

'I don't have a clue. If I did, I'd tell you.'

'DS Wood clearly doesn't like me. It could be him.'

'He might not be your biggest fan, but he wouldn't do that to you.'

'Do you think I should speak to Williams about this Jenkinson chap?' Chapman was surprised Anderson was again asking for his advice.

'No, she might take it the wrong way. I'd just let professional standards do their job.'

Anderson sighed. 'It won't look good if it was someone on the team.'

'I wouldn't worry . . . unless it was you,' Chapman said deadpan, wanting to see his reaction.

He looked stunned. 'What, no. I would never do such a thing . . .'

Chapman smiled. 'I was joking, guv.' Anderson let out a sigh of relief.

'On the plus side,' Chapman continued, 'it resulted in information that led to the recovery of the Rolex, the cash and the arrest of Liam.'

Anderson nodded. 'I want you to interview Liam with me. I've already had a quiet word with the CPS. They feel I've enough to charge Liam and if Russell and her team find De Klerk's blood or other evidence linking Liam to the crime scene, we'll have him bang to rights.'

Chapman had a nasty feeling Anderson was getting overconfident. 'That's a big "if,"' he said.

*   *   *

Arriving at John Walsh Tower, Jessica saw Diane and Taff's crime scene vans parked in the street. She read a text message from Chapman about the cash and Rolex needed for Liam's interview. He said photographs would do if they were going to examine them at the lab later in the day. Jessica didn't want to remove them from the evidence bags outside the lab, so she photographed them through the transparent bags and sent them to Chapman.

After putting on a crime scene suit, Jessica got in the lift and went to the fourteenth floor. When the lift door opened, she was surprised to see her colleagues sitting on their crime scene cases, eating cake with squirty cream.

'You've got to try this, it's delicious,' Taff said.

'Have you started on the crime scene yet?' Jessica asked curtly.

Diane put her plate down. 'We knew you were coming from the hospital, so we thought we'd wait until you arrived. Iris, the neighbour, offered us some homemade cake.'

'And we thought it would be rude to refuse,' Taff added.

'Time is of the essence . . . eating cake isn't,' Jessica said. 'Where's DS Wood?'

'With Iris. He said he'd brief us on what was done on the first search when you got here,' Diane told her.

'Thank you. I'll go and speak with him.' She went inside Iris's flat.

'Jess is in one of her tetchy moods,' Taff remarked.

'Remember, this is her first investigation in the Met, so she's going to be a bit more on edge.'

'Fair enough,' Taff said. 'Next time, we'll keep the cake until after the job's done.'

Jessica and DS Wood walked into the hallway as Diane and Taff were putting on their crime scene suits. Wood gave them details of the first search and informed them the cash and Rolex had been found under the sink in a zip-lock bag at the back of the unit.

'I finished my work on the glove marks recovered from the De Klerk house. I'm confident from the markings they are Sealskinz Ultra Grips,' Taff said.

'Isn't that illegal?' Diane said, looking shocked. 'Aren't seals a protected species or something?'

Taff laughed. 'It's a brand name. The outer layer is nylon with a waterproof membrane, and the inner lining is Merino Wool. The palms and fingers have a silicone grip pattern, and the thumb and index fingers are touchscreen compatible.' He removed a printed photograph from his pocket and showed it to Jessica and Diane.

'The fibres I found on the front door latch at the De Klerks were black Nylon,' Diane added.

'If those gloves are in the flat or were on Liam when he was arrested, it's nearly as good as his actual fingerprints,' Taff said.

'Good work, the pair of you. Do you have any details about the suspect?'

'From what I've picked up, only that he's young, has alopecia and his Christian name is Liam,' Taff said.

'OK.' Jessica turned to DS Wood and handed him the picture of the gloves. 'Did you see any sign of the Adidas trainers or gloves like these?'

'He wasn't wearing Adidas trainers when he was arrested, but I'll let Chapman know about the gloves in case Liam has them on him. Do you mind if I head off to the Jet garage? I need to pick up their CCTV. I won't be gone long.'

'Go ahead. Were the bins and washing machine searched?'

'Yes, and nothing connected to the crime was found.'

'What about the communal and recycling bins?'

Wood shrugged. 'Not as far as I know. Anderson organised the search, so you'd have to ask him.'

'Let's hope they haven't been emptied since Monday. Could you ask Anderson to organise a PolSA unit to search the bins? I'll brief them when they get here,' she asked, using the acronym for the specialist police search team.

'You'll be busy up here, so I'll call them, then brief them when I return from the garage. I forgot to mention that a laptop, PlayStation and Xbox are on the premises. We left them in situ and checked the serial numbers. They're the proceeds of a recent local burglary.'

'We'll take them to the lab for fingerprinting. Thanks for organising the PolSA team,' Jessica said.

After Taff had videoed and photographed the flat, they started looking around it. It was filthy, with a strong smell of sweat and dirty clothes strewn around the main bedroom. The bathroom toilet pan was covered in bits of excrement, adding to the stink. The bath had a ring of soap scum around it, as did the washbasin. Diane walked in, started to retch and turned away.

'You wuss. It's no worse than a decomposing body,' Taff said.

'They don't bother me. The only thing that turns my stomach in this job is human and dog shit,' Diane replied.

'You won't mind searching the bathroom then, Taff,' Jessica said, smiling. 'It shouldn't take long, then you can help me in the main bedroom while Diane searches the smaller one.'

'I don't want you anywhere near me after you finish in that sewer,' Diane grimaced.

Jessica went to the main bedroom and started her search with the wardrobe. There were three pairs of worn, tatty trainers in it and a pair on the bedroom floor, none of which were Adidas. Using an ultraviolet crime scene torch, she started checking all the dark clothing for any signs of blood.

'Come see what I found,' Taff shouted out from the bathroom. Walking into the hallway, they saw Taff holding up a dripping-wet, transparent waterproof bag containing a mobile phone.

'Please tell me that wasn't in the toilet,' Diane said, making a face.

Taff smiled. 'Well, it wasn't hidden in the bath.'

'That's gross.'

'I think he found it in the cistern, Di,' Jessica said, noticing the cistern lid was on the toilet seat.

'I've photographed it in situ. I'll take a few more for DS Wood, then bag and tag it for fingerprint examination. Then Guy can have a look at the data on it,' Taff said.

'Any sign of prints on the bag?' Diane asked.

'I need to dry it out at the lab before using a light source or powders. There's nothing else of interest in here, so I'll help you in the bedroom, Jess.' They meticulously checked all the clothing and trainers in the flat for bloodstains but found none. There was no sign of the Adidas Ultraboosts, Sealskinz gloves or a hydraulic door breacher, though Diane found a crowbar in the hallway cupboard.

'Looks like he's got rid of the clothing he wore and the door breacher, which suggests he's forensically aware and has a criminal record,' Taff suggested.

Jessica closed her eyes to think and didn't acknowledge his comment. Taff looked at Diane, who put a finger to her lips and raised her other hand, indicating he should be patient and say nothing. Jessica's head moved from side to side as if repeatedly scanning the flat. After a minute, she stopped, opened her eyes and turned to Taff. 'There's no photographs or memorabilia around, but there are some really worn work overalls on one side of the wardrobe, and large-size jackets. It could be the suspect is renting or hasn't lived here for long. The flooring in the hallway, living room and bedrooms is laminate, and vinyl in the kitchen and bathroom. They're all good surfaces for retaining footprints, and we need to light source them.'

'I get what you're thinking, but there will be all sorts of footprints in here, including all the detectives who were in here earlier.'

'I'm only interested in any that fit the Adidas marks we found at the crime scene. You can ignore everything else . . . for now. If we find any matching footprints, it shows someone was in this flat wearing those trainers, so it has to be either the suspect's or someone he knew who he let in . . . and that's powerful evidence.'

'We can't prove it was Liam that left the footprints,' Diane said.

'I know. But if we find matching footprints, he has to explain how they got here. Check the base of the wardrobes and hallway cupboard. It will be even more difficult for him to explain if there are matching prints in there.'

'A bit of reverse psychology,' Taff grinned.

Jessica nodded and looked at Diane. 'I want you to use Luminol on any matching footprints that Taff finds to look for blood in them. If we find even the minutest speck that matches Johan De Klerk's DNA, it can only have come from the trainers after the commission of the crime.'

'The way your mind works is amazing. What you've come up with was staring us in the face, yet we don't see it,' Taff remarked.

'If you trawl too deep, you can miss what's on the surface,' Jessica said.

'Was that another Sherlock Holmes quote?' Diane asked.

'No, a lady called Anna Travis. She's an agent on the FBI Behavioural Analysis Unit. I heard her say it at a lecture and never forgot it.'

'Jessica, have you got a minute?' DS Wood called out from the doorway. 'You might like to come and see what the PolSA lads have found.'

'What is it?'

'I wouldn't like to spoil the surprise,' he smiled.

Jessica picked up her crime scene case and followed him to the lift. On their way down she asked about other residents in the flat they were searching, and he told her that it actually belonged to a Winston Brown who was currently in Jamaica. Their suspect's mother had stayed there at some point but she had left and he had now been renting for a short while.

At the rear of the flats, eight search officers, dressed in protective overalls and gloves, had been carefully opening bin bags and sifting through the contents on large sheets of plastic they had laid out on the ground. The air smelt of the rotting meat, fish and other foods spread across the sheet. Wood pointed to a separate plastic sheet on one side, with an opened black bin bag on top of it.

'They found that bag which wasn't tied up. The officers had a quick look inside and noticed dark clothing in it. I thought it best to leave it in the bag and let you know before removing it.'

Jessica put on her hair cover, face mask and gloves before slowly removing black Adidas tracksuit bottoms and a matching hoodie from the bag. She shone her ultraviolet torch on the sleeves of the hoodie and saw what she thought might be a dried bloodstain. She needed to do a further test, so she took a container of Hemastix from her case and removed one of the three-inch plastic strips coated with a blood reagent on the tip. She put a tiny drop of sterile water on the tip, gently rubbed it on the stain and waited for any colour change. The orange tip slowly changed to green, then blue, indicating a high blood haemoglobin concentration.

'Probably De Klerk's blood,' Wood remarked.

Jessica nodded. 'Although it tested positive for blood, a Hemastix can't differentiate between human and animal blood. Diane will do a further test at the lab, check the clothing more thoroughly for other bloodstains, and raise a DNA profile.' She took a photo of the clothing and used more Hemastix before packaging them. She thanked Wood and the search team and asked him if he had managed to get the Jet garage CCTV.

'Only for the night De Klerk was attacked. Unfortunately, the system temporarily crashed the night the car was set alight. If the bastard drove there in the Range Rover, purchased a petrol can or filled one up while it was down, he might not be on CCTV, but I'll look through it back at the station. The garage gave me a copy of all in-store and petrol purchases for both nights, but I've yet to look through them.'

'If you want, I can get our new team member to view the CCTV and check the till roll, but he'll need a picture of Liam.'

'Mike Chapman told me about Guy Jenkinson. I was on the Counter Terrorism Command with him before moving to homicide. You're lucky to have him. I'll send you a copy of Liam's arrest photo.'

Jessica returned to the flat and told Diane and Taff about the clothing the PolSA officers had found. Diane looked forward to examining the items for blood.

'There was a roll of black bin liners in the sink cupboard where the Rolex and cash were found. I'll take the roll to the lab and examine the tear-off marks for a mechanical fit to the one containing the clothing. I'll check it for fingerprints as well.'

'I think we will all be very busy in the lab for the next few days,' Jessica said. 'Any Adidas footprints?'

Taff nodded. 'We've recovered some, which look the same as the ones at the De Klerk house. Unfortunately, there are other footprints over the top of them.'

'Probably from the detectives. I can ask Chapman to get elimination prints from their shoes if you need them,' Jessica said.

'A closer examination under the microscope should confirm if they are the same Adidas trainers, Jess. There were none in the living room, bedroom wardrobes or hall cupboard, but there were in the hallway. They went past the kitchen towards the lounge, ending by the bathroom, where I found some by the toilet. A couple were in the kitchen by the sink, and two more were travelling towards the front door. We photographed them all.'

'We used the luminol but didn't find any blood. I also checked the kitchen and bathroom sink waste pipes for blood but found none. Same with the washing machine pipes,' Diane added.

Jessica noticed the coir mat by the front door. 'Did you try luminol on the mat?'

'No, but I can do,' Diane replied.

'Let's bag it and take it back to the lab. If the suspect wiped his feet when he returned home, he might have left blood on the mat. There's also the chance of pollens or soil being recovered from where he stepped in the raised bedding at the De Klerk's. Good work, both of you. Is there anything else you can think of that we need to do here?'

'Not at present,' Diane said, and Taff shook his head.

'I'll ask DS Wood to arrange for the front door to be secured and new locks to be fitted in case we need to come back. You two head back to the lab and get cracking on the exhibits and other stuff we've seized today. The suspect can only be held in custody for thirty-six hours before being charged. It would be good for Chapman to put any positive forensic results to him in an interview. I'll do one last sweep in here and tell DS Wood what we've found before leaving. I'll see you in a bit.'

* * *

Chapman was informed that Liam was being booked in at the station. He went down to the custody suite, where Liam was being belligerent and refusing to give his full name or any other details. His lip was swollen, a large bandage was plastered to his forehead and the bruising from his fall had spread across his eyelids. Chapman thought he looked familiar but couldn't place him.

The Custody Sergeant again asked him for his name and date of birth. 'I got these injuries 'cause that officer assaulted me,' he said, nodding to one of the two detectives beside him.

'Do you wish to make an official complaint?' the Sergeant asked.

'I ain't saying nothing more till I see a solicitor.'

The Sergeant sighed. 'No skin off my nose, son. I'll inform the duty solicitor of your arrest while your fingerprints, DNA and photograph are taken.'

The contents of Liam's backpack and pockets were placed on the counter. Chapman noticed a pair of gloves, but they were made of black wool. Wearing latex gloves, he looked in Liam's wallet and found five hundred pounds cash and a NatWest debit card in the name of Mr L Wilson. Chapman asked if the bank card belonged to Liam, but he didn't reply. The detective searching him said it was probably stolen, and he'd check with the bank. The detective then uncuffed him. 'Follow me.'

Chapman spoke to the officer who Liam had accused of assault. 'Go to the office, check the bank card and type up your report. Also, get someone to take Liam's phone and the cash to the lab as soon as possible to examine the phone data and the cash for fingerprints.'

In the fingerprint room, the detective told Liam his fingerprints would be taken on a scanner and asked him to hold out his right hand. Liam put his hands in his pockets. 'I ain't doing nothing until I see a solicitor.'

Chapman had an intuition about why Liam might want to avoid giving his name and fingerprints. 'You wanted for a crime, or did you fail to appear in court?' Liam said nothing, just smirked at Chapman, who smiled back. 'My guess is there's an arrest warrant out for you, probably for burglary.' Liam licked his lips. Chapman nodded. 'Thought as much. Now, here are your choices. One, you cut the tough guy act and give your fingerprints and DNA swab voluntarily. Two, my colleague and I, or more officers, if necessary, will take them by force, which we are legally entitled to do. So, what's it to be . . . the easy way or the hard way?'

Liam's smirk turned to a look of unease. He took his right hand out of his pocket and held it up. The detective held it and placed Liam's index finger on the scanner. 'Thank you, Liam, or should I call you by a different name?'

Liam made a hissing sound. 'You'll find out in a couple of minutes.'

'Are you working, Liam?' He nodded. 'Where?' Liam didn't reply. 'I'm only asking because we need it for your custody record. You don't have to tell me, but we will find out.'

'I'm a night attendant at the Jet petrol station in Hollybush Hill.'

Chapman nodded slowly. He decided not to ask further questions until Liam was in the interview room and his answers were being recorded. Chapman watched as the detective scanned Liam's fingers, then looked at the computer screen to see if there was a match on the database. When he saw the name William John Palmer come up on the computer screen and his last arrest photograph, where he still had hair, he could hardly believe what he was looking at. He sat staring at the screen, his whole body tensed as he waited until Liam's DNA swab had been taken and he was placed in a cell. Then he hurried up the stairs to his office.

CHAPTER EIGHTEEN

Jessica was returning to the MSCAN office when she received a call from Chapman. 'Hi, did DS Wood tell you about the stuff we found at Liam's flat and the clothing in the bin?' she asked.

'Yes, that's fantastic work by you all, and all useful stuff to question him about in his interview. Sounds like you're in your car.'

'I'm just on my way back to our office.'

'Do you mind coming to the station first?'

'We've got a lot of examination work to do. Things are starting to pile up, and I'm nearly at Lambeth.'

'I need to speak to you about Liam.'

'Why? What about him?'

'I'd rather speak to you in person.'

'For God's sake, Mike, just tell me what this is about!' she said, becoming frustrated.

'Liam is short for William.' He paused, knowing how she was going to react to what he was about to say.

'Tell me something I don't know,' she said impatiently.

He took a deep breath. 'The person we arrested earlier is the William John Palmer who assaulted you ten years ago.'

Jessica was stunned. For a few moments she couldn't speak. 'Why didn't you tell me this before?'

'I didn't recognise him when we arrested him because of his alopecia and the injuries to his face. I would have told you straight away if I'd known it was him. I only discovered Liam's identity when his fingerprints were taken ten minutes ago. The detective who took his prints said he'd enter the details on HOLMES and inform your team that Palmer's fingerprints and DNA were on file . . .'

'You could have told me first! Who did he call?'

'I don't know, but probably Guy, as he's your HOLMES manager. It would have looked odd if I had told the officer to delay sending them. I called you as soon as I could.'

Jessica knew he was right but was that didn't make the situation any better. 'This could raise all sorts of problems. My involvement could be seen as a conflict of interest. I could be asked to withdraw from the investigation.'

'It might not come to that.'

'What did Anderson say about it?'

'I haven't told him yet. I wanted to speak to you first. For now, I think we shouldn't tell anyone.'

'Are you serious? It will just make matters worse in the end if we don't.'

'Please come to the station, and we can discuss the best way forward.'

She let out a huge sigh as she turned the car around. 'All right, I'm on my way.'

Driving to Barking, Jessica became increasingly concerned about other people finding out her connection to Palmer. She knew she would have to tell Anderson and feared he would want her off the case. She contemplated calling Commander Williams first but decided to wait until she had spoken to Chapman.

As she approached Chapman's office, she passed a couple of people in the corridor and felt as if they were staring at her. She unconsciously pulled at her hair, making strands come loose to cover more of her face, until the band holding it in place snapped. She entered Chapman's office without knocking.

'That was quick,' he said, with a look of surprise at her wild-looking hair.

'Do you have an elastic band?' she snapped.

'It suits you. Just hang on a moment.' He rifled through his desk drawer and brought out several elastic bands. She chose one, scooped up her hair with one hand and quickly wound it into a tight topknot.

She stood by his desk. 'I've thought about things on the way here. We need to declare our previous involvement with William Palmer and withdraw from the investigation. If we don't, it could lead to misconduct allegations and disciplinary action.'

Chapman could see from the moment she came into his office that she wasn't her usual calm and collected self. He thought her decision was wrong and impulsive. 'Can we discuss it first?' he said, pointing to the chair beside his desk.

'I'm fine standing. Do you agree with me or not?' she asked bluntly.

'Would you like a cup of tea or coffee?' he asked, wanting to give her time to think and calm down.

'For Christ's sake, Mike, this is a serious situation, so just answer the question with a simple yes or no.'

'So, my opinion doesn't count then?'

'I didn't say that.'

'Please, Jess, sit down and listen to what I have to say before making any hasty decisions.'

Reluctantly, she did as Chapman asked. 'Go ahead,' she told him.

'OK, look, it's not unusual for a police officer to arrest the same person more than once, so my involvement in the investigation would not be a conflict of interest. Your name isn't on Palmer's criminal record file, but mine is, so I will have to inform Anderson that I arrested him on suspicion of sexual assault.'

'And what will you do if he asks who the victim was?'

'I doubt he will, since it was an arrest without charge ten years ago.'

'You didn't answer my question.'

'I'll tell him I wasn't the investigating officer, and it was so long ago I can't remember. The thing is, Jess, this investigation needs you and your team. You shouldn't have to withdraw because of a scumbag like Palmer.'

'I appreciate you're only trying to help me, Mike, and if William Palmer is guilty of assaulting De Klerk, then I hope he goes to prison for a long time. But the fact is, I'm not prepared to risk my future, or the team's, by hiding my connection to him.'

'OK, whatever you want to do, I'll support you, but I still think you should keep quiet about it for now.'

'You forget my name will be on the crime scene and forensic reports, which Palmer and his legal team will be entitled to read if he stands trial. I don't care how long ago it was. My concern is that Palmer will remember me and tell his lawyers that I was once his probation officer and I made a sexual assault allegation against him. The fact that he wasn't charged due to lack of evidence works in his favour. They will use it against me pre-trial or in court, alleging my evidence is biased, or worse, fabricated.'

'But that could happen even if you withdraw from the investigation.'

'I know, and that's why I'd rather declare the connection between me and Palmer here and now. It will also help negate false allegations against me and show I have nothing to hide.'

'You could wait until after we interview Palmer. If he confesses to the crime, his solicitor won't need full disclosure, and Palmer will be none the wiser about your involvement.'

Jessica shook her head. 'Let it go, Mike. It is what it is, and I'm not bothered about it. I mean that truthfully, I am not bothered and you have to believe me. I'll soon have another case to deal with . . . but hopefully, the offender will be no one I know,' she said, trying to make light of the situation.

Chapman forced a smile. 'Shall we go and see Anderson and tell him together?'

'I don't feel like speaking to him right now. I'd blow a gasket if he said the wrong thing. I want to tell Commander Williams personally, but you can tell Anderson, then if he wants to speak to me he can. I only ask that he keep it to himself and not tell everyone what Palmer did to me.'

'I promise you, Jess, I'll make sure Anderson says nothing to the team. I can also promise you that I'll tell him just before the interview that I arrested Palmer years ago. That way, he won't have time to ask for chapter and verse. Then, after the interview, I'll tell him about you.'

'Thanks, that will give me plenty of time to talk to Commander Williams. I'm going to head back to the lab now.'

Chapman lifted a property bag out of his desk drawer. 'I've got a mobile phone that was in Palmer's pocket. Could you take it back to the lab for Guy to examine?' Jessica hesitated for a moment, then nodded and took the phone from him. 'He also had a NatWest debit card in the name of Mr L Wilson. We thought it was nicked, but it wasn't. He recently opened the account using his date of birth and first name, Liam, and has his work wages paid into it. Palmer's wanted on a warrant for failing to appear in court two years ago on a burglary charge, so that's probably why he used a false name.'

'Makes sense. I better get on my way.'

'I'm sorry this has happened, Jess. You've done all the hard work and now you're the victim of circumstances beyond your control.'

'That's one way of looking at it. I hope the interview goes well.'

'Anderson's leading it . . . so it might not go to plan.'

'Will it be video recorded?'

'Yes. I can send you a copy. Will you be OK when you see his face?'

'Anderson's not that ugly,' she replied, making light of his concern. 'You know what I meant.'

'It's better to see his face now than in court, but I don't think it will bother me one way or the other.' Chapman suspected she was putting on a brave face on it. He remembered the night Palmer tried to rape her. She was in a state of traumatic shock, which had upset him to the extent that he'd wanted to give Palmer a beating. At the time, he had resisted the temptation, not because he feared being investigated, but for her sake. He knew if he'd beaten Palmer up as he badly wanted to, it could be used at trial to get the jury on Palmer's side. When he learned that Palmer wasn't going to be charged, he wished he had.

'We've got an interview viewing room with a TV in it. You can stay here and watch it if you like.'

'Thanks, but I need to get back to the office and see how things are going. I'll get Diane and Taff to watch the interview recording. If Palmer chooses to talk, his answers will be of interest and could help them to focus on specific items for forensic examination that might refute his account of events.'

'I can set up a secure link to the Met Net so you can watch it live. Palmer's solicitor hasn't arrived yet, so I reckon it will be at least a couple of hours before we interview him, which gives you plenty of time to get back to your office.'

'Good idea.' As she got up to leave, Chapman said he'd email her a link to the site and a password to gain entry. She gave him a sad smile that made him want to go round his desk and hug her tightly, but instead he stood up.

'I know you want to step back from being involved in the investigation, but I'd value your opinion on the interview.'

'Marks out of ten?'

He smiled. 'With your psychological expertise, I'm interested in how you interpret Palmer's body language and how he answers questions – if he chooses to. I've told Anderson it's best to do a short interview first, let Palmer stew for a few hours, then go back and hit him with all the hard evidence. I'd value your thoughts before the second interview, how we should approach it and what questions might get him to talk.'

'I'll do it, but only if it's just between us.'

'Of course, that's what I was thinking anyway. Would you like to discuss it somewhere away from the office?'

'Over the phone might be easier if it's in between interviews.'

'Maybe after the second interview we could go for a drink?' he suggested, expecting a refusal.

'That's fine by me. Let me know what time and where you'd like to meet,' she said, picking up her bag.

'Thank you for understanding, talk later.' She closed the door after her.

* * *

Jessica took the quickest route back to Lambeth via the Rotherhithe Tunnel, but the traffic was still slow and she could feel her frustration building. She wanted to return to the MSCAN office well before the interview started to speak with Diane, Taff and Guy about her withdrawal from the investigation. Although she trusted them, she didn't want to reveal the full details of what Palmer did and hoped they would respect her decision.

Driving towards the electric gates for the underground parking facility, she noticed Commander Williams and the Laboratory Director standing and talking together by the foyer entrance. She parked her car in the first available bay, hurried into the building and saw Williams entering the lift.

'Can you hold the doors, please?' Jessica called out as they started to close. Williams pressed the button to open the doors. 'Afternoon ma'am. If you've got time later before you return to the Yard, could I speak with you about the De Klerk case?'

'As it happens, I've come to see you about the case.' Williams smiled and pressed the button for the fourth floor.

'Oh, right. I thought you might be here for a meeting with the lab director,' Jessica said, wondering why Williams hadn't called her before coming to Lambeth.

'No, we just happened to bump into each other outside and had a quick catch-up.'

'Are you aware of the latest developments in the case?'

'If you mean William Palmer's arrest, then yes, I am.'

Jessica sensed Williams knew more than she was letting on. 'Have you spoken to DI Chapman?'

'I think we best have this conversation in your office.'

Jessica hoped that Chapman hadn't betrayed her trust and was about to say something when the lift stopped on the third floor. Two people got in and pressed the button for the fifth floor, where the canteen was. Jessica decided that it was best to say nothing until they were alone. Exiting the lift on the fourth floor, Williams followed her to the MSCAN offices.

Guy Jenkinson was at his desk inputting data on the HOLMES computer when he saw Commander Williams. He stood up. 'Good afternoon, ma'am.'

'Good afternoon, Guy. But really, you don't need to get up.'

'Force of habit,' he said, giving her a mock salute. He turned to Jessica. 'A detective on DCI Anderson's team called to say a fingerprint scan confirmed that the arrested man was William Palmer, also known as Liam. I gave Taff and Diane all the details to compare Palmer's fingerprints and DNA against those recovered from items seized at the De Klerk's house and the flat. Also, five hundred pounds was found in Palmer's wallet, which is now with Taff for fingerprinting.'

'OK, thanks, Guy,' she said.

'I can tell you that Palmer's lengthy criminal record started when he was thirteen with petty theft and progressed to burglary and handling stolen goods. He was . . .'

'Thanks, Guy,' Jessica interrupted, 'but DI Chapman has already told me about Palmer's criminal record.' She noticed how Williams looked at her as Guy spoke about Palmer.

Guy held up a phone. 'This is De Klerk's mobile. Unfortunately, the only prints and DNA on it were his own. Would you like me to download and examine the data for recent calls, texts and messages?'

Jessica looked at Williams. 'I raised examining the phone with DI Chapman before Palmer's arrest. He authorised it on the grounds the data may assist the investigation and lead to reasonable lines of enquiry . . .'

'But you're worried, now that Palmer's been arrested, the legality of doing that has changed,' Williams said.

Jessica nodded. 'I'm not very au fait with the legal side of digital examinations.'

'I think I have a solution,' Williams said. 'Palmer's due to be interviewed this afternoon, so I would advise waiting until that's done. If he denies everything or goes "no comment", I'd say there are reasonable grounds to examine the phone for any possible connection between them.'

Jessica realised Williams must have spoken to Chapman or Anderson about Palmer's arrest. She removed an exhibit bag containing the phone from her handbag, handed it to Guy and told him it was in Palmer's possession when he was arrested. She asked him to check who the registered owner was and access the data on it, working backwards from midday to two days before the crime occurred. Guy said Taff had told him about the phone found in the cistern at Palmer's flat, and if he'd finished with it, he'd start working on that as well and compile a list of the same numbers that had been called or sent messages on both phones.

'That would be great. Thank you, Guy.' Jessica walked towards her office with Williams.

'Sorry. One other thing,' Guy said. She stopped and turned. 'I looked up Springbok Wines Limited on Companies House. The company was in credit, with assets of just over one point five million pounds in the last financial year, which suggests there could have been a large amount of cash in the safe. That's it. I'll go and see Taff and Diane in the lab.'

'How are you coping since Palmer's arrest? Williams asked as they entered Jessica 's office.

Jessica sighed, 'Chapman told you, didn't he?

'Yes, but not right away . . .'

'He knew full well I wanted to tell you. He's betrayed my trust,' Jessica interrupted, deeply upset.

'It was Anderson that called me first.'

'Chapman said he'd tell him after Palmer was interviewed. How could he do this to me!'

'Please, just sit down and listen to me, Jess,' Williams said softly but firmly, then sat on the sofa and tapped the cushion for Jessica to sit next to her before continuing. 'Anderson was aware of Palmer's criminal record and noted his arrest by Mike Chapman ten years ago for an attempted rape while he was on probation. He was understandably curious and looked up the original crime report. The victim's name was redacted, but her profession wasn't. He remembered what you said in your MSCAN interview about being sexually assaulted and contacted me.'

'He was worried I'd screw up his investigation, was he?' Jessica said.

'No, he was worried about your welfare and how knowing about Palmer's identity might affect you. He saw your car in the yard at Barking and guessed you were with Mike Chapman, but he didn't want to stick his nose in for fear of upsetting you. He called me because he thought it might be better if I spoke to you, woman to woman, so to speak.'

'Does Anderson want me off the investigation?'

'He never raised it as an issue, but Chapman told me you did.'

'What else did he tell you?'

'That you saw a conflict of interest because of your connection to Palmer and thought you should step away from the investigation.'

'I don't have much choice.'

'Chapman, like Anderson, is concerned for your well-being, but neither of them wants you off the investigation. However, we all realise that you may not wish to continue under such stressful circumstances. But the choice is yours.'

'I won't deny Palmer's arrest came as a shock, but none of you need worry as I know I can cope.'

'Are you sure? Because his arrest has clearly upset you.'

'Honestly, ma'am. I'll be fine.'

Williams wasn't so sure but gave her the benefit of the doubt. 'Would you like to continue working on the case?'

'I'd love to, but my actions might be perceived as biased against Palmer. His lawyers could challenge the forensic evidence and allege I had a vendetta against Palmer and made the evidence fit the crime.'

'I won't deny that could happen, but the critical question is whether a fair-minded person, having considered all the facts, would believe you could be biased.'

'Even if they didn't, my continued involvement could be a big risk.'

'There are ways of minimising the risk.'

'How?' Jessica asked, surprised by Willams's remark.

'You only knew the suspect as Liam until DI Chapman informed you of his full name and previous convictions. It was then you realised William Palmer was the person who sexually assaulted you ten years ago. It was a very personal and sensitive issue, so rather than speak to a male officer, you immediately informed me. We discussed all the details of the case and your involvement from the get-go. As a fair-minded senior officer, I believe you are unbiased, honest and always act with integrity. Your history with William Palmer will not bias your thoughts or conclusions, and the forensic evidence will speak for itself. I concluded that it is safe and appropriate for you to be involved in the investigation, and I will stand by my decision, regardless of who questions it.'

'Thank you, Ma'am.'

'Is there anything else you wish to discuss?'

Jessica wasn't about to disagree or challenge her decision. 'No, ma'am.'

'Problem solved then. From what Anderson told me there's enough evidence to charge Palmer. If he's found guilty, he will spend a very long time behind bars. I'd best get back to the Yard. Keep up the good work.' Williams then started to type a text message on her phone as she left.

Jessica breathed a huge sigh of relief. It was as if an enormous weight had been lifted off her shoulders. She also realised she had misjudged Anderson and decided to thank him personally for supporting her and for his concern about her welfare.

A few minutes later, Jessica's phone pinged. It was a text message from Chapman: 'Sorry for not telling you Williams was involved.

I was under strict orders to say nothing until she spoke to you. For what it's worth, I agree with her decision and I'm glad you chose to remain on the investigation.'

Jessica realised Williams had texted Chapman, and probably Anderson too, to tell them about the conversation they'd just had. She texted back: 'I understand. Thanks for your support. I'm looking forward to watching the interview and having a drink later. God knows I need one!'

CHAPTER NINETEEN

Jessica laid her notepad, pen and a bottle of water neatly on the table before switching on her computer and opening the link to the interview room at Barking. She could feel herself getting tense, not knowing how she would react to seeing William Palmer's face after so many years. The interview room appeared on the screen, but it was empty. She opened the water bottle, took a sip and sat back, awaiting Palmer and the interviewing officers' arrival.

A few minutes later, the door opened, and a tall, well-built, bald male entered the room. She couldn't see his face as his head was down, but she knew it must be Palmer. He was followed by a short man in a dark blue suit, who Jessica assumed was his solicitor. Anderson and Chapman then entered the room, and they all sat down at the table, Palmer and his solicitor on one side and the officers on the other. Only then did she get a good clear look at him and instantly felt her heartbeat quicken. With his completely bald head, large dark eyes with no eyebrows, pointed nose and thin lips, he looked freakish. She realised she would never have recognised him if she hadn't known who he was. Anderson turned on the digital recording machine and gave his name, the date, time and interview location. He then said the other officer present was Detective Inspector Michael Chapman.

Palmer kept his head down while Anderson asked the others present to identify themselves. The solicitor gave his name as Matthew Baldwin, but Palmer said nothing, and Anderson again asked him to state his name. Jessica watched as he slowly raised his head and scowled at the camera.

'I am Liam John Palmer,' he said assertively and pointed to his head. 'I got these injuries because the officers who arrested me beat me up for no reason!'

Anderson informed Palmer that he and his solicitor were welcome to make an official complaint of assault, which he assured them would be thoroughly investigated. 'Do you prefer to be called William or Liam?'

'Everyone calls me Liam these days,' he replied with a shrug.

Anderson cautioned him and asked him if he understood. Palmer nodded, and Anderson explained what the police had found at the De Klerk's house, including graphic details of De Klerk's injuries. 'He remains in a coma,' he added. Palmer remained silent and seemingly emotionless as he listened. 'Can you tell me where you were on last Saturday night and the early hours of Sunday morning?'

'No comment,' Palmer replied.

'We made enquiries at the Jet Garage, Hollybush Hill, where you work. They told us that you had the weekend off and didn't start work again until 9 p.m. on Monday. Is that correct?'

'No comment.'

'Is there anyone who can account for your movements on the night of the crime?'

'No comment.'

'I appreciate your solicitor may have advised you to give "no comment" answers. However, this is your opportunity to tell us where you were and what you were doing on the night Johan De Klerk was beaten and stabbed. Failure to do so could harm your defence if you are charged.'

'No comment.'

'Johan De Klerk's sixty-thousand-pound Rolex watch was stolen during the break-in. We also believe a large sum of cash was taken. Do you know anything about that?'

'No comment.'

Anderson put a photograph on the table and slid it towards Palmer, who leaned forward to look at it. 'We have positively identified the Rolex watch in the photograph from its serial number. It's Mr De Klerk's. There's two thousand pounds in cash next to it. Have you seen these items before?'

'No comment.' Palmer slid the picture back and yawned. Jessica could tell he was faking it, trying to appear unconcerned. She also noticed his dirty fingernails when he slid the photograph back across the table.

'We searched your flat early this morning while you were at work. We found the watch and the money hidden under the kitchen sink. Can you explain how they got there?'

Jessica watched as Palmer's eyes opened wide with surprise. He shook his head and was clearly about to say something when his solicitor nudged him. Palmer looked desperate as he turned to his solicitor, who shook his head.

He licked his lips, looking nervous. 'No comment,' he said quietly.

'This information was not disclosed to me before the interview,' Baldwin said with a stern look.

'We are not obliged to disclose all our evidence to you, Mr Baldwin,' Anderson replied calmly.

'Well, I have not had the opportunity to discuss this development with my client, and I'd like to do so.'

'Certainly. But before we take a break, I'd like to inform you that Mr De Klerk's Range Rover was also stolen during the aggravated burglary, most likely as a getaway vehicle. It was recovered on Tuesday morning after being set alight. The location is not far from your client's flat and very close to the petrol station where he works.' Anderson put a photograph of the burnt-out vehicle on the table. Jessica saw Palmer take a deep breath and nervously exhale as he looked at the photograph.

'You just said my client was working on Monday night from 9 p.m. He does a twelve-hour shift, so it can't have been him that set the car alight,' Baldwin said quickly.

'You're right about Liam working that night, but we cannot be sure he remained in the garage all night as he works alone.'

'Their CCTV should confirm it,' Baldwin said.

'We've already obtained the CCTV. The strange thing is that it went down during the early hours of Tuesday morning, and nothing was recorded for about two hours.'

'Between what times?' Baldwin asked.

'One to three a.m., which would cover the time we think the Range Rover was set alight.'

'If the till receipts show sales between those times, my client can't have left the garage.'

'I have an officer checking them as we speak, Mr Baldwin.'

'Is there anything else you'd like to surprise us with DCI Anderson?' Baldwin asked.

Anderson handed him a photograph of the PlayStation, laptop and Xbox. 'We found these items in Liam's flat and checked the serial numbers. They were stolen during a burglary two months ago in Chigwell, along with jewellery valued at two hundred thousand pounds. We'd like to know how Liam came to be in possession of the items and if he knows where the stolen jewellery is.'

Baldwin was about to say something, but Liam spoke first. 'I didn't steal the laptop and game boxes. I bought them . . .'

Baldwin nudged Palmer to stop talking. 'I'd like to use the private consultation room to speak to my client.'

'Certainly. I'll get one of the custody officers to organise it. Take your time and let me know when you're ready to recommence the interview.' Anderson switched the digital recorder off, and he and Chapman left the room.

As the door closed, Liam turned to Baldwin with a desperate look. 'The cops are fitting me up! I've never even heard of this De Klerk bloke . . .' Baldwin pointed to the camera and told him to say nothing more until they were in the private consultation room. A custody officer then entered the room and asked them to follow him. Jessica watched as Palmer left the room. She noticed he was dragging his right foot and assumed he'd injured his leg when he tripped, trying to avoid arrest.

Jessica texted Chapman, saying that she would speak to the rest of her team regarding any forensic results and call him in about twenty minutes. She then went to the main office, where Diane, Guy and Taff were still seated around the computer screen on which they had watched the interview.

'Underneath all that bravado, Palmer's shitting himself. He's clearly lying,' Taff said, and the others nodded in agreement.

'I thought Anderson was pretty good in the interview. He didn't get flustered, and I liked how he sprung the stuff about the car and CCTV near the end,' Diane remarked.

'Palmer looked really worried at that point and wanted to talk, but Baldwin shut him off again. What do you think, Jessica?' Guy asked.

'I agree Palmer is hiding something. But he could just be an accomplice of the intruder.'

'I definitely think someone else is involved,' Guy said, and they all looked at him.

He picked up a mobile phone and his A4 notepad from his desk. 'This is the phone Taff found in the toilet. The surface had been wiped clean, so no DNA or fingerprints were recovered. Palmer also had a personal iPhone, which I've yet to examine.'

'So, Palmer could have used that burner phone to communicate with someone else involved in the break-in,' Taff suggested.

Guy held it up. 'It is a cheap Android with prepaid minutes and no formal contract. I retrieved the number via the SIM card and contacted the service provider. It's been live for seven days. No standard calls or text messages have been sent or received on the phone, but internet connections were made, the last one being early Tuesday morning, then it was turned off at 8 p.m. that evening.'

'What was its last cell site location?' Jessica asked, opening her notebook and taking a pen from her pocket.

'A mast in Montague Road E11, the same street as John Walsh Tower. Cell site analysis showed it was used for internet connections on Monday at 4 a.m. and again on the evening De Klerk was assaulted. The phone has WhatsApp, which allows users to communicate via the internet. Unfortunately, all the data has been erased, and no backup was created. WhatsApp does not store any data relating to messages or calls as everything is end-to-end encrypted.'

Taff sighed. 'So, we'll never know what calls or messages were made or received?'

'I've got some data recovery software programs I can use. Fingers crossed, I might be able to retrieve the WhatsApp data,' Guy said.

'How long will it take?' Jessica asked.

'Not too long. I can link the phone to my computer right away and let the software run while we're talking.'

'Go ahead. That's good work, well done,' Jessica said.

'Palmer will have difficulty explaining the phone away, especially as it was used just after the break-in and the after the car was set alight,' Taff said.

'Baldwin will probably just advise Palmer to go "no comment" again,' Diane said.

'I'm not so sure that's a good thing, now the evidence is mounting up against him. Hopefully, Palmer will see he's deep in the prover-bial and start talking in the second interview,' Taff said.

'If he lies about it, he'll only be digging a deeper hole for him-self,' Guy added as he plugged the phone into his laptop.

'Chapman said he intended to hit Palmer with all the incrim-inating evidence in the second interview and see how he reacts. With that in mind, do you have any other forensic updates besides the phone stuff for me to give him? Jessica asked.

Taff nodded. 'I've examined the knife recovered from De Klerk's back, and there were Sealskinz glove marks on the han-dle indicating the person holding it used their right hand. I also examined the two tumblers from the cinema room. The one with the cheetah had Johan De Klerk's fingerprints on it, and the one with the water buffalo had someone else's, but they were not on the database and they weren't Michelle De Klerk's. I didn't find anything on the Rolex watch: it had been wiped clean like the burner phone.'

Diane took over. 'I swabbed the inside of the watch clasp and found a minute trace of DNA, which probably came from sweat. I'm using PCR to amplify it, and hopefully I'll get a result in another day or two, but it's obviously most likely De Klerk's.'

'What's PCR?' Guy asked.

'Polymerase chain reaction. It involves using short synthetic DNA fragments called primers to select a segment of the genome to be amplified. Multiple rounds of DNA synthesis follow this to amplify that segment, producing millions to billions of copies of a specific segment of DNA, which can then be studied in greater detail.'

'Bet you wished you never asked,' Taff smiled.

'No, I get it . . . I think,' Guy said.

Diane continued. 'I've completed the DNA work on the items seized from De Klerk's house but haven't found any DNA that matches Palmer or anyone on the database. As expected, I'm seeing either Johan or Michelle's DNA profile.'

'What about the found cash in Palmer's flat?' Jessica asked Taff.

'For now, and to speed things up, I just examined the top and bottom banknotes in the bundle. I recovered fingerprints from the two notes that matched Johan De Klerk's using black powder suspension and infrared light. Other recovered prints were not on the database, so they could be from anyone who handled the cash at any time. I'm afraid Palmer's prints were not on them, but I did find marks that matched the Sealskinz gloves and what I believe to be washing-up gloves.'

'Palmer had black woollen gloves on him when he was arrested,' Jessica told them.

'It's odd that the Sealskinz weren't with the clothing in the communal bin,' Guy remarked.

'If he wore the Sealskinz to drive the car, he might have thrown them in the fire after he set alight to it.' Diane suggested.

'But why then dump the other clothing in the bin?' Guy said. 'And what about the Adidas trainers? They haven't been found either.'

'On that subject, I can confirm that the trainer marks in Palmer's flat are the same Adidas trainer marks we recovered from the De Klerk house,' Taff said.

'He must have disposed of them elsewhere as well,' Diane said. 'Having previous convictions for burglary, Palmer will be forensically aware and likely know that gloves and trainers hold a lot of sweat, which is good for raising a DNA profile.'

'Are there any other forensic results that might help Anderson and Chapman in the next interview?' Jessica asked. Taff said he was still working on the black bin bag from the communal bin and the roll of liners recovered from Palmer's flat and hoped to have some results late afternoon. 'What about the money Palmer had in his wallet?' Jessica asked.

'I've applied the black suspension powder and raised finger-prints on some of the bank notes. I need to enhance them with infrared lighting, and then I can enlarge and check them against Palmer and Johan's prints. Be about twenty minutes before I can give you the results.' Diane said she'd examined the Adidas cloth-ing recovered from the bin bag. Small traces of blood were on the bottoms and the hoodie, which she would test for De Klerk's DNA.

'Was there any blood on the coir mat we took from Palmer's flat?' Jessica asked her.

'No, and there were no traces of pollens or soil from the De Klerk's Garden. However, I did find a few tiny grey granules embedded in it. Mass spectrometry testing revealed they contained traces of magnesium, iron, calcium, sulphur and humic acid . . . the components of a slow-release compound fertiliser.'

'How do you know it's fertiliser?' Taff asked.

'I tested the soil sample you gave me from the De Klerk's Garden, but the compounds weren't the same. I had a hunch, called Wanstead golf course and spoke to the head greenkeeper, and guess what . . . ?'

'Their fertiliser contains the same compounds as the pellets you found in the mat,' Taff said, looking impressed.

Diane nodded. 'I can't say positively it's from their golf course, but the only other golf club in the area is the Ilford Club, about two miles away. I also called them, and they use a different type of fertiliser.'

'That's a great piece of work, Di. Palmer will have difficulty explaining how those pellets got on his mat,' Guy remarked.

'Not necessarily. He could say he went for a walk on the golf course, or it was an innocent cross-transfer,' Diane said.

Jessica shook her head. 'Put together with what we know about the burner phone and CCTV going down, it's good evidence, so well done. Unless there's anything else, I better call Mike Chapman and tell him about your results. Guy or I will let you know when Palmer's interview is about to restart.'

Jessica called Chapman, who asked her how she felt when she saw William Palmer.

'At first, I was nervous, and like you, I wouldn't have recognised him. But to be honest, it didn't bother me. I was more interested in what he had to say and his behaviour.'

'What did you think?'

'Hard to say as he didn't really answer any questions. But body language wise, I think he's hiding something and may have committed the crime or at least been an accomplice.'

'Accomplice? What makes you say that?' Jessica told him about the burner phone and the other forensic results. 'That's great work. Anderson will be happy. Also, DS Wood went back to the Jet garage and they didn't have any sales receipts for petrol cans on Monday and Tuesday. But interestingly, they did a stock check a week ago and had five on the shelves, but there were only four today. It looks like someone either shoplifted a can or Palmer took it.'

'How long has he been working at the garage?' Jessica asked.

'Five months.'

'What does the manager think of him as an employee?'

'Very good, always on time and a hard worker.'

'When do you think you'll be starting the second interview?'

'Palmer's solicitor is still talking to him, but hopefully soon. I'll text you.'

Jessica was about to end the call when Guy walked in, holding an A4 printout and looking pleased. 'I've cracked the WhatsApp messages. Palmer broke into the De Klerk's and then contacted someone else who must be involved. There's a bloody tracker on the burner phone as well.'

'Did you hear that?' Jessica asked Chapman.

'A bit of it. Turn on your speakerphone.'

Jessica did so and nodded to Guy to carry on. 'The burner phone from Palmer's flat had been used to make contact via WhatsApp messages, apart from one call. The messages are to one other number, which is also registered to a burner phone. The communications are short, to the point and started on Friday afternoon at 4.08 p.m.'

'Go slowly so I can write them down,' Chapman replied.

'On Friday afternoon, Palmer got a message saying, "he's going away Saturday morning, back Monday." Palmer replied, "will do job early hours Monday." He got a thumbs-up emoji reply. Then, on Monday at 4 a.m., Palmer sent a message saying, 'job done, call later'. This was followed . . .'

Chapman interrupted. 'Slow down, I'm trying to catch up.'

'Guy will send you a printout of everything,' Jessica said.

'That would be helpful for the interview but carry on anyway.'

'Palmer then received several repeated messages saying, "Contact me now" and "Where the fuck are you?" Whoever sent the messages started calling Palmer's number, but he didn't answer. At 3.10 p.m. Monday, Palmer called the other burner number, and the conversation lasted a few minutes.'

'Is this still all on WhatsApp?' Chapman asked.

'Yes, every contact was made using it. The next one was on Tuesday at 3.48 a.m. Palmer sent a message saying, "car torched", clearly referring to the fact the Range Rover had been set alight, which we know happened in the early hours of Tuesday morning. There was no further contact between either phone. Palmer's was switched off at 8 p.m. last night and recovered at his flat this morning. I hope that all made sense.'

'Yes, thanks. What about cell mast locations and the owner of the other phone?'

'Before it went dead, Palmer's burner phone was last picked up by the cell mast in Montague Road. The other phone is also a burner with the same service provider. It went live at the same time as Palmer's, and the first cell tower to pick them up was in Leather Lane, Holborn at 6 p.m. last Wednesday.'

'Do we know the other phone's current location?'

'No, it's gone dead, but it was last live near a mast in Caroline Street, Birmingham, on Tuesday morning. I've asked the service provider to send me a detailed cell site analysis log for all the calls and messages sent and received, but that could take a day or two. It's also more difficult because WhatsApp calls are encrypted and made online.'

'Can we trace an IP address?' Jessica asked.

'No, both phones were using a free VPN,' Guy replied, referring to a virtual private network used to hide an IP address.

'You mentioned something about a tracker at the beginning,' Jessica said.

'Palmer's burner phone has a hidden tracker app on it. It doesn't record where he's been on his phone, but it sends information about location, calls and texts to someone else, who can view it through a web portal.'

'Looks like whoever gave Palmer the phone doesn't trust him,' Jessica remarked.

'Certainly does. The Leather Lane connection is interesting. There's a street market there with lots of different stalls. Could be Palmer's selling jewellery from his burglaries to a dodgy trader,' Chapman remarked.

'The PlayStation, laptop and Xbox in his flat were proceeds of a burglary where two hundred thousand pounds worth of jewellery was stolen,' Jessica said.

'I'll get one of the team to speak to the property owner and request photos of the stolen jewellery if they have any. Great work, all of you.'

As Chapman was about to end the call, Taff came in with a big smile and holding his thumbs up. 'I found Johan De Klerk and Palmer's fingerprints on some of the cash from Palmer's wallet. There were also a couple of marks from the Sealskinz gloves. All three were on one of the notes. The odds of that happening by chance are a million to one. The money must have been stolen from De Klerk.'

'This just gets better and better,' Chapman said.

'There's more,' Taff said. 'I spoke with the scene of crime officer who dealt with the burglary in Chigwell where the property found in Palmer's flat was stolen from. He sent me copies of the footprints they recovered. They were Adidas Ultraboost with the same tread as the ones in Palmer's flat and De Klerk's house.'

'The second interview with Palmer will be interesting and full of surprises . . . mostly for him,' a delighted Chapman said.

CHAPTER TWENTY

Jessica had been in her office for nearly an hour, reviewing all her notes and ensuring no forensic opportunities had been missed. Her mobile pinged with a text message from Chapman informing her that the second interview with Palmer would start in twenty minutes. She logged into the Met web link on her desktop computer, and the empty interview room appeared on the screen. Jessica then told Guy she would watch the interview alone and make notes. 'I'll let Diane and Taff know,' he said.

'Thanks. Do you have Palmer's criminal record?'

'Yes, I also contacted social services and got a copy of their file on him. I haven't had time to read it all, but I've printed it off.' He handed her the file.

'I double-checked Palmer's burner phone but couldn't find anything else on it. I've downloaded all the data from his personal mobile, so I'll start looking through it. Do you want me to continue working on De Klerk's mobile, too?'

'So far, there doesn't appear to be any direct connection between Palmer and De Klerk, so I don't think it will take us any further. Make Palmer's phone the priority for now.' He gave her a thumbs-up and she returned to her office to look at Palmer's file.

Sitting at her desk, she did some deep breathing before opening the file. Seeing Palmer as he was now hadn't triggered any traumatic memories, but this might be different. The first thing she saw was a photograph of Palmer as a sullen-looking teenager, and she was instantly taken back to the time she'd first met him as a trainee probation officer working with a youth offenders team. He was fourteen or fifteen and had convictions for theft, criminal damage and burglary. Back then, he was often referred to as Will or Willy, which she suspected might be why he now preferred to be called Liam. Reading the social services file, Jessica realised how much she had forgotten about him. At the age of fourteen, he was diagnosed with attention deficit hyperactivity disorder, commonly known as ADHD, due to his hyperactivity and impulsiveness. Alongside his ADHD, he was also diagnosed as having a conduct disorder on account of his antisocial behaviour and criminal activities.

And Jessica had never been aware of what she read next. Palmer's ADHD was believed to have started when he was eight years old after a severe head injury. His mother had called an ambulance and said he had fallen over and banged his head. The hospital, due to the nature of the injury, told the police that they suspected William had been assaulted.

A detective from the child abuse unit carried out an investigation and suspected the father, an alcohol and drug abuser with a history of violence, had deliberately smashed William's head against a wall. The father denied assault, and the mother stuck to her story. Specially trained officers interviewed William, but he repeatedly said he fell over. They concluded that his denial of the truth was due to a fear of further brutality at the hands of his father. A report was sent to the Crown Prosecution Service, but they decided there was insufficient evidence to charge the father. Social Services became involved, but shortly after the incident the father died from a heroin overdose, and William was allowed to stay with his mother, even though she had a drinking problem.

Jessica felt some empathy for Palmer after reading what had happened to him as a child, but it would never excuse what he did to her and how it had affected her life. She recalled the problems in her family life and how her father, Roger, constantly chastised and belittled their mother, Eileen, in front of them. Jessica never saw him physically assaulting her, but he often snarled, pointing a finger and telling her cruelly how she was overweight and needed to be a better wife and mother for him and the children. Being so young, she thought all fathers behaved similarly. He was never very affectionate to her and instead favoured David, buying him more expensive Christmas and birthday presents. Looking back, she knew it was intended to wound her. The odd thing was that at the same time, he was forever bragging about her and David's non-existent successes at school, making Jessica uncomfortable and leading school friends to tease them both mercilessly.

Jessica remembered the night she and David, aged eleven, saw two large suitcases in the hallway and wondered if their father was going away on a business trip, which he had been doing more and more frequently. It seemed odd to them as he usually just took an overnight case. They had sat silently by the bannisters on the upstairs landing, clinging to each other as they listened to their father speak to their mother as if she were a piece of dirt. Although it was many years ago, every word her father said was still engrained in her memory.

'You are a waste of space, Eileen. I don't love you, and I don't think I ever have. Everyone agrees I deserve better . . . so I'm leaving you whether you like it or not. My solicitor is drawing up divorce papers, and I'm putting the house on the market.'

'But where will the children and I live?' a shocked Eileen asked.

'I've rented a flat, and you can stay here with the kids until the house is sold. I am not an unreasonable man, Eileen. I'll give you a lump sum from the sale and pay child support. I have put down an offer on a bungalow in Petts Wood for you and Jessie, which has been accepted. It will be more than adequate for the two of you, and

there is no onward chain, so hopefully, you will be able to move there in a month or two.'

'What about David?' she asked in shocked tone.

'A son needs his father. Once I have found a suitable property, David will live with me.'

'But what about his schooling?'

'I will send him to a boarding school, which will be in his best interests if he wants a successful career.'

'But we can't afford that . . .'

'There is no more we, Eileen. I'm leaving tonight. My solicitor will contact you,' he concluded brusquely.

Jessica remembered David's distress as he pulled himself from her embrace and ran down the stairs. She followed, watching as David held their father tightly around the waist. She grabbed her mother's hand and held on tightly. Tears ran down David's cheeks as he begged. *'No, Daddy, please don't go, please stay with us. I don't want to leave school and all my friends.'* Roger put his hands on David's shoulders, straightened him up and leaned down so they were face to face.

'You shouldn't have been eavesdropping. I'm only thinking of what's best for you, son. Boarding school will make a man of you. With a good education, you can achieve whatever you want in life.' David was still crying, but his tone changed as he stepped back from his father.

'No . . . I want to stay with Mummy and Jessie!'

'You can for now, but I've made up my mind, and you'll do as you're told.'

'You can't make me!' David shouted, then rushed to his mother and Jessica's side.

Roger's eyes hardened as he stepped forward, pointing a finger at Eileen.

'This is your fault. You've poisoned him against me.' Eileen ushered the children behind her for their safety, and for the first time, Jessica witnessed her mother stand up against their father.

'I won't let you take the children. They need to be together with me. I'll fight you for custody and take every penny you've got.'

'Fine. See you in court then, but don't come running to me for help when you can't cope,' he sneered. Roger slammed the front door shut as he left. It was the last time they saw him. Jessica remembered their mother trying her best to comfort them that night, saying she loved them with all her heart and that they would all be safe and happy in their new home.

Jessica took a deep breath and sat upright. Although they were harrowing memories, they made her more angry than sad, appalled at her father's cruelty. It wasn't until eight years later, her mother told her – though not David – that shortly after Roger left, she discovered he had been having an affair with his twenty-two-year-old secretary, and the supposed business trips had been nights spent with her. At the time, Jessica had said that it must have hurt her terribly when she found out, but her mother said it was a blessing in disguise as it enabled her to get a better divorce settlement and avoid a custody battle in court.

Jessica felt a deep sadness when she thought about her mother. However, she found some comfort in the fact that she was no longer suffering from the debilitating pain of cancer. Jessica missed her mother deeply and recalled the happy times they shared every day, but she had never been able to come to terms with her father's cruelty to such a kind and gentle woman. She often wondered if he had remarried and had another family who suffered like they had. She knew the experience had profoundly affected her own life and explained some of her reluctance to form steady relationships with men, not wanting to end up a victim like her mother. Being devoted to her work, on the other hand, had helped her to feel strong and independent.

She took a deep breath, exhaled and continued reading Palmer's file. Between the ages of sixteen and twenty-three, he'd had five convictions for theft and shoplifting, four for burglary, two for criminal damage and one for arson. He had spent time in prison on two occasions, totalling one year. She scanned the details of his convictions and couldn't find anything relating to an assault or threat of violence during any of them. The arson conviction was for setting a skip alight.

Jessica looked at the details of the burglary charge for which he had failed to appear in court. The crime had been committed two years earlier, just after 1 a.m., while the occupants of the semi-detached house were asleep. Palmer had entered the rear of the premises through a side gate, then forced a kitchen window open with a crowbar. He'd been searching through the living room cabinet drawers when he heard the deep growl of an Alsatian behind him, and a man asking, 'Can I help you?' He fled through the open window, then ran in front of a car and was taken to hospital. He was treated for a fractured skull, broken leg and dislocated knee before being released six weeks later. He was immediately arrested and admitted to the offence before being released on bail to appear in court.

She closed the file. She knew she ought to feel sorry for him, especially given his family history. But as she imagined the look of terror on his face on seeing the snarling dog, she couldn't help smiling.

CHAPTER TWENTY-ONE

Jessica was making notes on her iPad when she saw Palmer and his solicitor, Baldwin, enter the interview room, followed by Anderson and Chapman. They all sat in the same places, and Anderson turned on the digital recording machine. Everyone introduced themselves as before, and Anderson again cautioned Palmer, who said he understood. Anderson put a photo of the stolen laptop, PlayStation and Xbox on the table. Jessica thought Chapman might lead the second interview, but Anderson opened the questioning again, this time with a soft approach.

'I'd like to pick up where we left off, Liam. You were asked how you came to have those items in your flat and replied, "I didn't steal the laptop and game boxes. I bought them." Would you like to elaborate on that?'

Palmer looked at Baldwin, who, to Jessica 's surprise, nodded. 'I bought them at a local car boot sale about a month ago.'

'For how much?'

'About three hundred and fifty quid.'

'That was a pretty good deal for property worth about a thousand pounds.'

'He wanted more, but I got him down. I wouldn't have bought the stuff if I'd known it was stolen.'

'Can you describe the man who sold it to you?'

'Short guy in his fifties with grey hair.'

'And would you be able to recognise him again?'

'I might . . . I'm not sure.'

'OK, we'll move on then. Have you ever been on Wanstead golf course?'

Palmer laughed. 'I've never played golf in my life.' Jessica picked up that he now appeared more confident.

'What about walking around it?'

'I've never been anywhere near it.'

Baldwin interjected. 'May I ask what playing golf has to do with the reasons for my client's arrest?'

Anderson smiled. 'Just curious, that's all. What were you doing last Sunday night and Monday morning, Liam?'

Palmer shrugged. 'I was at home watching TV and playing games on the Xbox and the PlayStation until the early hours. I got up Monday at about midday.'

'Did anyone visit you at your flat on Sunday or Monday?'

'No. I was on my own.'

'Did you go out at all?'

'Not on the Sunday. On Monday I went to the pub at lunchtime, had a couple of pints and a burger, then went home to bed and left for work at about eight fifteen.'

'Which pub?'

'The Bell on the High Road.'

'Did you leave your work at all during the night, specifically between one and three a.m.?'

'No, I didn't.'

'Are you sure?'

'Of course I am. If I did and customers came along, they'd complain to the manager that no one was there to serve them.' He was adamant, but Jessica could tell he was edgy now.

'Have you checked the till receipts?' Baldwin asked.

'Yes, we have, and there were no sales between two and three a.m.'

'It's not unusual for zero sales at that time of night. I never left work and had nothing to do with that car being set alight,' Palmer said, looking even more agitated.

'Where exactly was the car found?' Baldwin asked.

'On Wanstead golf course, about a mile from the garage. We did a test run from the garage by car at thirty miles an hour. We were there within two minutes. The quickest route back on foot took twenty minutes. Driving to the dump site, setting the car alight and walking back could all be done in under half an hour.'

'I can't walk that fast. I've got foot drop,' Palmer snapped back.

'What's foot drop?' Anderson asked.

Baldwin answered for him. 'Liam was hit by a car two years ago. He broke his leg, dislocated his knee and fractured his skull. He can't lift his right foot properly, so it drags on the ground when he walks.'

'Can't be that bad. He managed to run from my officers when we arrested him this morning,' Chapman said.

Palmer pulled up his right trouser leg and lifted his leg. 'I have to wear an ankle foot support to help me walk better. It makes the drag less noticeable but doesn't help me to walk any quicker.' Jessica made a note to request Palmer's medical records while Anderson continued.

'Our forensic team found fertiliser pellets embedded in your doormat. They're identical to the pellets used on Wanstead Golf course . . .'

Baldwin interrupted. 'That is ridiculous, DCI Anderson. Anyone visiting his flat could have left them on his mat, or it could have been an innocent cross-transfer onto my client's shoe.'

'I am aware of that, I just felt it's something Liam should know, in case it jogs his memory about being on the golf course.'

'How many times do I have to tell you? I've never been on that bloody golf course, and I didn't set light to the car.' Liam pursed his lips and sat back defiantly with his arms crossed, but he was looking more worried.

'Do you own any trainers like these?' Anderson asked as he put a picture of the Adidas Ultraboosts on the table.

Liam shook his head, pointing to his shoes. 'I wear Skechers all the time. They're lightweight and make it more comfortable for me walking. Like I just told you, I got a bad leg.'

Anderson put down a picture of the gloves. 'Have you ever owned any Sealskinz gloves like these?'

'No, I've only got a pair of woollen gloves. Would you like to know what underwear I've got on?' Palmer asked with a smirk.

'I know this may be frustrating, Liam, but we are investigating a serious crime. Johan De Klerk's house in Victoria Park Road, Hackney, was broken into around 2 a.m. on Monday . . .'

'For fuck's sake, I don't know the guy, and I've never been to Hackney in my life!' Palmer interjected.

Anderson continued calmly. 'Please, just let me finish, Liam. During the burglary, he suffered a fractured skull and was repeatedly stabbed. At present, he is in a coma, he should be conscious very soon and hopefully will be able to identify the man who attacked him.'

'Good, because then he'll be able to tell you it wasn't me.'

'I told you in the first interview that we found De Klerk's Rolex and a large sum of cash in your flat.' He put the photographs on the table. 'You previously chose to give a "No Comment" answer when I asked about them, but I'd like to give you another opportunity to explain how they came to be in your flat.'

Palmer shook his head in apparent despair. 'I don't know! I've never seen that stuff until now.'

'I find that hard to believe, seeing as it was hidden under your kitchen sink,' Anderson said.

'Then someone else must have put it there.'

Anderson frowned. 'Are you seriously suggesting someone

broke into your house and put them there to frame you?'

'Yeah, and I think it was him.' Palmer pointed at Chapman.

'That's a very serious allegation to make, Liam,' Baldwin said, sounding genuinely surprised.

Palmer looked straight at Chapman. 'He arrested me years ago for something I didn't do. They tried to fit me up, but it was all fucking lies, and I was never charged.'

'Have you arrested my client before, DI Chapman?' Baldwin asked.

'Yes, about ten years ago, when I was night duty CID. The case was allocated to Detective Sergeant Blake to investigate . . .'

'Is Blake also involved in your current investigation?' Baldwin interrupted.

Anderson answered. 'No, and for your information, DI Chapman didn't recognise who Liam was until his fingerprints were taken. When he was identified as William Palmer, DI Chapman immediately informed me about the previous arrest.' Jessica winced as she watched the screen. She was seriously worried now that the revelation of Liam's previous arrest could lead to her and Chapman's removal from the investigation. She also worried that Anderson might reveal that she'd been the victim and was now in charge of the team dealing with the forensic investigation. It felt as if everything was unravelling.

'Why didn't you tell me this before?' Baldwin asked Liam.

'Because I didn't recognise him at first. Then when I was told his name it came back to me. I was thought it would look bad if I said anything, but I had no choice when they started trying to fit me up again.'

'What were the circumstances of the previous arrest?' Baldwin asked.

Anderson answered. 'I can assure you it has no bearing on this case. I wouldn't have allowed DI Chapman's continued involvement if I'd felt it had. As you well know, Mr Baldwin, it's not uncommon for police officers to arrest the same person more than once, and we are talking about something unrelated that happened ten years ago.'

Baldwin looked at Liam for an answer. 'They said I tried to rape a probation officer. She told them a pack of lies, and they believed her. I was . . .'

'That's not true,' Chapman interrupted.

'Let my client finish, please, officer,' Baldwin frowned.

'I was only fifteen, and she came on to me, but I wasn't interested. She didn't like that I turned her down, so she made it all up to get back at me. My mum told Chapman I was at home all night, but he still arrested me.' Palmer glared at him, breathing heavily. Palmer's false accusation made Jessica clench both her fists tight with anger. He hadn't come up with that story when he was arrested ten years ago, and she wished she was in the room now to challenge his lies. She took a few deep breaths to calm herself down and listened carefully as Chapman responded.

'I met the victim that night, and from the state she was in, I had no doubt she was telling the truth. She didn't hear the offender break into her flat but woke up to find him standing by her bed, masturbating. He jumped on her, put his hand over her mouth and tried to rape her. Then, when she managed to scream, he ran off. Although he wore a balaclava, the victim recognised his voice and named William Palmer as the person responsible. The grounds for his arrest were completely justifiable, and I had no further involvement in the investigation,' Chapman said, matter-of-factly.

'I take it the CPS decided there was insufficient evidence to charge Mr Palmer,' Baldwin said.

'That is correct,' Anderson said. 'On the grounds that a reliable identification couldn't be made and there was no supporting forensic evidence. Now, getting back to the current investigation . . .'

Baldwin wasn't finished. 'Rape, attempted rape or any form of sexual assault are very traumatic for the victim and can also be for the officer investigating. From DI Chapman's tone when speaking about the incident, I feel he may still feel animosity towards Mr Palmer. His objectivity and impartiality are therefore questionable, constituting a clear conflict of interest.'

'I decide who will investigate this case, Mr Baldwin, not you. DI Chapman has done everything by the book, and I consulted with the commander in charge of major crime investigations, who agreed there is no conflict of interest. If you wish to make a formal complaint, feel free to do so after the interview, but first, there is other incriminating evidence we want to question Liam about.' Anderson nodded at Chapman to take over.

Chapman put three footmark photographs down on the table.

'These are photographs of footmarks recovered from your flat this morning. They are from Adidas Ultraboost trainers. You said earlier that you don't own that style of trainer. Can you tell us how those footmarks came to be in your flat?'

Palmer shrugged. 'Someone who came to the flat I suppose.'

Chapman put down three other photos of the same trainer. 'Would you agree the tread marks on these photos are the same as the other ones on the table?'

Palmer didn't even look at them. 'If you say so.' Chapman asked him again to look closely at them, which he did. He agreed they were the same type of footmark.

'This is absurd,' Baldwin complained. 'My client is not a footprint expert.'

'It doesn't take an expert to see the similarities, Mr Baldwin. I'm sure you will too if you take a closer look.'

'As my client said, a visitor could have left them in his flat,' Baldwin replied.

'That's true, but the second set of pictures are footmarks from Johan De Klerk's house left by the intruder who stabbed him. Our footmark expert has positively identified the marks in Liam's flat as coming from the same Ultraboost trainer that left marks at the crime scene. There are also matching footmarks in blood at De Klerk's house.'

Chapman laid photographs of the bloodstained footmarks on the table. 'We didn't find any Ultraboost trainers in your flat, Liam, so either you disposed of them after the crime, or someone came to your flat and left the footmarks before or shortly after the crime was committed. Which was it?' Chapman asked.

Baldwin could see the implications of the footmark evidence and shook his head at Liam, encouraging him to make a 'no comment' answer, but he ignored him. 'It must have been someone who visited me . . . or you put them there like you did with the money and the watch,' he replied angrily.

'You said earlier that no one visited your flat on Sunday or Monday.'

Palmer suddenly looked worried. 'Maybe someone did. I'm confused and can't remember now.'

'The five hundred pounds we found in your wallet. Does it belong to you?'

'Of course it does. It isn't nicked if that's what you're thinking.'

'That's a lot of cash to carry around,' Chapman remarked.

'I don't like using my bank card apart from withdrawing money. I know how much I'm spending when I've got cash in my pocket.'

'Are you saying you got that money from a cash point?'

Palmer nodded. 'It's all legit money.'

'That's still a lot, considering you can only draw out two hundred a day.'

'I was saving up to get a bike,' Palmer said, looking down at the table.

'We had the money in your wallet examined for fingerprints, and yours were on it.'

'Of course they were!' Palmer replied, obviously confused, as was Baldwin.

'So were Johan De Klerk's, along with marks from the Sealskins gloves, which were next to your prints on one of the notes. Our fingerprint expert said the odds of that happening by chance are a million to one.'

'I don't understand what you're saying! You're confusing me!' Palmer's voice had risen noticeably.

'The money in your wallet must have been in Mr De Klerk's possession at some point, and the only reasonable explanation is that you broke into his house, assaulted him and stole his money.'

'No, no, this is not right. You must have put the stolen money in my wallet as well!' Palmer shouted.

Baldwin put a hand on his arm. 'Just stay calm, Liam, this is all evidence not disclosed to me before the interview.'

Chapman shrugged, 'Life is full of surprises, Mr Baldwin. We also found De Klerk's fingerprints and some from the gloves on the cash hidden under the sink, again indicating it was taken from Mr De Klerk's house. The gloves and the trainers haven't been recovered because Liam disposed of them, probably when he set light to the Range Rover.' He looked at Liam, steely-eyed.

Palmer looked genuinely scared as he turned to Baldwin. 'No, no, he's lying. I didn't do it. This is all a fit-up.' Jessica had to admit she was enjoying watching Palmer squirm and was impressed by how Chapman had confronted him bit by bit with the incriminating evidence. It reminded her of Commander Williams's remarks about 'boiling the frog'.

'Do you own any other mobile phones besides the one you had on you when arrested?'

'No . . .' he said nervously.

Chapman put a photograph of the phone recovered from Palmer's flat on the table.

'This is a burner phone. Have you seen it before?'

'No, never.'

'It's been used to communicate solely through WhatsApp messages and calls with another burner phone. The first message received on it last Friday said, "he's going away Saturday morning, back Monday". Johan De Klerk was due to be away from his home over that period but cancelled his trip at the last minute.' He tapped the photo, 'The reply sent from this phone was, "will do job early hours Monday." Then, on Monday at 4 a.m., not long after the break-in, this same phone sent a message saying, "job done, call later".' Chapman paused to let it all sink in.

'Why are you looking at me like that?' Liam protested. 'I'm telling the truth. I swear to God I don't know anything about that phone.'

Chapman raised his eyes. 'It was also used to call the other burner at 3.10 p.m. on Monday and last used on Tuesday at 3.48 a.m. A message saying, "car torched" was sent to the other . . .'

'For fuck's sake, I've never made any calls or sent messages on that phone! Why are you doing this to me?' Liam screeched.

'Has cell site analysis been done on the phone you allegedly found at Liam's flat?' Baldwin asked Chapman.

'Some, yes, but it's still ongoing. I can tell you it was switched off at 8 p.m. last night. The last recorded location at that time was a cell mast in Montague Road, fifty metres from where Liam lives.' Chapman placed another photo on the table. 'Is that your bathroom toilet cistern, Liam?' He nodded, looking confused by the question. He started rubbing his eyes nervously. 'We found the burner phone in a waterproof bag hidden inside the cistern. Our lab said it had been wiped clean of fingerprints and DNA. Can you explain how it got there?'

Baldwin put his hand on Liam's arm to stop him from talking, but he shrugged him off and exploded with rage, swiping his hand across the table and scattering the photographs across the floor.

'It's you!' he shouted. 'You put it there. You put everything in my flat to frame me!' His lips were flecked with spittle and he seemed close to tears.

'We found these Adidas tracksuit bottoms and this hoodie in the communal bin at John Walsh Tower. Do they belong to you?' Chapman asked, holding up a photo.

'No, they don't, and you know it!' Liam wailed.

'The clothes had blood on them, which is being DNA tested. We believe it will be Johan De Klerk's blood, and we believe the clothing is yours.'

'I never went to his house or stabbed him.' Liam sunk his head in his hands and started to cry.

Chapman didn't say anything. 'Can you tell me how Liam came to be a suspect?' Baldwin asked Anderson.

'Anonymous information to Crime Stoppers after a press release. The informant said a man called Liam was trying to sell a Rolex watch to him in a local pub on Monday and . . .'

'I told you that, I fucking told you I was in the pub Monday lunchtime!' Liam burst out. 'But I didn't try to sell anyone a watch. You can ask the landlady, Pauline. She'll tell you I'm not lying.'

Chapman started speaking again. 'The informant gave us a description that matched Liam's and said he lived in a flat in John Walsh Tower, which we now know is owned by a Winston Brown.'

'Then this Winston Brown would have a key to the premises. He may have committed the crime and put the stolen property in the flat,' Baldwin suggested.

'Unlikely, as Winston's been in Jamaica for some time now. We believe he used to be in a relationship with Liam's mother and sublet the flat to him,' Chapman replied.

'The informant could be responsible,' Baldwin argued, but he sounded like he was grasping at straws now.

'There was no sign of forced entry,' Anderson said, 'so Liam must have let the informant into his flat or given him a set of keys. If so, this is his opportunity to tell us who the other person involved in the crime is. At present, everything points to him being responsible for the attempted murder of Johan De Klerk.'

Liam put his head in his hands. 'I didn't do any of this. I swear to you, I am telling you the truth, it's someone else.'

'Then tell us who that someone is,' Anderson said.

'I swear, don't know . . . if I did, believe me, I'd bloody tell you,' Liam pleaded.

'We've shown you overwhelming evidence that proves you were involved, and you've repeatedly lied to us.' Anderson said.

'I'm not lying.'

'You are, and you know it, Liam. The money in your wallet with Johan De Klerk's fingerprints and yours proves you were involved in the crime,' Chapman said.

Liam was crying uncontrollably as he turned to Baldwin, 'Please tell them to believe me, you got to make them believe I'm telling them the truth, I never done it.'

'I think you shouldn't answer any more questions, Liam,' Baldwin replied, stoney-faced.

'If you know anything at all about the crime, it would help you to tell us,' Chapman said.

There was a brief silence before Liam replied, his head bowed as he wiped his nose with his hand. He sounded almost childlike. 'She wasn't making it up – I lied, I got me mother to lie for me, she was so pissed she never knew what day it was. I'll admit it now, because you got to believe me that I'm telling the truth, it was me that broke into her flat, but I swear to God I didn't try to rape her,' Liam sobbed. Jessica was stunned. Why had Liam suddenly made this admission? Was it just guilt, or did he naively think it was a way out of his present dilemma?

'I would advise you not to say anything more, Liam,' Baldwin said, really concerned now.

Liam shook his head. 'It's me that could go to prison, not you. I'm prepared to admit what I did to that woman if it makes them believe I didn't stab that man or steal his money.'

'I hear what you say, but I strongly advise you to say nothing more for now,' Baldwin insisted.

'Just let me make my own decisions. I'm not listening to you anymore, you're full of bullshit. I want them to know so they'll believe me,' Liam said as he rubbed the tears from his eyes. Baldwin shook his head and sighed, knowing his advice was not going to be taken.

Anderson handed Liam a tissue. 'Tell us what happened with the probation officer.'

A distraught Palmer nodded as he blew his nose. 'Her name was Jessica. She had curly red hair and was really nice to me. I fell in love with her but knew she'd never love me back. I followed her home one day to find out where she lived. It was a ground-floor flat in Peckham. I'd use my electric scooter, go to her flat at night, hide behind a bush and watch her through the window with binoculars.'

'Were you hoping to see her naked in the bedroom?' Chapman asked.

'Yes, but I never did. She always wore a nightdress or towel when she closed the curtains.'

'Did you masturbate when you watched her from the bushes?' Anderson asked. Liam nodded, and Jessica felt a cold shiver run through her body. 'How long were you watching her for?'

'A couple of weeks.'

'How did you break into her flat?' Chapman asked, knowing the method of entry was important in case Liam changed his story later or said he deliberately lied, thinking it would help him in the De Klerk case.

'Through the kitchen window at the back. It was old and easy to force open quietly with a screwdriver. I was never going to rape her. I couldn't do that to her. I just wanted to see her in bed.'

'Masturbating while watching her, then breaking into her house suggests an intention to sexually assault her,' Anderson said.

He shook his head. 'I just wanted to be near her.'

'What happened when you went into her bedroom?' Chapman asked.

'She was wearing a nightdress, but it was hanging off her shoulder to one side and I could see part of her breast. I got an erection and started to masturbate. I wanted to see more of her body and slowly pulled the bed sheet back, but she woke up.'

'Were you still masturbating then?' Anderson asked.

'Yes, I could see the fear in her face and knew she was about to scream. I jumped on her and put my hand over her mouth. I said I wasn't going to hurt her, but she pulled my hand away, started to scream and I ran off home.' Palmer bowed his head, twisting the now sodden tissue between his fingers. He muttered something that was almost inaudible but sounded like a wretched apology.

As Palmer recounted the events of that terrifying night, Jessica felt as if she was being transported back in time. Everything he said was exactly as it happened, but she had no idea he had been watching her night after night and masturbating. She suddenly realised that the rest of the team were watching the interview in the main office and she wondered if they would work out that she was the victim. Jessica suspected Diane, who knew she used to be a probation officer, might figure it out but trusted her not to say anything to the others.

'Were you wearing a balaclava at the time?' Chapman asked.

'Yes. I threw it in a bin on the way home.'

'And you persuaded your mother to lie for you.'

Liam nodded, 'She was drunk, I told you, so pissed-up she didn't know what I was doing. But I knew she'd protect me, because I had stuff on her.' He looked up. 'I'm ashamed and sorry for what I did, but I wasn't going to rape her.'

'I find that hard to believe after the way you stalked your victim and broke into her house.' Chapman glanced up at the camera, knowing Jessica was watching.

'Will Liam be charged with a sexual offence?' Baldwin asked.

'I hope so, but that will be a decision for the CPS,' Anderson replied bluntly.

'Will I go to prison?' Liam asked, his voice shaking.

'A judge will decide that, but it's highly likely. Admitting that crime is to your credit but continuing to lie about your involvement in the De Klerk case isn't helping you. If found guilty, you could go to prison for attempted murder, which carries a life sentence.'

Liam looked shocked, as if he'd thought by admitting the sexual assault the other crimes would be dismissed. 'But you got to believe me, it had nothing to do with me. If I knew anything about it, I swear before God, I'd tell you.' He began sobbing again.

Chapman shook his head. 'You're lying, Liam. All the evidence we have points to you being involved in the burglary and assault on

Mr De Klerk. The calls and messages sent from the burner phone recovered in your toilet cistern suggest you were the person who broke into the house and stabbed him.'

'It wasn't me!' Liam shouted, standing up with his fists on the table.

'Sit down!' Chapman commanded. 'That's a lie, and you know it.'

'If you know, Liam, or can think of anyone who might be involved, then I suggest you tell the officers,' Baldwin said. Liam slumped back in his chair and put his hands over his face.

'I'm giving you one last chance to tell us the truth, Liam,' Anderson said, but Liam didn't answer.

'I don't think there's anything more to be achieved by continuing this interview,' Baldwin said.

Anderson nodded. 'I will call the Crown Prosecution Service and seek their advice on which crimes Liam should be charged with. This interview is concluded.'

Liam looked devastated. 'Wait a minute, please, you have to believe me. I haven't committed any crimes since the burglary when I got run over. I got a place to live and a job. I've worked hard, and I don't want to lose it all, so please just let me go.'

'You need to speak with Mr Baldwin, Liam,' Anderson said as he turned the tape off. He and Chapman left the room.

CHAPTER TWENTY-TWO

Jessica could feel her heart racing as she switched off the live link. She sat back in her chair and ran her hands through her hair. Hearing Palmer's admission had brought back an intense visual recall of everything that had happened that night. It was so vivid, it felt as if she was back in her bedroom and he was once again looking at her through the eye holes of his balaclava and licking his lips before he pounced on her. Jessica doubted Palmer was telling the truth when he said he had no intent to rape her, but although his admission suggested he would plead guilty, there was always a chance he might change his mind, and it would be another harrowing experience giving evidence against him.

Jessica thought about her meetings with him as a probation officer. She wondered if she had missed any signs of him being obsessed with her, but nothing came to mind. He found it hard to engage in conversation, was withdrawn, and disliked talking about his family life. Due to his ADHD, he was hyperactive and impulsive, but as far as she could recall, he was never disruptive or aggressive, unlike some of the young offenders she dealt with. She wondered if Palmer had suffered from limerence, a very intense desire, infatuation, or obsession with a person that is often uncontrollable, which people with ADHD were often more prone to. She was also aware that teenagers with ADHD may have a higher-than-normal sex drive and trouble with impulse control and resisting temptation.

Reflecting on Palmer's condition made Jessica think of something that she, Anderson and Chapman might have inadvertently failed to consider. She picked up his criminal record file and flicked through his arrest entries. She found exactly what she feared might be there when looking at his arrest for the attempted rape by Chapman.

Jessica hurried through to the main office, where Guy, Diane and Taff were huddled together discussing Palmer's second interview. Jessica wondered if they were talking about her, but that wasn't her main concern.

'Looks like Palmer's up shit creek without a paddle,' Taff said with a smile.

'Guy, I'm not very knowledgeable about police custody procedures, but would an adult with ADHD need an appropriate adult present during an interview?' Jessica asked.

'Depends on the circumstances. PACE, the Police and Criminal Evidence Act, states that anyone who is known or suspected to have a mental disorder or mental vulnerability must be interviewed with an appropriate adult present.'

'Can a solicitor be the appropriate adult?' Jessica asked.

'It's extremely rare, and only if they are not acting as a solicitor. I take it you are asking because you think Palmer might have ADHD.'

'I know he has. It's in his file. When Palmer was arrested as a juvenile for the attempted rape, he had an appropriate adult present during the interview. I think he should have had one for both the interviews with Anderson and Chapman.'

'I don't get what the problem is,' Taff remarked.

'If the police have breached their statutory duty to provide an appropriate adult, it could have serious ramifications in court. A judge could rule the interviews as inadmissible evidence,' Guy told him.

'Oh, shit. That's not good,' Taff said.

'Anderson and Chapman may not be responsible for the error,

though,' Guy continued. 'The Codes of Practice state that if the custody officer believes the detained person is a vulnerable adult, they must arrange for an appropriate adult to be present during the interview. But if Palmer or his solicitor didn't mention his ADHD, how were they to know?'

'But shouldn't they have looked at his previous convictions before interviewing him?' Diane asked.

Guy shook his head. 'There's no regulation that says you have to, and you might well only look at the more recent arrests and convictions anyway. Palmer's been arrested several times since the attempted rape, both as a juvenile and an adult. Did he have an appropriate adult present for any of those interviews?' he asked Jessica.

'As far as I can see, only as a juvenile.'

'Under PACE, when a juvenile is questioned by the police, the presence of an appropriate adult is required by law, so that may be why they were present, and it had nothing to do with his ADHD.'

'Let's hope so. Thanks, Guy. You've made me feel a bit easier about it,' Jessica said.

'Ultimately, any decision about the validity of the interviews would be down to the CPS or the judge trying the case. Watching Palmer in the interview, I would never have thought he had ADHD or any form of learning difficulty. He's simply lying,' Guy said.

'But what if he is telling the truth?' Jessica said. They looked at each other in surprise.

'You can't seriously think Chapman planted everything in Palmer's flat,' Taff said.

'Of course not,' Jessica said. 'But some things about this investigation don't make sense. We need to dig a bit deeper. Our priority now is to identify who has the other burner phone. I also want to review all the evidence from the De Klerk's house and Palmer's flat.'

'Someone might have given the bin bag to Liam to dispose of,' Guy suggested.

'Palmer's fingerprints weren't on it, but there were also marks from the Sealskinz gloves,' Taff added.

'I'll take swabs from the waistband of the trackie bottoms and the collar of the hoodie to test for the wearer's DNA. If it isn't Palmer's, then it's unlikely he dumped the clothing,' Diane said.

'Check if there's any hairs in the hoodie. If there are, they can't be Palmer's, for obvious reasons. Taff, did you fingerprint the cistern cover?'

'No. I didn't think finding Palmer's prints on it would prove anything.'

'I'm interested to know if any marks from the Sealskinz gloves are on it.'

Taff sighed. 'Sorry, Jess, I should have done that.'

'Don't be silly. None of us thought of it at the time.' Jessica pulled a set of keys from her pocket and handed them to Taff. 'DS Wood sent these over. They're for the new locks on Palmer's flat.'

'I'll go look at the cistern lid after this meeting,' Taff said, putting the keys in his pocket.

'Will he need a warrant? Diane asked.

'Not if the one issued covers multiple entry. There will be a copy of it on HOLMES. I'll have a quick look now,' Guy said and went to his desk.

'Palmer might have been holding the phone and other stuff for someone,' Diane suggested.

'It's possible, but from his reaction in the interview, I don't think so. And the clothing in the bin could have been put there to make us think Palmer disposed of it,' Jessica said.

'Well done for asking for the bins to be searched,' Diane said. 'This unknown suspect appears to be very forensically aware.'

Jessica nodded. 'I agree. Whereas Palmer doesn't strike me as being that bright. If he committed the crime, it's more likely we would have found the Ultraboost trainers and Sealskinz gloves at his flat or in the bin.'

Taff nodded. 'We didn't find a hydraulic door breacher or any crowbars at Palmer's either. There was no tool kit or anything to suggest he was an active burglar. So maybe the unknown suspect still has the items we're missing.'

Jessica agreed. 'Palmer doesn't appear to be a smoker either. There were no ashtrays or cigarette butts in his flat, and he had no cigarettes on him when arrested, nor was he ever in the Paras. All of which suggests he may not be the owner of the Zippo lighter.'

'It's a multiple entry warrant, so another search is fine,' Guy said, returning from his desk. 'What do you make of the money in his wallet with De Klerk's and the glove prints on it?' he asked Jessica.

'It's a bit odd, and he did seem very nervous when asked about it. For me, he either removed some money from the stash under the sink or someone gave it to him, possibly as a form of payment for doing something, which could be why he's lying about where he got it from.'

'The other person could be a hardened criminal, and Palmer's scared of him,' Guy suggested.

'That's a possibility. Can you identify Palmer's IP address and see if he was online playing games during the relevant times?' Jessica asked, referring to the Internet Protocol address, a unique numerical label assigned to any device connected to a computer network.

Guy nodded. 'I can check his phone, laptop and the game boxes. They record the date, time and location of his internet connections, websites visited and online services accessed. I'll need to ask the internet provider for a more detailed record, which will require a warrant.'

'See what you can get from the items you mentioned first,' Jessica told him.

'Is there any way you can trace who sent the anonymous information to Crimestoppers?' Diane asked Guy.

'No. Their system is designed to protect your identity and cannot physically trace your IP address. When you fill out an online form, your device's IP address is overwritten, masking it. However, if we can find the device we think might have been used, the browsing history, cookies and cache might confirm if he visited the Crimestoppers site. If he's deleted them, the service provider might be able to help us. If he used a virtual private network, though, the data becomes unreadable to the service provider and network administrators.'

'The DNA you found on the Rolex watch – can you have a result by tomorrow morning, Di?'

'I'll do my best.'

'I'm not saying Palmer wasn't involved in the crime in some way, but as you can see, a lot of things don't add up or fit with his personality. Is there anything else you think we should be looking at to prove or disprove Palmer's involvement or identify our unknown suspect?' They looked at each other, but no one answered.

'Are you going to tell Anderson about what we've just discussed?' Diane asked.

'I'll have to, but first I want to know what results Guy gets from his digital examinations. I then need to draw up a report detailing all the evidence that shows Palmer is or isn't involved in the crime. It will no doubt upset Anderson and some members of his team, but no matter what anyone thinks of Liam Palmer, it would be wrong to let an innocent man go to prison for something he didn't do.' They all nodded their agreement, then Jessica got up and headed to her office. Diane watched her go, then turned to Taff.

'She never ceases to amaze me. I mean, I was emotionally distressed listening to that piece of shit. I can only imagine what it was like for her.'

Taff nodded. 'She keeps a lot hidden, that one.'

'Maybe that's not such a good thing,' Diane said, getting up.

Jessica had just started typing her report when there was a knock at the door, and Diane entered. 'I just thought I'd ask how you were feeling after the interview.'

Jessica smiled ruefully. 'I thought you'd guess it was me Palmer was talking about.'

'I haven't said anything to the others, and I don't intend to.'

'Thanks, I appreciate that.'

'Do Anderson and Chapman know?'

'Yes, and I have to say Anderson was actually very understanding. He spoke with Commander Williams, and that's why she was here earlier. Thankfully, they both agreed there was no conflict of interest and decided I should remain on the investigation.'

'That's good. Anderson must realise how much he needs you. Anyway, I'll let you get on with your report.' She turned to leave.

'You don't need to worry about me, Di. Watching the interview hasn't made me an emotional wreck or anything.'

Diane gave her a sympathetic look. 'It must have been terrifying for you. I was close to tears when Palmer was talking about it. I know he confessed, but to accuse you of coming on to him was sick beyond belief.'

Jessica shrugged. 'He felt trapped and thought making false allegations against me and Chapman was his way out.'

'So, you don't think he was going to assault you before he ran off?'

'I did at the time, and it was a terrifying experience, but I've learned to cope with it.'

'Through your yoga and meditation?'

'That's helped, but I had a lot of counselling before I started meditating. You might find this hard to believe, but hearing Palmer confess has made me feel better, maybe given me some kind of closure. And strange as it may sounds, I now have some sympathy for him.'

'How can you feel sympathy after what he did to you?'

Jessica told her about the terrible childhood Palmer had endured, living with an alcoholic mother and a violent, drug-addicted father. Diane winced as Jessica described how Palmer's father smashed his head against a wall when he was eight, which probably caused his ADHD.

'That's tragic, and I understand why you feel some sympathy for him, but it doesn't excuse what he did to you. If it was me, I'd still like to punch the living daylights out of him.'

'I'm not saying it does excuse what he did to me. But from the way he reacted, I believe he feels genuine remorse.'

Diane looked sceptical. 'Well, just hear me out – do you not think he might have confessed because he thought it would help him wriggle his way out of the other things he's accused of?'

'Yes, but probably just through desperation, if he's being accused of an attempted murder he didn't commit.'

'Well, he's lying about something, so he's only himself to blame,' Diane said.

'It's not in my nature to see someone suffer for something they might not have done.'

'I know. And that makes you a good person,' Diane said. 'But you have to think of yourself as well. You know I'm a good listener if you ever need to talk.'.

Jessica got up and embraced her. 'I know,' she said as they hugged each other tightly.

CHAPTER TWENTY-THREE

Jessica was reviewing the forensic evidence and writing her report when Chapman called. 'Sorry, I was in a meeting with Anderson and then speaking to the CPS. How are you after the interview? I was worried about how upsetting it must have been for you, listening to Palmer's story about you fancying him.'

'Hearing him say that and then recounting what he did to me was quite harrowing, but I also feel a sense of relief that he finally confessed. What did the CPS say?' she asked, not wanting to dwell any more on the interview.

'There is sufficient evidence to provide a realistic prospect of a conviction, so they recommend charging Palmer with attempted murder, aggravated burglary and arson.'

Jessica was taken aback. 'Even though it's clear from the burner phones and other evidence that someone else was involved?'

'They considered it a joint enterprise crime, which means Palmer can be convicted if he planned it with another person, was present, helped or encouraged others to commit the crime, even if he didn't participate in the offences himself.'

'I see.' Jessica wondered if it was the right time to raise her concerns about Palmer's involvement.

'What did you think of the interview?' Chapman asked.

'I thought you and Anderson worked well together. I liked how you casually showed Palmer the photographs and asked harmless questions before challenging his answers with more direct ones. It revealed he was lying about some things.'

'Anderson is over the moon and he's delighted with you and your team's quick results. He even phoned Williams to sing your praises. You might get a commendation on your first case! All we need to do now is identify the other person or persons involved, and the case is closed. Have you got any forensic updates that might help us on that?'

'Yes, I have. We can discuss them when we go for a drink later.'

'Slight change of plan there, I'm afraid.'

'Oh, right. Are you bailing on me?'

'I need to go to The Bell, a pub on Leytonstone High Road.'

'Any particular reason?'

'Palmer said he went there Monday lunchtime, and the anonymous informant said he tried to sell a Rolex in a local pub. I thought it might be worth popping in and asking a few questions.'

'I can meet you there if you like,' Jessica said, eager to speak to him face-to-face.

'It's a bit of a dive, you know, the sort of place frequented by criminals. I could meet you at The Bull in Chislehurst around eight if that's not too late.'

'No, that's fine. I fancy doing a bit of detective work.'

'OK, do you want to come here first and we'll go in my car?'

'Sounds like a plan. I've got a report to finish, so I'll be with you about six.'

*   *   *

Jessica had just finished her report and printed copies for Chapman and Anderson when Taff rang. 'You were right about the cistern lid. Prints from the Sealskinz gloves and Palmer's are on it. Luckily, whoever changed the lock left the old one in the kitchen. I'll examine the interior components at the lab under a microscope and look for any fresh scratches or tool marks. If someone did fit Palmer up, they could have picked the lock to get in there.'

'Good thinking, Taff. There's no need to come back here. You can do it first thing in the morning.'

'I'd rather get it done right away. I'll head back now and let you know the result later.'

'Thanks. I'm off to Barking to see Chapman and update him on our findings, so I'll see you tomorrow.'

'I doubt he or Anderson will be very pleased.'

'Well, all we can do is present them with the forensic evidence as we find it. What they do with it is up to them.'

When she arrived at Barking, Jessica called Chapman and said she was in the yard. She locked the car, then untied her hair and fluffed it out. 'That suits you,' he said when he saw her.

She smiled. 'If you have curly red hair as a kid, you get teased a lot and learn to keep it tucked away. I feel more myself like this.'

'So, what's the latest on the forensic evidence?' he asked as they got in his car and he pulled out of the yard.

She took her report from her briefcase. 'I don't think you'll like it, but . . .'

'You're going to tell me anyway,' he smiled. Jessica read from the report, covering everything she had discussed with her team earlier. She also told him about the prints on the toilet cistern and lock that Taff was going to examine.

Chapman frowned. 'Anderson's not going to like it. He's convinced Palmer's our man.'

'Do you honestly think he could scale the De Klerk's garden wall with his bad leg?'

'He managed to run away with no problem when we went to arrest him.'

'Going down a few flights of stairs is not the same as climbing over a twelve-foot wall.'

Chapman sighed. 'All right, if it makes you feel better, I suppose he could have been stitched up.'

'It's not about making me feel better. It's about finding out the truth!' she said sharply.

'Believe it or not, that's what we were trying to do in the bloody interview!' he replied.

'If you're worried about telling Anderson, I'm happy to do it,' she said.

'I'll tell him tomorrow,' he said, shaking his head. 'But no doubt he'll want to speak to you about it.'

'Then let's just do it together.'

'He'll want to know why you're defending Palmer.'

'I'm not defending him. I'm just doing my job, as are the rest of my team.'

'But you do agree that Palmer is involved in some way?' he said.

'I believe he is hiding something. It is odd that the CCTV cameras went down at the garage the night the car was set alight, for instance.'

'There's also the missing petrol can.'

'Yes, but we can't prove he stole it.'

He slapped his hand on the steering wheel in exasperation. 'Why are you defending him, after what he did to you?'

'For Christ's sake, don't you start as well,' Jessica retorted. 'What Palmer did to me has nothing to do with the current investigation.'

'I'm sorry, I didn't mean to upset you.'

She took a deep breath. 'I just think it might be worth interviewing Palmer again. Now he's had time to think about things, he might be more forthcoming.'

'There are legal issues around questioning a suspect after they've been charged unless new information has come to light.'

'What about speaking to Palmer, off the record.'

'I'm not putting my job on the line for him.'

'But you'll let him go to prison for a crime he might not have committed.'

'Palmer should have thought of the consequences before he got involved,' he said stubbornly.

'Look, can we just drop it for now, go to the pub and make some enquiries?' Chapman said, trying for a more conciliatory tone. Jessica didn't reply, and neither spoke for the rest of the journey to the pub.

Ten minutes later they passed The Bell, as Chapman drove slowly along Leytonstone High Road, looking for a parking spot. Two large signs said 'All the Great Sporting Action – Sky Sports' and by the front entrance was a large blackboard sign saying 'Live Karaoke Every Friday, Regular Bingo, Live Bands and Quizes', spelt with one z.

Chapman eventually found a parking space and asked Jessica if she had the RingGo app on her phone to pay online. 'Can't you put a police sticker on the dashboard?'

'I would normally. But around here, it'll get the car keyed or the tyres slashed.'

'That's good to know. Are we likely to get mugged as well?' she said, raising her eyebrows.

'I did say it was a rough area, but you insisted on coming.'

'No. You said the pub was a bit of a dive, and if the outside is anything to go by, you were right.'

'You can wait in the car if you want.'

'If it's going to be vandalized, I'd rather come with you.' He laughed, the tension between them broken.

*　*　*

The Bell was a traditional pub with an open interior and large arches leading to a dining area on one side and a pool table and darts board on the other. The long bar was wood with several bar stools in front of it and tables and chairs to one side. It was only 6.30 and the pub was quiet; a few people were sitting at the bar, and some were in the dining area having a meal. The décor was a bit run down, but the inside was reasonably clean and tidy. Jessica noticed TVs on nearly every wall, showing different sports.

'There's more TVs in here than Curry's,' Jessica said, which made Chapman smile.

'What'll you have to drink?' he asked.

'A glass of Sauvignon Blanc if they've got it,' she said. While he was getting the drinks, Chapman discreetly showed the young barmaid his warrant card and asked to speak to the landlord or landlady. She told him the manager was away on a golf trip, but his wife Pauline was out the back and she'd fetch her.

Chapman and Jessica sat at a corner table, and after a couple of minutes, a lady with short-cut blonde hair in her early fifties approached them and introduced herself as Pauline Holland, the landlady.

'How can I help you, officers?' she asked.

Chapman leaned forward, speaking quietly. 'We were wondering if you had anyone in here trying to sell a watch on Monday or Tuesday just gone.'

'What sort of watch?'

'A man's Rolex, with a black face and a diamond-studded dial,' Chapman said.

'No, definitely not. Me and my husband run a decent pub. If we think someone is trying to sell hooky gear, we give them a warning and say to do it elsewhere, or you're barred.'

Chapman got a picture of Palmer out of his pocket. 'Do you know this man?'

'Yeah, I've seen him in here before. He's as bald as a coot, so it's hard not to notice him. What's he been up to?'

'His name is Liam Palmer, and we heard he was trying to sell a Rolex in here.'

Pauline chuckled. 'Are you being serious? I'd soon know if he had, and believe me, he'd have been out on his arse before he knew it. Excuse me a second.'

'Is there anything else you can tell me about Liam?' Chapman asked.

Pauline shrugged. 'He comes in here now and again, but mostly at lunchtime 'cause he works nights, though I have seen him on the occasional Saturday night.'

'Has Liam ever tried to sell or buy any property you thought might be stolen?'

Pauline shook her head. 'No, never, and like I say, I'd soon know if he had. The older punters don't like troublemakers coming in here, so they always tell me or my husband who is up to no good. I give them a free pint to tell me what's going on. It's like having an extra pair of eyes and ears in the place. None of them have ever said Liam is a wrong 'un.'

'What do you make of Liam?' Jessica asked.

'What do I make of him? I dunno, seems a nice lad. He's quite shy, you know, pretty much keeps himself to himself. He likes a game of pool and often just plays on his own if it's quiet. He comes out of his shell a bit when he's pissed.'

'Is there anyone he particularly mixes with, or you'd consider a friend?' Jessica asked.

'Not really. If you talk to him, he'll talk to you, but mostly just about the latest computer games.'

'We found a stolen laptop and two games consoles at his flat. He said he got them at a car boot sale, but we think he bought them knowing they were stolen,' Chapman told Pauline.

'Liam's not the brightest, if you know what I mean. I'd say it'd be easy to pull the wool over his eyes.'

Chapman nodded. 'If, say, Liam wanted to buy a games console, an iPad or something like that on the cheap, is there anyone you can think of he might approach, but not in here necessarily?' Chapman asked.

Pauline looked around to see if anyone was listening, then leaned forward. 'You might want to speak to a real nasty bugger called Wheeler, aka The Dealer.'

'Wheeler handles stolen gear then?' Chapman asked.

'I didn't say that, but supposedly he's the man to go to if you want something cheap with no questions asked. He's a big bloke, too, and quick with his fists.'

'Has Wheeler ever caused any trouble in here?'

'He did once a couple of months back. Knocked a young lad out with a sucker punch from behind. My old man Mick doesn't stand for any nonsense. Wheeler backed off when Mick confronted him with a pool cue. He barred him. Thankfully, he's not been in since.'

'Do you know Wheeler's first name?' Chapman asked.

'No, I just know everyone calls him Wheeler or The Dealer. Hang on, I'll be back in a second.' Pauline went and spoke with the barmaid.

'I think it might be worth our while trying to find this Wheeler and having a chat with him,' Chapman said.

Pauline returned. 'Holly was born and bred around here. She thinks Wheeler's first name is John or Jim, and he might live in one of the tower blocks on Montague Road.'

'Did Holly know which one?' Chapman asked.

'No, but Liam lives in one of them as well. I also asked her if Liam and Wheeler were friends. She doubted it.'

'Do you know if Wheeler was ever in the military?' Jessica asked.

Pauline shrugged. 'No idea, but he's a big bugger and looks fit. If that's all, I need to finish my bookkeeping darlin'.'

'Thanks for your help. It's much appreciated. Can I buy you a drink?' Chapman asked.

'Not while I'm working, thanks. I hope Liam's not in any serious trouble. Like I said, he's a nice lad, and having worked in this business all my life, I know a wrong 'un when I see one.'

As they walked back to the car, Jessica's phone rang. It was Guy. They spoke for a few minutes while Chapman waited. In the car, Jessica told Chapman what she'd learned. 'Guy checked out the stolen games consoles and Palmer's phone use from Saturday night through to 7 a.m. Tuesday when the Range Rover was found.'

'And . . . ?' Chapman asked, already guessing what was coming.

'He was at home using the Xbox and PlayStation from 9 p.m. Sunday night until 3 a.m. Monday. According to the cell mast data, his phone never moved from his house. If the digital data is right, it's highly unlikely Palmer broke into De Klerk's house.'

'He had the burner phone, though,' Chapman replied.

'Palmer was playing against other people online throughout the night. On Monday, while he was at work, he used his phone to play games and watch TV shows virtually all night.'

'He could still have left to torch the car,' Chapman replied.

'Maybe, but his phone was linked to the garage's Wi-Fi all night and was never picked up by the mast nearest Wanstead Golf Course. The only movement shown is from his house to work and back.'

Chapman sighed. 'Shit, it looks like you were right about him being a fall guy. We need to know more about this bloke Wheeler.' He called DS Wood, who was still in the Barking office, and asked him to do an electoral roll check on both John Welsh and Fred Wigg towers for the names Jim and John Wheeler to try and identify a flat number. They sat patiently in the car, waiting for DS Wood to call back. But Jessica's phone rang first. It was Taff, and she put the call on speakerphone.

'The prints on the cistern are from the same Sealskinz gloves. I took Palmer's old front door lock to bits and did a cursory examination. From the scratch detail and marks inside, I'd say a battery-operated lock pick gun was used to open it. They're not cheap, the sort of thing a professional locksmith or experienced burglar would use.'

'OK, good work, Taff. Now go home and get some rest and tell Diane to do the same.' Shortly after she ended the call, Chapman's phone rang. He turned on the speakerphone, hoping for good news.

'No luck with a Wheeler living at John Walsh or Fred Wigg Tower blocks, I'm afraid,' Wood said.

'Bollocks, but thanks for trying, Julian. Anyone known to us going by those names?'

'I got a few possible hits with criminal records. The most likely one is a John Wheeler, white, aged thirty-four, six feet tall with crew-cut brown hair. He's got form for burglary, handling stolen goods and grievous bodily harm. He's been inside a couple of times but hasn't been nicked recently. I'll send you a photo.'

'Certainly sounds like the man we are looking for,' Chapman said.

Wood continued. 'There was something else that might of interest in his criminal record file. He's got a parachute regiment tattoo.'

'Now we're getting somewhere. What was his last known address?' Chapman asked eagerly.

'Westbourne House, Romford Road, in Forest Gate.'

'That's a halfway house for prisoners on parole,' Jessica said, recalling it from her probation officer days.

'Correct. Wheeler was released from prison eighteen months ago and sent there to transition back into the community.'

'That's not far from here.' He started the car.

'I wouldn't bother,' Wood said. 'I rang the manager, who told me Wheeler left in a hurry about a year ago after he beat the shit out of another resident. He's still wanted for questioning about it and hasn't been seen since. I'll carry on digging to see if I can find his current whereabouts.'

'OK. If Anderson's still there, don't say anything. I'll bring him up to speed when I get back,' Chapman said.

Wood laughed. 'He went home ages ago. Now Palmer's been charged, he's all cock-a-hoop.'

'He might not be for much longer,' Chapman said despondently. 'It's looking more likely Palmer is a patsy and had nothing to do with the De Klerk stabbing. The money, the Rolex, it's all a set-up to put him in the frame.'

'Jesus Christ, are you serious?' Wood asked, stunned by the news.

'Yes. It's more likely this guy Wheeler might be involved with someone other than Palmer.'

'I wouldn't want to be in your shoes when you tell Anderson,' Wood laughed.

Chapman ended the call, sat back and let out a big sigh. 'So close yet so far. If it was Wheeler who broke into De Klerk's, stabbed him and fitted up Palmer, he'll be long gone by now.'

'I doubt he's as smart as he thinks,' Jessica said. 'I'm confident you'll find him.'

'Well, let's bloody well hope so. I'll drop you back at the station, then call Anderson. You may as well go home. I'll ring you later with an update.'

Jessica sat back in the passenger seat. She thought about Wheeler and possible ways of locating him, and one came to mind. 'If Palmer and Wheeler are connected, they must have made contact somehow,' she said.

'Agreed, but we don't know where or when. Palmer denied being involved or knowing anyone who was. The landlady at The Bell said he was a loner . . .'

'If they know each other, Palmer may have John Wheeler, The Dealer or JW in his phone contacts or even an email address. If he does, we can track the current location of Wheeler's phone to try to locate him. And if we get a possible number, the service provider may have a home address for Wheeler.'

'That's good thinking. Give Guy a call.'

'I told him to go home. My team has worked their backsides off today, and they all need some rest. I'll text Guy and ask him to check Palmer's phone again first thing in the morning.'

'OK, we're all tired. Time to call it a day.'

Arriving back at Barking, they saw DS Wood getting into his car. Chapman beeped his horn to get his attention and they both went over to talk to him.

'Any luck in tracing an address for Wheeler?'

'No, if I had, you know I'd have called you. On a positive note, though . . . the hospital rang earlier and said De Klerk is recovering more quickly than expected. He's been moved from the ICU to a private room, although he hasn't regained consciousness yet. But they're hoping he will in the next twenty-four hours.'

'Good, because we need to speak to him about the contents of his safe,' Chapman said.

'Sorry to be rude, but this is for Mike's ears only,' Wood said, taking Chapman to one side. Jessica shrugged and headed towards her car, leaving them to talk in private.

'Has Anderson turned up?' Chapman asked.

'No. He's probably in his pinny cleaning the house while his wife watches TV.'

'So what's up then?'

'You remember DS Richard Stubbings? He left the job three or four years ago.'

'Yeah, after being sacked for gross misconduct. As I recall, he was caught accessing sensitive data and suspected of passing it on to a private investigator he knew.'

'It was a misunderstanding, and no payments were ever involved,' Wood said.

'We both know that's a load of bollocks. But why are you bringing him up?'

'We joined the job together and are still in touch. Stubbs called me and said he's got some info on the De Klerk case but wants to speak privately. I'm off to meet him in the pub.'

'Why didn't he contact you before now?'

'He was in Spain working on a case and only got back last night. Stubbs's work partner saw the news, told him about it this morning and he called me this afternoon.'

'Don't tell me Stubbings is working for the private investigator he passed information to.'

Wood grinned. 'I've always said you're a good detective. Whatever the info is, Stubbs is wary about talking over the phone. It might be something or nothing, but I won't know until I speak to him.'

'Be careful. He might be tapping you for information to pass onto the press.'

'For fuck's sake, Mike. I wasn't involved in the press leak, and nor was Stubbs.'

'I didn't say you were. I'm just saying to be careful. I'm not a fan of Stubbings. I always thought he was an arrogant prat who strutted around like he was God's gift.'

'He's not all bad, and he's kept his nose clean since he left the job. If you're that worried, why don't you come with me.'

'No, thanks. I can think of better things to do than socialising with Stubbings. Just be careful, Julian, and for God's sake don't tell him anything about the case.'

'I'm not stupid, Mike. I'll let you know how I get on tomorrow.' Wood got back in his car.

'What was that all about?' Jessica asked, sitting in her car with the door open.

Chapman leaned in. 'He's got an informant who might have some useful information, but somehow I doubt it. I'm going to leave it until the morning to tell Anderson about Palmer, Wheeler and our conversation with Pauline Holland. I don't feel like arguing with him over the phone.'

'In that case, I'm not letting you do it alone. We're in this together, and Anderson needs to hear all the facts . . . from both of us,' Jessica said.

'Thanks, I could do with your support. Anyway, we're both knackered and need to get some sleep. Shall we meet here early and review everything we've got before speaking to Anderson?'

'Yes. I think that would be useful. What time?'

'There's a lot to discuss, and Anderson usually gets in between eight and nine. Is between six and six thirty too early?'

She shook her head. 'That's fine by me.'

'Convincing him that Palmer might be innocent won't be easy . . .'

'Only a fool would ignore the evidence. That said . . .'

Chapman laughed and eased her car door shut as she started the engine. He stood watching her drive out. 'You're quite something, Jessica Russell,' he said to himself.

* * *

As DS Wood entered the Rose and Crown in Woodford Green, he saw Richard Stubbings sitting in the corner, reading the paper. 'I'll have a pint of Guinness, Stubbs,' he said as he approached.

Stubbings got up and winced as he shook Wood's hand.

'How are you doing, Stubbs?'

'Not bad, mate. Bloody sciatica is not getting any better though.'

'You have had that for months now. Have you been to the doctor?'

'Yeah. He said it might be nerve damage, put me on meds and gave me a load of exercises to do. Even suggested fucking Pilates. All bollocks, so it looks like I'm stuck with it.'

'Sorry to hear that.'

'I can live with it. The pain is not too bad, but it's given me a limp.'

'How's work going?'

'Just had an interesting job in the Costa del Sol. I spent a week in Marbella, with all expenses paid by the client.'

'What was that about then?'

'Following a cheating husband. He spent every night in the Navy Bar in Puerto Banús. The place is full of expensive, gorgeous hookers. The guy's got his own haulage company and is loaded. Anyway, I managed to befriend him, and he even treated me to a night of debauchery with two gorgeous tarts. I got a few pictures of him shagging one of them. The result is his wife wants a divorce and half of everything he's got, which is a bloody fortune. I felt a bit sorry for him. I mean, it wasn't as if he had a proper bit on the side. Guinness, wasn't it?'

Wood shook his head in dismay as Stubbings limped to the bar. He could tell he was trying to big up his private investigator job and actually wished he was still a detective investigating murders and serious crimes. But then again, Stubbs only had himself to blame.

'Cheers, Woody,' Stubbings said as he handed him his pint.

'Cheers. So, what have you got for me on the De Klerk case?' Wood asked, taking a sip of his Guinness.

'This is strictly between us, OK? The client made me sign a non-disclosure agreement. If they found out I gave you any information, it could destroy me financially and the PI company I'm a partner in.'

'You know you can trust me, Stubbs.'

'I wouldn't be sitting here talking to you if I didn't. We go back a long way, Woody, and we always had each other's backs.'

Wood put his pint down. 'Don't take this the wrong way, but what do you want from me in return?'

'Nothing, apart from the next round. The thing is, I can't stand the client.'

'Are we talking about a male or female client?'

Stubbings looked around, then leaned forward, speaking quietly. 'We're talking about Michelle De Klerk, aka "that bitch Belsham". I think she might be involved in what happened to her husband.'

'Are you serious?' Wood asked.

'Deadly serious. Take it from me. She's only interested in herself and her career. There's a jeweller called Nathan Cole you need to check out and a friend of hers called Chandice Bramston you need to talk to. Just don't mention my name for Christ's sake.'

'There's always a way round, Stubbs,' Wood said reassuringly. 'Just tell me everything you know.'

CHAPTER TWENTY-FOUR

Michelle De Klerk sat beside her husband's bed in the private room he'd just been moved to, wanting to be there when he woke up. She watched his heart monitor, willing it not to stop beating, and felt a sense of relief as she noticed his eyes twitch and his fingers move during the night. Exhausted, she wrapped a blanket around herself and eventually fell into a deep sleep. Around 2 a.m., the night nurse entered the room. She moved quietly, checking Johan's pulse and heart monitor, careful not to disturb Michelle. After completing her task, she left to prepare her report, dimming the room lights on her way out.

About an hour later, Johan began to stir and then, suddenly, he was awake. For a moment, he felt disoriented, taking steady, deep breaths. As his eyes adjusted to the semi-darkness, he focused on Michelle's sleeping figure beside him, but he couldn't understand why she was there or where he was or why there was excruciating pain coursing through his entire body.

He slowly began to take in the darkened room and tried to remember what had happened and how he had got there, but nothing made sense. His mouth was dry, and his tongue felt too big for his mouth. He closed his eyes, feeling as though he was trapped in a nightmare. Another hour passed; he felt less pain but was still unable to lift his head. This time, however, he found that he could form words.

'Michelle, Michelle . . . wake up,' Johan croaked weakly. He closed his eyes then tried again.

She shot up, hardly believing he was awake, throwing the blanket aside and crossing to the bed. He was struggling to sit up.

'Oh my God, my love, I'm here, I'm here, let me help you, don't move.' Michelle eased one of his pillows up, then perched beside him, taking hold of his hand and kissing it.

'I've been trying to wake you for ages,' he said, sounding groggy.

'I was exhausted. I've been here for you all the time. How are you feeling?'

'Really rough. My body aches like hell, and my throat is killing me. Can you give me some water?' he rasped.

Michelle went to the bottle beside her chair. She held it gently to Johan's mouth. He took a few sips and then licked his lips.

'What day is it?'

'It's Thursday morning now. Someone broke into the house and assaulted you in the early hours of Monday morning. You were badly injured, and the doctor put you in an induced coma.' She couldn't tell whether he took in what she had just said.

'What hospital am I in?'

'Hackney. Can you remember what happened?' He was about to say something when Michelle touched her mouth, indicating he should keep quiet. She went to the door, opened it and looked down the corridor, but no one was there. Johan started to ask her what she was doing, but she shook her head and put her finger to her mouth again.

'I just wanted to be sure no one is eavesdropping.'

'I don't understand . . . I feel terrible,' he said in a hoarse voice.

'I need to talk to you, it's very important, Johan, so for God's sake just listen to me.'

'Yes, yes . . . OK.'

'The police have been asking questions, and I don't know the answers. You need to tell me what happened.'

He closed his eyes and winced in concentration. 'I remember

hearing a noise downstairs . . . then when I went to look, someone attacked me.'

'The doctor said you're lucky to be alive,' she told him.

He took a slow, deep breath. 'The safe . . . did they . . . ?'

'For Christ's sake, it doesn't matter, Johan.'

'It does . . . to me, Michelle,' he croaked, and she helped him to take another sip of water.

'All right. The police asked if I knew what had been stolen. I said I didn't. But they took your Rolex and the Range Rover, which they then set on fire.'

'Foken bliksem!' he muttered in Afrikaans, then closed his eyes, wincing in pain.

'Who are you talking about, Johan? Do you know who broke into our house and assaulted you?'

He licked his lips. 'Of course not. If I did . . . I'd tell you. I feel ill, Michelle, and my head is killing me. Maybe you . . . should call for a nurse?'

Although his heart rate didn't change, Michelle suspected he was lying. 'What was in the safe, Johan?'

He took another deep breath. 'Cash . . . lots of it . . . I was going to take it to the bank . . .'

'Are you involved in some sort of tax fraud?' she asked.

'No . . . course not. If a client wants to pay cash, I don't object. I put it all through the books.' He licked his lips again and asked for some more water.

'How much cash?' she asked, picking up the water bottle.

'Not much.'

'How much is not much?' She helped him take a few more sips and asked him again. His voice was stronger now and his mind seemed to have cleared.

'I don't know . . . fifty grand . . . maybe a bit more.'

'Did you get a look at the man who attacked you?'

'No . . . he was wearing a balaclava.'

'Do you know a man called Liam? He's about twenty-five and bald.'

'What? No . . . Michelle, I'm feeling really bad. I need the doctor.'

She leaned in closer, almost touching his face. 'Listen to me, Johan. The police got a tip-off and searched this man's flat. They found your Rolex watch and a large sum of cash. When I last spoke to the police, they hadn't tracked him down yet. They aren't telling me much, and I didn't want to ask too many questions until I spoke to you. They only found two thousand pounds. If you're telling me the truth, that still leaves forty-eight thousand. Are you sure . . .'

'For fuck's sake, Michelle . . . it's you that's making my heart rate go up . . . why are you asking me all these questions?'

'I know when someone is lying to me . . . especially you!'

'Jesus Christ, Michelle, I'm the one who was attacked. Why are you talking to me like I'm a piece of kak?' he said, breathing heavily.

'Because I know when you're talking crap. The police will want to interview you and ask about the contents of the safe. I need to know what you're going to say.'

'The same as I just told you . . . for God's sake just leave it alone.'

'If you've been up to anything dishonest, the police will find out, and I'll get dragged into it. Do you understand what I'm talking about? I can't be involved, not with my career.'

'I haven't done anything wrong.'

'I sincerely hope not because the police have your phone and computers. If they find anything suspicious . . .'

'There's nothing to worry about, so don't keep going on about it. I really need some pain medication.' He screwed up his face in agony.

Michelle stroked his face and whispered to him. 'We are in this together, Johan. We will have a baby to raise in five months, so I'm prepared to do whatever's necessary to protect you. But I can't do it if you don't tell me the truth, so let's start again. What happened?'

Johan's face puckered and it looked as if he was going to start crying. 'Come on, Johan, I'll call for help in a minute, just tell me what happened.'

He sighed and took a few breaths to compose himself. 'I fought with him in the living room. I gave him a good beating and thought I'd knocked him out. I went to the kitchen to get a knife, just to threaten him with so he'd get out . . . but he hit me with something from behind. I think I managed to call the police. The next thing I felt was a searing pain in my back from when he was stabbing me . . . then I must have passed out.'

'Why didn't you call the police when you first heard him downstairs?'

'I don't know. I'd just woken up . . . I was confused. I wasn't sure if somebody was really in the house, so I went downstairs to check it out.'

'Do you think Cole was involved in what happened?'

Johan grimaced. 'Why do you ask that? I haven't had anything to do with him since what happened with Chandice's ring.'

'You promise me that's the truth?'

'I've had nothing to do with him, I'm telling you.'

'When the police searched this man Liam's flat, they found jewellery stolen in another burglary. I know that Cole deals in stolen jewellery. He removes the stones, makes new rings and necklaces and sells them on.'

'How do you know that?' he asked, frowning.

'For heaven's sake, are you stupid? Why do you think I warned you never to see Cole again? I deal with plenty of criminals in my job. After what Cole did to Chandice, I started asking some of my clients a few questions about him and got answers that were worrying, to say the least.' She didn't mention that she had hired a private detective to investigate Cole.

'I swear, I haven't had anything to do with him since then.' He started coughing, and his breathing got heavier.

Michelle could tell he was still lying. She got up, put on her coat and picked up her handbag. Johan looked worried. 'Where are you going?'

'Home. I've had enough of your lies, Johan. From now on, you can fend for yourself!'

'No, please, Michelle, don't go. I can't do this without you,' he pleaded.

'My mind is made up, Johan,' she said, hoping he would reveal more.

'All right, all right . . .' a sullen-looking Johan nodded. 'I was seeing him, but I'm not now.'

'I want to know what the pair of you were up to!'

He let out a long sigh. 'Long before the incident with Chandice's ring, I was at Cole's shop. He knew I had a warehouse in Hackney and asked if any empty ones were for rent. I told him the one next to me was about to be vacated.'

'What did Cole want with a warehouse?'

'He said he was considering buying a CVD machine and would need somewhere to keep it.'

'What's that?' She asked.

'It's short for chemical vapour deposition. A CVD is used to make high-quality synthetic diamonds. Cole said he was looking for a business partner . . . I asked him about making diamonds, and he told me how everything worked. He said they were cheap to produce and you could make a big profit when you sold them.'

Michelle raised her eyes. 'Don't tell me you became his partner and started selling fake diamonds.'

'They aren't fake. They are real diamonds, man-made. Cole assured me it isn't illegal to own a CVD machine and make lab diamonds to sell. I checked it out . . . he was telling the truth.'

'Why didn't you tell me about it?' she said, trying to keep calm.

'Because I didn't want you to find out my debts were mounting, and I was struggling to keep the business going, that bloody mortgage. The money from the lab diamonds enabled me to turn things around.'

Michelle bowed her head, gave a sharp intake of breath. Things were going from bad to worse. 'You are so fucking stupid. There's no way a man like Cole would do things legally and above board. Surely you must have suspected he was up to no good after what he did to Chandice?'

'It crossed my mind that he might tell clients the lab diamonds were mined so he could bump up the price . . .'

'Which means Cole was deceiving you as well. Anyone in their right mind would have challenged him about it.'

'I was worried he might say he didn't want me involved in the partnership.'

'You're unbelievable, Johan. How much was the CVD machine?'

'Hundred and fifty grand, split between us. I got a loan for my seventy-five, but I quickly made enough profit to pay it off. It was a profitable business.'

Michelle shook her head in disbelief. 'Where is this machine?'

'In the warehouse next door to mine.'

'Do you rent it?'

'No, Cole does.'

'How long has this partnership been going?'

'A year or so.'

Michelle was so shocked she had to sit down. 'This is all

unbelievable. Did you ever stop to think a purchaser might suspect the diamonds were lab ones and get a second opinion?'

'No one ever has, which made me think everything was legit.'

'I think you knew from the start what Cole was up to. You didn't walk away because greed got the better of you,' she said, picking up her handbag and standing up, as if she was leaving. She knew it would make him react.

'All right . . . when I discovered Cole was passing off the lab diamonds as mined ones, I told him it was risky and that if we got caught, we could both end up in prison. He said he knew other jewellers who did it, and they had never been caught. It's almost impossible to distinguish between a lab-grown diamond and a natural one unless you've got expensive high-tech equipment. Cole also made fake certificates to show customers their provenance.'

'This just gets worse and worse. How could you be so stupid? Did you not stop to think how what you're doing could destroy our marriage? If you had walked away, Cole couldn't have done anything about it without incriminating himself.'

'I told him a few weeks ago you were pregnant, and I was having second thoughts about our . . . partnership. He was upset and asked me to reconsider. I said I'd think about it, but that was because he still owed me money for the lab diamond sales.'

'If you cared about me, you'd never have got involved with him in the first place!'

'I got involved because I didn't want you to think I was failing . . . I did it for you . . . I thought everything was above board and it would solve my financial problems, which it . . .'

'I don't believe you!' she hissed.

'I'm telling the truth . . . I told him I didn't want to be involved with him anymore.'

'When did you tell him that?'

'He came round the house last Friday with my money, and I told him then.'

She was standing at the end of his bed looking down at him. 'And what did he say to that?'

'He got angry . . . tried to persuade me to carry on. We argued a bit, but I told him I couldn't risk all you and I had together, and he eventually accepted it. He said he would find a new partner and shook my hand. I was so relieved . . . I thought he'd go nuts. He even said he'd pay me back some of the cost of the CVD machine.'

'How much money did he give you last Friday?' Johan closed his eyes and she nudged the end the bed with her knee. 'How much did he hand over to you?'

'A hundred and fifty thousand.'

Michelle looked stunned. 'In cash?'

'Yes . . . my payments were always in cash so I could put them through the books as wine sales.'

'That tells me you knew the diamond sales were crooked,' she sneered. 'And you put the money in the safe?' Johan nodded. 'You just told me there was only fifty thousand in it.'

'OK . . . I didn't want you to know what I was up to with Cole.'

'You keep lying to me! Tell me how much was in that safe, Johan!' she demanded.

'In total . . . including my legitimate business earnings . . . there was about two hundred and fifty thousand.'

Michelle shook her head in disbelief. 'Did Cole know you put the money in the safe?'

'He was in the study when I did it.' Michelle had to sit down again. She pressed her hands to her stomach and then rubbed her hands over her swelling belly. She was trying to think through everything Johan had told her, trying to make sense of it, but some things just didn't add up. Now that she knew Cole had been in her house on Friday, and the burglary had happened overnight on Sunday, she suspected Cole might somehow be involved. But why would he give Johan all that cash and steal it back a couple of nights later? He could have simply refused to pay Johan what he owed him, and as it was the proceeds of a crime, there was nothing Johan could have done about it.

'What are you thinking?' he asked nervously.

'What else was in that safe, Johan?'

'Nothing, just the cash.' He tried to look her in the face but his eyes betrayed him, unable to hold her gaze.

She knew that look, a look she'd seen hundreds of times in court, and when she had questioned Johan about her friend's ring all those months ago, he'd had it on his face then too. She knew he was lying. 'All right, Johan, stop acting like a dumb teenager for once and tell me the truth. If Cole was behind the burglary, there had to be something else in that safe he wanted, and I need to know what it was.'

'I told you, Michelle . . .'

'Stop lying, or I swear to God I will walk out on you here and now!'

He let out a sob. 'Please . . . don't leave me. I'm sorry I got us into this mess, but I know we can work things out.'

She snorted. 'There's no "we" involved. It's going to be down to me to get you out of this shit. You have to listen to me, and do exactly what I tell you to do, do you understand?'

Hearing footsteps, Michelle froze. She quickly picked up her blanket and told Johan to lie back and close his eyes.

'Keep your eyes shut and don't move . . .'

'Why? I'm awake now . . .'

'Just do as I tell you,' Michelle said, returning to sit in the easy chair, the blanket over her knees.

'I thought I heard voices,' the nurse said on entering.

'I was told to keep talking to him to help Johan wake up,' Michelle said. 'I thought I saw his hand moving just now.'

'Yes, sometimes you get an involuntary twitch. I'll check the IV drips and then leave you in peace.' Michelle remained silent, watching the nurse go about her task, half afraid Johan would open his eyes, but he thankfully remained completely still, his eyes firmly shut.

After a few minutes, the nurse left, closed the door behind her and then suddenly reopened it. Michelle got up, afraid Johan would give himself away.

'Would you like a cup of tea?'

'I'm fine, thanks. I have some water, but I'll press the call button if I need anything.' Michelle waited until she heard the nurse's footsteps receding, then nudged the edge of the bed. 'She's gone. Now if you want me to sort this out, understand that if you lie to me again, I will walk out of here and that's it, we're over. Understand? So, tell me, what was in the safe that Cole was so desperate to get his hands on?'

He licked his lips. 'Michelle . . .'

'Tell me.'

'Diamonds. Uncut diamonds . . . stolen diamonds.'

'Stolen diamonds? Where the fuck did they come from?' she demanded.

'From South Africa. They were hidden in wine boxes and shipped here.'

Michelle had to take a deep breath, hardly believing what he had just told her. She paced up and down, trying to calm herself, then stopped again at the end of his bed. 'I can't see your parents or sister Mariette being involved, but I can when it comes to your brother Duante. Am I right?'

Johan nodded. 'Yes, but it was Cole who asked me if I could get a hold of any rough diamonds from South Africa.'

'What, to sell them on the black market and go halves with you?'

'That's what I thought he wanted to do, but he said you need a Kimberley Certificate to prove legitimate ownership, or no reputable dealer would be interested in them. He said he knew a few dodgy dealers, but they would be unwilling to pay anywhere near the market price for stolen diamonds, with or without a certificate. Cole felt it was too risky to try and sell them right away, but he said he had a plan where we could both make a lot of money.'

Michelle felt like breaking down in tears. It was hard to even look at him. 'A plan . . . and what exactly was that . . . ?'

'To show wealthy people the stolen uncut diamonds with false provenance and certificates showing they were mined in South Africa and high value. Cole would offer to make rings, brooches and other specially designed jewellery at a reasonable price for interested clients but then use lab diamonds instead of the mined ones, making a huge profit.'

'And you decided to seek Duante's help.'

'I knew he had contacts in the South African jewellery business, but I didn't tell him about Cole or his plan. I just said I was in financial trouble, didn't want our father to find out and asked him if he could source a few diamonds for me that I could sell to a dodgy jeweller I knew. He said he would ask around, but getting the diamonds might take a few weeks.'

Michelle crossed to the hospital room window, the blind was partially down, and she eased it up a fraction. Looking out onto the car park, she tried to digest everything Johan had told her. She remained standing with her back to him as she asked how Duante acquired the diamonds. Johan explained that his brother got hold of a diamond mine worker from a nearby shantytown. This worker would hide a homing pigeon in his lunchbox. He carefully packed rough diamonds into small sackcloth bags, binding them to the bird's feet and under each wing. When no one was watching, he would send the pigeon flying home with the diamonds.

Michelle could hardly believe what she was hearing. She recalled watching a TV programme about diamond smuggling with Johan when they were last in South Africa. 'I hope you are ashamed of yourself. Those kids steal stones worth hundreds of thousands to a jeweller but only get pennies per carat themselves. The guards beat them and break their fingers if they get caught stealing. Some have been murdered, and the companies hush up their deaths. How could you be part of that?'

'No one got hurt, and anyway, the smuggling has stopped now.'

'How many diamonds did your brother smuggle over?'

'Thirty or forty in different sizes and carats.'

'How much are they worth?'

'I don't know exactly. Cole said some are worth a lot of money, others not much.'

'And how long has this scam been going on?'

'About five months, maybe a bit longer.' She couldn't believe this had all been going on under her nose without her noticing. While she was going through IVF treatment and then having the joyous and long-awaited confirmation she was pregnant, her husband was dealing in stolen diamonds to pay off debts she knew nothing about. She took a deep breath, resisting the temptation just to walk out.

'So tell me, if Cole showed clients the stolen diamonds, why were they in your safe?'

'He said that it would be safer if I looked after them. When he needed some to show a client, I would take them to him, or he'd come to me and give them back to me afterwards.'

'So you felt you could trust him?'

'I had no reason not to. We were partners. I even gave him some diamonds to keep on Friday as a parting gift.'

She put her hands to her head. 'I can't believe how naive you are, Johan. Can you not see Cole has played the long game with you?'

'What do you mean?'

'Just think about it, Johan. He manipulated you from the start to get the big payoff. He probably never showed any buyers the stolen diamonds. He just wanted you to think he had. How many times has he been to our house?'

'Just a couple of times.'

'Then he's aware we have no CCTV or other security. Did you mention anything to him about going to the christening over the weekend?'

'He asked if he could give me the money on Saturday, but I said I was away for the weekend and Friday would be better.'

'Why didn't you come with me to the christening?'

'Because I wanted to put the cash Cole gave me through the books.'

She shook her head. 'If you had come with me, you wouldn't be lying here now. Can't you see Cole got someone to break into our house? He knows you can't tell the police the diamonds were stolen. And you can't claim all that cash back on the insurance as they will want proof the money was from business sales.'

'Look, I'm sorry I ever got involved with Cole, all right, but I did it for us. If my business went under, I thought we might lose everything.' His eyes welled with tears. He reached out for Michelle's hand, but she pulled away.

'Don't you dare give me all that "I did it for us" crap. If your business was failing, you should have told me. I would have helped you find a way round it. We could have sold the house.'

'I couldn't tell you. That house was what you'd always wanted, we worked so hard to make it perfect, the perfect home for a family . . .' Tears started running down his cheeks.

'If you cared about me and the child we are expecting, you would never have contemplated getting with a scumbag like Cole,' she said bitterly.

'I was planning for our baby's future . . .' he said feebly.

'Well, your plan has gone tits up, hasn't it!' she retorted.

'There are still some diamonds hidden in wineboxes at my warehouse that Cole doesn't know about'.

'Shut up! That can't solve our problems. We don't know what Liam Palmer will say when he's interviewed. If he implicates Cole in the break-in, then Cole will be arrested.'

'If the police didn't find the diamonds and the cash at Liam's, Cole must have it.'

Michelle was shifting her weight from one foot to the other, the way she often did when waiting to enter the court room, her mind ticking over.

'Cole's a shrewd bastard, so he'll probably have devised a cover story, laundered the cash and sold the diamonds already. If the police interview him, he'll just say he knows you because you bought jewellery from him and rent the warehouse next door.'

'What should I say if they ask me about Cole?'

Michelle felt drained. She needed more time to think it all through. She looked over at him and sighed. He seemed so piti-ful, with his bruised face and the thick bandages around his head, his blue eyes looking pleadingly towards her, like a child. But she felt only anger. If they were going to get through this, though, she couldn't show it. She had to give him the confidence to do what needed to be done, to make him feel they were working together. She moved to his bedside and took hold of his hand, then bent her head to kiss his forehead.

'I'm here for you, Johan. I'm never going to abandon you, however foolish you've been. But you will need to do exactly what I tell you, all right? So, darling, when the police speak to you, tell them you can't remember anything about what happened. It's all still a blur. I'll talk with Doctor Babu and tell him how concerned I am about your memory loss. Hopefully, he'll say you are not medically fit to be interviewed. That way, I'll have more time to speak with Anderson and try to find out what's happening in the investigation. Then I can tell you what to say.'

'Who's Anderson?'

'He's the DCI leading the investigation. He's not very experienced, so we should be able to pull the wool over his eyes. The same with the family liaison officer, DC Owens. However, there's a woman, Jessica Russell, who's in charge of the forensic investigation – she's smart, and she can spot a liar.'

Johan let out a long breath. 'I don't know what I'd do without you, Michelle. I'll do my best to fool them, but I'm worried they won't believe me.'

'You just have to use what's happened to you as an excuse for being unable to remember things.'

'What if they find out about the CVD machine?' he asked, a tremor of panic in his voice.

'It's not a problem for Cole if it's legal. If they ask you, say you knew he made lab diamonds but you hadn't purchased any from him. Did you use your own phone to contact him?'

'No, I used a burner phone and WhatsApp.'

'Where's the phone now?'

'I went to the warehouse on Saturday to sort out some paperwork.

It's hidden in the air vent next to my desk. Look, Michelle, I know I've only got myself to blame for what's happened, but you don't need to get involved.'

'Well, I am involved now. So just listen to me and do exactly what I tell you.'

CHAPTER TWENTY-FIVE

Feeling exhausted, Jessica went straight to bed when she got home. David had left a message saying he had gone to see a film at the Odeon in Orpington and wouldn't be back until late. She fell asleep almost instantly and slept soundly until her alarm woke her at 5 a.m.

She went to the bathroom to shower and tried to open the door, but it was locked.

'Let me know when you've finished, David. I'll be in the kitchen.'

'You can go next, as long as you're quick,' David replied. She turned sharply and saw him standing by his bedroom door in his pyjama shorts.

'Who's in the bathroom?' a shocked Jessica asked. She heard the door being unlocked.

'Donna, this is my sister, Jessica. This is Donna,' David smiled. Jessica turned and saw a slim, attractive girl in her late twenties with long, wavy blonde hair standing in the bathroom doorway with a towel wrapped around her.

'Really good to meet you, Jessica,' she said with a big smile. 'David has told me a lot about you. I'm a real fan of all those forensic TV shows. Your job must be so fascinating and gruesome.'

Jessica was so surprised that she wasn't sure what to say. 'Er . . . nice to meet you too.'

'I'd love to chat about your work, but I'd better get dressed for my rounds,' Donna said as she kissed David on the cheek, walked into his bedroom and closed the door.

'How long have you known her?' Jessica whispered, as they walked towards the kitchen.

'Donna only started at the post office yesterday. But we hit off just like that.'

Jessica turned and faced him. 'Are you serious?'

He grinned. 'We've known each other for about six months and have been dating for two. She's also into cycling and she's joined the Petts Wood club. We've been away together on a few cycling trips.'

'So, you weren't with friends like you told me.'

'Sometimes there was a group of us . . . on others there wasn't. Is it a problem?'

'Of course not. I'm pleased for you. But I don't understand why you didn't tell me you were in a relationship.'

'I didn't know I had to.'

'But why didn't you?'

'Because I knew you'd start asking me loads of questions and worrying if she was right for me.'

'No, I wouldn't.'

'Yes, you would. You can't help it. You've always worried about me when there was no need to.'

'It's because I care about you and wouldn't want to see you get hurt. Is it serious?'

He raised his eyes. 'There you go, worrying.'

'It is a reasonable question to ask.'

'And the answer is yes. I like her a lot, and I think she feels the same about me.'

'Why didn't you bring her to the house before now?'

'Her name's Donna!' he snapped.

'Sorry. It's just a bit of a surprise, that's all. I'm pleased to have met Donna and I'm glad you're together. Maybe we could all go out for a meal, then I can get to know her better.'

'Yeah, that would be nice – as long as you don't get called out to a crime scene in the middle of dessert.'

'I might have to work on Saturday, but I'll make sure to get the night off.'

'I'm going to a party with Donna on Saturday night. What about tomorrow evening?'

'Let's pencil it in, but I can't promise as it's really hectic at work. You book somewhere you and Donna would like to go and the meals on me. What does she like, food-wise?'

'She loves seafood, especially prawn linguini. I'll book Quattordici in Chislehurst for seven thirty.' 'Sounds good. I'll do my best to be there.'

'Just so you know, I've told Donna about the past and my problems with depression. She really understands because she's had her own issues to deal with over the years.'

Jessica nodded. 'It's good that you told her and that she's confided in you. Right, I better get a move on. I've got to be at the office at half six. You OK if I use the bathroom first?'

He nodded. 'I got an email from the doctor about my creatine kinase levels. I've got an appointment with the neurologist tomorrow morning at Guy's. I got in earlier than expected due to a cancellation.'

'That's good news. I can ask DCI Anderson for a few hours off work to go with you.'

'Donna's taken the day off to go with me. You'd probably have to spend hours in the waiting room while the tests are done. I know you're not comfortable sitting about doing nothing,' he smiled.

'Are you sure you want to go out Friday evening after your appointment?'

'Of course. I can't eat or drink anything for twenty-four hours before it, so I'll be famished. And don't worry if you're stuck at work. We can all go out another time.'

'I'll do my best to be there.' She opened the dishwasher and looked inside. 'Glad to see you rinsed and stacked the plates neatly for a change.'

He laughed. 'That was Donna.'

*   *   *

Arriving at Barking, Jessica went to the ladies' room. Looking in the mirror, she remembered Chapman saying that having her hair down suited her. She removed the scrunchie and puffed her hair before going to his office.

'How do you want to approach things with Anderson?' she asked as she walked in.

'I think we should just be frank with him. The forensic evidence speaks for itself. I'll let him read your report first if that's OK with you.'

'Of course. He might not like it, though.'

'If Anderson wants to throw his toys out of the pram, then so be it. Everything you've said so far makes sense. He'd be a fool not to listen, but the choice is his.'

About half an hour later, Jessica got a phone call from Guy. 'You're in early,' she remarked.

'I wanted to get to work on Liam Palmer's mobile phone asap.' She put the speakerphone on. 'I found a contact for a J. Wheeler. There have been no recent calls from Palmer's phone to Wheeler's. However, Wheeler's number called Palmer on Monday at 6 p.m., and the call lasted about two minutes. Cell site analysis revealed that the call was from the Montague Road mast. I had the number pinged for the phone's current location, and it's still live and in the same area.'

'Looks like Wheeler does live in one of the tower blocks,' Chapman said. 'Have you got an address?'

'His mobile is pay-as-you-go, so there's no registered address, I'm afraid.'

'That's no surprise, given he's a wanted man,' Chapman said.

'The last call Wheeler received was just after midnight on Wednesday morning. I haven't got the caller's details yet, but I'll let you know as soon as I do. I'll keep digging and start looking at all the calls, texts, etc made by Wheeler. Hopefully, that will give you the names of a few people you can speak to who might know his current whereabouts. I'll send an email with what I've got and Wheeler's phone number.'

'Thanks, Guy. Good work.' Jessica ended the call.

'So we've got a definite connection between Palmer and Wheeler now,' Chapman said. 'The question is why Palmer has failed to tell us about him.'

'He could be frightened of him. It doesn't look like Palmer was a random choice to be the fall guy.'

'I agree. Palmer tried to put on the hard man act, but I reckon he's a soft touch and easily led. The stolen games consoles and laptop he had in his flat were probably bought from Wheeler and the proceeds of a burglary he committed. You're right, you know.'

'Aren't I always,' she smiled.

'I mean what you said yesterday about re-interviewing Palmer.'

'I thought you said there were legal implications about doing that?'

'Stuff the legality. It's the truth that matters, and we need to find Wheeler.'

They went to the custody suite, and Chapman took Jessica to a room with a one-way mirror so she could see into the interview room without being observed. 'You could get into trouble for this,' she warned him.

'Honestly, I don't give a shit,' he shrugged. 'He'll be in court later this morning and then remanded in custody. Speaking to him on the inside without a solicitor will be almost impossible. And we're up against the clock. This could be our last chance to see what he knows about Wheeler.'

Jessica nervously watched Chapman enter the interview room and wait for Palmer to be brought in. After a few minutes, a bewildered-looking Palmer was led in. As soon as he saw Chapman, his eyes opened wide with panic, and he turned quickly, trying to leave the room. The custody officer accompanying Palmer gripped his arm and led him towards one of the chairs.

'It's OK. You can let him go.' Chapman put his hand on Palmer's shoulder. 'There's nothing to worry about, Liam. Please sit down.'

'My solicitor said you can't talk to me again now I've been charged,' he said.

'This isn't being recorded, Liam. This is all off the record. I'm here because I need your help, not to have a go at you, and if . . .'

'Help me! You don't believe a word I've said. I don't want to talk to you anymore, so just take me back to my cell.'

'I admit I didn't believe you during the interviews, Liam. But I've learned things since then that have made me change my mind.'

'How do I know you're not lying and trying to blame me for something else I didn't do?' Liam asked suspiciously.

'Look, Liam, I know you didn't break into De Klerk's house. And you're right about someone trying to frame you. But I need to ask you some questions to prove it.'

Palmer twitched and chewed at his lips. 'All right, I'll listen to you, but can I go back to my cell when I want to?'

'Of course.' Palmer reluctantly sat down, looked over to the closed door and then at Chapman. 'Do you want a drink?' Chapman asked. He shook his head. 'Our forensic team examined your phone and the games consoles. We know you were playing games on the night De Klerk's house was broken into. The same with your phone on the night the car was set alight, so we know you're not responsible for either of those crimes.' Palmer let out a trembling sigh of relief. 'And you'll be pleased to know your fingerprints and DNA were not on the watch, cash or burner phone found in your flat.'

'You see, I told you I'd never seen them before. What about the clothes in the outside bin?'

'Forensics are still looking for wearer DNA on them, but I believe you were telling the truth when you said they're not yours.'

'Yeah, that's right, I was telling the truth. So the charges will be dropped and I can go home?'

'I can't make that decision, Liam. It will be up to DCI Anderson and the CPS. But if you answer my questions, it could help you. You have to be honest with me, though.' Chapman showed him the photo of Wheeler on his phone. 'Do you know this man?'

Palmer glanced at it, then quickly looked away. 'No, I've never seen him before.'

'You barely looked at it, Liam, which makes me think you do know him.'

'I swear. I've never seen him before.' His voice trembled, and he started licking his lips.

'Are you frightened of him?'

'If I don't know him, how can I be frightened of him?'

'His name is John Wheeler. I think he's the person who's trying to frame you for breaking into the house and stabbing Johan De Klerk.'

'I want to go back to my cell. I've got nothing more to say to you.'

'Did he give you the money in your wallet?'

'No. Please, just let me go back to my cell.'

'If I'm going to help you, Liam, I need you to tell me the truth.'

'I am. I don't know him.'

Chapman sighed. 'The thing is, Liam, the money in your wallet had your prints and De Klerk's on it, so it had to have been stolen from him. I don't think you stole it, but I can't help you if you don't help me, Liam.'

'I can't help you because I don't know him.'

'What are you so worried about?'

'I'm not worried.'

Chapman sighed again. 'I can see that you are, Liam. Has Wheeler threatened you?' Liam looked at the floor. 'Have it your way. Wait here, and I'll get the custody officer to take you back to your cell.'

Chapman got up and left the room, then went to see Jessica next door. 'Liam must be terrified of Wheeler, but I don't know what else I can do to get him to open up.'

'Can the charge of attempted rape be dropped to indecent exposure?'

Chapman hesitated. 'If that's what you want, and the CPS agree, I don't see why not.'

'Then let me speak to him.'

'I don't think that would be a good idea.'

'I'm not worried about being in the same room as him.'

'All right, but I'm staying in there with you. Give me a minute to explain that someone else wants to talk to him.'

'What are you going to say?'

'I'm going to big you up,' Chapman said, walking out before she could say anything.

The custody officer showed Chapman back into the room. 'I want to go back to my cell,' Liam pleaded.

'The custody officer is busy, but he'll be back here in a minute or two. There's something I think you should know.'

'What?'

'The lady in charge of our forensic unit watched your interviews and believed what you said might be true. So much so that she looked at all the evidence again and concluded you were telling the truth. She convinced me you didn't break into the house or assault Johan De Klerk, and Wheeler set you up for the crime. If not for her, I wouldn't be talking to you now and trying to help you.'

Liam looked surprised. 'Why would she do that for me?'

'Because she cares about what happens to you. She doesn't want to see you convicted of a crime you didn't commit. She put her job on the line for you. Honestly, at first, I didn't believe her. I was convinced you were guilty, but now I know you're not.'

Liam looked gobsmacked. 'Can you thank her for me? Nobody ever done nothing for me like that.'

'You can do that yourself . . .'

Jessica took the cue, passing the waiting custody officer positioned outside as Chapman had instructed him, and entering the room. 'This is Jessica Russell, head of our forensic unit,' Chapman said. Palmer's eyes opened wide with shock. He started to push his chair back from the table as if he needed to get away from her.

'Don't worry, Liam,' she said. 'I'm not here to shout or scream at you. Thank you for telling DI Chapman what happened in my flat that night. It can't have been easy, and I understand why you didn't admit it back then.' Liam seemed bewildered, putting his hands on the table and then back on his lap. He bowed his head, unwilling to look at her. Chapman glanced at her anxiously, but she seemed relaxed and unconcerned. She let the silence lengthen.

Eventually Liam coughed and wiped his lips with his hand. He still wouldn't look at her. 'I'm sorry for what I did. I didn't mean to frighten you. You were always kind and tried to help me when you were my probation officer. All I knew as a kid was that my dad beat my mother, who was always drunk, and she took the punishment out on me. It was never my dad who grabbed my hair and slammed my head against the wall until I was unconscious. It was her. But I had to tell social services it was my dad who did it so she could keep custody of me and not lose her benefits. I've been living a lie my entire messed-up life.'

Jessica was shocked but tried not to show it. 'That's all in the past, Liam. It's the present and what happens to you now that's important. I think you know the man in the photograph, but I understand if you're frightened of him . . .'

'I don't know him. I've never seen him before,' he said stubbornly.

'DI Chapman has enough evidence to arrest Wheeler, but we don't know where he is.'

'I don't know either. Please, I appreciate you standing up for me, I really do, but now I just want to go back to my cell.'

Jessica spoke softly, leaning forward. 'If he's arrested and charged, he can't hurt you. We know he's trying to frame you for a crime you didn't commit. Neither of us wants to see you go to prison for something you didn't do.'

Chapman took up the baton. 'We know Wheeler lives in one of the tower blocks on Montague Road, but we need the exact address. I understand why you're frightened of him, but like Jessica said, if we arrest him, he can't hurt you.'

Palmer looked hesitantly at Jessica for reassurance. 'Liam, I want you to know that I have asked that the charge for the offence against me be dropped to indecent exposure.'

'You'd do that?' Palmer asked.

'If you help us, I will talk to the CPS and ask that they consider granting you bail. I can also ask that you be considered for witness protection and given a place to live well away from Wheeler.'

He closed his eyes, shaking his head from side to side. 'Listen, I've seen what this bloke can do . . . I saw him smash a kid's face in the pub for not doing anything, and I know he almost killed another bloke at his hostel . . . he said he'd cut my throat if I ever said anything to anyone, I'm so scared of him . . . how do I know he won't find me and hurt me again?'

'You have my word, you will be protected,' Chapman said.

'And mine.' Jessica said quietly.

Liam sniffed, then wiped his nose with the back of his hand. He took a deep breath. 'Flat 78 Fred Wigg Tower. There, I done it.'

'Are you sure, Liam?' Chapman asked. 'The last thing I want is to force entry to the wrong flat.'

'I am telling you the truth. He got me the laptop, the PlayStation and Xbox, and I went there to collect them.'

Chapman nodded. 'OK. Thank you, Liam. There are a few other questions I'll need to ask you about your involvement with Wheeler, but right now, I'm going to go and arrest him. As soon as I've done that, I'll let you know. Is that OK?'

Liam looked to Chapman first, and then to Jessica. 'Am I going back to my cell?'

'Yes, I'll see you get some breakfast.' Chapman was in a hurry to get going as the custody officer entered. Chapman hurried out and Liam and Jessica both stood up.

Hesitantly, Liam put his hand out, reaching towards her as if to shake her hand.

She stared at him. 'Don't touch me,' she said quietly. She walked out as the custody officer took Liam by the arm.

It was 7.30 a.m. when Chapman tried calling Anderson, but there was no answer. He sent a text message saying there had been a significant development in the investigation and that he needed to search a suspect's address and arrest him if he was there. Jessica was standing beside him as he put his phone down.

'We need to go to Wheeler's flat right away. He may not be there, so we might have to set up a surveillance operation. Hopefully, you and your team will find some incriminating evidence. I'll need a full forensic search on the premises, so I'd like you to come with us and see what you'll be dealing with.'

'Yes, of course. I don't expect Anderson will be very pleased, though.'

'Sod him. He should have answered his phone. Mind you, it's probably better he didn't. He'd have told us to wait until he got here and wasted valuable time. I'll see if anyone's in the main office who can come with us. You get down to the yard, I'll only be a few minutes.'

Chapman drove to Fred Wigg Tower with Jessica and DC Bingham, who had got into work early. On arrival, they met two uniformed officers waiting around the corner in a marked patrol car. They then all took the lift to flat 78. Chapman knocked on the door and waited, but there was no answer. He knocked again, but still no one came to the door.

'Bollocks,' he muttered to himself. 'I'll need a warrant to force entry. For now, we'll set up an observation post. That'll give us time to brief Anderson and get the warrant, then he can decide whether to go in.'

Jessica got her phone out, dialled Wheeler's number, put her ear to the door, and listened. 'I can hear a mobile ringing. It's unlikely he'd go out leaving his phone behind. He could be in there.'

Chapman turned to one of the uniformed officers. 'You got a door ram in the patrol car?'

'Yes, guv.' He hurried off.

Chapman crouched down and opened the letterbox. 'This is the police, Wheeler!' he shouted. 'Open the door now, or we'll force it open.' There was still no reply, and when the officer returned with the ram, Chapman took it from him.

'Don't we need a warrant to enter, guv?' Bingham asked.

'No. Wheeler is suspected of attempted murder, and we think he's refusing to let us in, so we have reasonable grounds to enter by force, arrest him and search the premises. Get your tasers out just in case,' Chapman instructed the uniform officers. He swung the ram back and struck the door hard a few times before the lock gave way with a sound of cracking wood. 'Armed police! Stay where you are, Wheeler!' Chapman shouted, standing back to let the officers, with their tasers raised, enter first.

The contents of the hallway cupboard were strewn across the floor. The officers, followed by Chapman and Jessica, cautiously stepped over a rucksack, hoover and assorted coats, checking the kitchen and bedrooms before approaching the living room.

Chapman sniffed a few times and looked at Jessica. 'Is that smell what I think it is?' he asked.

Jessica nodded. 'Let's hope it's an animal, not Wheeler.'

The living room had been ransacked. A man was slumped back in an armchair with a bruised face and a trail of dried blood from his nose and mouth onto the front of his shirt and trousers. Chapman looked at the photo of Wheeler then passed it to her.

'I'd say that's him,' she said, looking closely at the body. Chapman put on some latex gloves and checked for a neck pulse, just to be sure. 'Looks like someone got to him before we did,' she said, removing a pair of latex gloves from her handbag and putting them on. She took the man's hand and lifted it. 'The arm muscle isn't fully stiff, which suggests rigor mortis is on its way out. It can last up to twenty-four hours, sometimes longer, then the stiffness disperses, and the muscles become flexible.'

'How long do you think he's been dead, then?' Chapman asked.

'It's best to call out a pathologist. They can give you a better time of death estimate than me.'

'At a guess?' Chapman asked.

'A day and a half, maybe two, tops.' Chapman asked one of the uniform officers to call the local station and ask them to contact the local coroner's office, requesting a pathologist attend the scene. He then crouched down and looked at the man's trainers.

'Adidas Ultraboost.'

'And pair of Sealskinz gloves are on the coffee table beside a passport,' Jessica added. She picked up the passport and removed the folded piece of A4 paper tucked inside it. She opened the passport and showed it to Chapman.

'It's in the name of Colin Heart but with Wheeler's photograph.' She then unfolded the piece of paper. 'A printed copy of a one-way, business class ticket for Colin Heart. Emirates Airways to Dubai for 9 a.m. yesterday morning. Looks like Wheeler was in a hurry to get out of the country.'

'Well, he won't be getting a refund,' Chapman said.

'Dubai's an odd place to go if you're on the run,' Jessica said, frowning.

Chapman shook his head. 'Not these days. A growing number of criminals on the run are heading to the Middle East. It's become a popular alternative to the Netherlands and the Costa del Sol in Spain. There are large expat communities and a regular flow of tourists, which allows fugitives to maintain a blend in.'

'There's a suitcase in the bedroom with a few bits of clothing in it, and a lot of clothes strewn around the floor,' a uniformed officer told them. They both had a look. Some folded clothes were still on the bed, but other clothing was scattered over the floor, and the bedroom wardrobes and dressing table drawers had also been searched. Jessica nodded to the case. 'The inner lining's been ripped out. I wonder what they were looking for.'

Chapman shrugged, 'Could be the watch and the cash, but it

doesn't make sense that Wheeler would plant it on Palmer and leave the UK without it. You can't survive in Dubai without money. Maybe there was more in that safe we don't know about.'

'As this is a suspected murder, I think we should remove ourselves in case of any cross-contamination,' Jessica said. 'I'll call my team out. They can photograph and video the scene before we start the forensic examination. Can you take me back to Barking? I need to get my car. All my equipment's in it.'

'I better ring Anderson.'

'Are you going to tell Liam?'

'Yes, but I need to ask him about the phone call with Wheeler first and what else he knows about him. Do you think he could be involved in Wheeler's murder?'

'No, and be honest, neither do you. But I expect Anderson will.'

Jessica called Guy and asked him to tell Diane and Taff to come to the scene and for him to collect Wheeler's mobile phone and laptop so he could start working on them. Chapman called Anderson, who was still at home. He said he hadn't seen Chapman's text as he was charging his phone. Chapman briefly explained his visit to the pub, the information about Wheeler and the discovery of his body. Anderson was livid and told Chapman to call the MSCAN team to the scene and to get his 'arse' back to the station. 'I expect a thorough explanation for your actions, in particular your failure to keep me informed about what you're doing at all times!'

Travelling back to Barking, Jessica asked Chapman why he hadn't told Anderson she was with him at the pub or mentioned they had spoken to Palmer. 'I thought it best to wait until I talked to him personally. He was angry enough as it was.'

'We're in this together, Mike, so we'll talk to him together.'

He grinned. 'Yes, ma'am.'

CHAPTER TWENTY-SIX

Palmer looked anxious as he entered the interview room. His eyes were bloodshot and puffy as if he'd been crying. 'Did you find Wheeler?' he asked nervously.

Chapman nodded. 'Yes, we did.'

'Does he think it was me that grassed him up?'

'No, he doesn't, and he never will,' Chapman replied in a confident tone.

'There's nothing for you to worry about, Liam,' Jessica said quietly.

'Just take a seat, and I'll explain everything,' Chapman said. 'We need to interview you to clarify some points and allow you to comment on information that has come to light since you were charged. Are you happy for me to do it without a solicitor representing you and with us both being present?' Chapman asked.

'What have I done now?'

'Nothing. I just need to ask you a few questions about Wheeler and your relationship with him.' Palmer looked at Jessica for reassurance. But he had to look away as she returned his look coldly.

'Will what I say be used in evidence against Wheeler?' Palmer asked.

'No, it won't, but it will help us clear a few things up and be to your credit if you can help us,' Chapman replied.

Liam again looked at Jessica. 'OK,' he said quietly. Chapman switched on the recorder and went through the caution. 'Do you know a John Wheeler who lives at 78 Fred Wigg Tower?'

'Yes.'

'How did you meet him?'

'I met him in the pub a few months ago. I used to play pool

with him sometimes until he got barred for punching this kid out because he'd switched the TV channel. He just fucking went for him, busted his face open, so we weren't what I'd call friends. He scared the life out of me.'

'Was that The Bell on Leytonstone High Road?' Chapman asked.

'Yes. Sometime after that, I was playing pool with him and he asked me if I was interested in buying some second-hand electrical stuff. I asked him what it was, and he said a couple of games consoles and a laptop. When we left the pub, he took me to his flat and showed me the stuff. It was in good nick, so I bought it.'

'What, there and then?'

'No. He gave me a couple of days to get the money and said to ring him when I had it and then come and collect the stuff, which I did.'

'How much did you pay for it?' Chapman asked.

'Three hundred and fifty quid.'

'Did you think it was stolen property, or was that a fair second-hand price?' Chapman asked, deliberately giving Palmer a chance to sound good, but he didn't twig.

'When I gave him the money, he poked me hard in the chest and told me I wasn't to tell anyone. That's when I thought it might be stolen. Then one night, I was just coming out of my flat and I saw him in the road, and he was just standing there staring at me. It freaked me out because it meant he knew where I lived.'

'Did he ever try to sell you any jewellery?'

'No. Not interested in that stuff, just video games, like what he sold me.'

'Did you have any dealings with Wheeler after that?' Chapman asked.

'No, he scared me, the way he was outside my flat. Somebody told me he'd done this bloke in at some place he was living, so I didn't want to go near him. I know the landlord of the pub wasn't keen on him being around and . . .'

Jessica interrupted him by holding up her hand. 'Listen, Liam, we've examined your mobile phone. Wheeler called you on Monday around 6 p.m., and you spoke with each other for a couple of minutes. Is that right?'

A worried-looking Liam nodded. 'I only did what he asked because I was scared of him.'

'I understand, but we need to know what he asked you to do,' Chapman said briskly.

'He said he had a car he needed to get rid of and claim the insurance on. He wanted a can of petrol but was worried he might get seen on the cameras. It was me who turned them off. He paid me five hundred quid for doing it and letting him have the petrol and a can.'

'Did you not think that was a lot of money for a can of petrol and switching the CCTV off?' Chapman asked.

'I wasn't going to argue.'

'Did you see the car?' Chapman asked.

'No. He must have parked it up the road somewhere and walked to the garage.'

'Did he threaten you?'

'When he gave me the money, he said if I told the police or anyone about the car, he'd come after me. I was shit scared. That's why I didn't tell you about him.'

'Do you know anyone Wheeler's close to? Chapman asked.

'No. Will I have to give evidence against him in court? What if he finds out what I've told you?'

'I couldn't tell you this earlier because I didn't want it to influence your answers. We found Wheeler at his flat, but he was dead. He can't hurt you.'

Palmer gasped. 'He's dead! What the fuck happened to him?'

'The post-mortem will determine the exact cause of death. However, it looks like he was tortured, possibly to extract information,' Chapman said.

'Oh my God, will they come after me as well?' He suddenly looked terrified.

'No, they won't, because whoever else is involved with Wheeler doesn't know what you told us and never will,' Chapman said calmly.

'What will happen to me now?'

'We will speak to the CPS, and I'm confident they will drop the charges regarding the De Klerk case. As I said before, I'm going to ask that the attempted rape charge be dropped to indecent exposure. However, you'll still have to go to court for that and the burglary charge you were wanted on a warrant for.'

'But you will protect me, right?

'Of course I will, but I can't make the decision to release you right now. You're going to have to go back to your cell and you'll appear in court later this morning. I'll let Mr Baldwin, your solicitor, know what's happened. He can apply for bail on your behalf, but it's up to the magistrate.'

The interview door suddenly burst open, and a red-faced Anderson entered the room with the custody officer in tow. 'This interview is terminated,' he shouted, leaning over and turning off the recorder. 'Take him back to his cell, immediately!' he told the custody officer. He turned to Chapman and Jessica. 'The pair of you in my office now!' The custody officer grabbed a terrified Palmer by the arm and lifted him from his seat.

'Take your hands off him,' Chapman warned angrily. 'He's not a threat to anyone.' He put a hand on Palmer's shoulder. 'Don't worry. You'll be OK. We'll tell him everything you told us.'

'Too bloody right you will!' Anderson bellowed.

Jessica turned and looked at Anderson harshly. She waited for Palmer to be taken out before speaking. 'I think you need to take some time to calm down before we speak to you, and I want to call my team for an update.'

Anderson looked flustered. 'Twenty minutes, no longer.' He turned and stalked out of the room.

Jessica looked at Chapman. 'Might as well get some breakfast.'

He shook his head, smiling to himself. 'Now I get why Taff calls you Dragon.'

*　　*　　*

DS Wood parked near the gated entrance to the impressive-looking house. With its double frontage and prestigious location in Kingston upon Thames, he reckoned it was worth three and a half to four million pounds. He pressed the intercom on the gate and a well-spoken female voice answered. Wood introduced himself, holding up his warrant card for the camera. 'Sorry for disturbing you, but I'd like to speak to Chandice Bramston.'

'I'm Chandice Bramston. May I ask what it's about?'

'I'm investigating a series of jewellery frauds and believe you might have been a victim.'

'Does it concern that jeweller in Hatton Garden?'

'If you mean Nathan Cole, then yes, it does,' Wood replied, and the gates opened. He walked up the driveway, the gravel crunching under his feet as he admired the landscaped front garden. When he reached the house, the door opened. Chandice was in her late thirties, dark-skinned, with high cheekbones and emerald green eyes. She was wearing tight-fitting leggings, a sports bra, an Armani tracksuit top and fluffy slippers. Wood thought she might easily have been a model.

'May I see your warrant card again, please?' He removed it from his pocket and held it up for her to see. Chandice took it from him without saying anything and looked closely at the photograph and then his face before returning it. 'Please come in. I'd be obliged if you could put a pair of those slippers on.' She pointed to a wooden box filled with slippers from upmarket hotels. 'Excuse my attire, but I just returned from my morning gym session. Please come through to the kitchen. I was about to have a glass of Bucks Fizz. My little reward for a hard workout. Would you like one?'

'I'm fine, thanks,' he said, thinking she certainly didn't look very sweaty if she'd been to the gym.

'Don't worry, I won't tell your superiors you were drinking on duty,' she smiled.

'Go on then,' Wood smiled back.

'What makes you think I was a victim of Cole's?' she asked, as she expertly popped the cork from a bottle of Dom Perignon.

'Through an informant who has connections to Cole.'

She poured a splash of orange juice and champagne into two glasses, handed one to Wood, raised her glass and said, 'Cheers.' Wood did the same, and they both took a sip. 'Who was this informant of yours?' she asked, calmly but steely-eyed.

'I'm sorry, Mrs Bramston, but I can't tell you that for legal reasons. I can only say that I was told Cole might have stolen some of your jewellery.'

Her eyes narrowed further. 'How did you get my name and address?'

Wood could tell she was wary and realised that getting information from her wouldn't be easy. She seemed very sharp, and he knew he needed to be careful not to say anything that would reveal his involvement in the De Klerk investigation and then lead back to Stubbings. He sipped his champagne to give him time to think.

'The informant gave me your surname and said you lived in Coombe Park. I checked the voters' register, and the only Bramstons living in the area were Patrick and Chandice.'

She nodded. 'Patrick's my husband.'

'I also looked for your name on our crime report system but couldn't find it, so I thought it best to speak to you personally in case you were a victim, knowingly or otherwise.'

'Theoretically I was a victim, but I chose not to report the matter for personal reasons, which I'm not prepared to divulge.'

'I respect that, of course, but it would be helpful if you could tell me what happened.'

'How do you think I can help your investigation?' He wondered if Chandice was fishing for information, possibly to pass on to Michelle De Klerk. He knew Stubbings had never interviewed Chandice, but Michelle might have told her about him.

'I suspect Cole may have used different methods to scam several people, and they may not even realise they were victims. I could arrest him right now on reasonable suspicion, but if I don't know all his methods, an interview could prove worthless. I want to build a watertight case before an arrest.'

Her eyes narrowed. 'I despise Cole for what he did, but I'm not prepared to give evidence against him. Doing so could implicate a dear friend, who, like me, was an innocent victim. She's suffering enough as it is right now, and I don't want to add to her distress. I want to build bridges, not destroy them.'

Wood was pretty sure the dear friend was Michelle De Klerk. 'My informant was once close to Mr Cole, but no longer. And like you, they can't stand the man. I was told you were introduced to Cole by a woman called Michelle, as you needed a ring resizing.'

'It sounds like you know rather a lot,' she said curtly.

He shrugged. 'Bits and pieces, but not the full details. That's

LYNDA LA PLANTE | 335

why I need to speak to you and other victims personally.'

'Michelle wasn't a victim of Cole. Well, not directly. But I need to know that you won't speak to her. As I said, she's in a bad way emotionally.'

'What you tell me will be in the strictest confidence, and I won't approach her unless I have to for the sake of the investigation.'

Chandice paused for thought. 'Her name is Michelle De Klerk. You might know her as Michelle Belsham, KC.'

He feigned surprise. 'Yes, I've come across her in court. She's well known to the CID as a highly-respected defence barrister.'

Chandice laughed. 'She told me the police refer to her as "that bitch Belsham". She considered it a compliment.'

'I have heard her called that,' Wood conceded. 'I didn't know her married name was De Klerk.'

'She's a tough lady, Michelle, but she's a totally different person outside of her work. Her husband, Johan, was stabbed during a burglary the other night and is critically ill in hospital.'

Wood tried to look shocked. 'That's awful. Now I see what you meant when you said she's under a lot of stress. It must be very distressing for you as well.'

She sighed. 'It is. But she didn't tell me about it. I saw it on the news. Under the circumstances, I didn't want to call her, so I sent her a text just saying I'm always here for her if she needs me. Sadly, I haven't received a reply.'

'She's obviously focusing completely on her husband, but I'm sure she'll contact you soon,' he said.

'I hope so, but somehow I doubt it. I think she's embarrassed about what happened with Cole and now it's awkward for her to talk to me. Which is so sad – we've been friends since university when we studied law together, and we were each other's chief bridesmaids.'

'Are you also a barrister then?'

'I wanted to be at one time, but then I decided to become a solicitor and specialise in human rights issues.'

'Are you still practising?'

'No. I haven't done any legal work since I had my son eight years ago, and I also have a daughter aged six. I do sometimes wish I was still practising.'

'What does your husband do?'

'He's a banker.'

Wood didn't want to push her, but he was aware time was getting on. 'What happened between you and Michelle that caused the falling out?'

'Cole, to put it bluntly. Just give me a minute.' Chandice walked out and he remained sitting on the high stool looking around at the state-of-the-art kitchen. He reckoned the massive glass fronted fridge-freezer must have cost more than his entire one-bedroom flat. He turned as Chandice walked back in and perched herself on the stool beside him. She opened a small velvet case.

'This is my engagement ring.' She slipped it onto her finger. 'The blue Ceylon sapphire is twelve carats, and the halo of diamonds around it are eighteen. The sapphire was originally in a necklace belonging to my husband's deceased grandmother. My husband had the ring specially made for me.'

'By Nathan Cole?'

'Good lord, no. Garrard's, the former Crown Jewellers, designed it. It's quite similar to Princess Diana's engagement ring.'

'Can I ask how much it cost.'

'Seventy thousand,' she said coolly.

Wood whistled. 'I'm definitely in the wrong business. So what happened?'

Chandice topped up their glasses with champagne. 'You might

not believe it, but I wasn't always as slim as I am now. In fact, I was always a bit chubby, so I started dieting and going to the gym. As a result, my fingers got more slender and my wedding and engagement rings were no longer a snug fit. I told Michelle I was worried about them falling off. She recommended a jeweller her husband knew in Hatton Garden and took me to meet Nathan Cole. His shop was very impressive, with some very expensive and elegant jewellery, though I do also distinctly remember how it stunk of cigar smoke.'

He was eager to get her back on track. 'And he resized your rings?'

'Yes, and I asked him to polish them as well. I left them with him for a few days, then I discovered a few months later that Cole had swapped the sapphire for an inferior stone.'

'How did you find out?'

'I attended the London Jewellery Show at Kensington Olympia last December. They had stalls with experts who were doing free jewellery evaluations. I thought, for insurance purposes, I would see what the ring was currently worth. I was knocked for six when two experts looked at it and said the sapphire was almost worthless. It had been made in a lab apparently. My husband had photos, valuations and letters proving the provenance of the original sapphire, so we knew for certain it had been swapped.'

'What did Michelle say when you told her?'

'She was with me at the show and was as shocked and upset as I was. I wanted to report it to the police, but she asked me to wait until she'd spoke to Johan. I was very angry and told her Cole was a thief and she should know better than anyone that he ought to be punished. I told her she'd got a week to sort it out, or I would inform the police.'

Wood pointed at the ring. 'I take it that's the real sapphire?'

She nodded. 'Michelle came round and collected the ring from me. A couple of days later, she called to say it was all sorted and I went to her house to collect it. Johan was there but didn't say much, other than apologising. Anyway, maybe I shouldn't have said it, but I said to her that maybe she should get her engagement ring checked out too, a big solitaire diamond. Michelle got upset, we had a blazing row, I think she thought I was inferring her husband had something to do with what had happened. It ended up with me storming out of the house, and we haven't spoken since.'

'Did you get the ring double-checked?'

'You're telling me I did. The expert at Olympia had given me his card. He re-examined it and confirmed it was a 12-carat Ceylon sapphire, and the diamonds were genuine too.'

'You were lucky to get it back.'

'I know, and if I hadn't done, I would have reported it to the police. Having heard what you've said about Cole, maybe I should have done.'

'I understand why you didn't,' Wood said reassuringly. 'You weren't to know other people had been victims.' He chuckled. 'I'll bet Michelle put the fear of God in Cole when she confronted him!'

Chandice smiled ruefully. 'She's definitely not the sort of person you want to upset. But actually she said it was Johan who spoke to Cole. I don't know if you've met him, he's a giant of a man, built like an ox, though he's really as soft as shit. Michelle said he told Cole he'd call the police and ruin his business if he didn't return it. Cole said he'd taken the sapphire out to clean it and accidentally put the wrong one back in.'

'That's pretty lame,' Wood said, rolling his eyes.

'I thought it was all a bit odd, but before we had the row, Michelle asked if it could be the end of the matter, and I agreed. We haven't spoken or seen each other in about six months.

I called and left messages but never got a reply, so I gave up. I also think there might have been another agenda, but maybe I shouldn't mention it.'

'What was it?' Wood asked, thankful for the champagne which seemed to have loosened Chandice's tongue.

'Well, poor Michelle was desperate to start a family. I remember her saying to me that part of her wanting to marry Johan was that she reckoned they'd have beautiful children. She made me laugh when she said they'd be perfect if they had his looks and her brains. But it didn't work out as planned for them. I think she had a miscarriage and eventually had to have IVF treatment. Whether or not it was successful I don't know, but in the meantime, I had my two. To be honest, I felt she was envious, I mean she tried not to show it, but she was getting desperate.'

'What did your husband think about it all?'

'About the ring?'

'Yes, how did he react?'

'I thought it best not to tell him. He'd have confronted Johan and Michelle. That's another reason I can't make a statement. So I'd appreciate it if you didn't speak to him.'

'That's fine, I don't need to,' Wood assured her, wondering if it was Michelle who had persuaded Chandice not to say anything to her husband.

'Do you know how the De Klerks got to know Cole?

'I know what you're thinking, officer, but I can assure you neither of them was involved.'

'I understand, but you'd have to say her persuading you not to report it has allowed Cole to steal precious stones from other people.'

'I know, and that saddens me. Michelle has achieved a lot in her career and hopes to be made a judge one day. I think she was worried that if Cole was arrested and the press found out she or Johan were involved, they would use it against her and her reputation would be sullied. I love her dearly, I really do, and I just decided it was best to do as she asked.'

'The media are like vultures these days,' Wood remarked. 'Purely out of curiosity, how did they meet?'

'Michelle was a junior barrister when they met. We went to South Africa on holiday together about ten years ago. Johan was the guide on our safari. He was instantly besotted with Michelle. I felt like a gooseberry on that trip.' She smiled at the memory.

'He gave up the safari work to be with her in the UK?'

'Not exactly. On a trip that Johan was leading, a rampaging female elephant protecting her young charged at the jeep and overturned it. A woman in her seventies was trampled to death. The company was sued, and Johan lost his job. It was in the papers over there but I don't think it made the news here in the UK.'

'What's he doing now?' Wood asked, hoping to discover something he didn't know. He realised that the article about Johan and Michelle meeting at a rugby match was a lie to cover up the safari incident, so he wondered what else they were hiding.

'Johan's father, now let me think . . . yes, Pieter runs a winery in Wellington, just outside Cape Town, which the family has owned for over a century. Johan was never interested in the wine business but started working for his father after the safari incident. He had wanted Michelle to move to South Africa, but she was ambitious in her career and determined to become a Queens Council, as it was back then, which she eventually did. Johan approached his father about opening a wine business in London, which he agreed to. I think Johan has been quite successful, and then they recently bought this incredible property, not that I have been there as yet, but I was told there was a huge amount of construction work done, a cinema in the basement, but you know what they say, behind every great man . . .'

'There is a great woman. Sounds like they have a very successful marriage.'

'Like all married couples, they have their ups and downs. Mind you, Michelle is the one who rules the roost and keeps him in line. Johan can get a bit loud when he's had a few, but he's a pussycat really.' She poured herself another glass of champagne. 'Detective?'

'No thank you, I'm driving. But I'll have to try one of Johan's wines sometime. Can you get them in supermarkets?'

Chandice laughed. 'Good lord, no. His wines are far too expensive. He mostly supplies top restaurants, but you can get them online.' She removed a bottle of Pinot Noir from a rack under the kitchen counter. 'This is one of Johan's family's wines. Take it with you and try it when you get home.'

He looked at the label with its animal logo. '"Springbok Wines, a Taste of the Cape". That's very kind of you. I look forward to having a glass or two. And thank you for taking the time to talk to me.'

Chandice opened a kitchen drawer and started to rummage around inside it. 'I'm sure I've got it here somewhere.'

'Got what?'

'Nathan Cole's business card. I don't know why I kept it. It's of no use to me, so you may as well have it. Ah, here it is.' She handed him the card.

He took it from her. 'How would you describe him?'

'An arsehole and a little shit would be most appropriate,' she replied frankly. Wood smiled. 'But I suppose I'd say he's quite short, about five foot six, bald on top and has dyed black hair on the sides. I'd say he's in his mid-fifties.'

Wood nodded. 'That pretty much fits with what other people have said.'

'If you can put Cole behind bars without our involvement, I will be very pleased, and I'm sure Michelle will be as well.'

'As promised, I won't be approaching Michelle or Johan. A few victims are willing to make a statement and give evidence against Cole, and I'm sure I'll find more. I hope you and Michelle can find a way to restore your friendship and that her husband makes a full recovery.' Chandice suddenly looked worried. 'Are you all right?' he asked.

'I've just had a thought. Do you think Cole might be involved in what happened to Johan?'

Wood hadn't expected her to make the connection and had to think quickly. 'That's a very good point you've made and one the investigating team should consider if they don't already know about Cole. But to be honest, I very much doubt Cole had anything to do with it. He has no criminal record, no history of violence and from what I've learned about him so far, he's just a con man.'

'Thank you, Julian. You've been very kind and understanding.'

'Thank you again for being so forthcoming.' Wood left and got in his car.

He drove around the corner, parked up and took a small portable recorder from his jacket pocket. He checked it was still recording before switching it off. He then took out his pocketbook and started to make notes of his conversation with Chandice. He would have plenty to tell Chapman, but he needed to make sure none of it led back to Richard Stubbings, so this might have to be an edited version.

CHAPTER TWENTY-SEVEN

Anderson sat at his desk while Jessica and Chapman stood in front of him. 'What the hell are you two playing at, interviewing Palmer after charge and without a solicitor? You've broken Code C of the Police and Criminal Evidence Act, so anything he said is inadmissible as evidence.' He was clearly still angry but managing to keep his voice level.

'I'd beg to differ, sir. Code C also states that an interview after a charge can be conducted to prevent or minimise harm or loss to some other person or the public and in the interests of justice.'

Anderson shook his head. 'Oh, a legal buff as well as a fool. Your irresponsibility could now lead to the case against Palmer being thrown out by a judge.'

'There is no case against him. He was . . .' Chapman started to reply, but Anderson wouldn't let him.

'Now you think you know better than the CPS lawyers, who, let me remind you, said there is clear evidence of a joint enterprise and Palmer's involvement in the attempted murder of Johan De Klerk!'

Chapman was unable to disguise his annoyance. 'We just dismissed everything Palmer said without looking at all the evidence. Apart from Jessica, that is. He's been set up. He had nothing to do with the burglary or the assault on De Klerk.'

'Have you lost your mind?' Anderson asked incredulously.

'The landlady of the pub told us about Wheeler, and Palmer, to his credit, gave us his address. Wheeler broke into De Klerk's house, and now it looks like he's been murdered!' Chapman concluded.

'You failed to inform me about what you were doing, and that's neglect of duty.'

'I sent you a text. I thought you would call me. I couldn't sit on my arse and do nothing. Go ahead, discipline me and send an innocent man to prison if that's what you want. But I—'

Jessica butted in. 'Can the two of you please stop arguing. It's getting us nowhere.'

'You need to read the forensic and behavioural report Jessica prepared,' Chapman said, taking it from his jacket pocket.

'Why has he got it before me?' Anderson asked Jessica.

She removed another copy from her handbag. 'I only compiled it yesterday and haven't had the chance to give it to you until now.'

'You could have left it on my desk,' Anderson huffed, grabbing the copy from her.

'I wanted to give it to you personally and discuss the reasoning behind my observations and conclusions.'

He didn't seem to have answer to that. 'What's happening at the crime scene where you found Wheeler's body?'

'It's been cordoned off, and Jessica's team are attending,' Chapman said. 'A pathologist has been called to examine the body and estimate the time of death.'

'Do the video and photography,' Anderson said, looking at Jessica. 'But I want to see the body in situ. Call your team and tell them the forensic examination can start after I've done that.'

She took her phone out. 'Since I compiled the report, other things have come to light that we need to discuss, but time is of the essence. The body can be left in situ while Diane and Taff examine the scene. We need to identify whoever else is involved with Wheeler, and quickly.'

'Very well, but I need you two to tell me everything, chapter and verse, after I've read this. A coffee wouldn't go amiss either.'

Chapman said he'd get them all a coffee. Jessica called Diane. She informed her she was with DCI Anderson and Diane was not to touch or move the body as he wanted to see it. Diane asked about examining the scene, and Jessica said it was OK to proceed with that after the video and photography were completed.

After finishing the call, Jessica sat quietly while Anderson read her report. She noticed his look of irritation gradually turn to one of concern. She hoped he was beginning to realise that Palmer was not involved in the crimes he was accused of. Chapman returned with the coffees and looked at Jessica with raised eyebrows, wondering how things were going. She gave him a wink.

A few minutes later, Anderson finished reading. 'That's a very detailed report, Jessica. We may have misjudged Palmer's involvement in the crime. The messages to and from the burner phones show two people were involved, so it doesn't absolve Palmer completely. He may even be responsible for Wheeler's death.'

'He gave us Wheeler's location. Why on earth would he do that if he'd killed him?' Chapman argued.

'Other things that absolve Palmer have come to light since I wrote my report,' Jessica added.

'Enlighten me then,' Anderson said, turning the report over so he could make notes on the back.

Jessica told him about Guy's digital examinations, which revealed Palmer was playing online games or watching films during the night De Klerk was assaulted and then when the Range Rover was set alight. She then told him about the Sealskinz glove marks on Palmer's cistern lid and Taff's discovery that the lock on Palmer's front door had been picked.

'When we found Wheeler's body, he was wearing Adidas Ultraboost trainers, and there was a pair of Sealskinz gloves on the table, alongside a fake passport and one-way flight ticket to Dubai for Wednesday morning,' Chapman added.

Anderson nodded. 'I hear what you're saying. It looks like

this man Wheeler committed the crime, but it doesn't account for the money in Palmer's wallet that had De Klerk's fingerprints on it.'

'That's because Wheeler stole it from De Klerk, then gave it to Palmer as payment for turning off the CCTV system at the garage and giving him a can of petrol,' Chapman said.

Jessica took over. 'Guy managed to identify Wheeler's phone number from Palmer's mobile. Wheeler rang Palmer on Monday evening to arrange switching off the CCTV and . . .'

Anderson raised his hands. 'Slow down a minute, it's hard to put all this information in context. Go back a bit and tell me how you learned about Wheeler.'

Chapman explained why they went to The Bell and their conversation with the landlady, when decided Palmer knew more about Wheeler than he was letting on.

'Palmer is terrified of Wheeler, but he eventually gave us his address.'

Anderson sighed. 'You did the right thing. I just wish you'd spoken to me before interviewing Palmer or going to Wheeler's flat. Tell me what Palmer said when you interviewed him.'

'I can't remember everything, word for word. Being off the record, I didn't record it or take notes.'

'Lucky I did then,' Jessica said, producing her iPhone.

She saw the look of surprise on Anderson and Chapman's faces. 'It's not illegal, is it?'

'Never mind about that. I want to hear it,' Anderson said.

'I thought it might be useful for my behavioural analysis of Palmer,' Jessica said, turning on the recording.

Anderson made more notes while listening to the interview. 'It's all quite plausible,' he said when it was finished. 'And I can understand why Palmer would be frightened of Wheeler. But how do we know he didn't murder Wheeler and take the proceeds of the burglary?'

'That's highly unlikely, sir,' Chapman replied. 'As I said . . .'

'I know, I know. Palmer gave you Wheeler's address. But maybe that was just to put you off the scent. Maybe he's cleverer than you think.'

Jessica felt he was clutching at straws to cover up his errors. She needed to get him back on track without belittling him or appearing condescending. 'Palmer has attention deficit hyperactivity disorder.'

Anderson raised his eyebrows. 'That's news to me.'

'I read his criminal record and his social services files. His father deliberately smashed his head against a wall when he was eight, but he wasn't diagnosed with ADHD until some years later. Palmer suffers from racing thoughts and obsessive worrying.'

'Well, I'd be worried if I were in his shoes,' Anderson retorted.

'Palmer's brain is a constant flow of thoughts, which he finds hard to control,' Jessica continued. 'They interfere with his daily life, making it difficult for him to focus on any one thing at a time. He becomes fixated on things that worry him, going over them repeatedly in his mind, which leads to anxiety and stress and makes it difficult for him to complete tasks or make decisions.'

'Are you saying he's retarded?' Anderson asked.

'We don't use that word any longer,' Jessica said, trying to be patient.

Anderson waved a hand dismissively. 'Whatever he is, the fact is Palmer is capable of committing a crime, as borne out by his previous convictions and the assault on you.'

'That may be so,' Jessica agreed. 'But I don't believe he's capable of killing a man like Wheeler and then successfully covering his tracks. And do you honestly think Wheeler would have left all that cash and the Rolex with someone as unreliable as Palmer?' Jessica asked pointedly.

Anderson frowned. 'I was just playing devil's advocate. Unless there's anything else, I think we should go to the crime scene.'

* * *

Jessica drove to Fred Wigg Tower in her car, and Chapman took Anderson. She arrived first, and as she approached the building, she noticed a tall, attractive woman with cropped dark hair standing by the foyer lift. She looked to be in her early forties and was casually dressed in a tight-fitting roll-neck jumper and trousers. It was only the black leather pilot's case she was holding that provided a clue to who she might be.

'Hi, are you the pathologist?' Jessica asked.

'Yes. I'm Doctor Nicki Giorgini.'

'I'm Jessica Russell, in charge of the forensics team.'

'I read a report Commander Williams sent us about the new MSCAN team and recall your name,' she said with a warm smile as they shook hands.

'This is our first major investigation as a unit,' Jessica said as the lift doors opened, and they stepped in.

'Coincidentally, this is also my first case since I joined the Greater London Forensic Pathology team,' Nicki said. 'I was based in Manchester but jumped at the opportunity when I was offered a job down here.'

'Well, it's a pleasure to meet you,' Jessica said.

'You too,' Nicki said.

They got out of the lift, and Jessica called out to Taff and Diane, who were inside Wheeler's flat. They came out and she introduced them to Doctor Giorgini. She noticed the glint of appreciation in

Taff's eyes, and so did Diane, who frowned at him. Taff said that he'd used a handheld fingerprint scanner on the right index finger of the body and could confirm from the criminal database that it was John Wheeler. Diane added that Guy had taken Wheeler's phone and laptop to the lab for examination.

'Great, you carry on, and we'll catch up after I've briefed Doctor Giorgini about the investigation.' She then gave Nicki a brief outline of the De Klerk case and explained how Wheeler fitted in.

As Nicki was putting on protective clothing, Chapman and Anderson arrived. When they were introduced to Nicki, Jessica saw Chapman had the same look in his eye as Taff. While they were all suiting up, Jessica nudged him.

'You looked a bit smitten there.'

'I was surprised to see a female pathologist, that's all. She's not really my type.' He looked at Jessica, and she found herself blushing.

When they were all suited and gloved, Jessica asked Taff and Diane to join them on the landing. 'Have you found anything of interest?' she asked.

'I recovered footprints using ESLA in the hallway, and a few were on either side of the armchair,' Taff said. 'They could be the suspect's prints, but I'll need to eliminate them against yours, DI Chapman's and the uniform officers. I looked at the trainers Wheeler was wearing. I'm confident the footmarks at De Klerk's house and Palmer's flat came from them. Same with the Sealskinz gloves on the coffee table. The rucksack in the hallway had these items in it.' Taff showed them photographs of a small crowbar, a battery-operated hydraulic door breacher and lock pick on his iPad.

'It would seem Wheeler was a professional burglar,' Anderson remarked.

'I'm willing to bet when I do striation mark tests, we'll find these tools were used at De Klerk's house and the lock pick tool to gain entry to Palmer's flat.'

'Good work, Taff. How'd you get on Diane?' Jessica asked.

She got out her iPhone. 'I've done a lot of DNA swabs. I can test them back at the lab, but I also searched the bedroom. There's a photo album with pictures of Wheeler as a paratrooper. There's one where he's lighting a cigarette with a Zippo lighter. I photographed and enlarged it. If you look closely, you can just make out the paratrooper crest.' Diane handed her phone to Taff to show them while she nipped into the flat, quickly returning holding a clear exhibit bag.

'I also found this neck support travel pillow,' she said, holding it up.

Anderson didn't look impressed. 'He was about to fly to Dubai, so . . . ?'

'It's got a zip opening. You can put small items of clothing or other stuff in it too . . .'

'My wife has one, so I know how it works, thank you,' Anderson said dismissively. 'If that's all, I'd like to see the body now.'

Diane pretended she hadn't heard him. 'Curiosity got the better of me, and I thought I'd see what he'd stuffed it with.' She took her phone from Taff and showed them a picture. 'It was full of socks stuffed with cash. I only counted the amount in one sock. It was forty thousand pounds. There were six socks, so I'll let you do the math.' Anderson looked embarrassed. 'I'll fingerprint the cash at the lab. A lockbox on the living room floor had been cut open with a small angle grinder we found on the coffee table. I did a swab test for drugs and got a positive for cocaine on the outside of the lockbox and on the coffee table where there were also some visible white powder remnants.'

'Maybe whoever killed Wheeler forced the lockbox open and

took the contents but missed the cash because they didn't think to look inside the travel pillow,' Chapman suggested. Jessica asked Taff to examine the inside of the lockbox for fingerprints and Diane to check for DNA.

'How long will it take to get a result?' Anderson asked.

'I can do rapid DNA testing on it and hopefully have a result by tomorrow morning, but it's expensive,' Diane said. Jessica looked at Anderson enquiringly.

'We're up against the clock,' he said. 'Whoever's involved with Wheeler might flee the country as well. I need answers, and quickly, so go ahead.'

'I think Wheeler may have a girlfriend or paid for a prostitute to visit him,' Diane said.

'What makes you think that?' Anderson asked with a puzzled look.

'I found five empty Durex sachets in his bedroom bin. There were no used sheathes, so he probably flushed them down the toilet.'

'I'll take a DNA swab from his penis while I'm here. Vaginal fluid might help you to identify who she is,' Nicki remarked. 'Can I look at the body now?' Jessica led her to Wheeler's body, followed by Anderson and Chapman. Taff and Diane waited outside.

'Your jaw nearly hit the floor when you met Nicki,' Diane remarked.

'Well, she is quite attractive . . . for a pathologist.'

'She's probably a lot older than she looks,' Diane retorted.

'Meow! A bit like you then,' Taff replied.

Diane punched his arm. 'Just remember it's rude to stare.'

Inside the flat, Chapman noted that the smell of decomposition was worse than when they'd first arrived. Nicki suggested it might be because the central heating had come on. Anderson removed a Vicks nasal stick from his pocket and took a deep sniff in each nostril.

'That doesn't actually help, you know,' Nicki told him.

'Well, I can't smell the body now,' Anderson replied.

'You will, and a lot better in a minute or so. Vicks clears your nasal passages, allowing you to smell things better,' she smiled. Nicki photographed Wheeler's body before using an infrared ear thermometer to check his body temperature. She then looked closely at the bruises on his face. 'I'd say from the colouring, some of these injuries are a day or two old and some maybe three. The most recent one is to his nose, which looks broken and probably occurred at or around the time of death. Considering the early stages of decomposition and the rigor and livor mortis, I'd estimate he died two days ago between 6 p.m. and midnight.'

'He must have booked the flight on Tuesday. If we can find out what time he did that, it will help narrow down his time of death,' Anderson said.

'Guy is already working on Wheeler's phone and laptop, so that might give us some answers,' Jessica said.

'Have we made any enquiries with his neighbours?' Anderson asked Chapman.

'Not yet, but I've asked Andy Bingham to organise it.'

'Where's DS Wood? As a supervising officer, he should organise it.'

'He's following up on a lead. Probably be a dead end, but I thought he should check it out.'

Nicki was looking at Wheeler's hands. 'It looks like he was restrained. There are rope marks on his wrists and traces of sticky tape around his mouth and nose. This looks interesting,' Nicki said, looking closely at the back of Wheeler's head before removing some plastic tweezers from her bag.

'What is it?' Anderson asked.

'A small piece of black masking tape. It must have come loose when the tape was removed from his mouth.' Nicki carefully removed it from Wheeler's hair before placing it in a small plastic container.

'Taff might get a fingerprint off it. And it might be useful for a mechanical fit if we can find the roll of tape it came from,' Jessica observed. Nicki undid Wheeler's shirt buttons, revealing some round red marks on the upper centre of his chest.

'Cigarette burns?' Anderson asked.

'From the circumference, I'd say they're from something bigger, like a cigar.'

Jessica looked in the ashtray on the table. 'There's a lump of ash that's bigger than a cigarette.'

'That's definitely cigar ash. My grandad used to smoke them. Whoever did this taped Wheeler's mouth while they were torturing him,' Chapman said.

'But when they removed the tape, he still didn't tell them where the cash was,' Anderson said.

'He may have died before he was able to,' Nicki said. 'He's got some heavy bruising to the upper left side of the abdomen, which I'd say is at least three days old.'

'What do you think caused it?' Anderson asked.

'Could be a kick, or he was hit hard with a blunt instrument like a baseball bat or a lump of wood. However, I don't think his external injuries would have killed him. He may have serious internal injuries or had a heart attack, but I won't know until I open him up in the mortuary.'

'Could he have choked on his vomit if his mouth was taped?' Anderson asked.

'It's possible, but I didn't see any vomit inside his mouth. That's not to say some may not have got stuck in his throat. A full post-mortem should tell us more. I can do it at the new East London Forensic Centre when we finish here. Is that OK for you all?' Everyone nodded.

'I'll just be two ticks. I want to ask Di and Taff to search the stairwell, foyer, and outside for any discarded cigars,' Jessica said.

'I was just thinking the same thing. I can get some uniform officers to assist,' Anderson said. Chapman glanced at Jessica and shook his head, knowing it had never crossed Anderson's mind.

Outside the flat, Jessica's phone rang, and she answered a call from Guy. He said he had carried out a cursory examination of Wheeler's phone and the laptop. She returned inside to put him on speakerphone so the others could hear.

'Just before 8 p.m., Tuesday night, Wheeler used the laptop to book an Emirates Airways flight to Dubai, which cost two thousand eight hundred pounds. He paid with a credit card in the same name as the passport. Around the same time, he ordered an Uber for midnight to take him to Heathrow. I contacted the company, who said the driver turned up, waited outside for five minutes and tried calling him but got no answer and left.'

'Looks like he might have been killed between 8 p.m. and midnight then?' Chapman suggested to Nicki, who nodded.

'I know you're busy, but I've also got some info from the service provider on the missing burner phone if you want it,' Guy said.

'Yes, please. DCI Anderson and DI Chapman are with me,' Jessica said.

'You might recall I said it was last used in Birmingham. Well, whoever contacted Wheeler on it was staying at the Bloc Hotel, Caroline Street.'

'Do you know that for certain?' Anderson asked.

'Yes, because they made the mistake of using WhatsApp on the free Wi-Fi provided by the hotel. Unfortunately, I can't give you a name or a room number.'

'I'll get someone to make enquiries with the hotel. Great work,' Anderson said.

'Something about the hotel's location might also interest you. It's in the heart of Birmingham's jewellery quarter, with over a hundred retailers, diamond dealers and workshops.'

Chapman nodded to himself. 'When the burner phones went live, the first cell tower to pick them up was in Leather Lane, Holborn, last Wednesday evening. Leather Lane is the next street down from Hatton Garden, London's jewellery quarter and the centre of the UK diamond trade.'

'It seems likely the lockbox contained jewellery, then,' Anderson suggested. 'I need to ask Michelle De Klerk about it.'

'When I first met Michelle, she told me she didn't know what Johan kept in the safe in his study, but she thought it might be some cash. They had jewellery in a bedroom safe, which wasn't broken into,' Jessica reminded him.

'Be interesting to see where they bought their jewellery. A dodgy dealer would have their details and might get someone like Wheeler to steal it,' Chapman said.

'Would you like me to examine De Klerk's laptop to see if there's anything relating to recent jewellery purchases?' Guy asked over the speakerphone.

'Good idea,' Anderson said, 'but let me apply for a warrant first.'

Diane came into the living room. 'Found this on the road just down from the flats. Might have been discarded when someone was getting in a car,' she said, holding up an exhibit bag with a cigar inside.

'I thought we might find one. You can fast-track it for DNA.

Fingers crossed we get a hit on the database and can make a quick arrest,' Anderson said, looking pleased.

'We may as well call for the undertaker's van now. We can do the fingernail work, DNA swabs and fibre tapings here, which will take about twenty minutes, and then he's good to go,' Jessica said.

'That sounds good to me, Jessica,' Nicki replied.

Jessica looked at Diane. 'How long do you reckon it will be before you finish here?'

'About an hour or two, less if we had extra help.'

'If it's all right with you, sir, I'd like to send Diane and Taff back to the lab so they can start examining what we've recovered here,' Jessica asked Anderson. 'I'll ask for some local SOCO's to attend and take over. I'll brief them on what's required, then meet you at the mortuary.'

'Fine by me,' Anderson replied.

'I'll start taking the DNA swabs and other samples from Wheeler for Diane to take back to the lab and work on,' Nicki said as she unzipped Wheeler's trousers, then pulled down his underpants to take the penis swab. An embarrassed Anderson quickly asked Chapman to take him back to the station so he could brief the team and organise the urgent enquiries. They both hurried out of the room. Nicki shook her head. 'What is it about men and penises?'

'Probably worried they would feel inadequate if they saw Wheeler's,' Jessica replied, and they both laughed.

CHAPTER TWENTY-EIGHT

Jessica followed the undertaker's van to the East London Forensic Centre in the Borough of Waltham Forest. The new state-of-the-art facility, fitted with the latest technology, provided comprehensive invasive and non-invasive post-mortem examinations, vital for several faith communities.

Mike Chapman was waiting by the entrance and waved when he saw Jessica. 'Anderson won't be attending. He's got a lot to be getting on with at the office.'

'Is that a polite way of saying he's squeamish or he's run out of Vicks?' she smiled.

'Definitely squeamish. He phoned his wife on the way back to the office. He said he might be home late. I could hear her shouting at him and saying she'd throw his dinner in the bin if he wasn't home by seven.'

'What did he say?'

'That he now had a murder to deal with connected to the De Klerk case and wasn't going to let the team down. She wasn't happy and accused him of letting *her* down. He told her there was a first time for everything and ended the call. She tried ringing him back, but he put the phone on silent.'

'Good for him.'

'She might be waiting for him with a rolling pin, though. The next murder we end up investigating might be Anderson's,' Chapman laughed. As they were about to enter the mortuary, Chapman's phone rang. He told Jessica he would catch up with her. He waited until she had gone inside to answer.

'Where the fuck are you, Julian?' Chapman demanded.

'On my way back to the nick. Where the fuck are you?' Wood retorted.

'I'm not in the mood for silly games. Anderson asked where you are, and I've had to cover your back. You know that bloke Wheeler I asked you to check out?'

'Yeah, you found him?'

'Yes, no thanks to you, but he didn't say much.'

'With his record, I didn't expect him to.'

'He's fucking dead, Julian! Someone tortured and murdered him.'

'Jesus Christ. You serious?'

'No, I'm making it all up because I've nothing better to do. I want to know where you are and what the hell you've been doing.'

'All right, calm down, Mike. I've been out grafting and I got some interesting information from Stubbings and a woman called Chandice Bramston. I'm calling so we can meet somewhere private and chat about it before telling Anderson.'

'I'm just about to go into Wheeler's postmortem. I'll call you when I'm done.'

Jessica and Chapman put on protective clothing and entered the mortuary examination room, where Doctor Giorgini was already gowned and putting on some rubber gloves. Wheeler's body was still clothed, and Jessica took some frontal photographs before helping Nicki and a mortician turn the body over for more photography. Once this was done, they removed the clothing, and Jessica put them in exhibit bags. Nicki then put measuring scales by the various injuries to Wheeler's torso, and Jessica photographed them. Nicki made a Y incision on the torso, cut into the skin and muscle with a scalpel, and then folded back the flesh. She put a measuring scale on his ribs and asked Jessica to take some photographs.

'A few of his ribs are broken. It looks like one of them has ruptured his spleen, resulting in a slow internal bleed into his abdomen over at least two or three days. I'll need to remove and examine his internal organs to be sure.'

'Is that what killed him?' Chapman asked as Nicki cut through Wheeler's ribs.

'Two secs and I'll be able to tell you.' She lifted out his internal organs and placed them in a large bowl. She put his spleen on a chopping board, and Jessica took some photographs of it before Nicki examined it. 'Yup, his spleen has been punctured by a rib.'

'How would that little puncture wound kill him?' Chapman asked.

'When the spleen ruptures, it can easily bleed internally, leading to haemorrhagic shock and death.'

'What's haemorrhagic shock?'

'A life-threatening condition that occurs with major blood loss, which results in inadequate oxygen supply to the body's tissues and organs, which in turn causes death. A ruptured spleen is a medical emergency requiring swift diagnosis, intervention and sometimes surgery. If he'd gone straight to a hospital after the injury, he might have survived.'

'Would he have been in a lot of pain?' Jessica asked.

'Yes. Bleeding from the rupture can irritate a nerve that runs from your neck and down through the left side of your chest. Other symptoms are dizziness, disorientation, anxiety and nausea, to name but a few.'

'So, whoever or whatever caused his ruptured spleen was responsible for his death?' Chapman asked.

'Technically, yes. I'm certain the rupture didn't occur when he was gagged, bound and tortured.'

'Would the eggshell skull rule apply?' Chapman asked.

'That would be for the CPS and a court to decide, not me,' Nicki replied.

'What's the eggshell rule?' Jessica asked Chapman.

'The rule protects vulnerable individuals and ensures that a defendant is held accountable for the full extent of the harm they cause during an assault, regardless of the victim's pre-existing condition or vulnerability.'

'The torture with the cigar is grievous bodily harm and could be a contributing factor, but it's a very fine line in this case, DI Chapman. I'll need to do histopathology on his organs and brain before confirming the exact cause of death.'

'There were signs of a struggle between Johan and his assailant at the De Klerk house. If Wheeler was responsible, then it could be Johan broke his ribs and caused the ruptured spleen,' Jessica told them.

'That's a viable theory,' Nicki said.

'Now that Wheeler's dead, only De Klerk can tell us what happened,' Chapman said.

'Maybe whoever Wheeler contacted on the burner phone knows what happened,' Jessica suggested.

'At the moment, we haven't a clue who he is, and if he's left the country, we are screwed,' Chapman said dejectedly.

'I think we should stop speculating until I finish the post-mortem,' Nicki said as she removed the internal organs and put Wheeler's spleen in a separate container before opening the stomach to examine the contents. 'Can you photograph this for me, please, Jessica.'

'What is it?' Chapman asked.

Using tweezers, Nicki lifted the object from Wheeler's stomach. 'It's a condom with something wrapped in cling film and tape inside it. It looks like Wheeler's a drug mule and was trying to smuggle these to Dubai. When swallowed like this, it's harder to detect them using traditional X-ray or computed tomography imagery.'

'So it could have been drugs that were in the lockbox or stolen from De Klerk's safe,' Chapman suggested.

'How many are in his stomach?' Jessica asked.

'I can see three more, but I need to have a feel around in case there are others.'

'Rather you than me,' Chapman winced.

'If one had burst, the drugs in it would have killed him,' Nicki said, removing two more condoms from Wheeler's stomach.

'Diane said she found five Durex wrappers in Wheeler's bedroom bin,' Jessica reminded them.

'That's not a lot for a drugs mule. Generally, in postmortem cases with drug mules, I recover anywhere between thirty and fifty wrapped condoms,' Nicki said.

'I think we need to look inside one and see what we're dealing with,' Jessica suggested. Nicki put one of the condoms on a chopping board and, using a scalpel, slowly cut it open before carefully unwrapping the clingfilm and tape to reveal the contents. Chapman leaned in to get a closer look.

'Looks like different sizes of coloured pebbles. Is it some form of crack cocaine?' he asked.

Jessica was equally perplexed. 'I don't know. We can test them back at the lab.'

Nicki smiled. 'I've only ever seen this once before, during a presentation at a pathology conference last year. Unlike their polished counterparts, which display a brilliant sparkle, raw diamonds have a rough exterior and resemble ordinary rocks or pebbles.'

'They're fucking diamonds?' Chapman exclaimed. 'Excuse my French.'

'It looks like it. You'd best get an expert to look at them for a more definitive answer,' Nicki told them.

'How many are there?' he asked.

'There's five in the one I just opened, so assuming there's the same in each condom, that's at least twenty diamonds, maybe more.'

'What sort of value would we be talking about?' Chapman asked.

Nicki shrugged. 'I haven't a clue. I believe it would depend on the carat and type of diamond. You could be talking between a few thousand pounds to two hundred thousand, maybe more once they're polished and cut. There's a few really good-sized ones.'

'I'll arrange for a marked response vehicle to take the diamonds to the lab,' Chapman said.

'I'm perfectly capable of doing that,' Jessica said.

'I know, but you could be involved in an accident or a carjacking, and I'm not prepared to risk losing thousands of pounds worth of vital evidence. Or you,' he added with a smile.

The post-mortem lasted nearly three hours as Nicki examined all of Wheeler's internal organs, then cut open his skull and examined his brain. She also took blood, urine and hair samples to be examined for drugs.

'Is the spleen injury the definite cause of death, then?' Chapman finally asked.

'I don't know yet, but as I said before, it would have eventually killed him without medical intervention. Wheeler was a fit man with a healthy heart, but he might have died from takotsubo cardiomyopathy.'

'What's that?' Chapman asked.

'It's also known as broken heart syndrome. A weakening of the left ventricle, the heart's main pumping chamber, can occur when a person experiences severe emotional or physical stress. A rush of overwhelming stress hormones, like cortisol and adrenaline, put sudden stress on the heart, which Wheeler could have suffered when tied up and tortured. Again, without medical assistance, it could have killed him.'

'If that's how he died, whoever tied him up and tortured him is responsible for his death,' Jessica said.

'No one knows the exact cause of takotsubo syndrome, but it can lead to severe, short-term heart muscle failure, and in rare cases, it can be fatal. I need to X-ray his heart and do some histopathology and microscopy work before I can determine if that's how he died. I'll have a full report done by midday tomorrow and send it to you two and DCI Anderson.'

* * *

After the postmortem, Chapman and Jessica went to see Anderson, who was on the phone with Commander Williams. He smiled and pointed to the chairs, inviting them to sit. 'Yes, ma'am, I've informed the CPS. They agreed the current charges against Palmer should be dropped. However, he will be remanded in custody on the assault charge and burglary warrant.' He paused to listen before continuing. 'We all got it wrong, and if it wasn't for Jessica, an innocent man could have gone to prison for a long time. She's with me now, so I'll pass on your appreciation.' He ended the call and looked at her. 'As you probably guessed, Commander Williams has been very impressed with you and your team's work, as have we all.'

'Just doing our job, sir, and thank you for your support. We all appreciate it.'

'Just call me John or guv when we talk privately. I want to apologise to you both regarding my tunnel vision regarding Palmer. You'd probably have expressed your concerns earlier if I'd been more approachable.'

'I was also convinced Palmer was guilty as sin at first,' Chapman said.

'What will happen to him for assisting Wheeler by turning off the CCTV?' Jessica asked.

'Palmer helped us, so I took the view that with Wheeler being dead, there was insufficient evidence to charge him with assisting an offender. As far as I'm concerned there will be no further action on that matter.'

'You do have a heart after all,' Chapman smiled.

'I'm sure you'd have done the same, Mike. What were the results of the postmortem?' They informed him of Doctor Giorgini's findings, covering as much detail as they could recall. 'The takotsubo syndrome is interesting. That said, whatever the cause of Wheeler's death, the CPS feel there will be enough evidence to charge the person or persons responsible with murder . . . if we can find them.'

'We will, guv. I'm sure Jessica's team will come up trumps with a DNA or fingerprint hit on something from Wheeler's flat.'

'No offence, Jessica, but we can't bank on it' Anderson replied.

'None taken. I've had many a case where we thought we would get a result and didn't, but we will do our best.'

'DC Bingham has been leading the house-to-house enquiries at Fred Wigg Tower. Wheeler's flat is owned by his sister, who lives in Derby and rents it to him. She's married, so his surname wasn't on the voter register. So far, we haven't found a resident who saw anyone coming or going from the flat. A few knew who Wheeler was and weren't very complimentary about him. Some were glad that he was dead.'

'Live by the sword, die by the sword. Is there any news on Johan De Klerk's condition?' Chapman asked.

'I phoned Doctor Babu earlier. He's off the ventilator and was moved to a private room last night. He's still unconscious, but his eyes and hands have twitched, which is a good sign. Being a fit and otherwise healthy man, the prognosis is good.'

'Any idea on when we might get to speak to him?' Chapman asked.

'Doctor Babu thought De Klerk should have come round by now. He said he might overnight, but he'll reassess him tomorrow morning.'

'Have you spoken to Michelle De Klerk?' Jessica asked.

'Yes, I called her after my conversation with Doctor Babu. She was obviously still very distressed about her husband's condition, but I reassured her that the doctor was confident he could make a full recovery.'

'Did she ask about Liam Palmer?' she asked.

'She wanted to know if he had been charged. I said I'd meet with her tomorrow morning and discuss the recent developments, but she wasn't happy. She wanted to have some good news for Johan when he woke up.'

'So, Michelle knows it wasn't him now?' Jessica asked.

Anderson shook his head. 'Not yet. I said I'd rather speak to her personally and arranged to meet her at the hospital at six o'clock.'

'Are you going to tell her about Wheeler and the diamonds?'

'I'll tell her about Wheeler and the cash, not the diamonds. If they came from Johan's safe, I want him to tell me where he got them and why he had them when he wakes up.'

'I think that's a good move, guv. Are you taking Dawn Owens with you?' Chapman asked.

'No, I would have, but she called in sick this morning.'

'Nothing serious, I hope?' Jessica said.

'The office clerk took the call. She said Dawn had stomach cramps and seemed quite upset.'

'I've never known her go sick,' Chapman said. 'Knowing Dawn, she'll be upset by letting us down.'

Anderson nodded. 'I don't think there's much more we can do today, Mike. A lot now depends on the forensic work. Do you still feel we might have some results by tomorrow morning, Jessica?'

'Hopefully, but I can't say if they will be positive. Guy's working on Wheeler's mobile and laptop, and Taff's priority is the tape in Wheeler's hair. I've asked Diane to look for touch DNA on the diamonds as well.'

'Guy can examine De Klerk's laptop and PC now. We've got a warrant. A copy should have been sent to him,' Anderson said. 'I'm happy for your team to concentrate on whatever they think will get us the quickest result to identify any other suspects.'

'I'll let them know,' Jessica replied.

'You two have been up since the crack of dawn, so go home and get some rest. Tell your team to do the same, Jessica. We'll have another meeting at 10 a.m. tomorrow to discuss any new developments.'

'I was just wondering. Seeing as Dawn's gone sick, would you like me to accompany you to see Michelle?' Jessica asked.

'I appreciate your offer, Jessica, but you've had a long enough day as it is.'

'Honestly, I'm fine.'

'OK, I appreciate it. I'm sure she'll be more at ease with you there. I've got a couple of calls to make, then we can head off to the hospital.'

'I'll grab a drink and a sandwich in the canteen. Just let me know when you're ready to go.'

Before Jessica went to the canteen, she and Chapman had a brief conversation in his office. 'I reckon he's phoning his wife to tell her he'll be home late,' Chapman said.

'Looks like he's beginning to stand up to her.'

'Let's hope he makes it to work tomorrow!' Chapman laughed.

Jessica went to the canteen and ate a sandwich in a quiet corner. When she finished, she phoned Dawn. 'Hi Dawn, it's Jessica Russell. I just heard you'd gone sick and thought I'd call to see how you were.'

Dawn immediately burst into tears. 'I don't know what to do. DCI Anderson wanted me to go and see Michele De Klerk with him today, but I can't face her right now. I'm terrified I'll lose my job if anyone discovers what's happened.'

'Take a deep breath, Dawn, then tell me what's worrying you.'

'Is there anyone with you?' Dawn asked.

'No, I'm on my own. Whatever you say is just between us.'

'Thank you. I did something stupid and I think I could be in big trouble.'

'What did you do?' Jessica asked calmly.

'I told my boyfriend, Sam, about the investigation, you know, what happened to Johan De Klerk and who his wife was. I think it was him that told the media.'

'What makes you think that?'

'I remembered meeting his uncle at a family wedding last year. He said he worked for the BBC.'

'Do you know what department he's in?'

'I think he said he was a producer or something.'

'Did you speak to Sam about it?'

'He said he hadn't spoken to his uncle in ages and would never pass on what I told him. But I think he's lying.'

'Why?

'I don't know, just the way he reacted. I asked him again, and he got really upset. He said if I didn't trust him, then there was no point in continuing our relationship . . . then he stormed out.' Dawn burst into tears again.

'He might be telling the truth, you know.'

'But what if it was him and someone finds out?'

'Do you know his uncle's name?'

'It's his dad's brother, so I guess it will be Brian Moore.'

'I'll make discreet enquiries to find out if it was him. For now, don't say anything to anyone. And please don't get yourself all worked up about it. Sam may be telling the truth.'

'What if it does turn out to be Sam and his uncle?'

'Then you'll have to tell Anderson, but we'll cross that bridge when we come to it. Do you mind if I speak to DI Chapman about it?'

'I'd rather you didn't. He'll just tell Anderson.'

'I can assure you he won't. Chapman will support you, and I also think Anderson will be quite understanding. You're not the first police officer who's spoken to their partners about their work. For now, try to patch things up with Sam. Tell him you've been under a lot of pressure and you're sorry for doubting him. If we find out he lied to you, then my advice would be to dump him. I'll even come round and help you throw him and his belongings out the door.'

Dawn let out a little laugh. 'Thank you so much. You've made me feel a lot better.'

Jessica saw Anderson enter the canteen. 'I've got to go now, but let me know how it goes with Sam, and I'll call you when I find out more. Take care and chin up.'

CHAPTER TWENTY- NINE

DS Wood and Mike Chapman were sitting at a table in Mottingham's Prince of Wales pub. They both had pints of lager in front of them. 'What was Wheeler's cause of death?' Wood asked.

'Ruptured spleen.'

'Any idea who killed him?'

'Probably Johan De Klerk.'

Wood laughed. 'Right . . . a man at death's door has a miraculous recovery, nips out to Wheeler's flat to seek revenge and beats him to death. You're on the same planet as Anderson.' Chapman explained what they believed had happened. 'A bit of summary justice then,' Wood said.

'I'd have preferred it if Wheeler was still alive. We might have got him to tell us who else was involved and who the diamonds belonged to.'

'I might be able to help you with that,' Wood smiled.

'Just get to the point. I've had a fucking long day, and I'm knackered.'

'I had an interesting meeting with Stubbings last night, which led to an even more interesting one with a lady called Chandice Bramston.' He took out his notebook and put it down it on the table.

'Who's she?'

'Michelle De Klerk's best friend – or at least she was. They're not on speaking terms due to a mix-up over a very expensive sapphire ring and a dodgy jeweller.'

Chapman's eyes lit up. 'You got a name?'

'Nathan Cole. He owns a shop in Hatton Garden.'

'And . . . ?' Wood told Chapman how Michelle De Klerk

had introduced Chandice to Nathan Cole to get her engagement ring resized.

'Cole swapped the sapphire for a fake one, but Chandice twigged a few months later.'

'How did Stubbings get involved?' Chapman asked.

Wood grinned. 'You're going to like this. Michelle De Klerk hired him under her married name, but he recognised her as Belsham, the barrister. She made him sign a non-disclosure agreement before telling him why she wanted his services as a PI.'

'And why did she?'

'She suspected Cole was swapping diamonds and other gemstones for lab-made ones.'

'What exactly did she want Stubbings to do?'

'Find out as much as he could about Cole's activities. She never gave him Chandice's name. All she said was that Cole had ripped off a close friend with a fake sapphire ring, but as the real one had been returned, her friend didn't want to pursue the matter.'

'How did Stubbings find out this friend was Chandice?'

'Good detective work is his forte, but I'll tell you more after you get a round in.'

Chapman went to the bar and brought back two more pints. When he'd sat down, Wood continued. 'Stubbs started enquiring about Cole through informants and other contacts he still had, and . . .'

'Are some of them serving police officers?' Chapman interrupted, frowning.

'I didn't ask. But he found out that Cole used professional burglars to steal valuable jewellery from wealthy people. In the main, he targeted people who had purchased goods from him as he had their addresses. Cole then removed any precious stones and made new rings, necklaces, etc, to sell as legit pieces.'

'He could have been using Wheeler to do the burglaries, then,' Chapman remarked.

'Yeah, but Wheeler must have double-crossed him. I found out Cole smokes cigars, so it looks like he's the person who tortured Wheeler.'

'Which means he may do a runner . . .'

'He hasn't. Not yet anyway. I got my wife to call his mobile number this afternoon and ask if he could restore an old diamond ring. He said he'd need to look at it first. He's open for business at 10 a.m. except for Sundays and Mondays.'

'You're a crafty old bugger, aren't you.'

'I like to think so. Stubbs said he told Michelle everything he'd discovered and asked if she was going to inform the police. She didn't give him an answer but asked if there was any evidence that her husband was involved in Cole's dodgy dealings. Stubbs told her he hadn't found any but could do more digging if she wanted.'

'And did she ask him to?

'No. She paid him off and warned him he'd better not breach the non-disclosure agreement, or she'd sue him for every penny he had.'

'So Stubbings walked away, and that was the end of it?' Chapman asked.

'Of course he didn't. He's a detective, isn't he? He was suspicious of Belsham and wanted to know more, but knew he had to be careful.' He flicked through pages in his notebook.

'So is Johan linked to Cole's criminal activities?'

'Stubbs couldn't be certain, but he did some surveillance on Cole's shop and saw De Klerk entering the shop with a briefcase. He came out nearly an hour later . . . without the briefcase.'

'When was that?'

'A few weeks after his wife hired Stubbs.' He turned another few pages.

SCENE OF THE CRIME | 372

'So it looks like Johan could be involved in Cole's scams. The question is, does Michelle know, or is she involved as well?' Chapman said.

'Stubbs also followed De Klerk to a warehouse in Hackney Wick.'

Chapman shrugged. 'That's where he stores his wine.'

'Then Cole turned up while Stubbs was watching the place.'

'OK, that's more interesting. But he could have been buying some wine.'

'That's what I said to Stubbs, but he said Cole didn't come out with any wine . . . just the same briefcase that he'd seen De Klerk carrying.'

'Is he still watching Cole?'

'No. He got involved in other investigations and didn't have the time.'

'Did he tell Michelle?'

'He couldn't. He reckoned she might sue him for continuing the investigation behind her back.'

'So how did Stubbings find out about Chandice if Michelle didn't tell him?'

'Through LinkedIn, Facebook, etc. He guessed that Chandice Bramston was most likely to be the "close friend" Michelle was referring to.'

'He took a big risk talking to her. Wasn't he worried she might tell Michelle?'

'Stubbs didn't talk to her. I did. He gave me her name and said she lived somewhere in Coombe Park. I traced her address through the voters register and visited her this morning. I told her I was investigating Nathan Cole for fraud and theft. She's a smart cookie and was very cagey at first, but I got what I needed from her, and it confirmed that Stubbs was telling the truth.'

'Why did he wait until yesterday to speak to you?'

'He's been abroad. He didn't know about the De Klerk stabbing until he got home a couple of days ago.'

'What did Chandice tell you?'

'Chandice said Michelle is a very ambitious woman and would do anything to protect her reputation. Stubbs had the same impression.'

'Do you think Chandice might tell Michelle about your visit?' Chapman asked.

'They've not spoken since she got her sapphire back, and that's nearly 6 months ago, so I think it's unlikely. I know you'll have to tell Anderson about Cole, but I'd appreciate it if you could find a way to keep Stubbs's name out of it. Same with Chandice Bramston.'

'I'll do my best. How much did you tell Stubbings about the investigation?'

'Just what was on the news and a bit more detail about what happened during the burglary.'

Chapman gave him a suspicious look. 'Did Stubbings want anything in return for the information?'

'Not a sausage.'

'Why do you think he spoke to you then?'

'Two reasons. One because he's a friend and knows he can trust me. He doesn't like Belsham and is happy to see her get some comeuppance. A few years before Stubbs was dismissed, he was involved in a murder case where she represented the defendant, a wealthy businessman who was acquitted. I won't go into all the details, but Stubbs was convinced she coached him and basically prepared his answers. He felt she'd really fucked them over.'

'I don't think she'd risk her career doing that. Sounds like Stubbings is blaming her for his own mistakes. The fact that Michelle Belsham hired Stubbings isn't a crime, and she may well just be an innocent victim of Cole's.'

'Then why didn't she want Chandice to report the theft of the sapphire or report it herself?' Wood said bluntly.

'Fair point,' Wood conceded. 'Was it that redhead, Jessica Russell, that figured out Palmer wasn't involved?' Wood asked.

Chapman nodded. 'She's a real pro. She sees things other people miss.'

'She's pretty fit as well,' Wood winked.

'I wouldn't know about that,' Chapman replied with a shrug.

Wood grinned. 'Don't give me that crap. I've seen the way you look at her. Have you asked her out yet?'

'Look, I like her a lot, but I don't think she'd be interested.'

'If you don't ask, you'll never find out,' Wood said with a wink.

* * *

When Jessica and Anderson got to De Klerk's room in the hospital, the blinds were down. Anderson knocked gently on the door and few moments later Michelle opened it and stepped out into the corridor. Before she closed the door behind her, Jessica could see Johan lying motionless with his eyes closed.

'Has he still not woken up yet?' Jessica asked.

'Not yet,' Michelle replied with a sad expression. She suggested they go to the waiting room and talk there. Once there, Michelle sat down, while Anderson and Jessica remained standing.

'I wanted to give you an update on the investigation,' Anderson told her. 'I've brought Jessica along to answer any questions about the forensic side of things.' Anderson told Michelle about Liam Palmer's arrest and the subsequent withdrawal of all charges against him after it was discovered that John Wheeler had committed the break-in, assaulted Johan and framed Palmer for the crime.

'I'm pleased to hear you caught the real culprit and an innocent man was vindicated. Did Wheeler admit he was responsible for what happened to my husband?'

'No. When we found him, he was dead.'

She looked shocked. 'Murdered?'

'We're still awaiting the pathologist's final report. But Wheeler did have a ruptured spleen, which contributed to his death. We believe the injury may have occurred during the struggle with Johan,' Jessica said.

She frowned. 'If my husband did something to Wheeler, it must have been in self-defence.'

'Of course. And that wasn't Wheeler's only injury. Burn marks on his body indicate that he was tortured with a lit cigar shortly before he died,' Anderson said.

'Oh my God, this is just terrible. Have you any idea who might have done that to him?'

'Not as yet, but we believe they were involved in or at least aware of the break-in and were looking for the contents of Johan's safe,' Anderson told her.

'Did you find anything else you think might have been stolen from Johan's safe?' she asked.

'Yes. We recovered a large amount of money hidden in a travel pillow. Added to the five thousand found in Palmer's flat, it totals nearly two hundred and fifty thousand pounds. Do you know if Johan had that much cash in the safe?'

Jessica noticed a brief fare of anger in Michelle's eyes before she gave a small shake of her head, as if finding it hard to believe. 'That's a lot of money, but I don't know anything about it. You'll have to ask Johan when he regains consciousness.'

'Doctor Babu was surprised he hadn't woken up by now,' Jessica said.

'I know,' Michelle said sadly. Michelle gripped both arms of the chair and eased herself up, then stood with one hand resting on her belly. 'Thank you for updating me on the investigation. Is there anything else?'

Anderson shook his head. 'We'll let you know if there are any further developments.'

She nodded and left the room.

'What did you make of that?' Anderson asked Jessica when she had gone.

'I thought you handled her well. But it was interesting how she deflected the question of what was in the safe towards Johan. When you told her the actual amount of the cash, she looked annoyed before she managed to control herself.'

'And what does that tell us?'

'I'm not sure – but I'm wondering if Johan has already woken up.'

Anderson looked taken aback. 'I find that hard to believe. I mean, do you really think he has regained consciousness and has spoken with Michelle?'

'I don't know. I'm just raising it as a possibility based on my observations. I thought it odd that she didn't ask more about Wheeler or why he would break into their house.'

'Why?'

'Because barristers, like us, are naturally inquisitive. I thought she would want to know more about who was involved and why their house was targeted.'

'I think she's just focused on Johan and his recovery.'

'She makes that very clear, but I think she was also fishing for information but didn't want to go too deep in case she gave anything away. Also, people who already know the answers tend not to ask pertinent questions.'

'Do you think I should have mentioned the diamonds recovered from Wheeler's stomach?'

'No, I think you were right not to. I think it's good to keep something up our sleeve. Excuse me for a minute. I won't be long.'

'I'll wait here for you,' Anderson replied, thinking she was going to the toilet.

Jessica returned to the waiting room a minute later. 'That was quick,' Anderson said.

'I'm now convinced Michelle is lying, and she discussed the investigation with Johan before we got here.'

Anderson looked surprised. 'What makes you say that?'

'I just knocked on Johan's door. When Michelle opened it, I lied and told her we'd finished with Johan's laptop and phone and asked if she'd like them back . . .'

'Was Johan awake?' Anderson asked hopefully.

'No, he was still looked to be asleep, but I think he might be putting on an act.'

'Why?'

'When we first arrived and Michelle opened the door, I noticed a bottle of water on his bedside cabinet, which was three-quarters full. When Michelle opened the door a minute ago, it was nearly empty. It can't have evaporated into thin air.'

'Good work! Should we go and confront them, do you think?'

'No, let them stew for now. I'll go to the lab early tomorrow morning and speak with the team. Hopefully, we might have some more forensic results to present them with.'

* * *

Michelle peeked through the blinds, watching Jessica and Anderson walking down the corridor towards the lift. 'They've gone, Johan.'

He opened his eyes and sat up slightly. Michelle turned sharply and glared at him. 'Anderson said the man who broke into the house is called John Wheeler. Looks like they recovered the rest of the money from the safe when they found him.'

'What about the diamonds?' Johan asked anxiously.

'They never mentioned them, so they may not have found them.'

'But if this Wheeler guy has them, he might tell the police they were in my safe.'

'We don't need to worry about Wheeler talking to the police.'

'Why not?' Johan asked.

She held her hands over her stomach. 'Because he's dead. You ruptured his spleen in the struggle when he attacked you.'

'Jesus . . . did they say anything about Cole?'

'No. It looks like they don't know about him yet.' Michelle told him about Wheeler being tortured with a cigar and the money found in the neck pillow.

'So Cole killed Wheeler. That means he must have the diamonds,' she added.

'What if the police connect him to Wheeler's death and arrest him?'

'We've got to hope they don't, and if they do, hope that he doesn't drop you in the shit.'

'But you said he wouldn't do that because he'd implicate himself.'

'If there's forensic evidence that puts Cole or an accomplice in Wheeler's flat, that changes things. If Cole is charged with murder, I'm sure he'd say anything to get a reduced sentence.'

'Oh my God. What will we do then?'

'Stop whining!' she snapped.

'I'm sorry, Michelle. I think maybe I should just come clean and tell them everything . . .'

'For Christ's sake, shut up and give me time to think. The forensic woman, Jessica Russell, was with Anderson. I think she's suspicious. So we need to have a watertight story.'

Johan said nothing, waiting for Michelle to tell him what to do. 'I've got to go out for a while, but when I get back, I'll tell a nurse that you've woken up. You need to act disoriented and confused. Doctor Babu or another doctor will come and examine you. You'll probably be asked if you can remember what happened . . .'

'What should I say?'

'For now, you can't remember a thing. Do you think you can manage that?'

'I think so,' he said, sounding unsure.

'You've lied to me for months, so it shouldn't be a problem,' she said harshly.

'Where are you going?'

'To clear up the fucking mess you've created.'

CHAPTER THIRTY

When Jessica arrived at the MSCAN office early Friday morning, Guy was working on his laptop, preparing phone charts and other data for her. 'So, what have you discovered?' she asked him.

'With De Klerk's phone, I've concentrated on calls and messages for the week before the break-in. Most of them are between him and his wife. There's also voice and video calls on WhatsApp and Facetime to South Africa. It will take me a while to confirm the registered owners of those numbers, but I cross-referenced them against his contacts, and the calls were to Duante, Mariette and Pieter. As I recall from that article, that's his brother, sister and father.' He handed Jessica a printed list of all the calls, data and cell site analyses he had prepared. 'Last Friday morning, Johan called a UK mobile number, and the conversation lasted three minutes.' He pointed to it on the list. 'Cell site data suggests the call was made from his home to a phone registered to a Nathan Cole.'

'Has his name come up in the investigation before?' she asked.

'I checked on HOLMES, and it hasn't.'

'Does Johan make regular contact with Cole?'

'No. I've checked back six months, and the Friday call is the only one I can find.' Guy handed her another document. 'The phone is registered to Cole's business address, a jewellery shop in Hatton Garden. I looked it up on the net, and the details and other stuff about him are on this document.' He handed it to Jessica along with a printout of all the calls and messages between the two burner phones. 'We know that Palmer is not involved, and one of the burner phones was planted at his address, most likely by

Wheeler. We don't yet know who has the other burner phone.'

'You think Nathan Cole has it, don't you?'

Guy nodded. 'We know both burners went live in Holborn at 6 p.m. last Wednesday, and the cell tower was near Cole's shop. On Friday afternoon, a message was sent to Wheeler's burner phone stating, "He's going away Saturday morning, back Monday." Wheeler replied, "will do the job early hours Monday." To which he received a thumbs-up emoji reply.'

'Is there any way you can prove Cole used the burner to send that or any other messages?'

'There's evidence that strongly suggests he did. I checked the calls Cole made and the cell site locations. He used his business phone for a two-minute call on Friday at 4.06 p.m. Then, at 4.08 p.m., the "he's going away" message was sent on the burner phone. The cell mast that picked up both phones was in Hackney Wick, near De Klerk's house. I hope this all makes sense, and I'm not going too fast.'

'It does, and I hate to be a devil's advocate, but it doesn't prove it was Cole using one of the burner phones.'

'I agree it's circumstantial. However, there are more messages and calls that link Cole to the burner phones.'

'I'm all ears,' she smiled.

'On Monday, after the break-in, Wheeler's burner received several repeated messages during the day saying, "Contact me now" and "Where the fuck are you". Those messages were sent via the free Wi-Fi at the Bloc Hotel on Caroline Street, Birmingham. We also know that a cell mast in Caroline Street picked up the missing burner phone before it was switched off on Tuesday morning. I have also linked Cole's business phone to the hotel Wi-Fi and the Caroline Street mast, which makes the evidence that Cole used the burner even more compelling.'

'Brilliant, If Cole stayed at the hotel, he'd have a hard time denying it was him using one of the burner phones even if he's got rid of it.'

'He did stay there. I spoke to the hotel manager. She confirmed a Mr Nathan Cole was staying there at the relevant times.'

Jessica was elated. 'Anderson will be over the moon!'

Guy frowned. 'There's something else I've found that's a bit worrying. About two years ago, John Wheeler stood trial for GBH. He pleaded self-defence and was found not guilty. Thus, it's not on his criminal record.'

'What's worrying about that? It still shows his propensity to violence.'

'His defence council was Michelle Belsham KC.'

'My God, so she knows Wheeler.'

'It could just be a coincidence,' Guy shrugged.

'I don't believe in coincidences. I'll let Anderson know so he can read the case file.'

'Do you think the De Klerks might be tied up with Cole in something criminal, and it's all gone horribly wrong?' Guy asked.

'It's certainly beginning to look that way. De Klerk could have told Cole he would be away from Saturday to Monday. I think Wheeler and Cole must have known the diamonds and cash were in the safe. Anything of interest on De Klerk's laptop?'

'Not so far, but I still need to look at a lot of stuff on the hard drive. There's more work to be done on De Klerk's phone, too, but I'll concentrate on looking for calls and messages between him and Cole. I got a list of Cole's calls and messages from his service provider. I'm working my way through it to identify the recipients.'

'Anything of interest on Wheeler's phone or laptop?'

'I looked at the internet search history. He was on the Crime

Stoppers site, so I think it's safe to say he sent the anonymous tip about Liam trying to sell the Rolex. He also booked the Dubai flight on the laptop. Phone-wise, there's not a single call to or from Cole, but he did call Liam Palmer on Monday at 8 p.m.'

The office door flew open, making Jessica jump. Taff bounced in, smiling from ear to ear and waving a computer printout. 'What a result, boyos,' he shouted.

'Sounds like you just won the jackpot,' Guy said.

'I have. I lifted a partial print from the masking tape on Wheeler's head and ran it through the database. I got a few possible hits, but after comparing the friction ridge detail on the tape lift against all of the possibles, I'm confident this man left the print.' He handed the criminal record printout to Jessica, who glanced at it before reading the relevant details aloud.

'Christopher Bishop, aged forty-five, white male. Last known address flat twenty-eight, Fairmead House, Kingsmead Estate, Hackney. Occupation, minicab driver. Convictions for handling stolen goods, burglary, criminal damage and fraud.' She looked up. 'Fabulous, Taff, this is a significant result.'

'What was that name again?' Guy asked, and she repeated it. He picked up the paperwork from his desk and hurriedly flicked through it.

'Is the name familiar to you?'

'Yes. I'm sure it was on my list of numbers that Cole called after the crime.' He paused and continued looking. 'Got it. Cole used his business phone to call a mobile registered to Christopher Bishop. The call was made from Birmingham on Tuesday at 2.05 p.m. A second call to Bishop was made from a cell site near Euston station just after 5 p.m.'

'Could be Cole got a train back from Birmingham to Euston. What do you think Guy?'

'Cole called Bishop again at 8 p.m. on Tuesday, the night we believe Wheeler died.'

'Who's Cole?' Taff asked.

'Guy will explain it all to you. Has Bishop called Cole or Wheeler?' Jessica asked.

'Don't know yet. I'm waiting for the details of Bishop's calls to come through.'

'I've got a couple of other updates as well,' Taff said.

'Be quick then. I need to go to Barking and tell Anderson about all this new evidence.'

'Johan De Klerk and Wheeler's fingerprints are on the cash Diane found in the neck cushion. Footprints on either side of the chair don't match the elimination shoe prints I took from you or the officers. But using a light source and black powder, I lifted a detailed one from a *Radio Times* on the floor beside the chair. It looks like it's a Skecher size seven. I don't know the make of the other shoes yet, but I'll email you photos of them all. The tools in Wheeler's rucksack made the striation marks at the De Klerk house and the lock pick was used to open Palmer's front door.'

'Any prints on the lockbox?'

'Just Johan's on the inside.'

'Keep up the good work. Can you apologise to Di and explain why I didn't get a chance to review her results. Ask her to call me with an update as soon as possible,' Jessica said.

'Will do,' Taff replied.

She picked up her shoulder bag and hurried out of the office.

CHAPTER THIRTY-ONE

Arriving at Barking, Jessica went straight to Chapman's office, but he wasn't there. She saw DC Bingham in the corridor and asked him if Chapman was in. Bingham told her he was in the canteen with DS Wood. Jessica thanked him and hurried up the stairs. She saw Chapman and Wood sitting at a table, eating bacon sandwiches and drinking coffee.

'Guy and Taff have identified two new suspects.'

'That's good news. Who might they be?' Wood asked.

'A Hatton Garden jeweller called Nathan Cole and a minicab driver, Christopher Bishop. Have their names come up in yours or anyone else's enquiries?'

Chapman and Wood looked at each other, shrugged and shook their heads. 'What have those two fellows been up to then?' Wood asked.

'Guy linked Cole and Wheeler to using the two burner phones, and Bishop's print was at the Wheeler crime scene on the piece of tape. It also looks like De Klerk knows Cole.'

'How do you know that?' Wood asked.

'Because he phoned Cole on the Friday morning before the break-in on Monday.'

'Now that is interesting,' Wood said.

'How did it go at the hospital with Michelle?' Chapman asked.

'I think she's lying about Johan still being unconscious and may know more than she's letting on.'

'What makes you think that?' Wood asked.

'Just a gut feeling.' She looked at Chapman. 'I'll go into more detail when we talk to Anderson, but I'd like to do it now as he might want to take immediate action.'

'Let me finish this bacon sarnie and I'll come with you. Do you want a drink?' Chapman asked.

'No, thanks. I'll meet you in Anderson's office,' she gave Wood a nod as she left.

'Bet you'd love to,' Wood said in a low voice.

'Love to what?'

'Come with her.'

'Fuck off, Julian, and have some fucking respect. She and her team might have just saved you and me from revealing Stubbings as an informant.'

Jessica knocked on Anderson's door and Chapman followed her in. 'I've got some new information and forensic results for you,' Jessica said.

'Take a seat. I'll fill Mike in on what happened at the hospital with Michelle first,' Anderson said. He told Chapman what Michelle had said, and about Jessica spotting the water bottle.

'Very sharp,' Chapman grinned.

Anderson picked up his pen and opened his notebook. 'What have you got for me, Jessica.' She recounted everything she had discussed with Guy and Taff, then handed him copies of the mobile phone calls and cell site analysis Guy had prepared. She also gave him a copy of Christopher Bishop's criminal record. 'This is excellent work by you and your team. It looks like De Klerk is definitely linked to Cole, which makes me wonder if he's also connected to Wheeler somehow.'

'There is a tenuous connection between Wheeler and Michelle,' she said. 'She was his defence barrister in a GBH case.'

'Interesting. I don't wish to sound pushy, but has Diane got any DNA results yet?' Anderson asked.

'She was still working on the items when I left the office. I asked her to call me, but I haven't heard from her yet.'

'Would you mind calling her? The results might help us determine the best way forward.'

'Not at all,' Jessica said, pleased he had used the word 'us'. She called Diane.

'You must be telepathic. I'm still in the lab and I was just about to call you with my DNA results,' Diane said.

'I'm with DCI Anderson and DI Chapman. I'll put you on speaker on so they can listen. But don't get too technical,' she added. Anderson gave her a rueful smile.

'OK, starting with the diamonds. I found three DNA profiles, which come from Johan De Klerk, John Wheeler and the third from an unknown male. I ran it through the database but didn't get a hit. However, the unknown DNA matches the saliva DNA I recovered from the water buffalo glass Jessica found in De Klerk's cinema room. I'm still working on the saliva DNA from the cigar we found in Montague Road, but there are already similarities to the unknown DNA on the diamonds. I'm pretty sure they will match once I get a full profile. Did that make sense to you non-scientists?'

'It did,' Anderson said.

'That's great work, Diane. It proves that De Klerk and Wheeler handled those diamonds. I think we can all agree the unknown DNA is probably Nathan Cole's,' Jessica added.

'Who's Nathan Cole?' Diane asked.

'Guy will tell you all about him,' Jessica said.

'Thanks for all your hard work,' Anderson said, thinking that was it.

'I'm not done. I've more exciting results for you . . . if you'd like to hear them,' Diane teased.

'Fire away.' Anderson said.

'I recovered DNA from Wheeler's wrist and hand swabs. Naturally, his was there, but I also raised another profile and ran it on the database. I got a match to a Christopher Bishop. His DNA was either transferred onto Wheeler's wrists from the rope that was used to bind his hands, or Bishop held his hands while someone else tied them. I've got a list of Bishop's previous convictions. He . . .'

'We already know about them, Di. Taff found his fingerprint on the piece of masking tape,' Jessica told her.

'Nice of him to tell me,' she replied, obviously annoyed that Taff had stolen her thunder.

'I suspect he didn't want to disturb you while you were busy with the DNA work. Have you anything else for us?' Jessica asked.

'I found no foreign DNA on Wheeler's fingernail clippings or scrapings. I haven't done any tests on the lockbox yet, as extracting DNA from the diamonds seemed to be the priority. I also found Wheeler's DNA on the waistband and hoodie of the clothing dumped in the communal bins outside Palmer's flat. You were right, Jess. Wheeler must have put it there, probably as part of his effort to frame Liam. That's all I've got for you so far.'

'Thanks again, Diane. My team and I appreciate all your hard work,' Anderson said. Jessica thanked Diane and ended the call. 'This is all rather odd,' Anderson said, going over his notes.

'How do you mean?' Chapman asked.

'There's a connection between Cole and Bishop through phone calls, but nothing to connect Bishop to De Klerk or Wheeler.'

'If Cole doesn't have a driving licence, and Bishop is a minicab driver, maybe Cole uses him to get around,' Jessica suggested.

'Good thinking. We can check with Transport for London to see if Bishop has a cab licence,' Anderson said. 'If Cole has a driver's licence, DVLA will have his home address. However, there could be quite a few males with the same name that we'll have to sift through.'

'We can connect Michelle to Wheeler through the court case,' Chapman said, grateful that he wasn't going to have to reveal what Julian Wood had told him about her, Cole and Chandice's sapphire.

Anderson frowned. 'Yes, but that doesn't implicate her in any crime.'

'She went away for the weekend. We know she has a safe containing jewellery, which she may have purchased from Cole, thus connecting the two of them. She may also have known what was in Johan's safe and arranged the break-in,' Chapman said.

'That's stretching things a bit, Mike,' Jessica said. 'Although I think she's hiding something, I don't believe she'd have wanted any harm to come to her husband. If she was involved, she'd have wanted him away from the house when the break-in happened.'

'We don't know much about Cole, but Wheeler's a nasty bastard. Maybe he decided to break in no matter what and thought he could do the job without waking De Klerk, but it all went pear-shaped,' Chapman argued.

'You've never met Michelle. Do you honestly think she could be behind what happened to her husband?' Jessica said bluntly.

'You just said yourself that she's hiding something.'

'Yes, but I don't think she'd set Johan up. I think she was fishing for information yesterday so she could tell Johan what we knew. It could be she's actually trying to protect him.'

'Or herself. I'm just saying that we should be open-minded and not rule her out as a suspect.'

'Let's not start arguing with each other and focus on what we need to do next,' Anderson interjected. 'As I see it, we have enough forensic and phone evidence to arrest Cole and Bishop. I think we should interview them before we speak to De Klerk and Michelle.

Do you both agree?' They both nodded. 'Ideally, I'd like to know if the prints and DNA from the water buffalo glass and the cigar belong to Cole before we arrest him. If they aren't his, there's someone else we need to find,' Anderson said.

'Dawn Owens was going to enquire about any cleaners the De Klerk's employed. Do you know if she got a result?' Jessica asked.

Anderson checked on HOLMES. 'Doesn't look like it from her last report.' He ran a search using the word "cleaner". 'Here we go, there's an entry on the house-to-house enquiries. A neighbour of the De Klerks said they use the same house cleaner as them on Monday, Wednesday and Friday. She does the mornings at the De Klerks and afternoons at the neighbours. Her name is Janice something, but it doesn't appear she's been spoken to yet.'

'Is there a phone number for her?' Jessica asked.

Anderson nodded. 'I'll get one of the team to contact her, but I doubt she'll be able to tell us much.'

'Do you mind if I try calling her now?'

'Not at all.' Anderson read out the number.

Jessica dialled it. When the phone was answered, she confirmed it was Janice, introduced herself and put her phone on speaker. 'I'd like to ask you some questions about the De Klerks and when you last cleaned their house. Is that OK?'

'It's terrible what happened to Mr Johan. I feel so sorry for him and Mrs Michelle. Do you know how he is?' she said with an African lilt to her accent.

'Johan is recovering well, but still in the hospital.'

'Oh, thanks to God. I have been praying for them every day.'

'Can you tell me when you last cleaned the De Klerk's house?'

'It was last Friday morning.'

'And what hours did you work?'

'I do five hours.'

'From when?'

'7 a.m. to 12.'

'I take it you have a key to the premises.'

'Yes, Mrs Michelle trusts me, and I let myself in.'

'And do you clean the whole house?'

'Oh, yes. I clean everything. I am very thorough.'

'Do you do the basement areas as well? Including the cinema room?'

'Oh, yes. And the gym and Mr Johan's study.'

'We found two crystal glasses in the cinema room on the Monday morning after Johan was hurt. One glass had a cheetah engraving, and the other a water buffalo. Can you recall if you saw them there on Friday morning?'

'Oh no, they were not there. If they had been, I would have washed them by hand. I never put the crystal in the dishwasher.'

'And you're certain of that?'

'One hundred per cent. Mr Johan often leaves the glasses in the cinema room and popcorn on the floor, but I always make sure it is clean and tidy. I don't miss even a tiny speck of dust when I clean.'

'Was Michelle or Johan at home that morning?'

'Mrs Michelle was at work, and Johan was in his study. I remember it because I was going to hoover and dust the study, but he said not to bother as he was very busy.'

'Did anyone come to visit Johan while you were there?'

'No, if they did, I would know. I always answer the door when I am there.'

'Thank you, Janice. You've been very helpful. I'll let Michelle know she and Johan are in your prayers. I'm sure they'll appreciate it.' Jessica ended the call.

Anderson smiled. 'That was crafty.'

'If the fingerprints and DNA on the water buffalo glass are Cole's, it proves he was in the De Klerk's house and could only have got there after midday on Friday,' Jessica said.

'I'm going to organise arrest teams for Cole and Bishop. Mike, I'd like you to lead the team arresting Cole and DS Wood for Bishop. I'll monitor everything from here and keep radio contact with both teams. Unless there is anything else, I think it's time for the office meeting with the rest of the team.'

'Can you give me twenty minutes to speak to Julian and organise our teams?' Chapman asked.

'No problem. Is there anything else we need to discuss?'

'There's a way we can get Cole's fingerprints so that Taff can make an instant comparison before an arrest,' Jessica said.

'And what's that?' Anderson asked.

'Pay a visit to his shop, ask for an estimate on a ring or something.'

Anderson hesitated, then looked at her. 'Are you up for doing that?'

She smiled. 'I suggested it, so I guess I am.'

CHAPTER THIRTY-TWO

When they were in Chapman's car, Jessica told him about her conversation with Dawn Owens. 'At least it's not someone on the team,' he said. 'I'll make some discreet enquiries. Anderson won't be pleased, whatever the outcome, but I'll try and persuade him just to give Dawn a dressing down. Anyway, best keep it to ourselves for now.'

'Good, thank you.'

Chapman pulled up in Hatton Garden near the junction with Greville Street, behind the observation van. Taff jumped out of the observation van and got in the back seat of Chapman's car. 'This is all very exciting. I'd never been in an observation van,' Taff said, handing Jessica a small acrylic ring box. She opened the box, and Chapman removed a diamond ring from his pocket, wiped it with a tissue, and placed it on the velvet mounting inside the box. 'Where did you get the ring?' Taff asked.

'The exhibits storage room. It's from an unidentified body on a cold case murder. The pathologist said she was hit in the head with an axe, and her body had been in the ground for over a hundred years, which is why we were never able to identify her. At the time we had a jeweller examine the ring. He reckoned it was made in the mid to late eighteen hundreds. The diamond is two carat and worth thirty or forty thousand quid.'

'Nice of her to help – whoever she is,' Taff quipped. 'Wipe the box down before you hand it to Cole . . . and try and hold it by the corners when you do. It's a good surface to get prints off.'

'I know what to do, Taff,' she said curtly, and Taff returned to the observation van.

Jessica wiped the ring box clean, put it in her coat pocket and was about to open the car door.

'Are you sure you don't want to wear a wire?' Chapman asked. 'I brought one along in case you changed your mind.'

'There's no point. It's just a quick in-and-out job. Mind you, it would have been helpful to know what Cole looks like, but I . . .'

Chapman sighed. 'He's white, mid-fifties, about five foot six and bald, apart from dyed black hair on the sides.'

'How on earth do you know that?' Jessica asked with a quizzical expression.

'I'll explain it all to you later.'

'I'd like to know before I go into his bloody shop!'

'Julian Wood got some information through an informant, but I couldn't risk their identity being revealed.'

'Am I in any danger? Will Cole suspect I'm undercover?'

'Of course not. Look, I can do it if you're worried.'

'No,' she said firmly. 'We all agreed Cole would be less suspicious about a woman. But I'm really pissed off with you, Mike.'

'Sorry, I should have told you earlier. I'm . . .' She got out of the car, slamming the door.

When she got to the shop, she pressed the camera doorbell. After a few seconds, it buzzed and she walked in. The interior was very plush, with soft lighting and elegant display cases containing rings, necklaces, bracelets, earrings and watches. She immediately detected the distinctive odour of cigar smoke. There was a man matching Cole's description behind the counter.

'Good morning. How can I help you?' he smiled.

'I've got a diamond ring that belonged to my husband's great-great-grandmother. I wanted to enquire about having it cleaned and restored, or possibly having the stone remounted in a new ring.'

'Are you Mrs Wood?' He asked.

Jessica looked puzzled. 'My name is Chapman, Jessica Chapman.'

'Sorry, my dear. A Mrs Wood called me yesterday saying she wanted an old diamond ring cleaned and restored. I thought you might be her. Do you have the ring with you?'

'Yes, I do.' She took the box from her pocket and placed it carefully on the counter.

Cole opened the box and removed the ring, examining it with a jeweller's loupe. 'Do you have any provenance for the ring?' he asked.

'Unfortunately not.'

'The hallmark indicates it's a two-carat diamond, and the ring is twenty-four carat pure gold. It's definitely Victorian. It's a very nice piece and will look as good as new when cleaned up. Is it insured?'

'I'm not sure, to be honest. My husband deals with that sort of stuff.'

'I'd have to look at it more carefully, but I'd say it's worth at least forty thousand pounds.'

Jessica gasped, pretending to be surprised. 'Best I make sure it is insured then.'

'I can do you a valuation certificate if you like.'

'Thank you. How much would it cost to have it cleaned?'

'Forty pounds, which includes a polish. I can't do it right away, but if you leave it with me, I'll have it done in a day or two and let you know when it's ready for collection. Remounting would be a bit more expensive and take a few weeks. Honestly, it's such a lovely, historical piece, I wouldn't alter it.'

Jessica heard the door buzz. Cole looked at the CCTV monitor on his side of the counter and pressed the entry button. A man came in and quickly approached the counter. 'I need to have a word in private, Nat.'

Cole turned to Jessica with an ingratiating smile. 'Please excuse me for a moment, if you would.' Jessica saw the man's face as he walked past her to the rear of the premises, with Cole following behind. She recognised Christoper Bishop from his most recent criminal record photo. Jessica got out her phone to text Chapman, pretending to be absorbed by it as she listened to the two men's conversation.

'I got a phone call from my neighbour. He said four blokes were at my flat knocking on the door. From how he described them, it's got to be the old bill. He said they were now in the back of a big van. It's fucking obvious they are after me.' Bishop sounded very agitated, making it even easier for Jessica to hear.

'That's not good,' Cole sounded worried. 'We need to go to the warehouse and get the diamonds.'

'I just had a drive round here, and there's a van parked down the road. I think it's the filth. I reckon they must have found Wheeler.'

Jessica sent the text: 'Bishop here. Knows you're watching. Come quick!!'

'Shit. We need to get out of here,' Cole said.

'Where the fuck are we going to go, Nat?'

'We need to get to the Hackney warehouse. We can buy fake passports and get out of the country. Get your cab and meet me out the back. Fucking move it!'

Jessica was still standing by the counter as they returned. Cole picked up the ring put it back in the box, then handed it to her. 'I'm very sorry, madam. Something's come up that needs my urgent attention. You'll have to come back.' He put his hand on her back, ushering her towards the door.

Once she was outside, Cole locked the door behind her and moved the sign to closed. She looked across the road and saw Bishop heading towards his car. She then saw the observation van speeding up the road. 'Police! Stay where you are!' Jessica shouted at Bishop. He froze momentarily before opening the driver's door of his cab. She rushed towards him, grabbed the back of his jacket and pulled him into the middle of the street. As he turned, he slammed the palm of his hand into her chest and she lost her grip on his jacket, nearly losing her balance.

'Get off me, you fucking bitch!' Bishop growled with his fist raised. Before he could throw a punch, Jessica kicked him as hard as she could between the legs. He grunted in pain and fell to his knees, clutching his groin. Chapman and DC Bingham quickly grabbed Bishop and handcuffed him.

'Cole's gone out the back. Bishop was going to drive round and pick him up.' Jessica said.

'Caution him, Andy. I'll go and get Cole,' Chapman told Bingham.

'I'll help you,' Taff said, hurrying off with Chapman. As they turned into Hatton Wall, Chapman saw Cole running down the road carrying a shoulder bag. Taff was fast on his feet, quickly caught up with Cole, and rugby-tackled him to the ground.

'Going anywhere nice?' Taff grinned.

As Chapman handcuffed Cole, Taff opened the bag, revealing a large amount of cash and various pieces of jewellery. He showed it to Chapman. 'Good job, Taff. I must say he's sprightly for his age.'

'I used to be a fullback,' Taff said proudly.

Chapman read Cole his rights, arresting him on suspicion of the murder of John Wheeler and conspiracy to commit burglary. Cole didn't reply. Chapman handcuffed him and removed his mobile phone from his pocket, then handed it to Taff. 'Get Guy to have a look,' he told him. He took Cole's shop keys from his pocket. 'We're going to search your premises,' he said.

'You need a warrant to do that,' Cole said.

'You've been arrested for an indictable offence. That gives us the power to search premises that may hold evidence without a warrant – which is probably every bit of jewellery in your shop.'

Cole laughed. 'It's all perfectly legit. I've done nothing wrong.'

'Put this dreamer in the observation van,' Chapman told the other two officers on the arrest team. He pointed at Bishop. 'And get him to Barking.' He went over to talk to Jessica. 'Are you all right?'

'I'll survive. No thanks to you,' she added tersely.

'I'm sorry, but I had no idea Bishop was going to turn up. I should have thought of it.'

'He had his bloody taxicab parked up, for God's sake. You're lucky I released my pent-up anger on him, not you,' she said.

'I'm sorry . . .'

'For Christ's sake, stop apologising. I overheard Bishop say they must have found out about Wheeler. Cole said something about diamonds hidden in a warehouse.'

'De Klerk has a warehouse in Hackney Wick that Cole has been to.'

'You're full of surprises today, aren't you? How do you know that?'

'Stubbings was watching De Klerk and saw Cole go there empty-handed and come out with a briefcase.'

'My God, why didn't you tell me?'

'Because I was trying to protect Stubbings as the informant. I thought . . .'

'I don't want to hear anymore,' she said, holding her hand up.

'I'll be back in a minute,' he said.

Chapman got in the back of the observation van where a sullen-looking Cole was waiting to be taken back to the station. 'Do you know Johan De Klerk?'

'I'm not saying anything until I speak with a solicitor.'

Chapman lifted a bench seat and removed an exhibit bag and

crime scene shoe covers from the storage box. 'I want your shoes. You can wear these covers until you get to the station, where you'll be given some prisoner's plimsolls.' Cole didn't move. 'I can get my colleagues to hold you down while I rip them off your feet, or you can do it yourself. The choice is yours.' Cole sullenly complied, and Chapman put the shoes in the exhibit bag. 'You're in some deep shit, Cole, and you'd better hope your pal Bishop doesn't drop you further in it. I'll be interviewing you later, so I'll let you know what he says,' Chapman added, enjoying the worried look on Cole's face.

He gave the shoes to Taff, then went and spoke with Bishop and asked if he knew Johan De Klerk. 'Never heard of him,' Bishop replied.

'I've just spoken to your friend Cole, who was very cooperative. We can now put you in Wheeler's flat the night he was murdered, which means you could be going to prison for a long time, Christopher.'

'I don't believe you. Nat wouldn't say anything like that because it's not true.'

'Tying Wheeler up, then putting tape across his mouth so he couldn't scream when you tortured him with a cigar sickened me, so God knows what a jury will think.'

'Nat's lying to save his skin. I wasn't there when he did that.'

'So, you do know what I'm talking about?' Chapman grinned, realising Bishop was not the sharpest tool in the box.

Bishop looked flustered. 'I heard Nat talking to someone else about it . . .'

'That's crap. I also know about the warehouse you were going to take him to so you could get the diamonds,' Chapman said.

'He's lying. He asked me to take him to a customer to deliver some jewellery.'

'If I were you, I'd stop playing games and have a long hard

think about what else Cole might tell me before I interview you.'
Chapman started to walk away.

Bishop looked as if he was hyperventilating. 'Wait! Cole made
me go to Wheeler's with him as a bit of muscle. It was him that
tortured the poor bloke, not me. I'm not a violent person . . .'

'You were about to punch my colleague before she kicked you
in the nuts.'

'Come on! I just wanted her to back off so I could get in the cab,'
he replied, looking more freaked out.

'Where's the warehouse? Do you have a key for it?'

Bishop was struggling for breath. 'I don't know anything, honest, I just drive Cole around, I swear on my kids' life.'

'That's exactly what you'll be doing Bishop, twenty-five years
with no parole. So I'd suggest you better start talking – now!'

Bishop looked desperate. 'All right, all right, it's 383 Wick Lane,
next door to De Klerk's. It's a digital key entry lock. One zero six six.'

'And what can I expect to find there?'

'A machine for making diamonds. Cole's also hidden some
cash there.'

'Is Johan De Klerk involved in the diamond lab?'

Bishop nodded. 'They're running some sort of scam where they
swap real diamonds for lab-grown ones.'

'What's your part in it all?'

'I'm not involved in it. I swear on my life, I'm just a driver, I
drive Cole around and deliver jewellery to his customers.'

'De Klerk has a couple of drivers he uses to make wine deliver-
ies. Are they involved?'

He shook his head. 'Not as far as I know.'

Chapman nodded. 'All right, you've done the smart thing.'
He walked over to Jessica, repeating what Bishop had told him.
'I'll inform Anderson of everything that's happened here and about

the warehouses. We'll need warrants to search them. I'll get him to send more officers to search Cole's shop. Would you mind helping me in the meantime?'

'Oh, you want my help now do you? I'll be happy to – if you explain why you didn't tell me or Anderson about DS Wood and his informant. I'd also like to know what else Wood told you.'

'You drive a hard bargain, Jessica Russell.'

'I don't like being lied to, Mike . . . and don't you dare say sorry again!'

*   *   *

While they searched Cole's jewellery shop, Chapman told Jessica about the information Stubbings had given Julian Wood and what Wood had told him about his meeting with Chandice Bramston. 'After the incident with the sapphire ring, I now understand why you suspected Michelle might be involved, and you may be right. What I don't get is why you never said anything about it when we had the meeting with Anderson,' Jessica said, still annoyed.

'Because Julian asked me not to. If Michelle found out Stubbings was the informant, she'd sue him for breaching the non-disclosure agreement.'

Jessica snorted. 'That's pretty ironic considering Stubbings was dismissed for gross misconduct after leaking information to a journalist . . .'

'That may be, but he's still an informant, and you protect your informants. Now we've arrested Bishop, who looks like he's going to spill his guts, I'm still hoping I can do that.'

'That's not going to be easy because you'll have to ask Michelle about her friend Chandice and tell her about Cole's arrest. She's not stupid and will realise you got the information from Stubbings.'

'Michelle may well think it was Stubbings, but she'd have difficulty proving it with all the evidence we have against her husband. It would also show that she failed to report a crime and may have withheld information that would have assisted our investigation.'

'That's true.'

'Chandice has point-blank refused to make a statement, so she's out of the equation.'

'I won't say anything. I still think you should tell Anderson, but it's up to you. In some ways, I wished you'd never told me.'

By the time the other team members arrived, Jessica and Chapman still hadn't found anything of evidential value in Cole's shop, apart from his laptop, which Taff had taken back to the lab for Guy to examine. Chapman instructed an officer to look for mobile phones and any uncut diamonds. Chapman was eager to leave but waited until a detective arrived handing him warrants for the two warehouses.

'Can I come with you?' Jessica asked as they walked to Chapman's car.

'If you want to. You're sure you're not sick of the sight of me?'

She shrugged. 'I'm only following you out of idle curiosity.'

They got into a squad car with a driver and headed towards the warehouses. Jessica was quiet on the journey and Chapman sensed she was still upset with him. 'I know I've pissed you off, but I . . .'

'Do not start apologising again,' she snapped.

'I was going to ask if you'd like to go for a drink after work. I understand if you don't want to.'

'I can't. I'm going out with my brother and his girlfriend this evening – that's if I'm not still stuck at work.'

He nodded. 'Maybe some other time then. Where are you going tonight?'

'Quattordici's in Chislehurst.'

'I've been there. The food's really excellent.'

'I know, that's why I agreed to go there,' Jessica said. Chapman sighed. Maybe it was just time to shut up. 'Actually, work permitting, you can join us if you want,' she said casually.

'Really?'

'Yes. I don't fancy playing gooseberry with David and his girlfriend.'

'I'd love to. What time?'

'Table's booked for seven thirty. We'll probably have a drink in The Bull first at seven.'

Chapman smiled. 'Sounds good. We're here' he said as their squad car drew up. DS Wood was waiting in the street outside the warehouse with his team of three detectives.

'Nice work with Cole and Bishop,' Wood said, nodding to Chapman.

'Actually, Jessica did most of the hard work,' Chapman told him. They then went into the warehouse foyer to speak to the security guard and show him the search warrants. The guard escorted them to De Klerk and Cole's premises.

'I was expecting some sort of container,' Wood remarked on seeing the floor-to-ceiling windows and glass door entry. The blinds were all down.

'They call them warehouses, but they're really just large office spaces with desks and chairs etc, but renters store stuff in them as well,' the guard explained. 'There's a back shutter for loading and unloading goods. We have security cameras covering the street, back and lobby, so let me know if you need to see any footage.'

'How long do you keep the recordings?' Chapman asked.

'Ninety days before the recorded footage is overwritten.' While the guard opened De Klerk's door, Chapman entered the numbers Bishop had given him for Cole's unit.

'Have a look at the state of this place, Mike,' Wood said as Chapman was about to open the door. De Klerk's warehouse looked as if someone had thoroughly searched it. A filing cabinet had been opened and the contents were strewn around the floor. Boxes of wine had been opened, the bottles removed and put to one side. They went from De Klerk's warehouse onto Cole's, which looked untouched. 'What do you reckon that big machine is for?' Wood asked.

'Bishop said Cole had a machine for making diamonds,' Chapman told him.

Chapman sighed. 'This is the second time someone's got to a suspect's address before we have.'

'Do you want Jessica's team to examine the warehouses before we search them?'

'I'll get her to view it first.' He phoned Jessica, who was still in De Klerk's warehouse, and asked her to come in and have a look.

Jessica looked in from the doorway, surveying the scene. 'Someone was in a hurry to find whatever they were looking for in De Klerk's section. My team are very busy at the moment. It would be helpful if the divisional scene of crime officers carried out the photography and forensic examinations,' Jessica said.

'I'll take some pictures on my phone for Anderson, call him with an update and request the SOCOs attend,' Chapman said.

'Do you think Cole or Bishop were responsible for trashing De Klerk's section?' Wood asked.

Jessica glanced at him. 'I overheard Cole say he'd got diamonds hidden in his warehouse, but they were arrested before they could get here. And I can't see it being Wheeler, as he's been dead for a couple of days now.'

Wood nodded. 'Whoever did this must have known the entry number.'

'Not if they had technical knowledge and used a hacking device to break or bypass the key code and unlock the door. I think they found what they were looking for in De Klerk's office,' Jessica said quietly.

'How do you work that out?' Wood asked. They walked back into De Klerk's warehouse and Jessica gestured to the documents strewn over the floor and then pointed at the boxes containing bottles of wine.

'The boxes have been ripped open haphazardly, apart from the two over there on the floor next to each other that have been cut open neatly. I think whoever opened them knew where to look and what they were looking for.'

'Could it be a staged scene?' Chapman asked.

'It's possible, but I can't be certain as those two boxes may have been opened before the place was ransacked.'

'I'll get all the available CCTV from the security guard and head back to Barking with Jessica,' Chapman told Wood. 'Can you stay put, Julian, then brief the SOCOs when they arrive.' As they headed towards Chapman's car, he stopped and handed Jessica the car keys, saying he'd forgotten to tell Wood something.

Wood was inside De Klerk's warehouse, looking around when he saw Chapman. 'Don't take this the wrong way, Julian, but I need to ask you something about the break-ins.'

'You think it might have been Stubbings, don't you?'

'It crossed my mind. You said he'd been watching this place and he knew Cole was a hooky jeweller and De Klerk was involved with him. As I recall, Stubbings was also pretty good with computers and technical equipment.'

'You don't like him one bit, do you?'

'He's not my favourite person, no, and I don't trust him.'

'Well, I do, and I think you're out of order. Why would he give me all that information and then risk coming here? Stubbs isn't stupid, Mike. He knows that he'd go to prison if he got caught, and his life would be hell.'

'I hope, for both our sakes, this has nothing to do with him.'

Wood waited until Chapman had gone back to the car before calling Stubbings. He had a nasty feeling in the pit of his stomach. He'd tried his best to keep his name out of things, but if the stupid bastard had been thieving at the warehouse he'd landed himself right in it.

CHAPTER THIRTY-THREE

When they returned to the station, Chapman and Jessica went directly to Anderson's office. He was looking pleased with himself. 'Cole lives in a flat just around the corner from his shop. I've sent detectives and scene-of-crime officers to search both Cole's and Bishop's flats. So, tell me what happened in Hatton Garden.' Jessica described her interactions with Cole as she posed as a customer.

'She left out the best bit,' Chapman said with a smile. 'She put that toe-rag Bishop on the ground when he went for her.'

Anderson nodded. 'DC Bingham said you've got a mean right foot, Jessica.' She was relieved when Chapman moved on to what they'd found at the warehouses. 'Any idea who turned over De Klerk's place?' Anderson asked.

'I've been thinking about it on the way back here,' Chapman said. 'If a hacking device wasn't used, they'd have had to know the key code.'

'Michelle De Klerk?' Chapman nodded. 'What do you think, Jessica?'

'It's possible, but I don't think she'd risk being seen by the guard or picked up by the CCTV cameras.'

'She could have got someone to do the dirty work for her. In her line of work, she meets a lot of criminals,' Chapman suggested.

'I don't believe Michelle would risk her career by doing that.'

'I tend to agree with Jessica,' Anderson said. 'Get DC Bingham to look through the CCTV for the last couple of days to see if he spots anyone who is known to us or is acting suspiciously.'

'It might be worth sending it over to Guy with photos of all the suspects. He's a super recogniser who can identify faces, often after the briefest glimpse. He will quickly spot anyone of interest on the CCTV, even if they look different to the photos,' Jessica suggested.

'Agreed,' Anderson said.

'I'll upload the footage and photographs to HOLMES for him to review,' Chapman said. He just hoped it didn't turn out to be Wood or Stubbings caught on camera.

'I want you and DS Wood to interview Bishop first. He seems to be the weak link, and you can use his admissions against Cole when you interview him.'

'What about De Klerk? Bishop said he's involved with Cole in a jewellery scam,' Chapman said.

'Doctor Babu told me he's awake. But he's confused and not fit to be interviewed yet. Babu says he'll reassess him tomorrow.'

'If Jessica was right, it's all been a big act,' Chapman said.

'But we can't prove it, and I don't want to risk raising it with Doctor Babu. De Klerk's not going anywhere, and hopefully Bishop will give us plenty of ammunition to hit him with when he is fit to be interviewed.'

Jessica 's mobile pinged, and she looked at the text. 'Taff says Cole's right shoe matches the print on the magazine found on the floor beside Wheeler's body. The fingerprints on the water buffalo glass are also his.'

'Two more nails in his coffin,' Chapman remarked.

'What about the unknown DNA on the diamonds?' Anderson asked.

'Diane's doing Rapid DNA on Cole's mouth swab. It will take another hour to raise a profile, after which she can do a direct comparison and give us the result.'

'That's fine, as Bishop will be interviewed first, and Cole will want a pre-interview consultation with the duty solicitor.'

'Is it Baldwin?' Anderson nodded. 'Isn't there a conflict of interest if he represented Liam Palmer?' Jessica asked.

'Apparently not. I spoke with the CPS about it. They said that as the charges against Palmer in the De Klerk case were being dropped, there was no conflict, and, as the duty solicitor, he could represent Cole.'

'It could work to our advantage. Baldwin only knows what we questioned Palmer about. He has no knowledge of Wheeler's death or any of the latest forensic results, and we don't need to disclose our case to him fully.'

'I agree. I want you and DS Wood to interview Bishop. Jessica and I can watch from the viewing room.'

'What about Cole's interview?'

'You and I will do it together later. I suggest you inform DS Wood and prep for the interview with Bishop. Let us know when you're ready to start.'

Chapman nodded. 'Will do, guv.'

*   *   *

Chapman called DS Wood into his office to discuss Bishop's interview. 'Is there anything else you can think of we should ask Bishop?' Chapman asked.

'Nope, we've listed all the relevant questions we need to ask.'

'You recall when we were waiting for Palmer to turn up at his flat, I asked if you thought someone in the office had leaked information to the press.'

'Yes, and I told you it wasn't me.'

'I know it wasn't. But between us, it might have been Dawn's boyfriend. She told him about the investigation, and he has an uncle who works for the BBC.'

'She told you that?'

'No. Jessica spoke with her. Poor thing was in a dreadful state. She had an almighty row with her boyfriend, and he walked out on her.'

'Have you told Anderson?'

'Not yet, but at some point I'll have to. I don't want her kicked off the team. The problem is, if Anderson finds out I knew and didn't tell him, then I'm in the shit.'

Wood sighed. 'It had nothing to do with Dawn or her boyfriend. It was me. I called a journalist I knew, and he went to the BBC.'

'For fuck's sake, Julian, why didn't you come clean when I asked you?'

'Because I reckoned I could front out an internal investigation. I was pissed and furious with Anderson when I did it.'

'What did you hope to achieve?'

'Apart from pissing Anderson off? I thought it might lead to some useful information turning up, which it did, with Wheeler phoning Crime Stoppers.'

'He was trying to frame an innocent man!'

'I know that now. I also hoped Anderson might get kicked off the investigation, and they'd let you take over.'

'I can't believe you could be so stupid, with all your experience.'

'Like I said, I was shit-faced.'

'That's no excuse, plus you lied to me. It makes me wonder if you've been honest with me about what Stubbings told you. What about breaking into the warehouse?'

'You know everything Stubbs said has turned out to be correct. And I know for a fact he didn't break into the warehouse.'

'You've spoken to him, haven't you?'

'Yes. He went straight home after we met in the pub and was in Bath the next day on a case, and he's still there. He told me his wife could vouch for him and sent me pictures of receipts for meals he'd purchased in Bath and on the way there. He also gave me the name of the hotel where he's staying. I checked it out, and he was telling the truth.'

'Sounds like you don't trust him either.'

'It got me worried when you thought it might be Stubbs. I had to be sure. He was pissed off with me for thinking it might be him. I'm sorry I've put you in an awkward position by talking to that journalist. I deserve to be disciplined for what I've done.'

'You're treading on eggshells, Julian. I doubt you'll get dismissed, but you could be kicked back to uniform.'

'I'll tell Anderson it was me after we've interviewed Bishop.'

Chapman ran his hands through his hair, then let out a deep sigh. 'I must be mad, but I think there's a way out of this for you.'

'Forget it, Mike. I'm not going to let you risk your career over my fuck-up.'

'Dead men don't tell tales, Julian.'

'I'm lost . . . unless you're thinking of killing me.'

'It had crossed my mind. Seriously though, we know Wheeler gave Crime Stoppers the info about Palmer. Who's to say it wasn't him that contacted a journalist or went straight to the BBC? Maybe he wanted it on the news as part of his plan to frame Palmer.'

Wood thought about it. 'It's feasible – and virtually impossible to disprove now he's dead. Do you think Anderson will go for it?'

'Why not? It may also lead to the professional standards unit dropping their investigation, which he'd be pleased with.'

'Thanks, Mike, I owe you big time.'

'Too right you do. A bottle of Remy Martin VSOP might do the trick.'

'Expensive stuff.'

'Don't push your luck or it will be two bottles.'

*   *   *

Chapman turned on the recording equipment and cautioned a glum-looking Christopher Bishop, who'd said he was willing to be interviewed without a solicitor present. 'Let's start with how you came to know Cole,' Chapman began.

'It was about three years ago. I heard that Cole was buying stolen jewellery without asking questions. My days of breaking into houses were over, but I still handled stolen goods now and then. Anyway, I ended up working as a driver for him, delivering jewellery mostly.'

'What do you know about Cole's association with Johan De Klerk?' Chapman asked.

'I think initially he was just a client who bought some jewellery from him.'

Chapman showed him a photograph of Wheeler. 'Do you know this man?'

'Sure, Wheeler the Dealer. We shared a prison cell some years back, and I got to know him a bit more than I'd have liked. He's a nasty piece of work, definitely someone you don't want to cross. When we were banged up, he shanked a couple of inmates with a homemade knife. He's a pretty handy cat burglar but he mostly sells what he steals to buy cocaine.'

'What's his association with Nathan Cole?'

'Nat told me he needed someone to do a burglary at a big fancy house in Victoria Park Road. He didn't tell me who lived there, but he made me drive past it and took some photos on his phone. The back wall was about twelve feet high. I told him I was too out of shape to get over it so he asked if I knew anyone else who could do the job. I told him about Wheeler and introduced them.

Nat said to buy two burner phones and SIM cards, and I think he gave one to Wheeler.'

'You must have known it was De Klerk's house,' Chapman said.

'I didn't know where De Klerk lived then, and I didn't ask questions.'

'Tell us what Cole was doing from last Friday until his arrest earlier today.'

'Let me think a minute.' He paused briefly before continuing. 'On Friday morning, he called me and said he needed a lift. I picked him up in Hatton Garden and dropped him off at about three-thirty outside De Klerk's house. He said he had some business to sort out and told me to wait in the car. He came out about an hour later, and then I took him back to the shop.'

'When did you next see him?' Chapman asked.

'When we got back to the shop, Cole told me to pick him up from home at nine on Saturday morning, as he had to go to Birmingham on business. I dropped him off at Euston.'

'Did Cole say anything about Wheeler doing the burglary over the weekend?' Chapman asked.

'No. I didn't hear from him again until Tuesday afternoon. He sounded pretty pissed off on the phone and told me to pick him up from Euston. I was running late due to the traffic and didn't arrive until just after five. He was in a foul mood and furious with me for recommending Wheeler. I asked him what was wrong, and he said that Wheeler and a mate of his had fucked up and now he thought they were trying to rip him off.'

'This mate, you know his name?'

'No, he never said. I dropped him off at the shop and went home. I thought about going to see Wheeler to find out what had happened, then thought better of it.'

'So, you know where he lives?' Wood said.

'Yes. It's his sister's place.'

'Did you go to Wheeler's flat with Cole?' Chapman asked.

Bishop was sweating. He wiped his face with his hand, then swallowed. 'Yeah, on Tuesday night.'

'How did that come about?' Chapman asked.

'I was at home, and I remember it was late when Cole phoned me. He said to come and pick him up right away but didn't say why. When he got in the car, I could see he was fuming. He asked if I knew where Wheeler lived as he wanted to have it out with him and get his property back. I told him it wasn't a good idea as Wheeler can be a nasty bastard, especially if he's had any coke.'

'But Cole ignored you,' Wood commented.

Bishop nodded. 'He said he'd be reasonable with Wheeler and there was nothing to worry about. He wanted me with him because I knew Wheeler and he thought I could calm him down if things got heated.' Bishop reached for a bottle of water, unscrewed the cap and took a few gulps. His hands were shaking.

'So, what happened when you got to Wheeler's flat?' Chapman asked.

'I knocked on the door while Cole stood away from the spyhole. Wheeler didn't answer it at first, but I knocked again and said it was me and I needed to speak to him urgently. He opened the door and I walked in, then Cole rushed in from behind me with a gun in his hand.'

'What sort of gun?'

'It was an old revolver. Nat flicked open the cylinder to show Wheeler there were bullets in it and told him to sit in the arm-chair. Wheeler looked pale. He was clutching his side and groaning. Cole picked up a cushion to use as a silencer and held it to Wheeler's head. He told Wheeler he knew there was cash in De Klerk's safe and he wanted it – and something that sounded like a locked box. Wheeler said if there was any cash, his mate who did the job must have stolen it. He looked Cole in the eye and said he'd removed the diamonds from the lockbox and hidden them elsewhere for safekeeping.'

'Did you already know what had been stolen from De Klerk's?' Chapman asked.

'No, not until then.'

'But you just told us that Wheeler said he'd removed the diamonds, so you knew about them?'

'No, that was the first time I'd heard them mentioned. I'm telling you the truth.'

'What happened next?' Wood asked.

'Cole kept the gun to his head and said he'd better tell him where they were, or he'd blow his brains out. Wheeler laughed at him and said something like, "Go on then, if you've got the bottle, you little prick." He knew Cole didn't have what it takes to shoot a man in cold blood, and if he did, he'd never get the diamonds back.'

'We know from forensics that Wheeler's wrists were bound with rope and his mouth with black masking tape. If Cole was holding a gun, you must have done that.' Chapman said. Bishop took another drink and licked his lips nervously. 'If you want me to help you, you need to tell us everything,' Chapman said.

'I swear on my kids' life I didn't know Cole had brought that stuff with him. Look, I was shit scared at this point, with the gun and everything, so I just did as I was told. I thought Wheeler might make a fuss, but he didn't. He seemed to be in a lot of pain and it was like he had no fight left in him.'

'Did you punch Wheeler in the face?' Wood asked.

'No, that was Cole. He pistol-whipped him. I told him there was no need for all this heavy stuff, and he told me to shut up and search the flat.'

'Were you wearing gloves?'

Bishop nodded. 'There was a pair of Wheeler's on the coffee table.'

'Where's the rope and the tape now?' Wood asked.

'I threw it all in a bin on my estate, along with the clothes I was wearing, 'cause the rubbish collection was Wednesday mornings.'

Chapman realised the chances of recovering the items now were virtually nil. 'Well, you left a bit of tape on the back of Wheeler's neck, and forensics found your partial print on it. That's why we were after you.'

He sighed. 'I thought I must have fucked up somewhere.'

'You'd probably have got away with it if Wheeler hadn't died, as there's no way he'd have reported what happened to the police.'

'Maybe not, but he'd have come after me and Cole with a vengeance.'

'Did you find any diamonds?' Chapman asked, wondering if there were more than the ones recovered from Wheeler's stomach.

'No. Cole was livid, and that's when he started burning Wheeler with a cigar. It was horrible. I could smell his burning flesh and hear his screams from behind the tape. Cole said if he didn't tell him the name of his mate who robbed De Klerk's house and where the diamonds were, he'd keep going. Wheeler nodded, like he would, and I took the tape off his mouth.'

'What did he say?'

'He was in a terrible state. It was hard to make out what he was saying, he was groaning and gurgling that much, but I'm pretty sure he was saying he did the job on his own. Cole asked if his ribs were all messed up because of De Klerk, and he nodded. He asked Wheeler again if there was cash in the safe. He nodded, and I think he was about to say where it was when, suddenly, his eyes bulged, and he couldn't breathe, then his head slumped forward. I checked for a pulse, but he was dead.'

'What was Cole's reaction?'

'He was dumbstruck, then he started cursing at Wheeler. He wanted to search the flat again and started rooting around. After a few minutes, I said it was pointless, and he agreed we'd better get out.'

'For what it's worth, the money was hidden inside a travel pillow, and he'd swallowed the diamonds. It looks like he intended to sell them in Dubai.'

'Did he have a heart attack?' Bishop asked.

'It's possible. De Klerk caught him in his house and gave him a good beating, which ruptured his spleen and that could have led to his death.'

'So, we didn't kill him,' Bishop said, looking relieved.

'De Klerk had reasonable grounds to assault Wheeler. You and Cole didn't, so legally, you could be culpable of murder.'

Bishop looked shocked. 'I swear to you I never hurt him. It was all down to Cole. I was scared he was going to fucking shoot me.'

'Did Cole say anything on the way back to his place?' Wood asked.

'He told me to keep my mouth shut and get rid of the tape and my clothes. He said he'd give me five grand.'

'What's Cole's relationship with De Klerk?' Wood asked.

'Like I said before, I think they scam people.'

'Can you explain it in a bit more detail?'

'I don't know much about it, but Cole makes lab-grown diamonds in a machine. He told me it's all legal, and De Klerk got a cut of the profits.'

'What's the scam if it's all legal? Chapman said.

'I think Cole shows punters real uncut diamonds and then makes whatever jewellery they want with lab-grown diamonds that are worth about a quarter of what they're paying.'

'Where do the real diamonds come from?'

'I found a screwed-up Kimberley certificate for some mined South African diamonds in Cole's warehouse bin a few weeks back. De Klerk probably smuggles them in through his wine shipments from South Africa.'

'How do you know it was a fake certificate?'

'Well, you wouldn't throw it away if it was real. You need a genuine Kimberley certificate to make stolen diamonds look legit.'

'Sounds like you know a bit about it all,' Chapman observed.

'You learn a lot when you're banged up,' he said.

'They must have been making a lot of money,' Wood said.

'I don't know exactly how much, but I'd imagine you'd be looking at hundreds of thousands.'

Chapman whistled. 'Did you ever see Cole or De Klerk handling any uncut diamonds?'

'I saw De Klerk in the shop one time with Cole. There was a black box on the counter, which, looking back, was probably the lockbox Cole kept going on about. I saw what looked like little stones, but they must have been uncut diamonds. De Klerk closed it pronto when he saw me. I've also seen him in Coles warehouse a few times, so they must work the scam together. To be honest, I keep my nose out of their business. I'm just the gopher.'

'How long have they been producing these lab-made diamonds?'

'I don't know, but I found the fake certificate about three or four months ago.'

'What about De Klerk's wife, Michelle? Do you know if she's involved with Cole as well?'

'I've never heard her name mentioned.' Bishop looked as if he'd come to the end of his tether. 'Listen, what's going to happen to me? Am I gonna be charged? I've told you everything I know.'

'The CPS will decide that. Would you be willing to give evidence against Cole?'

'Will I get a shorter sentence if I do?'

'Possibly, but the CPS would have to accept a guilty plea to the charges before you give evidence against Cole. We would also give a letter to the judge saying how you admitted your part in the crimes and assisted us.'

'Cole's the one who got me into this fucking mess. So yes, I'll give evidence against him . . . and De Klerk if you need me to.'

After the interview with Bishop, Chapman went to see Anderson in his office. Jessica was with him, having watched the interview together in the viewing room. 'Nice work, Mike,' he said. 'And the search of Cole's shop turned up a loaded World War Two revolver hidden under the floorboards in the back office.'

'Good, that fits with what Bishop told us,' Chapman said.

'Do you think he was telling the truth about the rest of it?' Anderson asked.

'Bits and pieces, yes, but he's trying a bit hard to make himself look like a victim. He could have refused to take Cole to Wheeler's flat, but he didn't. Bishop doesn't have any previous convictions for violence, but he was prepared to assault Jessica to escape arrest.'

'Nicki Giorgini thought the more recent mark on Wheeler's face was a punch. I'd have expected a cut or a deeper bruise if it was a pistol-whip injury,' Jessica said.

Chapman nodded. 'I suspect Bishop was promised a cut of the cash or diamonds if he helped Cole. He also went straight to Cole's shop when he knew we were on to him. I reckon they're a lot closer than Bishop makes out.'

Anderson nodded. 'I thought you and Wood worked well together. I'd like the two of you to interview Cole. Be interesting to hear what he has to say now the evidence is beginning to stack up.'

'I suspect he'll go no comment or just deny everything. But I'm confident the CPS will agree he and Bishop should be charged. With that in mind, we should consider disclosing some of our evidence against him to his solicitor before the interview'.

'What about Bishop's interview? Will you disclose that?' Jessica asked.

'I was thinking about it as a possibility. It might get him to talk.'

Jessica raised her hand. 'Just a suggestion, but I think you might be better off holding back with Bishop's interview until you question Cole. I would tell Baldwin that you interviewed Bishop but don't disclose what he said. Then Cole might think Bishop hasn't told you anything, and it will come as a shock when he learns otherwise in the interview. Even if he makes no comment answers, his reaction on camera could be incriminating and good for a jury to see.'

'Very crafty, Jessica,' Anderson smiled.

'We'll play it that way then,' Chapman said.

Leaving Anderson's office, Chapman went to organise a meeting with Baldwin, who was due to arrive at the station. Jessica went to the canteen, hoping she might find DS Wood. She got herself a coffee and a sandwich, then spotted him at a corner table away from the other officers. 'Mind if I join you?' she said.

'Of course not, have a seat,' he said.

'I just wanted to say how well you seemed to work alongside Mike in the interview with Bishop,' she said.

'I've known Mike for a long time,' he said. 'He's a good bloke and a good detective; we get on well.'

'He told me how you got some new information that's proved really useful, about the fake sapphire and Michelle De Klerk's relationship with her friend, Chandice. You got to her via an ex-police officer is that correct? Don't worry, I'm not interested in the name.'

'Yeah, he'd been hired by Michelle, but he'd been working in Spain and didn't get to hear about the burglary until he returned. That was when he contacted me.'

'I see. So, you then went to see Chandice.'

'Yes. Look, I told Mike all about it.'

Jessica nodded and sipped her coffee. 'It would be very useful for you to repeat it all to me. It would give me an insight into her relationship with Michelle, and that would help me when I talk to her. You did make notes, didn't you?'

He started looking shifty. 'Yes, I don't have them with me now.'

'Why don't you start from the moment you arrived at her house. You'd be surprised how even the smallest details can give you a real insight into a relationship.'

Julian took a sip of his coffee. 'Look, I have to look out for this ex-copper. I don't want to get him into trouble. I mean I pretty well told Mike everything that she said to me.'

'I'm sure you did.'

'Then what do you want?'

'I may be wrong, but I think you are a very experienced officer, and I know from experience that jotting down notes when you are interviewing someone can often make them less cooperative. So, I would understand if you'd recorded the conversation without her knowledge.' Wood sighed, then took his mobile from his pocket. He scrolled through and then passed it to her.

CHAPTER THIRTY-FOUR

Jessica received the call from Chapman as she came out of the ladies toilet. DS Wood was standing waiting for her outside. She handed him his mobile. 'That was very interesting – and useful – thank you,' she said.

He put the phone back in his pocket with a frown. 'We'd better get a move on. Anderson's waiting.' They hurried to the viewing room, where Wood turned the recording equipment on. In the interview room, they heard Chapman opening with the usual introductions before he cautioned Cole.

Baldwin coughed. 'Before you commence the interview, DI Chapman, I'd like to inform you that Mr Cole has made a prepared statement that he would like me to read to you.'

'What's a prepared statement?' Jessica asked Anderson.

'It outlines the suspect's version of events and their response to the allegations against them. Because he hasn't had full disclosure, Baldwin hopes it will stop further questioning and reduce the impact of adverse inferences at trial.'

'So, the interview will be over after Cole's statement is read out?'

'No. Thanks to you and your team, there's incriminating forensic evidence to put to Cole that has not been disclosed to Baldwin. Cole may well give "no comment" answers, but that will harm his defence if he suddenly comes up with an explanation at trial.'

'Go ahead,' Chapman said, and Baldwin cleared his throat before proceeding.

'Firstly, I want to state that I am innocent of the crimes I am accused of and believe that John Wheeler and Christopher Bishop are responsible.

I admit to knowing Johan De Klerk. He's a charming man and a customer of mine. We first met eight or nine months ago when he bought some jewellery for his wife as a birthday present. I also sold Johan a Rolex watch, which Mr Baldwin has told me was stolen from him during a burglary, which I know nothing about.

I get along well with Johan, but we had a slight falling out last December over a ring belonging to his wife's friend Chandice. Michelle brought her to the shop to have her diamond and sapphire ring resized and polished. Chandice left the ring with me, but after I'd removed and polished the sapphire, I accidentally put a different one back in the ring. They all thought I had deliberately made a switch to keep the sapphire and sell it on.

They were understandably angry when they discovered what had happened, and Johan came to the shop. Thankfully, I found the original sapphire in a drawer with many others. Johan was satisfied that it was a genuine mistake and apologised for accusing me of any wrongdoing. I accepted his apology, and that was the end of the matter.

Last Friday, I received a phone call from Johan. He asked me to come to his house in Victoria Park Road, Hackney, to discuss the sale of some diamonds he had acquired. I was driven to Johan's in the afternoon by Christopher Bishop, a cab driver, who I regularly use as I don't have a driving licence. I can't recall when I arrived, but I think it was between three and four p.m. I told Bishop I wouldn't be long and to wait for me.

Johan invited me to his cinema room in the basement, which also had a bar. He gave me a cognac in a water buffalo engraved glass. We sat in the cinema seats, and he showed me a black lockbox containing numerous rough, uncut diamonds. I examined them and asked where they came from. He said South Africa and asked if I wanted to buy them. I suspected they were stolen or purchased on

SCENE OF THE CRIME | 424

the black market and told Johan I wasn't interested. He asked if I knew anyone who would be. I said I didn't, and he'd have difficulty selling them to reputable dealers like me, as rough diamond imports must be accompanied by a Kimberley Protocol certificate, which he didn't have. He told me he could get the certificates from a friend in South Africa, but I still wasn't interested.

Johan didn't say anything or pressure me, and I didn't ask any further questions about the diamonds, but I think he understood why I didn't want to get involved in illicit or stolen goods. We talked for a while, and I left. On the way back to my shop, without thinking, I told Bishop about the diamonds Johan had tried to sell me, and I believe he must have informed John Wheeler.

About two months ago, Wheeler came to my shop. I'd never met him before, and he mentioned he knew Bishop and tried to sell me jewellery that had obviously been stolen. I told him to get out and spoke harshly with Bishop, saying I'd sack him if he sent other criminals to my shop. Bishop was apologetic, and then he told me he'd met Wheeler in prison. After that, we didn't speak about the incident.

Mr Baldwin informed me that I am suspected of using a burner phone to communicate with John Wheeler. I totally deny this, and I believe the messages and calls on these phones were between Bishop and Wheeler. On Saturday morning, I went to Birmingham on business. I don't like trains, and Bishop drove me there. He stayed in a nearby cheaper hotel, but I don't know which one. I believe he used the burner phone to contact Wheeler. Any calls I made on my phone to Bishop were to request his services as a driver or to deliver purchased goods to clients, for which I paid him.

Mr Baldwin also informed me that I am suspected of being involved in the death of John Wheeler, who was gagged, bound and tortured to reveal the whereabouts of the property stolen from Johan De Klerk. Again, I deny this, and I don't even know where

John Wheeler lives, but I suspect Christopher Bishop does. I also believe Bishop tortured and killed Wheeler because he wanted the property he'd stolen from Johan De Klerk's house.

I am aware that the police obtained my phone records showing that I called Christopher Bishop on Tuesday at 2.05 p.m. while in Birmingham and again just after 5 p.m. near Euston station. I do not deny either of these calls. Bishop was in Birmingham with me, and I called him to say I was ready to go home. On the way, and while travelling through Euston, I remembered I had an important letter to post, and I asked him to stop when I saw a post box. He said he'd drop me off and go around the block, as there were traffic cameras, and he might get fined for stopping. I posted the letter and five minutes later he hadn't appeared, so I called him, and he said he was stuck in a side street due to heavy traffic.

I am also accused of trying to escape from the police when they came to my shop. This is sheer nonsense, and there is an innocent explanation. I had arranged for Bishop to pick me up and take me to a fellow dealer in Golders Green who wanted to purchase a quantity of jewellery from me. Bishop came to the shop, and I told him to drive around to the alleyway at the rear. This is because I don't like to go out the front with jewellery for fear of being robbed. Bishop didn't appear, so I looked around the corner. I saw two men walking towards me and thought I was going to be robbed. I had no idea they were police officers, so I ran.

In closing, I again deny all the allegations made against me. I believe that John Wheeler and Christopher Bishop were working together, and Wheeler robbed and assaulted Johan De Klerk. Something then happened that caused Bishop to go to Wheeler's flat, and while there, he attacked and tortured Wheeler, thereby causinghis death.

This statement is true.

Signed. Nathan Cole.

Baldwin slid the statement across the table to Chapman, who read it for himself and jotted down some notes. In the viewing room, Anderson had also made some notes during the reading of the statement. He turned to Jessica. 'So, it looks like Michelle knows Cole. Funny she's never mentioned it to us. It makes you wonder if she's also withholding information about other things.'

'I agree,' Jessica said, not letting on that it was something she already knew.

'He anticipated we might recover some diamonds and find his DNA on them. He's covering his back by saying he handled the diamonds at De Klerk's house.'

'Cole's clever,' Jessica agreed, 'but not as smart as he thinks he is. His story might have to change when he discovers the forensic evidence we have against him.'

In the interview room, Chapman looked at Cole and held up the statement. 'This is a fabricated load of nonsense, Nathan, and we can prove it. I didn't disclose this to Mr Baldwin, but we know, from Bishop's phone records, that he was in London while you were in Birmingham.'

Cole's expression didn't change. 'No comment.'

'There are some other flaws in your statement. The woman who came into your shop just before you were arrested was working undercover. She overheard you and Bishop talking in the back. Can you recall what you said to each other?'

'No comment.'

Chapman looked at his notes. 'Let me refresh your memory. Bishop told you the police were at his flat in Hackney and watching your shop. You replied, "We need to get to the Hackney warehouse. We can buy fake passports and get out of the country. Get your cab and meet me out the back."'

'No comment.'

'You have a warehouse in Hackney next to Mr De Klerk's where you make lab-grown diamonds. Is that correct?'

Baldwin held a hand up. 'This was not disclosed to me before the interview, DI Chapman. I want to discuss it with my client in private before you question him further.'

Cole put his hand on Baldwin's arm. 'It's all right. I'm happy to answer questions about it.'

'So, you admit owning a machine that makes diamonds?' Chapman continued.

'Yes, and it's not illegal. My lab diamonds are all certified by the International Gemological Institute. My clients know they are not buying a mined diamond. I run a reputable business.'

Chapman shook his head. 'You were running a scam with De Klerk. You showed clients falsely certified uncut diamonds and swapped them with lab-grown diamonds when you made rings or other jewellery.'

Cole laughed. 'That's ridiculous. If you check my books, you'll see everything is above board.'

'Why did you set up the lab next to De Klerk's warehouse?'

'I was aware he had a warehouse because of his wine business and asked if there were any spare premises there as I wanted to set up a diamond lab. Johan expressed an interest and helped fund the purchase of the machinery. In return, I give him a cut of the profits.'

'You didn't mention any of that in your prepared statement.'

'That's because there was nothing illegal going on. I'm sure Johan will tell you the same.'

'Is Mr De Klerk still getting a cut of the profits?'

'I gave him some money on Friday.'

'How much?'

'Quite a large sum, which I don't believe I'm obliged to disclose as it was a legitimate business payment. I should also add that after what happened at Johan's house with the uncut diamonds, I have decided to end our business relationship once he's discharged from hospital.

Chapman smiled. 'We've searched your warehouse. There were no diamonds and no cash.'

Cole's eyes widened, and he licked his lips. Wood laid two photographs on the table.

'This is a photograph of your Skechers shoes. They were removed when you were arrested. The photo next to it is the sole of your right shoe.' He put a photo of the shoeprint on the magazine on the table. 'This magazine was on the floor next to Wheeler's body, and the shoeprint exactly matches your right shoe. That puts you inside Wheeler's flat on the night he died, which was Tuesday . . . the same day you travelled back from Birmingham. Any explanation for that?'

'No comment.'

'You can't prove it got there on Tuesday,' Baldwin said.

Wood shrugged. 'I agree it's an assumption, but interestingly, the *Radio Times* is open at Tuesday's program listings, and your client's shoe mark is on that page. Our forensic team also found a cigar on Montague Road, and the saliva recovered from it matches his DNA.'

'No comment,' Cole replied automatically, but he was beginning to look anxious.

Chapman took over. 'You might think you're clever, Nathan, but you're not. We interviewed Bishop, and he's blaming you for everything. I have to say his version of events is much more credible than yours. That's why we know about your diamond scam with Johan De Klerk, and that you hired Wheeler to break into his house. Wheeler double-crossed you and attempted to steal the diamonds and the cash he stole from the safe. That pissed you off, so you went to his flat with Bishop. You held a revolver to Wheeler's head while Bishop bound and gagged him. You then pistol-whipped and tortured him by pushing a lit cigar into his chest and laughing while he screamed in agony.'

Wood put a picture of the revolver on the table. 'We found that under the floorboards in your shop. Our fingerprint expert examined it, and yours are all over it.'

'No comment.'

'I'm giving you one last opportunity to tell us the truth, Nathan,' Chapman said.

'No comment.'

'Then this interview is concluded. You will be charged after we've spoken with the Crown Prosecution Service.' Chapman turned the recorder off.

'I'd like a further consultation with my client,' Baldwin said, not looking at all pleased with him.

* * *

Chapman and Wood joined Jessica and Anderson in his office. He was on the phone with the CPS and thanked them for their advice before ending the call. 'Nicki Giorgini, the pathologist, rang me earlier,' he told them. 'She said Wheeler would have eventually died from his spleen injury, but the actual cause of death was a heart attack, most likely brought on by the trauma from being tortured.'

'Does that mean legally that Cole and Bishop killed him?' Jessica asked.

Anderson looked pleased. 'It certainly does, and the CPS said they are both culpable. There was no intent to kill Wheeler, but they can be charged with manslaughter.'

'Does it matter that they are both blaming each other?' she asked.

'It's the classic cut-throat defence,' Wood said.

'What do you mean?'

'Basically, it's where one defendant accuses the other of the crime to exonerate himself. Hence, they're trying to cut each other's throats,' Wood replied.

'The CPS may decide to hold separate trials or accept a plea to a lesser charge from Bishop, then have him give evidence against Cole at his trial,' Chapman added.

'Cole is also going to be charged with burglary and unlawful possession of a firearm,' Anderson added. 'Although Wheeler broke into De Klerk's house, Cole hired him to do so, and therefore, joint enterprise burglary is applicable.'

'Wheeler tried to kill De Klerk. Is that not joint enterprise as well?' Jessica asked.

'The CPS considered it but concluded it was unlikely Cole foresaw that Wheeler would stab De Klerk and nearly kill him,' Anderson replied. 'They didn't feel there was a reasonable prospect of a conviction.'

'What about Johan De Klerk? Will he be charged?'

'That will depend on what he says when we speak to him and any other evidence that comes to light. The diamonds are probably stolen, but it's nigh on impossible to prove who committed the theft unless Johan tells us, which is highly unlikely.'

'I don't mind going to South Africa and making enquiries,' Chapman said with a grin.

Anderson laughed. 'Sadly, I think it would be a wasted journey.'

'I'll take that as a no, then,' Chapman smiled.

'Sorry to keep asking questions, but I'm getting lost in a sea of legality and a bit confused about what crimes Johan has committed and, for that matter, Michelle,' Jessica said.

'There are various customs offences he could be charged with,' Anderson explained.

'After his near-death experience, he'd probably just get a suspended sentence or hefty fine.' Chapman commented.

'But he won't get the diamonds or the cash back, will he?'

'If we can't prove they were the proceeds of crime, he might,' Chapman replied.

'As for Michelle,' Anderson continued, 'it depends on what she says when we interview her. If we have enough evidence to prove she lied to us to protect Johan, the CPS will consider obstruction of justice and making a false statement as possible charges.'

'Will Cole and De Klerk be charged with any sort of fraud regarding the lab-made diamonds?' Jessica asked.

'They could be, but identifying the people who bought jewellery from them and persuading them to make statements could be a laborious task.'

'And Cole will probably have destroyed any records of his dodgy sales,' Chapman added.

'You could put out an appeal to the public,' she suggested.

'We'd have to get an expert to examine all the gemstones, which would be costly. As a homicide and serious crime unit, we don't have the time or resources to investigate it. Williams has told me to pass it on to the fraud squad, which I'm happy to do,' Anderson said.

'Now that we know Michelle and Cole are connected, will we interview her today?' Chapman asked Anderson.

'I'd rather do it tomorrow morning. Hopefully Johan will be well enough to be interviewed but that depends on what the doctor says. It will also give us time to assess everything we've got and decide on our approach.'

'Who's going to do the interviews with the De Klerks?' Chapman asked.

'You and I will speak to Johan,' Anderson told him. 'Dawn Owens said she'll be back at work tomorrow, so I'd like her to interview Michelle with Jessica.'

'Do you not think it would be better if Jessica spoke with Michelle?' Chapman suggested.

'Legally, I think it will be better if a police officer asks the questions, as what she says may need to be used in evidence against her or her husband. Jessica and I will prepare a list of questions for Dawn to ask.' Anderson smiled. 'What you have all achieved in under a week is remarkable, and I'm grateful for the long hours and hard work you've put in . . . especially you and your team, Jessica. Please thank them for me. Once Bishop and Cole are charged, I want everyone to call it a day. We'll regroup here at 8 a.m. tomorrow morning.'

'Any news from Guy regarding the warehouse CCTV?' Chapman asked Jessica.

'Let me call him.' She dialled the office number and when Guy answered, she put the speakerphone on. 'Hi. I'm just calling to ask how it's going with the warehouse CCTV.'

'I'm afraid I haven't seen Cole or Bishop,' Guy answered, 'but Michelle De Klerk went to the warehouse just after 7 p.m. yesterday evening.'

'Are you sure?' Anderson asked, clearly shocked.

'She arrived in a silver Mercedes SL sports car and was in the building for about an hour. She came out with a full black bin bag, put it in the boot, went back into the building, came out with two carrier bags, got into the car and drove off.'

'She'd know the key code. It must have been her who ransacked Johan's warehouse,' Wood said.

'Or she staged it to look like a burglary,' Anderson added.

Jessica wasn't so sure. 'It's obvious there are CCTV cameras at the warehouse. Considering she was furious with her husband for not setting up security cameras at their home, she must know his warehouse is covered. I can't see Michelle being so stupid as to commit a crime knowing she'd be caught on camera. We told her Johan's warehouse had been broken into, so she might have gone there to look at the state of the place and get some of Johan's belongings.'

'Or that's what she wanted us to think, and everything *was* staged. She could have the diamonds and cash in the bin bag,' Wood said.

'I'll keep working on the CCTV and see if I can find anything else of interest,' Guy said.

'Good work. I want you and the rest of the team to finish at 5 p.m. and get some well-earned rest,' Anderson told him.

'Thanks, guv. I'll let the others know.' He ended the call.

On her way to her car, Jessica phoned Guy and asked him to send her a copy of the CCTV footage of Michelle De Klerk. She also asked him to contact the hospital and ask for copies of the CCTV footage covering the corridor by De Klerk's room and the hospital entrance for Thursday and Friday and send them to her.

Getting into her car, she was initially wondering what she was going to wear that evening, but she couldn't stop thinking about Michelle De Klerk and her mysterious visit to the warehouse. She was obviously an extremely clever woman, with a thorough knowledge of the law, who must have known she would be caught on camera. So, what was she up to?

CHAPTER THIRTY-FIVE

When Jessica got home, David was in the kitchen on his laptop. She told him she'd invited a colleague, Mike Chapman, to join them for dinner and hoped he didn't mind. 'Not at all. I'll have someone sensible to talk to while you and Donna natter away. Is it anything serious?' he asked with raised eyebrows.

'I like him, but we're just friends,' Jessica told him. 'I said to meet us in The Bull at seven.'

'I can't remember the last time you went on a date.'

'It's not a date,' she said, shaking her head.

'How's Donna getting to The Bull?' she asked, changing the subject.

'She's coming here about quarter to seven. Do you mind driving?'

'That means I can't have a drink then.'

'No, we can get a cab back if you're over the limit and you can pick up the car in the morning.' Jessica didn't say anything as she only intended to have a couple of drinks. 'How's the investigation going?' he asked.

'Hard to believe, but its nearly all wrapped up. Just a few loose ends,' she said, not wanting to talk about the De Klerk's.

'Was your new boss pleased?'

'Over the moon actually. MSCAN is off to a cracking start.'

'Long may it continue,' David said with a smile.

'Right, I better go and get ready. Are you OK with me using the bathroom first . . . or is Donna in there?

'Very funny. I'll jump in the shower after you.'

As she walked to her room, she suddenly remembered something and returned to the kitchen. 'I'm really sorry, David. I was so wrapped up in the investigation that I forgot you were going to the hospital today.'

'It's all right. I know your head's all over the place. It always is when you're on a case.'

'So how did it go?' she sat down opposite him.

'I had a consultation with a specialist called Doctor Bennett. She asked lots of questions, took another blood sample and did a physical examination to test my muscle strength. I then had an MRI scan and a . . .' he paused as he looked at his laptop to make sure he pronounced it right, ' . . . an Electromyogram test which is used to detect neuromuscular abnormalities.'

'Was it painful?'

'It stung a bit when the nurse put the needle into various muscles, and they're still a bit tender. Doctor Bennett also took some muscle tissue samples for microscopic testing, but it takes a week or two to get the results back.'

'Did Doctor Bennett give you a diagnosis?'

'She thinks I have a disease called Polymyositis.'

'What's Polystisis?' she asked, pronouncing it wrong.

David laughed. 'Watch my lips. It's pol-ee-migh-oh-SIGH-tu-hss. You can abbreviate it to PM, but maybe not, as that means dead body examinations to you, doesn't it?'

'Right, got it, but what is it, and what does it do to you?'

'It's a form of myositis and generally happens to men aged thirty to sixty. You can have it for months or even years before it is diagnosed. It affects the muscles, their connective tissues and sometimes the joints, causing chronic muscle inflammation and weakness.'

'But how did you get it?' she asked, beginning to feel seriously concerned.

'They don't know for sure what causes it. Doctor Bennett did say it could be a genetic disorder. She advised that you get a blood test done.'

'I'll book an appointment on Monday,' she said.

'I'm still trying to get my head around everything, but this website says . . .' he looked at his laptop again, '. . . it causes the immune system to turn against the body and attack its own tissues, blood vessels, fibres and joints. Some think it's started by a virus or the combination of a viral infection and a defective immune system.'

'Is it curable?'

David shook his head. 'Looks like I'm stuck with it. But don't worry . . . it's not contagious,' he said with a grin.

Jessica couldn't bring herself to ask if it was life-threatening. 'Can it be treated?'

'There's no cure, but there is medication to help manage the symptoms like steroids and immunosuppressants. Doctor Bennett emailed me different exercises I can do to help restore my muscle strength and arranged a physiotherapy appointment.' He smiled. 'She even recommended meditation, so I hope you can help me with that.'

'Of course. It'll be nice to have someone to do it with,' she said, trying to be upbeat.

'Don't look so worried. Although it's a chronic illness, it's rarely fatal. I'll learn how to adapt and cope with it so I can live as normal a life as possible.'

She was close to tears. 'I'm so sorry, David. It's hard to know what to say, but I'll do everything I can to help you.'

He got up from his chair and hugged her tightly. 'I know you will. That's why I love you.'

'And I love you,' she replied, hugging him tighter as she started to cry.

David stepped back and wiped the tears from her eyes. 'Don't you start, or you'll get me going.'

'You're very upbeat about it all,' Jessica said, grabbing a sheet of kitchen roll, wiping her eyes and blowing her nose.

'I wasn't when Doctor Bennett first told me. If it wasn't for Donna being there, I think I'd have had a total meltdown. Donna told me it wasn't the end of the world and to be positive. She said onwards and upwards and live the best life possible, even when facing hard times or an uncertain future, and that's what I intend to do.'

'Donna is a very astute lady. I'm pleased she's there for you.'

'She's already helped me find online sites and blogs where people with Polymyositis talk positively about living with the disease. It's all quite inspiring, actually.'

'As are you, David. I'm really proud of the way you are handling this.'

David looked at his watch. 'We better get a move on, or we'll be late. You don't want your new boyfriend thinking you're a no-show.'

She wagged a finger at him. 'I told you, he's just a friend.'

'I'll be the judge of that. Now, get a move on.'

Jessica had a quick shower, and while she got dressed, she thought about David's diagnosis and how it would affect his life. She knew nothing about his disease other than what he had told her earlier and decided to look it up on her iPad – then quickly regretted it. Although David had spoken about some of the problems he would face, he hadn't mentioned the serious complications.

She read that if the oesophagus muscles are affected, swallowing and digestive problems could occur, leading to weight loss, malnutrition and aspiration pneumonia, as you're more likely to breathe food or saliva into your lungs. Breathing problems were also mentioned. If your chest muscles are affected, shortness of breath and respiratory failure could occur. It also raises the risk of heart disease, lung disease, cancer and other connective tissue diseases, such as lupus or rheumatoid arthritis. Most worrying was the estimation that about one in ten people who have poly-myositis die from it or related diseases, and the condition slowly gets worse.

Jessica closed the iPad and threw it on the bed, wishing she'd never looked at it. She decided to wait until another time to discuss David's illness in more depth. If he was determined to be so posi-tive, she knew she had to be the same. However, she couldn't stop herself fearing for David's future and worrying about the return of his depression, especially if he and Donna were to split up.

David was still getting ready when Donna arrived, and Jessica managed to have a quick chat with her in the kitchen. She thanked her for all her support at the hospital. 'It can't have been easy for you.'

'I was glad to be there for him, Jessica. My mother had motor neurone disease and died from it a few years ago. David's illness is not as severe, but he will face many of the same problems MND sufferers have, like muscle weakness, dysphagia and respiratory problems. Being positive is a must for him and those close to him, and I'll do everything I can to keep his spirits up and help him deal with it. I know from experience it will be a tough time for you as well, but if ever you need someone to talk to, I'm a good listener.'

'Thank you, Donna. I'm so glad my brother's met someone as kind and considerate as you.'

Donna smiled. 'I know our relationship came as a bit of a sur-prise to you. It's a bit of a whirlwind romance, but we are very fond of each other and want to have a long and lasting relationship. And in case you're wondering, he told me about his depression. That's something else I know a bit about, so it doesn't faze me. You mustn't worry. I think we're going to be all right.'

Jessica felt relieved. 'Well, he was very secretive about you, which is typical of him, but David clearly thinks the world of you. I better tell him to hurry up or we'll be late. Oh, I've also invited a colleague from work. His name is Mike Chapman. I think you'll like him.'

'Is he . . . ?'

'No, just a friend,' she said firmly.

Donna grinned. 'You never know, perhaps that will change this evening.'

The pre-dinner drinks at The Bull went well, Jessica thought. Chapman looked tired, but he was friendly and seemed to be enjoying himself. The lively conversation continued through the meal, and she was relieved to see how well Mike and David got on. She had also really taken a shine to Donna and was pleasantly sur-prised to find how smart and well-read she was. She was also very interested in Jessica's work and asked lots of thoughtful questions.

Midway through the meal, Jessica's phone started ringing. 'This better not be work,' she sighed, looking at the number. 'OK, defi-nitely not work. It's a plus one number followed by eight, zero, four.'

'Plus one is the code for America,' Chapman said.

'Probably a cold call wanting you to buy bitcoins. I wouldn't answer if I were you,' David said.

'You're probably right,' Jessica was about to end the call when Donna, who had checked the number on her phone, spoke up.

'Eight zero four is the area code for Richmond, Virginia.'

Jessica suddenly realised where it might be from and asked them to excuse her while she answered the call. 'Jessica Russell speaking. How can I help you?' she asked as she stepped outside.

'Good evening, Jess. This is FBI Agent Anna Travis. I'm sorry if I've interrupted your evening, but I'm off on holiday tomorrow and wanted to call you before I go.'

'Anywhere nice, ma'am?' Jessica asked, not wanting to jump in and ask if she was calling about the FBI Behavioural Analysis course.

'The Maldives with my husband to chill out and soak in the sun. Please, call me Anna.'

'How can I help you, Anna?'

'I've got a bit of good news. You have been selected for the Behavioural Analysis course at our headquarters in Quantico.'

'Thank you so much. I can't tell you how honoured I feel to have been selected for such a prestigious course.'

'It's twelve weeks and very intensive, including a lot of physical fitness tests I'm afraid.'

'I'm looking forward to the challenge. When does the course start?' Jessica asked.

'I can't give you an exact date, but probably early next year. I'll put you down as the first reserve should anyone be unable to attend an earlier course.'

'Thank you so much, Anna. Does Commander Williams know?'

'Yes, I spoke to the Commander just before I called you. She was telling me all about the major part you're playing in a current investigation. Like her, I was most impressed with your powers of observation, especially about the water bottle. That was very canny of you. It also takes a lot of guts to speak up when you think someone is innocent of a crime and your colleagues don't. You're to be commended for that, Jess. Commander Williams said you are a very special woman, and from what I've heard about you I agree with her.'

Jessica could feel herself flushing. 'Thank you for your kind words.'

'Keep up the good work, and I wish you continued success in your future endeavours. Take care, and we'll speak again soon.' Anna ended the call.

Jessica hurried back to the restaurant to tell everyone her good news. Chapman ordered a bottle of champagne to celebrate, and they all raised a glass. When the last plates had been cleared away, David suggested returning to The Bull for a drink. Jessica said she was tired and wanted to get some sleep, but David and Donna decided they would go to the pub and get a cab home. Jessica hugged them both and told them to enjoy the rest of their evening. Chapman said he was also tired and would call it a night and get a cab home.

'That's OK, I can drop you off. It's only just down the road,' Jessica told him.

On the journey to Chapman's flat, Jessica told him how thrilled she was to have been selected for the behavioural analysis course. 'I know it's a cliché, but it really is a dream come true.'

'I'm pleased for you. You deserve it,' he told her. 'Now, if you drop me off by the petrol station, I can walk from there.'

'Don't be silly. I'll drop you at your house.'

'It's a flat. My wife got the house when we divorced,' he replied. He gave her directions, and a couple of minutes later she was parking outside his block.

'Thanks for coming tonight. It was fun. And you and David got on well.'

'He's a nice bloke, your brother, and he's got a great sense of humour. Donna's lovely as well. They make a great couple.'

'I like her too. It's a bit of a whirlwind romance, but she's very kind and obviously cares a lot for David. I just hope that it lasts.'

'If first impressions are anything to go by, I'd say it will. Would you like to go out for another meal sometime . . . just the two of us?' Chapman asked.

'Yes, that would be nice.'

'Do you want to come in for a coffee?' he asked sheepishly.

'Thanks, but I'm really tired. Maybe next time.' He leaned in to kiss Jessica on the cheek, but at the same moment, she turned her head toward him and he accidentally kissed her on the lips. They both froze and exchanged surprised glances. She didn't seem offended, so Chapman put his hand behind Jessica's neck, drew her closer, and began to kiss her. She instantly pulled away.

'I'm sorry, Mike, I'm not ready for this yet.'

Chapman felt he'd messed up. 'Sorry. I was out of order.'

'It's OK. I'm not upset with you. It's just that I haven't been in a relationship for a long time, and my last one didn't end well.'

He looked worried. 'I hope I haven't ruined our friendship.'

'Of course not. I like you a lot. I wouldn't want that to happen.'

'I'll see you in the morning, then,' he said. He got out of the car and gave her a limp wave goodnight. Jessica could see he was upset as he walked with his shoulders slumped toward the flats and didn't look back. She knew he must be feeling rejected, and it would play on his mind all night. As she started to drive off, part of her wished she had been more open and honest with him. It wasn't the first time she had used that excuse, but it wasn't fair to him, and now she wished she hadn't. She slammed her foot on the brake, and as her body lurched forward, the seat belt pressed into her chest. She jumped out of the car and called out his name, but the communal entrance door had just closed behind him. She ran to the door and banged on the glass to get his attention. It made him jump, and he turned sharply. He quickly opened the door.

'Can we talk, please?' she asked nervously.

'Of course. Are you all right?' he asked, looking concerned.

'Yes, I'm fine, but I feel I owe you a proper explanation about why I'm avoiding a relationship with you.'

'Do you want to come in?'

'No, let's just talk out here for a minute.' There was a low wall near to the entrance to the flats and they went over and sat side by side.

'You don't need to explain anything, Jessica. After what Liam Palmer did, it's understandable. I was there that night, so I know how it affected you. Seeing his face and reliving it all over these past few days must have been horrendous for you.'

'Mike, it was a long time ago, and a lot has happened in my life since then. And you're right, it wasn't easy, reliving everything. But his confession and discovering about his awful childhood has actually given me some sort of closure.'

'That's a good thing then.'

'Yes, it is. But it's not just what happened with Palmer that makes me wary of relationships with men. I won't bore you with all the details, but my father was a narcissist and a bully. He treated my mother like she was a piece of dirt and showed no love towards any of us. He abandoned us when we were kids, and thankfully, I've never seen him since.'

'He sounds a right bastard,' Chapman said.

'He was, but I got over him. It affected David a lot more, and he had a hard time, then our mother died and he went off the rails, so I moved back in with him. But I'm not telling you all this as some kind of excuse because it isn't.'

Chapman was unsure what to say next. It felt as if she was somehow skirting around the real reason for her reaction when he'd kissed her. He reached out and took hold of her hand. 'I heard what you said to Palmer after the interview.'

'Really?'

'Yes, I'd never heard that tone of voice. I think he went to shake your hand to thank you and you said, "Don't touch me" and walked out.'

'Yes, I did. You know, for a long time after what he did, I had nightmares every night. I couldn't sleep if there was any creaking sound on the stairs – the slightest noise would freak me. Even though he was only a teenager, I never saw him as that, but as this huge monster all in black with his face hidden by his black hoodie and the awful growling sounds he made when he attacked me, like an animal. It took a lot of therapy for that image to fade and for me to be able to get on with my life.' He was surprised when she suddenly laughed softly, shaking her head and pulling her hand from his. 'Seeing this bald, pitiful creep, with his dirty fingernails, his yellow teeth and crippled leg . . . if I'd seen him like that years earlier, it would have taken a lot less time to get over that image of the black hooded monster. He disgusted me and it made me angry that I had wasted so much anxiety on such a pathetic creature. I actually found it a very positive experience.'

'Well, that's good to know.'

Again, she surprised him by giving a soft laugh. 'I know I am going a roundabout way to explain why I've had problems with relationships, but in all honesty, it is not why I don't think it's a good time for me to begin one with you. I really like you a lot, but I'm going to be going to Virginia and right now my career is too important to me to embark on any kind of relationship.'

He nodded. 'I understand, and thanks for being so open. All you've achieved in your life after so much heartache and pain is remarkable, and you should be very proud of yourself.'

'It might sound odd, but this investigation has really helped me understand how to cope with the emotions of my past.'

'Good for you. Can I ask if a plutonic relationship between us is acceptable?'

'It's pronounced platonic, but yes, it is.' Jessica leaned forward and kissed him on the lips. 'Thanks for being so understanding. I'll see you tomorrow morning.'

* * *

Arriving home, Jessica poured herself a glass of Sauvignon Blanc and sat at the kitchen table with her iPad to look at the warehouse and hospital CCTV Guy had sent her. As usual, Guy had been very thorough, sending her the sections she needed along with notes giving the exact timings.

Jessica first looked at the hospital CCTV for Thursday and noted that Michelle was by the lift on Johan's floor at 5.45 p.m., and left the hospital through the main entrance a couple of minutes later, which wasn't long after she and Anderson had spoken with her.

She then watched the warehouse CCTV. Michelle arrived in her Mercedes, parked opposite the entrance and went inside at 7.04 p.m. She was wearing the same clothing she had on at the hospital. At 7.35, she left the building, carrying the black bin bag, returning to bring out two heavy-looking carrier bags. She looked at Guy's notes, which said Michelle returned to the hospital at 8.50. She fast-forwarded the video to that time and noticed that Michelle was wearing different clothing. She assumed Michelle must have gone back to her house to change.

Guy also noted that Michelle left the hospital just before midnight and didn't return until eight Friday morning, carrying a briefcase. By this time, Jessica and the team had been made aware that Johan had regained consciousness but needed complete rest. She assumed Michelle had gone home for the night to get some sleep so she'd be ready for the next round of questions. She closed her laptop, giving it a small pat. She would do the same thing, get a good night's sleep and be prepared for her. Michelle was a formidable opponent, and Jessica knew she could not afford to put a foot wrong.

CHAPTER THIRTY-SIX

On Saturday morning, Jessica went to Barking for a meeting with Anderson, Chapman and Dawn Owens. Anderson said he'd spoken with Michelle the previous evening, and she was happy to talk to them this morning. She'd asked if there had been any further developments, but he'd only told her they had identified other suspects who had yet to be interviewed.

'Is Johan fit to be interviewed as well?' Chapman asked.

'Doctor Babu said De Klerk appears to be suffering from post-traumatic amnesia, which is not uncommon after a serious head injury. He said it can last for a few hours, days, weeks or even, in rare cases, months.'

Chapman looked dubious. 'How convenient for him. Surely a doctor could tell if he's putting it on?'

'I didn't want to challenge Babu's diagnosis and give anything away. He said a short interview of about half an hour would be enough for now. We can still ask Johan questions, and if we can subsequently prove it was all an act, we can use it against him. I told Doctor Babu we'd be at the hospital around ten., so we've got about an hour and a half to get our ducks in a row.'

When they got to the hospital, they went straight to De Klerk's room. Anderson knocked on the door and Michelle opened it, but the bed was empty. She was wearing makeup, expensive-looking jewellery and a tight-fitting pale cream cashmere dress that made her pregnancy very obvious.

'Johan's been taken for a scan. He shouldn't be long,' she said.

'I wasn't expecting four of you,' she frowned.

'Due to your husband's condition, I wanted to speed things

up. I will be speaking with him, and DI Chapman will take notes. DC Owens needs to ask you a few questions, and Jessica will take the notes. If that's all right with you?'

She sighed. 'I suppose it will have to be. Johan is still very groggy. I told him it wasn't a good idea to stress himself by talking to you today. I suggested he wait until tomorrow, but he's stubborn and insisted he'd be fine.'

'We all appreciate his and your cooperation. We will be in the waiting room. Could you ask someone to tell us when Johan returns?' Michelle said she would, and they went to the waiting room.

'She looks ready for action,' Chapman remarked.

'How do you mean?' Anderson asked.

'You know, all dressed up with her warpaint on,' Chapman replied.

A few minutes later, a nurse came to the room and said that Johan was back in bed and ready to see them. Anderson asked Dawn and Jessica to stay in the waiting room and said he would ask Michelle to join them. Dawn waited until they had gone before speaking to Jessica. 'Do you mind asking Michelle the questions?'

'I think DCI Anderson wanted you, as a police officer, to do the interview.'

'I know, and I've got his list of questions, but you know so much more about the case than I do. I'm not fully up to speed with what's happened in the last couple of days and haven't had a chance to watch Cole or Bishop's interviews. I'm really worried I might ask something I shouldn't.'

Jessica knew it would be inappropriate to interrupt Anderson and ask his permission now that he was with Johan. But she couldn't help agreeing. 'All right, I'll do it,' she said. She just hoped Anderson wouldn't tear them both off a strip afterwards.

*   *   *

A tired and pale-faced Johan was sitting up in bed, sipping from a water bottle. The heavy bandages had been removed and the wound was covered with a large, padded dressing. His face still bore the tell-tale bruises from his attack, although the swelling had gone down, and he was also still attached to a drip, along with the heart monitor.

'Good morning, Johan. I'm glad to see you are recovering. I'm Detective Chief Inspector John Anderson, and this is Detective Inspector Chapman.'

Johan's voice was still a little hoarse, but he spoke clearly. 'Michelle mentioned that you were leading the investigation. I was pleased to hear you caught the person responsible for the break-in and the assault. Though it saddened me to learn from Michelle that he might have died from an injury I inflicted on him.'

'We realise that you were acting in self-defence, but we'll still need to ask you about it – along with other matters.'

'To be honest, I can't remember a thing about that night or the days before it. Michelle has told me what you think happened, so I know I'm lucky to be alive.'

'What are these "other matters" you need to ask Johan about?' Michelle asked.

'We arrested a jeweller called Nathan Cole and want to interview Johan about his association with him. Cole has also made criminal allegations against Johan which we need to put to him,' Chapman said. Johan looked shocked but didn't say anything.

'We both know Nathan. Has he got anything to do with what happened to my husband?' Michelle asked, sounding concerned.

'We believe Cole hired John Wheeler to break into your house.'

'Oh my God, Nathan? I can't believe he'd do that to me,' Johan exclaimed.

'I'm afraid there's evidence to suggest he organised the break-in. And, as I say, he has made some serious allegations against you.'

'You know you are entitled to have a solicitor present,' Michelle told him. 'It just can't be me.'

He sighed. 'I've done nothing wrong, so I'd prefer to get the interview over and done with as soon as possible. I'm happy to talk to you without a solicitor.'

'See what I mean about him being stubborn? You can change your mind about the solicitor anytime you want,' Michelle said, kissing him on the cheek.

Johan reached for her hand, and she held it. 'You must try to stay calm, Johan. Try to remember as much as possible and answer the questions if you can. You're not well, so if it becomes too stressful, say so, and DCI Anderson will terminate the interview.' Michelle looked at Anderson, who nodded in agreement. She gently released Johan's hand, blew him a kiss and left the room.

Anderson cautioned Johan and began to ask him about his relationship with Cole.

*   *   *

Michelle entered the waiting room, looking tearful. She tossed her hair back with one hand, sat down and looked at Jessica, who sensed she was ready to put on a performance.

'Are you OK?' Dawn asked.

Michelle nodded, wiping away a tear. 'I'm worried about Johan being interviewed and how the stress might affect him. He's still in a very vulnerable condition.'

'I take it DCI Anderson told you why he needs to interview him?' Jessica asked.

'Yes, but only briefly. Johan looked mortified when he said Cole had made criminal allegations against him and hired the man Wheeler to break into our house. It came as a shock to me as well, which is not good in my condition.' She took a deep breath and looked about to cry.

'Would you like some water or a hot drink?' Dawn asked.

'A tissue would be good if you have one. I've been through boxes of them.' Dawn opened her handbag and handed Michelle a packet of tissues. She removed one, dabbed her eyes, and blew her nose.

'Would you like some time to yourself?' Dawn asked.

'I'll be fine, thank you. Hearing Johan being falsely accused is just so distressing when he's the victim in all of this – I mean, he nearly died.'

Dawn's sympathetic cooings were beginning to annoy Jessica, who was becoming increasingly convinced it was all an act. 'If you don't feel up to it, we . . .' Dawn started to say, but Jessica took over before she could finish.

'Do you mind if Dawn takes notes while I ask you some questions?'

'No, that's fine,' Michelle said with a sniff.

'What's Johan's relationship with Nathan Cole?'

'I wouldn't call it a relationship. Johan has purchased jewellery from him a few times. He bought me a beautiful necklace and his Rolex watch from Cole. I've only met him once and found him perfectly pleasant, but then he did something to a friend of mine that made me realise he was dishonest.'

'Was that friend Chandice Bramston?'

'How did you know that?' a puzzled-looking Michelle asked.

'Cole told us that you and Johan thought he'd deliberately switched a sapphire on her ring. He said it was a genuine mistake, and he had no intention of stealing it.'

'Then he's a liar. Chandice and I had been friends for years until we met that horrible little man,' Michelle said bitterly.

'Can you tell me what happened?' Michelle told Jessica the now familiar story. 'How did this situation make you feel?'

'Obviously appalled, and deeply embarrassed."

'Did you believe Cole when he said it was an honest mistake?'

'Of course I didn't. Johan wanted to report it to the police, but I told him it was pointless.'

'Why did you think it was pointless?'

'We all knew Cole was lying, but I doubted the police could do anything as it would be hard to prove. I knew as a barrister there was insufficient evidence for the CPS to recommend charging Cole.'

'That might not have been the case if you had reported it,' Jessica said.

'Actually, Michelle is probably right. It would be hard to prove Cole intended to steal the sapphire,' Dawn remarked.

'Thank you, Dawn. I'm glad someone agrees with me,' Michelle said and looked at Jessica with a superior smile.

'Weren't you worried, as a barrister, that not reporting a potential crime might reflect badly on you?' Jessica asked, irritated by Dawn's interjection.

'To be honest, yes, I believe I was. I'm not the police's favourite person. I was worried that if they got involved, rumours would spread that I was associated with a common thief, and the press might get a hold of it. As a barrister, it wouldn't have looked good, but as I said, and your colleague Dawn agreed, there wasn't enough evidence to prove it.'

'Did Chandice not want to report it?' Jessica asked.

'Initially, yes, but she agreed about the lack of evidence. She also didn't want her husband to discover what had happened. He'd have been furious. The sapphire was a family heirloom. Looking back, maybe we should have reported it, but it's too late now,' Michelle sighed.

'You were in an awkward position, and I'm sure I'd have done the same thing if I were in your shoes,' Dawn said kindly. Short of slapping her, Jessica wondered how she could get Dawn to keep her opinions to herself.

'The really sad thing is that Chandice and I fell out over it, when she suggested Johan was in cahoots with Cole, and we haven't spoken since. She did leave me a message after what happened to Johan, but I haven't got back to her.'

'You should. My mum used to say a good friend is like a four-leaf clover. Hard to find and lucky to have,' Dawn smiled.

Michelle smiled back. 'That's very true. Chandice said in her text that she's always there for me if I need her. Right now, I feel like I do, and I'd be a fool if I didn't make the effort to rekindle our friendship.'

'What did you think when Chandice said Johan was in cahoots with Cole?' Jessica asked.

'Well, it was nonsense, obviously. Just something she said in the heat of the moment.' Michelle looked at Jessica. 'Do you know what my husband is accused of?'

'I'm not privy to information concerning that side of the investigation. It's best you speak with DCI Anderson.'

Michelle turned to Dawn. Jessica feared Dawn would tell her but was relieved when she heard her answer. 'I've been off sick the last couple of days and don't really know what's been happening on the investigation, I'm afraid.'

'Then I guess I'll have to ask DCI Anderson,' Michelle smiled.

'That's all we need to ask you for now,' Jessica said, 'but I expect DCI Anderson will want to speak to you after he's interviewed Johan. Would you like a coffee or some water?' Jessica asked.

'Actually, a decaf coffee would be nice, thank you.' Jessica asked

Dawn if she would go to the hospital canteen. When she had left the room, she turned to Michelle.

'I watched some video from your husband's warehouse yesterday. You went there on Thursday evening. Why was that?'

Michelle looked surprised but remained composed. 'I went to collect some of Johan's paperwork, which I had every right to do, and before you ask, his warehouse wasn't ransacked when I got there. I took a binbag of papers home, sorted them out later that night and took a briefcase with Johan's business paperwork to the hospital the next morning for him to go through.'

'Was he well enough to do that?' Jessica asked.

Michelle looked at her as if it were a ridiculous question. 'I took it so he could look at it when he felt well enough. I know he recently had a wine shipment. He'd been very excited to get orders from Harrods and Fortnum & Mason, and I wanted to check if I needed to get them delivered for him.' She laughed softly and shook her head. 'Johan desperately needs a secretary or a PA. His papers were all mixed up with receipts and orders, his diary was not up to date and there were even some unpaid bills.' Jessica nodded, feeling Michelle was lying and giving her too much information to cover it up. She waited for her to lapse into silence before leaning forward.

'Along with the bin bag, you removed two large carrier bags. That seems to be rather a lot of documents.'

'If you must know, I also removed some bottles of the best wine to hand out to the nursing staff and doctors as a thank you for saving Johan's life.'

'That's very thoughtful of you, and believable, Michelle. But I think your story about Cole is a well-constructed fabrication, and I've no doubt Johan's will be as well.'

Michelle returned her look steadily. 'I'm not particularly

bothered about what you think since I've done nothing wrong, and neither has Johan.'

'On Thursday evening, when DCI Anderson and I came to see you, I noticed that the water bottle beside Johan's bed was almost full. The same bottle was empty after speaking to you in the waiting room. It made me wonder if Johan was awake and drinking from it while we spoke to you.'

Michelle shook her head. 'Dear God, I think you are fixated on us. If you must know, I drank it. I'm pregnant, as you can see, and the stress is rather frightening for me. As soon as I returned to his room, I felt quite unwell and needed some water.'

'Come on, Michelle, don't take me for a fool. I think Johan has already confessed his sins to you. The pair of you must have discussed what you would say, though it must have been difficult not knowing the full extent of the police investigation.'

The look on Michelle's face changed from one of irritation to self-righteous anger. 'You might think you're good at analysing people, dear. You have no idea what it has meant to me to be expecting a baby, after the miscarriages and then the IVF, to have finally conceived naturally again is a special blessing. What I have been subjected to since Johan was almost killed is disgusting and agonising torment. I have been terrified of the damage it could have on my unborn child. As a woman, I would have thought you could at least show me some kindness and consideration.'

'I have every sympathy for you, Michelle, and for your unborn child, but like DCI Anderson and his team, I have a job to do and ...'

Michelle glared at Jessica as she interrupted her. 'You don't know me or what I'm capable of ... and you have to hope you never find out. You're clutching at fucking straws with your wild fantasies. Rest assured, I will report you and destroy your career if you throw further insinuations or accusations at me.'

Jessica remained calm in the face of Michelle's assault. 'I'm just giving my honest opinion. I think you would do whatever is necessary to protect your career and stop the truth from coming out, but pride always comes before a fall.'

Michelle dropped her act and stood up, looming over Jessica in an intimidating manner. 'The only downfall would be yours if I miscarried because of this awful harassment I am being subjected to.'

'Michelle, please . . .' Jessica tried to interject as it was obvious how emotional she was becoming, her hands clenching and unclenching.

'No, you nasty little bitch, you let me finish. I love Johan, and he loves me. He respects me and what I do for a living. He would never risk destroying our marriage or my career by getting involved in criminal activity with a man like Cole. Do I make myself clear?' She looked at Jessica with steely eyes. Jessica deliberately said nothing, hoping that Michelle would continue.

Dawn suddenly burst into the room, carrying two coffees and looking terrified. 'Anderson said to tell you Johan's collapsed. They think he might be having a heart attack,' she managed to say.

'Oh my God!' Michelle exclaimed, running past Dawn and out of the room, knocking one of the coffee cups out of her hand. It hit the floor, splashing hot coffee over Jessica 's legs as she leapt up and followed.

Anderson and Chapman were outside Johan's room. Michelle tried to go in, but a nurse said to wait outside as the room was full of hospital staff working on Johan's chest with a defibrillator.

'What have you done to Johan?' a terrified Michelle shouted at them.

Anderson started to reply. 'He was fine. One minute he was talking to us and then suddenly . . .'

'I don't believe you! You did something to him! This all your fault!' she screamed.

The door opened, and Johan was wheeled out, an oxygen mask over his face. A young doctor and two nurses were hovering over him.

'Please, out of the way,' the doctor said. 'We need to get him to ICU.'

Michelle turned on them, her eyes blazing. 'If Johan dies, you're to blame. You haven't heard the end of this . . . any of you!' She hurried off to be with her husband.

CHAPTER THIRTY-SEVEN

Anderson and the others went to the waiting room. They sat quietly, trying to take in what had just occurred and desperately hoping Johan made it.

'What happened?' Jessica asked, breaking the silence.

Anderson looked too shocked to answer, so Chapman stepped in. 'One minute he was fine chatting to us, and then he just went downhill fast.'

'I think he was having a heart attack,' a wide-eyed Anderson finally managed to say.

'Did you pressure him at all?' Jessica asked.

Chapman shook his head. 'No. Even though we'd started asking some pertinent questions about Cole and the diamonds, we took it easy.'

'Then he started getting short of breath. I just thought it was a ploy to stop the interview and give him time to talk to Michelle,' Anderson said.

'Clearly it wasn't,' Jessica remarked.

'Did Michelle tell you anything useful?' Anderson asked her. She recounted their conversation.

'Do you think she was lying?' Chapman asked her.

'Not about how she met Cole and the sapphire ring, but I think she knows exactly what Johan and Cole were up to and coached her husband on what to say. Michelle had an answer for everything and at the same time was fishing for information about the investigation. In my opinion she is an accomplished liar and I doubt we will ever get the truth out of her.'

'De Klerk gave us virtually the same account as Cole about how they knew each other, the incident with the sapphire ring, the diamond lab and all that,' Anderson said.

'Then why didn't he tell Michelle, if it was all legitimate?' Jessica asked.

'And if he'd fallen out with Cole, why did he invite him to the house?'

'Unfortunately, we didn't get that far,' Chapman admitted.

'Did he say anything about the smuggled diamonds?' she asked.

'That was when he suddenly clutched his chest and cried out in pain. We realised he wasn't putting it on and pressed the panic button.'

'Maybe all his lies caused his stress levels to go through the roof,' Dawn remarked.

Doctor Babu came into the waiting room. 'I'm sorry to tell you this, but Mr De Klerk passed away before we could get him to surgery. It looks like he had a heart attack.' For a moment they all stood in shocked silence.

'How is Mrs De Klerk?' Dawn asked.

'Obviously she's very distressed. She's with Johan, and I don't think it would be a good idea for you to speak to her. She thinks your line of questioning may have been over-aggressive, causing his heart attack.'

'I can assure you we were not aggressive at all,' a worried-looking Anderson said.

'What do *you* think caused the heart attack?' Chapman asked Doctor Babu.

'It could have been any number of things.'

'Could it happen due to stress while we were interviewing him?' Anderson asked.

'It's possible, but I'd like to ask how Johan behaved when you spoke to him. Did he say he was feeling any symptoms like chest pain?'

Anderson looked at Chapman, wondering who should answer. Eventually Chapman did. 'He was a bit croaky as his throat was dry. He kept taking sips of water. I noticed he had difficulty lifting the bottle to his mouth, but I thought he was just tired. He could still answer our questions, and at one point, he started rubbing his left arm.'

'I asked him if he was OK. He said yes, and it was just pins and needles,' Anderson added.

'Did his heart rate monitor show any change while you were talking to him?' Doctor Babu asked.

'We were paying more attention to him than the monitor, but his breathing did get a bit laboured. At first, we thought he was putting on an act, but when he clutched his chest and cried out in pain, the heart monitor started beeping and that's when I pressed the panic button,' Anderson told him.

'Obviously I can't be certain, but I don't think your questioning led to Johan's heart attack. Initially, due to the trauma he suffered, he had high levels of potassium in his blood, which we monitored and brought down with medication. A sudden increase in potassium levels can cause heart palpitations, shortness of breath, chest pain, numbness or a tingling sensation in the limbs.'

'Like the pins and needles Johan said he was feeling?' Anderson asked.

'Yes. All the symptoms you witnessed in Johan are an indication of severe hyperkalemia. It's a life-threatening condition that can cause a heart attack and requires immediate medical attention.'

'What would cause a sudden increase in his potassium levels?' Chapman asked.

'His brain injury, trauma, the blood transfusion, kidney problems or medication. We won't know until further tests and a postmortem are conducted. Obviously, due to the circumstances,

I have asked for a pathologist to come in as soon as possible to give the cause of death.' He looked at his watch. 'Thank you for your assistance. I've got other patients to attend to, so I'd best get on.' Doctor Babu quickly left.

'Looks like the doc doesn't want to commit himself to a cause of death yet. But it doesn't look like we're to blame,' Chapman remarked.

'With Johan dead, we'll have difficulty proving anything against Michelle,' Anderson said glumly.

'There's nothing more we can usefully do here. We might as well head back to the station.' Jessica contemplated telling Anderson about her 'off the record' conversation with Michelle but decided now wasn't the time, especially since she'd admitted nothing. She decided she would tell Chapman when they got back to the station.

'I'll meet you by the car. I need to wipe the coffee off my shoes in the ladies,' Jessica said, picking up the packet of tissues Michelle had left on the coffee table.

While cleaning her shoes, she wondered if Chapman and Anderson had been honest about their manner of questioning Johan De Klerk. Jessica felt drained as she looked in the mirror and puffed out her hair, then stopped and looked closely at her reflection. Only then did it hit her that it was all over with Johan dead, bar the case against Cole and Bishop.

Chapman was waiting for her at the hospital entrance. He gave her a depressed shrug of his shoulders, obviously feeling the same way about Johan's death and how it affected the case against Michelle, Cole and Bishop. He told her that Dawn had gone back to the station with Anderson, and he would give her a lift. 'Anderson said you can go home, and he'll meet with us in the morning. He's going to contact Commander Williams and give her an update. He wants the postmortem completed asap and to hold off on a press release until he's had time to assess the situation, the situation being a major fuck-up. He's worried sick about any accusations we caused De Klerk's heart attack.'

'It's not your fault he died,' Jessica said.

'He didn't just drop down dead, Jessica . . . he was in agony and couldn't breathe. We stood there like two pricks, then the heart monitor kicked in, bleeping and going crazy. It's knocked me for six, I can tell you.' Chapman was so wound up that he crashed the gears as he drove off.

'What does it mean for the case now that Johan's dead?'

Chapman sighed. 'There's enough evidence to proceed with the charges against Cole and Bishop, but that's it.' They didn't speak much on the rest of the journey to the station. When they arrived, Chapman parked next to Jessica 's car and said he'd see her in the morning.

'Do you fancy going for a drink somewhere? she asked as he switched the engine off.

'Do you mind if I don't. Anderson will be getting the team together for a briefing about what happened at the hospital. I also need to write my report and get my head around what happened. I think Anderson will be having a hard time as well.'

'I'll see you in the morning then.' He walked off without replying, leaving her standing on the pavement by her car.

* * *

When she got home, Jessica changed out of her coffee-stained stockings and left her skirt on a hanger, ready to be taken to the cleaners. Her depression hadn't lifted; in fact, her dark mood had got even worse. David was not home, so she paced around the kitchen aimlessly for a while, then opened a bottle of wine. After drinking half a glass, she topped it up and then physically jumped as her phone rang. She answered it, thinking it was David.

'Good evening, Jess. This is FBI Agent Anna Travis. I'm sorry if I've interrupted your evening, but I'm off on holiday in a few days and wanted to call you before I go. Quantico has residential accommodation, but it's pretty basic, like a campus. Some rooms are single occupancy, but most have two single beds, two desks, two dressers and communal male and female bathrooms.'

'I thought that might be the case, but I'm easy either way,' Jessica replied, making an effort to clear her head.

'I don't know about you, but I like to get away from the 24-7 pressure and relax. A friend has a great apartment that will become available shortly before you are due to join us. It's a tad expensive but worth it, and I wondered if you would prefer to move in there. My house is close by and it's not far from the academy.'

'I thought it would be a residential course.'

'The FBI recruits' course is, but you're attending the Behavioural Analysis course, so you don't have to stay on site.'

'The apartment sounds fantastic, thanks,' Jessica replied enthusiastically.

'Good. I'll send you the details. How's everything going as the MSCAN team leader?' Jessica was about to say it was going well, when she couldn't stop herself, and everything that had happened came pouring out. Anna encouraged her to give more details, and Jessica found it almost therapeutic to talk her through the complex investigation. Anna was a good listener, not interjecting or halting Jessica's detailed explanations.

'Did you think De Klerk was involved in diamond fraud with Cole?'

'Yes, and I also believe his wife lied to us regarding his

involvement and coached him on what to say . . . not that it matters now he's dead.'

'Do you think she might be involved in her husband's death?'

'A gut feeling tells me she could be, but there's no evidence, and I'm up against detectives that would disagree with my suspicions.'

'Do you trust your gut feelings?'

'Yes, I do, but I don't know how I will be able to prove they are correct.' Jessica waited for Anna to respond, but there was silence. She asked if she was still on the line.

'Yes, sorry, I was just thinking about the best advice I can give you . . . which would be to step back and go over everything you know. Identify all the evidence, write it down and construct competing hypotheses to produce the most likely explanation of events. I hope I'm not teaching you to suck eggs, but from what I've been told your intuition is usually correct. Keep digging, and you'll find the evidence you need to prove Johan De Klerk was, or wasn't, murdered.'

Jessica thanked Anna for her advice and said she'd let her know the outcome. No sooner had she finished the call than her mobile rang. It was Diane, who'd been told about De Klerk's death and wanted to know how she was. Jessica told her everything that had happened at the hospital and about Doctor Babu's comments.

'How does it impact the case, now that Johan's dead?' Diane asked.

'Chapman said Johan didn't reveal any incriminating evidence of a criminal connection between himself, Cole or Bishop, but they will be tried for Wheeler's death.'

'What about Michelle?'

'She was screaming her head off, but I didn't fare much better questioning her. She can spin a yarn, all right. It was quite a performance as the innocent heartbroken wife and upstanding barrister.

Truthfully, I think she's a liar and a narcissist, manipulative and utterly convinced of her own superiority. I wouldn't be surprised if she attempted to bring a case against Anderson and Chapman for harassment and causing her husband's heart attack.'

'Does that mean we're off the investigation?'

'I can't see any more arrests being made, but we've still got forensic work and reports to complete.'

'At least we earned a lot of kudos on our first case,' Diane said, trying to be positive. Just as Diane was about to end the call, Jessica asked if she could do something for her. 'Name it.'

'When we searched the De Klerk's property, I filmed the contents of Michelle and Johan's cupboards in the en suite bathroom. As I recall, there were a lot of vitamins and health supplements in Johan's. I'm sure there was a large plastic container of potassium. Could you check on the video for me?'

'Sure, any reason why?'

'Yes. Doctor Babu said that Johan had a high potassium count in his system when he was brought in.'

'I doubt daily potassium vitamins would cause a heart attack.'

'I know, but if he was taking a daily dose, we should let the doctor and pathologist know.' Jessica said, not wanting to reveal her suspicions about Michelle.

'I'll get back to you as soon as I've had a look,' Diane said, ending the call.

Sitting at the kitchen table, Jessica started following Anna Travis's advice and making notes, though it did all feel a bit pointless. She googled potassium and read that it provides electrolytes essential for several body processes, supports nerve and muscle function and helps maintain normal blood pressure. She then looked up potassium overdoses and read that, as Doctor Babu had said, too much potassium in your blood can cause an irregular heartbeat and result in a heart attack. Frustrated by her own lists of queries, she next called the hospital mortuary, asking to speak to Dr Giorgini, explaining it was about Johan De Klerk's postmortem. She was put on hold and transferred to various departments before she angrily demanded that if Dr Giorgini was there, she urgently needed to speak to her. She hung on as she was informed that Giorgini was examining De Klerk's body. It was another five minutes before she was able to speak to her.

'Sorry to bother you, Nicki, but there's something you might be able to help me with.'

'Make it quick, Jess. I'm in the middle of De Klerk's postmortem. Anderson wants the results asap.'

'This might sound a bit crazy, but could you inject someone with potassium or put it in a drink to bring on a fatal heart attack?'

'Obviously you're talking about De Klerk.'

'Yes. I know what Doctor Babu said, but I find it odd that one minute he's chatting away, and the next he's dying. De Klerk had potassium in his bathroom cupboard, but I'm unsure if they were capsules or tablets.'

'It would take a lot of them to kill him.'

'I know, but it means his wife, Michelle, had access to them.'

'In a drink, the potassium might taste bitter or salty. You could crush and dissolve tablets or capsules in water to create a liquid for injection, but you'd have to know what you were doing to make it work slowly until it became lethal. De Klerk has a lot of needle marks on him, some old and some new, but I'll check for any in unusual places. I need to get back to the mortuary now.'

Jessica knew Giorgini was an exemplary pathologist, and if there was any evidence that Michelle had somehow injected Johan with a lethal dose of potassium, she would find it. But now that she'd brought the idea up, it seemed too far-fetched. Was she just clutching at straws, now that there was no realistic possibility of proving Michelle was involved in any criminal activity, or was it an emotional reaction to Michelle's threats?

Diane rang back and told Jessica that Guy had enlarged the section she had filmed and the potassium was quick-release and in tablet form. She asked how many milligrams of potassium were in each capsule, and Diane said 275. She asked Diane to send her a copy of the potassium container and photos of the back and sides so she could see all the details about the manufacturer and daily dosage recommendations. Diane was about to ask some questions, but Jessica asked to speak to Guy, and so she handed the phone to him. Guy immediately asked about the potassium's relevance, but Jessica interrupted him.

'I need you to do something for me asap. I want you to review every case Michelle De Klerk has worked on. You might have to go back years, I know.'

'Christ, she's been a junior and senior barrister before becoming a KC and must have worked in God knows how many chambers.'

'I know. Just keep going back and see if there is any case, no matter how long ago, that is connected to hospitals, doctors, surgeries or drugs. Do a word search for potassium in each case and let me know immediately if you get a hit.'

'Will do.' She hung up, knowing Guy would do a thorough search. Part of her doubted he would find anything confirming her hunch, but she just couldn't let it go. She decided to get changed, go to Barking and speak with Anderson and Chapman about her suspicions.

* * *

Jessica tapped on Chapman's office door before entering. He gave her a glum look as she walked in. 'Anderson is with Commander Williams, and I don't have an update for you. Williams has informed the IOPC, who will carry out an investigation regarding Johan's death.'

'Why? Doctor Babu said you could interview Johan, and he agreed to be interviewed.'

'Belt and braces. Technically, it's a death in police custody as we were interviewing Johan under caution, so it's mandatory IOPC investigate. Which, in some ways, is not a bad thing as Michelle is bound to make a complaint.'

'There was a large container of potassium tablets along with the vitamins in Johan's bathroom cabinet. Diane sent me some photographs I took of them.'

He looked at her as if she was mad. 'What the fuck has that got to do with anything?'

'I think he could have been given a potassium overdose and that's what killed him.'

'Who by? His wife? "Excuse me, Johan, do you mind staying still while I stick this needle in you?" "Not at all, Michelle, go ahead."'

'There's no need to be sarcastic.'

'I'm not. I'm being realistic.' Jessica's mobile rang. It was Guy. 'I need to answer this.'

'Carry on, I need some coffee. I'll get one for you.' He stalked out of his office as she answered the call. Guy said he had been as thorough as possible in reviewing Michelle's cases as a senior barrister and KC but found no evidence of any case Michelle had been involved in with connections to potassium, hospitals, doctors' malpractice or drug dealing.

Jessica took a deep breath. 'Go further back, Guy. Look at when she was junior council and an apprentice barrister if necessary.

You must keep searching and let me know if you find anything.'

'OK, I'll try and find the chambers she first worked for.'

'Thank you.' Jessica ended the call and sat waiting for Chapman to return. He eventually kicked his door open, carrying two take-away cups of coffee, and put them on his desk. She picked one up.

He sighed. 'Look, I'm sorry for taking the piss. I know you have legitimate suspicions about Michelle. But the fact is we have no proof, and with him being fucking dead it's doubtful we will find any. It's case closed, and we all need to move on.'

Jessica stood up. 'Thank you for this. I'd be grateful if you'd let me know the postmortem result when it comes in.'

'Where are you going?' he asked.

'Home.' She slammed the door behind her as he raised his hands in a hopeless gesture of apology.

She sat in her car, drinking her cup of coffee and mentally going over the facts of Johan's death and her interview with Michelle. She was about to drive home when Guy called, with what she expected to be a further negative result.

'Are you sitting down?' he asked.

'What have you got?'

'I went further back as you requested. Thirteen years ago, when Michelle was not fully qualified, she was working for Sir Donald Griffith, an old-time QC with a very reputable chambers in Liverpool. She was a trainee barrister attached to his Chambers for two years before moving to London. He died ten years ago.'

'Don't keep me in suspense, what have you got?'

'The case was well covered in the press. Griffith was prosecuting a former Olympic hurdler who was accused of injecting his partner, also an athlete, with a fatal dose of potassium. It's not uncommon for athletes to use potassium in small amounts, as it's beneficial for muscular problems. The defence council's argument was that the victim self-injected the potassium and miscalculated the dose without realising it could be fatal. The victim then went to a bar with his partner and friends, where he died nearly an hour later. The friends testified that the victim appeared well and showed no signs of physical discomfort until a few minutes before the fatal heart attack.'

'Shit, so it *can* take time to become lethal?'

'Yes, and a doctor who specialises in toxicology testified at the trial that potassium can be a slow release into the system and is often hard to detect after death.'

'What was the verdict?'

'The defendant was found not guilty as there was insufficient evidence to prove he deliberately injected his partner with the fatal dose. I've got the court transcript and some other stuff I've researched.'

'Thank you, please send it over asap.' Jessica sat for a while, taking deep, calming breaths, before calling the hospital again and asking to speak to Doctor Giorgini. She had to wait for her call to be transferred, but managed to keep her impatience in check until she heard her come on the line. 'I'm sorry to call you again, but it's really important . . .'

Dr Giorgini interrupted her. 'This is all a bit much, Jessica. I have just finished the postmortem and need to speak to the coroner and DCI Anderson first. I shouldn't discuss the results and my findings until that's done . . .'

'I really need to know because we may need to act quickly.'

Nicki sighed, 'What I tell you is strictly between us for now. OK?'

'I won't tell a soul.'

'I used the hospital's equipment to check for potassium levels in Johan's blood and urine. They were dangerously high, and I have concluded that this was the cause of his heart attack. I can't rule out that he might have been injected with potassium. There were no needle marks in any unusual places, but that's not to say he wasn't injected in the same site as a previous injection to conceal a criminal act.'

'If his wife Michelle injected potassium in his body, he'd know and would have said something. But it's highly unlikely a nurse or doctor did it.'

'I agree, not even accidentally. I have narrowed down the time frame of the sudden increase in his potassium level, which was last checked at 8 a.m. this morning and was just above normal.'

'Johan was on an intravenous drip. Could it have been put in that?'

'It's possible, and it would cause a slow feed into his body. I'll speak with the coroner, then call Anderson and let him know my findings, but I won't mention we've spoken or anything about the drip. I'll let you do that. As you know, I've just started in London and I don't want to start pissing people off by not following procedure.'

'Is there any chance you could inform Anderson first in the next few minutes?' Jessica asked, knowing she was pushing it.

'You're like a dog with a bloody bone. I'll call him now.'

'Thank you, Nicki. I owe you big time.'

'Too right you do,' she laughed, ending the call.

Jessica wanted to run into the station but forced herself to sit in her car for ten minutes before calmly walking in. She intended to speak to Chapman first, but he wasn't in his office, so she went to see Anderson and saw that Chapman was with him.

'I thought you were going home,' Chapman said.

'I was about to leave, but I thought I'd see if the postmortem results had come in. I also got some interesting information from Guy that I thought you should know about.'

'That was perfect timing, Jessica. Dr Giorgini hasn't completed her report yet, but she just called me and said that Johan De Klerk's potassium levels in his blood were dangerously high and concluded it was the cause of his heart attack.'

'Did she say why she thought they might have been so high?'

'She said someone might have injected him with a fatal dose.'

'That's interesting,' Jessica said, pretending this was news to her. 'Especially since Guy has uncovered a previous case of potassium poisoning.'

Anderson held a hand up. 'Before you go any further, I also spoke with Doctor Babu again. He said sudden stress can trigger hyperglycaemia and, in some cases, contribute to an increased risk of heart attack, especially in individuals who have just been through a traumatic incident. If, as we suspect, Johan was lying, his stress levels would have gone up, which, coupled with his injuries, could . . .'

Jessica interrupted him. 'Michelle De Klerk was a junior barrister on a case involving potassium poisoning, which means she has knowledge of its use and its effects on the human body.' She had their undivided attention now, as she repeated her conversation with Guy.

'Bloody hell, this doesn't look good for her,' Anderson remarked.

'It's unlikely Michelle injected him with the potassium, but she could have put it in his drip bag. I think examining it for fingerprints and DNA needs to be done asap.'

Anderson nodded. 'Do it.'

'I can call Taff and Diane and get them to go to the hospital, seize the bag and search Johan's hospital room for discarded syringes and anything else of evidential value.'

'Tell them to ask Doctor Babu for permission to do the search,' Anderson instructed.

'We'll need to get Michelle's fingerprints. Should we do it covertly or ask her?'

'No need. I got her elimination prints at the hospital when I took Johan's the day after he was attacked. For now, she doesn't need to know anything about what we are doing.'

'I still don't understand how and when Michelle could have tampered with the drip bag,' Chapman said.

'It could have been before we arrived at the hospital and while Johan was having a head scan.'

'Remember, Michelle was alone in the room when we got there,' Anderson said.

'OK, but we need to tread carefully here. I mean, it could be possible for someone else at the hospital to have put the potassium in the drip bag.'

Jessica knew she had to make them concentrate and keep their focus on Michelle.

'Think about the timing. Michelle knew from the evidence at the previous trial exactly how long it would take for the potassium to become lethal. She knew the time we were expected to arrive at the hospital to interview her and Johan. If you remember, the window in his private room overlooked the car park, so she could see when we arrived. John having the scan gave her the window she needed.'

'Where did she get it, then?' Anderson asked.

'There were his and hers cabinets in the en suite to the master bedroom, which I searched and then recorded the contents on video. I noticed a large plastic container of 275 milligram potassium tablets and other vitamins in Johan's cabinet. I looked inside all the containers in case any contained illegal substances. As I recall, the potassium bottle was virtually full.' Before continuing, she showed them the pictures that Guy had sent her on her phone.

'Michelle could have dissolved a quantity of powder from the capsules in hot water and created a highly potent potassium liquid, which she then put in the drip bag.'

'If she did, she will probably have got rid of the container and empty tablets by now,' he remarked.

'The video and pictures I took prove that potassium tablets were in Johan's cabinet. If she got rid of them, she'd have difficulty explaining why, especially after Dr Giorgini's postmortem results. I don't think anyone else was involved in Johan's death. Michelle had the motive and the access to the potassium.'

Anderson stood up and clapped his hands. 'We need to interview Michelle De Klerk and search her house.'

'Are you going to arrest her?' Jessica asked.

'Not yet. I want to recover the drip bag and have it tested for fingerprints first. If Michelle's aren't on it or there's no sign it was tampered with, it will be hard to prove she did it. I'll call Commander Williams and update her. Mike, I'd like you to get the search warrant and organise a small arrest and search team and transport.' Chapman nodded. He was still uncertain about Michelle's guilt but didn't argue. It was almost like an afterthought when Anderson glanced towards Jessica, who was standing in front of his desk. 'Good work, and I'd like you to accompany us. We'll regroup as soon as we are all good to go. I'll call Doctor Babu now.' Anderson picked up his phone.

Jessica called Diane and asked her to go with Taff to the hospital, seize the drip bag and search Johan's room. She then had a ham sandwich and an orange juice in the canteen and then went and sat in the incident room, trying to slow her heart rate.

'I've got the warrants, and the arrest team and transport are good to go,' Chapman said.

Jessica smiled. 'I'm looking forward to this.'

CHAPTER THIRTY-EIGHT

Chapman drove Jessica, Anderson and DC Owens to the De Klerk's house, accompanied by two other detectives in an unmarked vehicle, who had been instructed to remain outside and enter the house only when their assistance was requested. As Chapman parked, they were surprised to see a CCTV security company van and a man by the front door fitting a video doorbell. They also noticed a CCTV camera attached to the house's front.

'Bit late for all that now. If they'd done it before, Johan may still be alive and this investigation would never have happened,' Chapman remarked. Anderson knocked on the door, and a handsome, blond, suntanned man answered, introducing himself as Johan's brother, Duante. Anderson introduced Chapman and Jessica and told him they were sorry for his loss. Duante explained that he had arrived that morning and his father was due the following day. He ushered them into the drawing room.

'The whole family is devastated, as you can imagine. What happened to Johan was . . . I don't have the words. We are planning to have a small funeral in England and then fly Johan's body back to South Africa. Michelle is resting right now. She's exhausted and, of course, worried for the baby, but she's been checked over by her obstetrician and all is well. Can I get you anything – tea or coffee?' Jessica watched him closely, feeling he was giving them too much information. Duante gave a deep sigh. 'Michelle's expecting a boy. Poor Johan would have been over the moon; he so much wanted to have a son. It's all just so sad.'

'Could you please inform Mrs De Klerk we'd like to speak to her?' Anderson asked.

'May I ask what it's about?' Duante asked.

'I'd rather tell her in person,' Anderson replied.

'OK, I will go and tell her you are here then. Are you sure I can't offer you something to drink?' Anderson refused for all of them. They stood awkwardly in the living room where Johan and Wheeler had fought before he was beaten and stabbed. Chapman walked around the room and then stood by the fireplace, looking at the array of silver-framed photographs. Although he had seen the photographs when he first came to the house on the Monday morning, he hadn't taken much notice of them before.

In the photographs Johan was as blond as his brother but much taller and more athletic-looking, with broad shoulders and a slim waist. He smiled broadly with gleaming white teeth. The few pictures of Johan and Michelle together looked like wedding pictures, and Chapman thought she appeared somewhat domineering, often unsmiling.

Chapman turned as Michelle walked in. She wore a dark maroon velvet floor-length dressing gown over silk pyjamas. Resting or not, she was perfectly made-up, her hair loose with a satin headband. 'I was wondering when you'd contact me. I am waiting to know when my husband's body can be released so we can arrange his funeral. My brother-in-law, Duante, is taking care of the arrangements, while I consider what action to take against you regarding the unwarranted harassment my husband was subjected to, so I . . .'

'I'll speak to the coroner and ask him to call you,' Anderson said. 'But I'm afraid there may be a second postmortem.'

'A second postmortem? Why is that necessary?'

'We have evidence that implicates you in the death of your husband,' Anderson said quietly.

'What are you talking about? What evidence? This is preposterous,' she said firmly but calmly.

'Mrs De Klerk, this is not a social visit. We'd like to interview you at the station . . .'

'I've nothing to hide. If there are questions you need to ask me, then go ahead.'

'Your husband's blood and urine samples showed high levels of potassium, which had not been administered by the medical staff. We suspect that someone injected or otherwise illegally administered the potassium, which led to his heart attack.'

'You can't seriously think that had anything to do with me,' Michelle replied, looking shocked.

'We need to question you about it and also Johan's involvement in diamond fraud,' Anderson replied.

'I've already told you I know nothing about that . . .'

Duante interrupted. 'My sister-in-law is pregnant and grieving the loss of her husband. I don't think this is an appropriate time to question her.'

'It's all right, Duante. I appreciate your concern, but you shouldn't get involved. It might be best if you left us for now.' He hesitated, sighed, then walked out of the living room into the hallway, closing the door behind him. 'Have you considered that a man like Cole could have bribed a doctor or nurse to administer the potassium?' Michelle asked Anderson.

'I assure you we are looking at every possibility,' he replied. Chapman looked at Jessica with eyebrows raised, wondering why Anderson was trying to placate Michelle.

'I hate to say it, but I also found Doctor Babu to be incompetent. He should never have allowed you to interview Johan,' Michelle said bluntly.

'Johan agreed to be interviewed,' Anderson replied.

'Because he was trying to be helpful. Johan's potassium levels were high when he was first admitted to the hospital due to his injuries and the stress he was under. It seems to me those levels rose again and led to his heart attack when you and DCI Anderson aggressively questioned him.' It was clear Michelle had an answer for everything.

Chapman was losing his patience with Anderson's approach. He handed her a copy of the search warrant. 'I'm sure I don't need to explain what this is, or that you can have a . . .'

'I don't need a solicitor. I'm perfectly capable of representing myself, and I have no problem with you conducting a search. I only ask that you don't leave the house in a mess or damage anything.'

'We'll put everything back as we found it, Mrs De Klerk,' Anderson said, frowning at Chapman for his abruptness.

'Do you mind if I get changed?'

'Not at all,' Anderson replied.

Chapman was wary. 'DC Owens and Miss Russell will accompany you while you dress, and search your bedroom. My colleagues and I will search the rest of the house.' As the three women walked into the hallway, Jessica saw a nervous-looking Duante hovering by the door and wondered if he had been listening to the conversation.

'May I remind you, I'm in charge of this investigation,' Anderson told Chapman with a frown.

'Can't you see she's playing games with you?' Chapman retorted. 'She's the one controlling the narrative when it should be us.'

'I'm not stupid, Mike, but being aggressive plays into her hands. I understand your concerns, but just be patient, and I'm sure we'll find the evidence we need to arrest and charge her.' Anderson walked off to call the search team in.

* * *

While Michelle got dressed, Jessica went into the bathroom. She was surprised to find the potassium tablets still in Johan's cabinet. She put on some crime scene gloves, photographed it, then opened the container and saw it was now almost empty, having been almost full when she last looked inside it. Jessica sighed, regretting that she hadn't photographed the contents when she first examined the crime scene. She put the potassium container in an exhibit bag, then in her shoulder bag, and went into the bedroom.

'Do you mind if I use my bathroom now?' a petulant Michelle asked. Jessica said she'd finished but didn't say what she had taken for now. While Michelle was in the bathroom, Jessica opened the walk-in closet, moving hangers aside to see the hidden safe. It was open, and again, she used her mobile to photograph it and the trays of jewellery inside before closing it.

While Michelle washed, dressed and put on makeup, Dawn and Jessica continued to search the bedroom but found nothing of evidential value or interest. Jessica went downstairs to speak with Anderson and Chapman. 'Where's Anderson?' Jessica asked Chapman.

'He's in the back garden talking to Duante, who's having a smoke. He's asking him if he knows anything about the diamonds. The rest of the team is searching the basement. But if Michelle stole the other rough and lab-grown diamonds from the two warehouses, she won't have hidden them here.'

'I agree, but she might have given them to Duante for safekeeping,' Jessica suggested.

'That's possible, but we don't have enough evidence to arrest him for anything.'

'I found the potassium container, and it's over half empty.'

'Taff can examine it for Michelle's fingerprints, but they won't be of much evidential value as she could say she shares his vitamin tablets or bought them for him.'

'You're right. She already knew about Johan's potassium levels when Anderson told her we think he was given a deliberate over-dose. She always has the answers. Is Anderson going to arrest her?'

'I thought he would have by now. I think he's being tentative because she's pregnant and blaming us for Johan's death. It seems he wants to play everything by the book and not upset her.'

'You think he's scared of her?'

'That's one way of putting it. Out of his depth is another. Have you heard from Taff or Diane about the drip bag?'

'Not yet. They're probably busy searching Johan's hospital room. I'll nip out the front and give them a call.'

'There was a filing cabinet in Johan's basement study, wasn't there?'

'Yes, it isn't locked. Why do you ask?'

'Something just crossed my mind that might help us.'

'What?'

'I'll let you know if I find it,' he said, walking off.

Jessica went outside and called Taff. 'How's it going? Any luck with the drip bag or syringes in Johan's room?'

'It's been a bit of a nightmare, to be honest. When we got here, Johan's room had been cleared out. Unfortunately, all the syringes and needles had been put in a sharps disposal box and taken to the incinerator. Fortunately, we managed to speak to the cleaner and traced the yellow clinical waste bag she used, but it had seven drip bags in it amongst a load of other waste. Plus, some of the bags had leaked, so everything was wet.'

'So, it's not looking good for us.'

'Actually, we might have struck lucky. The hospital let me use a lab to do some comparison work. I'm just examining the fourth bag and using a particle reagent spray, which makes fingerprints visible on wet surfaces. Among a number of prints I've got what I'm pretty sure is Michelle De Klerk's left thumbprint on one side and index finger on the other side, which implies she held the bag.'

'How sure are you the prints are Michelle's?'

'Ninety-five percent, particularly as there are two matching prints. I'm confident further comparisons back at our lab will confirm they are hers.'

'Any needle marks in the bag?'

'No, but she could easily have injected potassium into it through the self-sealing additive port.'

'You're a bloody star, Taff. We can examine the bag's contents for potassium at the lab.'

'It's empty. It could have leaked out or have been deliberately emptied.'

'Even a tiny trace is good evidence.' Jessica returned to the house to speak to Chapman and found him in the basement study.

'Take a look at this.' He handed her an Aviva life insurance policy.

Jessica looked over the policy and then waved it in her hand. 'Talk about a motive. Bloody hell. Michelle gets a million pounds if Johan dies!'

'Yep, but in fairness, her life insurance is for the same amount. I doubt she would kill him for the money, but it's something else we can use to put pressure on her.' Jessica told him about her conversation with Taff and Michelle's fingerprints. 'No doubt she'll anticipate we'd search Johan's hospital room, but the evidence against her is getting stronger,' Chapman smiled.

'Can I ask Michelle about her prints being on the drip bag? She doesn't like me, so it might spark a reaction that could be to our advantage.'

'I don't think Anderson would approve.'

'Anderson can't object while he's in the garden with Duante. Michelle said she doesn't want a solicitor and all this farting around is getting us nowhere.'

'All right, but if Anderson says anything, it was my idea, as you're the forensic expert. We best go and see if she's come downstairs yet.'

A few minutes later Michelle walked into the living room wearing a designer tracksuit, slippers and the same maroon velvet dressing gown to find Jessica sitting in one of the armchairs while Chapman stood to one side.

'I would like to ask you some questions regarding some forensic issues. Is that OK with you?'

Michelle took a sip from the bottle of water she was holding, then sat opposite her. 'So, what do you want to ask me?' She sat back, crossed her legs and put her hands on her belly.

'Do you recall I took a set of elimination prints from you at the hospital?'

'Yes, which I willingly gave you.'

'The thing is, I've just spoken to our fingerprint expert. He found your left thumb and index fingerprints on the saline drip bag in Johan's room.'

Michelle shrugged. 'That doesn't surprise me.'

'You're not a nurse. So why did you need to handle the bag?' Chapman asked.

'I don't deny I touched the saline bag, but it was after Johan's death. I went to his room to collect my belongings and his briefcase, which had all his paperwork. I noticed the stand had fallen, and the saline bag was loose on the floor. I assumed it must have got knocked over while they tried to resuscitate Johan. I picked the stand up and the bag, then put it back on the hook. Were there any other fingerprints on it?' Michelle asked calmly.

'Yes, but we suspect they belong to nurses or doctors who attended to Johan.'

'Then that must make them suspects, even more so as I didn't touch that bag until after he died. It also supports the fact that Nathan Cole may be involved.'

'Your husband's life was insured for one million pounds. That's a lot of money that will now come your way,' Chapman said.

'This is absurd. My life is insured for the same amount, and I don't stand to gain much. My husband left many debts he had incurred mishandling his business.'

Jessica looked at Chapman, who nodded and stepped back, indicating that he would let her ask the pertinent questions. Jessica removed the exhibit bag containing the potassium capsule container from her bag and held it up. 'This was in Johan's bathroom cabinet. I photographed all the vitamins and looked inside the bottles. When your house was a crime scene, I looked in it, and it was nearly full. Now it's half empty, and Johan can't have physically taken them. Can you explain that?'

'Do you have any proof that the number of tablets has decreased?'

'I know what I saw,' Jessica said firmly.

'You didn't photograph the contents. So, you could be mistaken.'

'I don't think so.'

'That answer implies you're not sure. As you know, Johan was a fit and very athletic man. I was aware he took several vitamins and supplements daily, including potassium.'

'Do you know why he took potassium?'

'He said it prevented cramps, but I know very little about its health benefits.'

'Do you have any knowledge of what an overdose of potassium can do to a person's body?'

'I can't say that I do.'

'Do you know what level of potassium would be required to affect someone's heart?'

'No, I don't, and I am beginning to find your questions repetitive. You know I wasn't present when my husband had his heart attack. In fact, DI Chapman said he seemed fine when they initially spoke to him.' Jessica started to ask another question when Michelle leaned forward. 'If this line of questioning is a pathetic attempt to exonerate your two detectives from instigating the pressure on my husband that caused his heart failure, you are trying my patience.'

'An overdose of potassium was found in Johan's blood, and you knew exactly how long it would take to kill him after tampering with his intravenous drip.'

'That is ridiculous. Where do you think I was able to acquire the technical knowledge to administer a lethal dosage when I was not even in the same room?'

'You didn't have to be. You knew how long you had, you knew what time DCI Anderson and DI Chapman were going to interview your husband. In other words, you created the perfect alibi.'

'This is ridiculous, and I'm tired of your false accusations. If you have evidence I killed Johan, then arrest me. If not, then kindly get out of my house and leave me to mourn his death.'

'You're a liar, Michelle,' Jessica said. She removed a folded piece of paper from her bag and held it up. 'This is a copy of a newspaper article concerning an Olympic hurdler accused of murdering his partner by administering a lethal potassium injection.' Jessica read out the pertinent details of the case then looked at her. 'Ring any bells?' Michelle's eyes narrowed, but she didn't reply. 'A doctor who testified in the case gave details about potassium levels in the body and how long they could take to cause a fatal heart attack.'

'I don't know anything about that case.'

'Another lie, Michelle. Thirteen years ago, you were a junior barrister working in Sir Donald Griffith's chambers. He was prosecuting council in the case, and you assisted him.'

'I don't remember it.'

'We've got a copy of the court papers, and your name is on them. You attended the trial and assisted Sir Donald every day. You were aware that the defendant was found not guilty. You thought if he could get away with it, so could you. Am I right?'

Michelle screamed in fury, hurling the water bottle at Jessica, making her dodge out of the way. Michelle jumped up, the maroon velvet dressing gown spreading like wings as she reached for her. Chapman grabbed her as she spat and struggled, still trying to get to Jessica.

'Michelle De Klerk, I am arresting you on suspicion of the murder of Johan De Klerk. You do not have to say anything, but it may harm your defence if you do not mention when questioned something which you later rely on in court. Anything you do say may be given in evidence . . .' It was over as fast as it had begun. Michelle collapsed, sobbing, as Chapman helped her into an armchair.

'What the fuck is going on?' Anderson shouted as he ran into the room.

'She's had a bit of a meltdown, and I've arrested her on suspicion of murder,' Chapman replied calmly.

Michelle kept her head bowed, saliva dripping from her mouth as she sobbed. She cried, 'My Baby, my baby' and clutched her stomach as if in pain.

'Go call an ambulance for her, Mike, and tell Dawn to come in here.'

'It's all an act. Her fingerprints were on the drip bag and . . .'

'Do as I fucking say!' Anderson barked, looking at Jessica. 'The pair of you go back to the station. I'll speak to you later.'

CHAPTER THIRTY-NINE

It was early evening. Jessica and Chapman were in The Bull having a drink but not feeling like celebrating. 'Well, that was an eventful day,' Chapman said dryly, sipping his lager.

'Yes, we managed to enrage Michelle and Anderson simultaneously,' Jessica sighed.

'He wasn't as annoyed with us as I thought he would be.'

'That's because he knows Michelle is as guilty as sin.'

'It all seems like an anti-climax now that she's been de-arrested, though,' Chapman sighed as he systematically shredded a beer mat.

'Why did Anderson do that?'

'Because she'll be in the hospital for a day or two. She won't do a runner, and having an officer guard her day and night is costly. He can re-arrest her when she's discharged or just arrange for her to attend the station for an interview.'

Jessica shook her head in disgust. 'I'm glad her baby is all right, but the whole thing at her house was a big act for me. Being in the hospital gives her more time to think and get her story straight.'

'Anderson knows that, but he doesn't want to give her another reason to complain.' Chapman pushed the shreds into a pile.

Jessica grabbed his hand. 'Would you please stop doing that, it's irritating.'

'Sorry.'

'Don't start all that again.'

'Start what?'

'The compulsive apologising. Did Anderson question Duante about the diamonds?'

'Yes, but of course he denied being involved in the smuggling and wouldn't believe that his brother would do such a thing.'

'No doubt Michelle coached him as well,' Jessica sighed.

'It's hard to understand why she killed Johan. Do you think it was just because she had the perfect opportunity and would get the million pounds insurance?'

'I don't think money has ever been as important to her as her career. She couldn't risk being dragged into Johan's crimes or him confessing what he'd been up to.'

'It will still be all over the press.'

'But with Johan dead, she can speak for him and come out with the perfect story.'

'If the CPS say there's enough to charge her, she could still be found guilty and end up in prison.'

'Michelle has a good chance of being found not guilty,' Jessica replied.

'What makes you say that?' he asked.

'She's an expert liar who can spin a yarn and twist things to her advantage. To win over the jury, she'll portray herself as the innocent, tearful wife, a pillar of society and celebrated KC. She'll also use her pregnancy to get their sympathy.'

'How can you be so sure she'll succeed?'

'It's what she does for a living, and she's had years of practice convincing a jury she's right and the prosecution is wrong. It's pure theatre, Mike, and Michelle knows how to win over her audience.'

'You broke her when you brought up the Liverpool potassium case, though.'

'I played her at her own game and drew her in to show she was lying. She never thought we would look back so many years.'

'The potassium in the drip bag will be her downfall.'

'I wouldn't be so sure of that.'

He looked puzzled. 'Why not?'

'Johan's drip bag was empty. If we find any potassium, it will probably be minute traces.'

'I know that, but Johan wasn't being administered potassium, so Michelle had to have put it in there.'

'Di sent me pictures of the clinical waste bag and its contents.' Jessica showed him on her phone. 'The drip bag that leaked contained a pre-mixed solution of potassium. This next picture is Johan's bag. As you can see, the drip valve has come off and there's no tubing connected to it.'

'So, what's the problem?' he asked, looking confused.

'Cross-contamination. Some of the potassium from the leaked bag could have got into Johan's drip bag.'

Chapman laughed. 'The chances of that happening must be minuscule.'

'I agree, but as a forensic expert, I would have to say that while highly unlikely, there's a chance it could happen. The fact that the potassium bag leaked will have to be disclosed to Michelle.'

Chapman let out a long sigh. 'It never rains but it pours. Who would have thought that what appeared to be a straightforward case could hold so many twists and turns?'

'Believe me, Mike, nothing is ever straightforward in this job.'

*　　*　　*

Michelle De Klerk spent two days in hospital before being released. After a thorough search of her home, no large sums of cash or uncut diamonds were found. The chemistry lab found small traces of potassium in Johan's drip bag and agreed with Jessica's 'improbable but possible' view regarding cross-contamination.

During her interview under caution, Michelle readily answered questions but said nothing that could implicate her in the diamond scam or any attempt to pervert the course of justice. She had a smirk on her face when she heard about the potassium drip bag that had leaked and continued to blame Anderson and Chapman for her husband's death.

Anderson asked the Crown Prosecution Service if he could charge Michelle with murder, but they wanted to read and review all the forensic and police evidence first. Michelle continued practising as a barrister during the three months it took the CPS to decide that, due to insufficient evidence, there was not a reasonable prospect of conviction.

As the forthcoming trials for Bishop and Cole advanced with a certainty of their convictions and many congratulations for her team's excellent investigations, Jessica was already at work on her next murder case, knowing Michelle would now never be convicted of her husband's murder. She had no option but to accept the prognosis that there was insufficient evidence and no reasonable prosect of a conviction for Michelle De Klerk. She had even gone to watch her handle a defence trial in court. Seated partly hidden in the gallery, Jessica was able to watch the by now obviously pregnant barrister at work below in the court room. Wearing an immaculate wig, white starched collar and tails and black silks, she was a dominant and impressive figure. Acting as defence barrister for a suspected armed robber, she spoke eloquently and persuasively about how the defendant had been drawn into criminality due to tragic circumstances, losing his beloved young wife and unborn child.

Jessica watched Michelle virtually use her own almost full-term pregnancy, resting her hands on her swollen stomach to indicate the tragedy. She had seen enough and left the court, unable to accept that Michelle De Klerk had got away with murder, but the reality was that she had and pocketed the one million life insurance payout along with some rough-cut diamonds.

ACKNOWLEDGEMENTS

I would like to thank all the forensic scientists and members of the Met Police who help with my research. I could not write without their valuable input.

Cass Sutherland for his valuable advice on police procedures and forensics.

The entire team at my publisher, Bonnier Books UK, who work together to have my books edited, marketed, publicised, and sold.

A special thank you to Ben Willis and Bill Massey for their great editorial advice and guidance.

Nikki Mander who manages my PR and makes it so easy and enjoyable.

The audio team, Jon Watt and Laura Makela, for bringing my entire backlist to a new audience in audiobooks. Thanks also for giving me my first podcast series, *Listening to the Dead*, which can be downloaded globally.

Allen and Unwin in Australia and Pan Macmillan SA in South Africa and all my foreign language publishers, thank you for doing such fantastic work with my books.

All the reviewers, journalists, bloggers, and broadcasters who interview me, write reviews, and promote my books. Thank you for your time and work.

Dear Reader,

Thank you very much for picking up *The Scene of the Crime*, the first book in my brand-new forensic crime series. I hope you enjoyed reading the book as much as I enjoyed writing it.

If you enjoyed *The Scene of the Crime*, then please do keep an eye out for news about the next book in the series, which will be coming soon. You may also enjoy my Jack Warr series – *Buried, Judas Horse, Vanished, Pure Evil* and *Crucified are all* available now. And if you would like to delve into the Tennison series, all ten novels – *Tennison, Hidden Killers, Good Friday, Murder Mile, The Dirty Dozen, Blunt Force, Unholy Murder, Dark Rooms, Taste of Blood* and *Whole Life Sentence* – are available to buy in paperback, ebook and audio. I've been so pleased by the response I've had from the many readers who have been curious about the beginnings of Jane's police career. It's been great fun for me to explore how she became the woman we know in middle and later life from the Prime Suspect series. It's been a pleasure to revisit the Trial and Retribution series after its television success and I am thrilled to return to it in print – the first two books in the series are available to buy now.

To discover more about my life and career, please do pick up a copy of my memoir, *Getting Away With Murder*. It was such fun to write, and I'd love to hear what you think.

If you would like more information on what I'm working on, about any of my series, you can visit www.bit.ly/LyndaLaPlanteClub where you can join my Readers' Club. It only takes a few moments to sign up, there are no catches or costs, and new members will automatically receive an exclusive message from me. Bonnier Books UK will keep your data private and confidential, and it will never be passed on to a third party. We won't spam you with loads of emails, just get in touch now and again with news about my books, and you can unsubscribe any time you want.

Finally, if you would like to get involved in a wider conversation about my books, please do review *The Scene of the Crime* on Amazon.co.uk, Waterstones.com or on Goodreads, on any other e-store, on your own blog and social media accounts, or talk about it with friends, family or reader groups! Sharing your thoughts helps other readers, and I always enjoy hearing about what people experience from my writing.

With many thanks again for reading *The Scene of the Crime*, and I hope you'll return for the next in the series.

With my very best wishes,
Lynda

INTRODUCING
JACK WARR

The gripping and twisty series
from the *Sunday Times* bestselling author

Lynda La Plante

BEFORE PRIME SUSPECT THERE WAS

TENNISON

DIVE INTO THE ICONIC *SUNDAY TIMES* BESTSELLING SERIES.

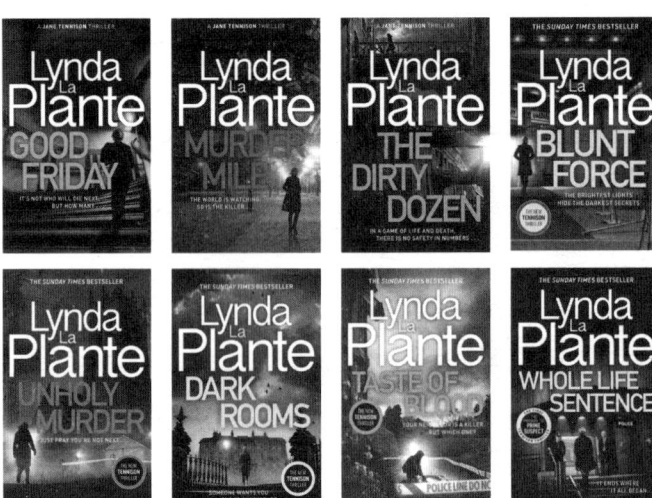

Now brought to a close with
the final epic instalment . . .

WHOLE LIFE SENTENCE